THIS PRESENT DARKNESS

MorenoT34135

Other Crossway Books by
FRANK E. PERETTI

This Present Darkness / audio cassette and CD
Piercing the Darkness
Piercing the Darkness / audio cassette and CD
Tilly
Tilly / audio cassette; also VHS and DVD
Prophet

THE COOPER KIDS ADVENTURE SERIES
The Door in the Dragon's Throat
Escape from the Island of Aquarius
The Tombs of Anak
Trapped at the Bottom of the Sea

THIS PRESENT
DARKNESS

FRANK E. PERETTI

CROSSWAY BOOKS

A PUBLISHING MINISTRY OF
GOOD NEWS PUBLISHERS
WHEATON, ILLINOIS

This Present Darkness

Copyright © 1986, 2003 by Frank E. Peretti.

Published by Crossway Books
      a publishing ministry of Good News Publishers
      1300 Crescent Street
      Wheaton, Illinois 60187

Cover design and illustration: Kirk DouPonce, UDG / DesignWorks

Printed in the United States of America

ISBN 1-58134-528-3

Library of Congress Catalog Card Number 86-70279

DP		14	13	12	11	10	09	08	07	06	05
72	71	70	69	68	67	66	65	64	63	62	61

*For we do not wrestle
against flesh and blood, but
against the rulers, against
the authorities, against the cosmic powers
over this present darkness, against the
spiritual forces of evil
in the heavenly places.*

EPHESIANS 6:12 (ESV)

Foreword

People often ask me, Which of your books is your favorite? Of course, as any parent would speak of his children, I reply that I prize all of my books, and it's hard to pick a favorite. Each book is unique, reflecting a particular time in my life, a stage of growth, something I was learning, pondering, and experiencing. You can almost trace Frank Peretti's spiritual journey by reading his books.

But having said all that, I can tell you that *This Present Darkness* holds a special place in my heart because it was my very first novel, written during a time of dark discouragement and bitter struggle. I was in my mid-thirties, I'd pursued many dreams with no enduring success, and now I was a frustrated, burned-out former minister working in a ski factory with only one dream left: to be a writer. When Crossway Books called me to say they would publish my book, that was probably *the* pivotal moment of my life.

What inspired this book? Nothing in particular and a lot of things in general. Twenty-five years ago, the drug tripping of the sixties was "maturing" into the neopaganism of the late seventies, and demons—and their doctrines—were gaining a weird, glassy-eyed respect from the popular culture; *Star Wars* was a smash hit movie that dazzled us with sights, sounds, and spectacle from other worlds; Superman and Indiana Jones were reviving the mystique and appeal of the "superhero." Somewhere in all this mix of spirit and spectacle, I envisioned a story that would convey the dangers and workings of warfare in the spiritual realm. I envisioned a movie-of-the-mind, a fiery-winged flight through dimensions never dreamed of, blade-to-blade encounters with the ugliness of spiritual evil, and the triumph, the blazing white light of God's holy angels, slingshot to victory by the prayers of struggling saints. For five years I dreamed, fantasized, and "played pretend" on paper, on and off, frequently abandoning, always returning to the project, the vision, the one thing I just had to finish before I died, published or not.

Seventeen years ago—three years after it was finished—*TPD* was in print. After a slow start, it leaped suddenly from store shelf obscurity to front-counter celebrity, and stayed on the bestseller lists for nearly ten years, breaking publishing barriers and records alike. Of all the books I have written, *This Present Darkness* has been the most popular. Of all the topics I've addressed in my books, spiritual warfare seems to be the one topic with which I will always be identified, probably to my grave.

Today, fifteen years after the publishing of the sequel, *Piercing the Darkness,* I don't talk much about spiritual warfare. I've moved on to learn and write about other topics as God leads me. But that's the nice thing about books: Even though the author has moved on to other things, the books remain. *This Present Darkness* is still speaking the same message to new generations, in many countries, in many languages. God is still using my feeble effort from years ago to open eyes, change hearts, and save souls. Do I find that satisfying, fulfilling, and awe-inspiring? Ohhhhh yes, and from the days in the factory until now, I have never been able to comprehend the vastness of God's power and purpose. I can only stand in wonder and give thanks for what He has done.

—Frank E. Peretti
May 19, 2003

1

Late on a full-mooned Sunday night, the two figures in work clothes appeared on Highway 27, just outside the small college town of Ashton. They were tall, at least seven feet, strongly built, perfectly proportioned. One was dark-haired and sharp-featured, the other blond and powerful. From a half mile away they looked toward the town, regarding the cacophonic sounds of gaiety from the storefronts, streets, and alleys within it. They started walking.

It was the time of the Ashton Summer Festival, the town's yearly exercise in frivolity and chaos, its way of saying thank you, come again, good luck, and nice to have you to the eight hundred or so college students at Whitmore College who would be getting their long awaited summer break from classes. Most would pack up and go home, but all would definitely stay at least long enough to take in the festivities, the street disco, the carnival rides, the nickel movies, and whatever else could be had, over or under the table, for kicks. It was a wild time, a chance to get drunk, pregnant, beat up, ripped off, and sick, all in the same night.

In the middle of town a community-conscious landowner had opened up a vacant lot and permitted a traveling troupe of enterprising migrants to set up their carnival with rides, booths, and portapotties. The rides were best viewed in the dark, an escapade in gaily lit rust, powered by unmuffled tractor engines that competed with the wavering carnival music which squawked loudly from somewhere in the middle of it all. But on this warm summer night the roaming, cotton-candied masses were out to enjoy, enjoy, enjoy. A ferris wheel slowly turned, hesitated for boarding, turned some more for unboarding, then took a few full rotations to give its passengers their money's worth; a merry-go-round spun in a brightly lit, gaudy circle, the peeling and dismembered horses still prancing to the melody of the canned calliope; carnival-goers threw baseballs at baskets, dimes at ashtrays, darts at balloons, and money to the wind along the hastily assembled, ramshackle midway where the hawkers ranted the same try-yer-luck chatter for each passerby.

The two visitors stood tall and silent in the middle of it all, wondering how a town of twelve thousand people—including college students—could produce such a vast, teeming crowd. The usually quiet population had turned out in droves, augmented by diversion-seekers from elsewhere, until the streets, taverns, stores, alleys, and parking spots were jammed, anything was allowed, and the illegal was ignored. The police did have their hands full, but each rowdy, vandal, drunk, or hooker in cuffs only meant a dozen more still loose and roaming about the town. The festival, reaching a crescendo now on its last night, was like a terrible storm that couldn't be stopped; one could only wait for it to blow over, and there would be plenty to clean up afterward.

The two visitors made their way slowly through the people-packed carnival, listening to the talk, watching the activity. They were inquisitive about this town, so they took their time observing here and there, on the right, on the left, before and behind. The milling throngs were moving around them like swirling garments in a washing machine, meandering from this side of the street to the other in an unpredictable, never-ending cycle. The two tall men kept eyeing the crowd. They were looking for someone.

"There," said the dark-haired man.

They both saw her. She was young, very pretty, but also very unsettled, looking this way and that, a camera in her hands and a stiff-lipped expression on her face.

The two men hurried through the crowd and stood beside her. She didn't notice them.

"You know," the dark-haired one said to her, "you might try looking over there."

With that simple comment, he guided her by a hand on her shoulder toward one particular booth on the midway. She stepped through the grass and candy wrappers, moving toward the booth where some teenagers were egging each other on in popping balloons with darts. None of that interested her, but then . . . some shadows moving stealthily behind the booth did. She held her camera ready, took a few more silent, careful steps, and then quickly raised the camera to her eye.

The flash of the bulb lit up the trees behind the booth as the two men hurried away to their next appointment.

They moved smoothly, unfalteringly, passing through the main part of town at a brisk pace. Their final destination was a mile past the center of town, right on Poplar Street, and up to the top of Morgan Hill about a half mile. Practically no time at all had passed before they stood before the little white church on its postage-stamp lot, with its well-groomed lawn and dainty Sunday-School-and-Service billboard. Across the top of the little billboard was the name "Ashton Community Church," and in black letters hastily painted over whatever name used to be there it said, "Henry L. Busche, Pastor."

They looked back. From this lofty hill one could look over the whole town and see it spread from city limit to city limit. To the west sparkled the caramel-colored carnival; to the east stood the dignified and matronly Whitmore College campus; along Highway 27, Main Street through town, were the storefront offices, the smalltown-sized Sears, a few gas stations at war, a True Value Hardware, the local newspaper, several small family businesses. From here the town looked so typically American—small, innocent, and harmless, like the background for every Norman Rockwell painting.

But the two visitors did not perceive with eyes only. Even from this vantage point the true substratum of Ashton weighed very heavily upon their spirits and minds. They could feel it: restless, strong, growing, very designed and purposeful . . . a very special kind of evil.

It was not unlike either of them to ask questions, to study, to probe. More often than not it came with their job. So they naturally hesitated in their business, pausing to wonder, Why here?

But only for an instant. It could have been some acute sensitivity, an instinct, a very faint but for them discernible impression, but it was enough to make them both instantly vanish around the corner of the church, melding themselves against the beveled siding, almost invisible there in the dark. They didn't speak, they didn't move, but they watched with a piercing gaze as something approached.

The night scene of the quiet street was a collage of stark blue moonlight and bottomless shadows. But one shadow did not stir with the wind as did the tree shadows, and neither did it stand still as did the building shadows. It crawled, quivered, moved along the street toward the church, while any light it crossed seemed to sink into its blackness, as if it were a breach torn in space. But this shadow had a shape, an animated, creaturelike shape, and as it neared the church sounds could be heard: the scratching of claws along the ground, the faint rustling of breeze-blown, membranous wings wafting just above the creature's shoulders.

It had arms and it had legs, but it seemed to move without them, crossing the street and mounting the front steps of the church. Its leering, bulbous eyes reflected the stark blue light of the full moon with their own jaundiced glow. The gnarled head protruded from hunched shoulders, and wisps of rancid red breath seethed in labored hisses through rows of jagged fangs.

It either laughed or it coughed—the wheezes puffing out from deep within its throat could have been either. From its crawling posture it reared up on its legs and looked about the quiet neighborhood, the black, leathery jowls pulling back into a hideous death-mask grin. It moved toward the front door. The black hand passed through the door like a spear through liquid; the body hobbled forward and penetrated the door, but only halfway.

Suddenly, as if colliding with a speeding wall, the creature was knocked backward and into a raging tumble down the steps, the glowing red breath tracing a corkscrew trail through the air.

With an eerie cry of rage and indignation, it gathered itself up off the sidewalk and stared at the strange door that would not let it pass through. Then the membranes on its back began to billow, enfolding great bodies of air, and it flew with a roar headlong at the door, through the door, into the foyer—and into a cloud of white hot light.

The creature screamed and covered its eyes, then felt itself being grabbed by a huge, powerful vise of a hand. In an instant it was hurling through space like a rag doll, outside again, forcefully ousted.

The wings hummed in a blur as it banked sharply in a flying turn and headed for the door again, red vapors chugging in dashes and streaks from its nostrils, its talons bared and poised for attack, a ghostly siren of a scream rising in its throat. Like an arrow through a target, like a bullet through a board, it streaked through the door—

And instantly felt its insides tearing loose.

There was an explosion of suffocating vapor, one final scream, and the flailing of withering arms and legs. Then there was nothing at all except the ebbing stench of sulfur and the two strangers, suddenly inside the church.

The big blond man replaced a shining sword as the white light that surrounded him faded away.

"A spirit of harassment?" he asked.

"Or doubt . . . or fear. Who knows?"

"And that was one of the *smaller* ones?"

"I've not seen one smaller."

"No indeed. And just how many would you say there are?"

"More, much more than we, and everywhere. Never idle."

"So I've seen," the big man sighed.

"But what are they doing here? We've never seen such concentration before, not here."

"Oh, the reason won't be hidden for long." He looked through the foyer doors and toward the sanctuary. "Let's see this man of God."

They turned from the door and walked through the small foyer. The bulletin board on the wall carried requests for groceries for a needy family, some baby-sitting, and prayer for a sick missionary. A large bill announced a congregational business meeting for next Friday. On the other wall, the record of weekly offerings indicated the offerings were down from last week; so was the attendance, from sixty-one to forty-two.

Down the short and narrow aisle they went, past the orderly ranks of dark-stained plank and slat pews, toward the front of the sanctuary where one small spotlight illumined a rustic two-by-four cross hanging above the baptistry. In the center of the worn-carpeted platform stood the little sacred desk, the pulpit, with a Bible laid open upon it. These were humble furnishings, functional but not at all elaborate, revealing either humility on the part of the people or neglect.

Then the first sound was added to the picture: a soft, muffled sobbing from the end of the right pew. There, kneeling in earnest prayer, his head resting on the hard wooden bench, and his hands clenched with fervency, was a young man, very young, the blond man thought at first: young and vulnerable. It all showed in his countenance, now the very picture of pain, grief, and love. His lips moved without sound as names, petitions, and praises poured forth with passion and tears.

The two couldn't help but just stand there for a moment, watching, studying, pondering.

"The little warrior," said the dark-haired one.

The big blond man formed the words himself in silence, looking down at the contrite man in prayer.

"Yes," he observed, "this is the one. Even now he's interceding, standing before the Lord for the sake of the people, for the town . . ."

"Almost every night he's here."

At that remark, the big man smiled. "He's not so insignificant."

"But he's the only one. He's alone."

"No." The big man shook his head. "There are others. There are always others. They just have to be found. For now, his single, vigilant prayer is the beginning."

"He's going to be hurt, you know that."

"And so will the newspaperman. And so will we."

"But will we win?"

The big man's eyes seemed to burn with a rekindled fire.

"We will *fight*."

"We will fight," his friend agreed.

They stood over the kneeling warrior, on either side; and at that moment, little by little, like the bloom of a flower, white light began to fill the room. It illuminated the cross on the back wall, slowly brought out the colors and grain in every plank of every pew, and rose in intensity until the once plain and humble sanctuary came alive with an unearthly beauty. The walls glimmered, the worn rugs glowed, the little pulpit stood tall and stark as a sentinel backlit by the sun.

And now the two men were brilliantly white, their former clothing transfigured by garments that seemed to burn with intensity. Their faces were bronzed and glowing, their eyes shone like fire, and each man wore a glistening golden belt from which hung a flashing sword. They placed their hands upon the shoulders of the young man and then, like a gracefully spreading canopy, silken, shimmering, nearly transparent membranes began to unfurl from their backs and shoulders and rise to meet and overlap above their heads, gently undulating in a spiritual wind.

Together they ministered peace to their young charge, and his many tears began to subside.

The *Ashton Clarion* was a small-town, grass-roots newspaper; it was little and quaint, maybe just a touch unorganized at times, unassuming. It was, in other words, the printed expression of the town of Ashton. Its offices occupied a small storefront space on Main Street in the middle of town, just a one-story affair with a large display window and a heavy, toe-scuffed door with a mail slot. The paper came out twice a week, on Tuesdays and Fridays, and didn't make a lot of money. By the appearance of the office and layout facilities, you could tell it was a low-budget operation.

In the front half of the building was the office and newsroom area. It consisted of three desks, two typewriters, two wastebaskets, two telephones, one coffeemaker without a cord, and what looked like all the scattered notes, papers, stationery and office bric-a-brac in the world. An old worn counter from a torn-down railroad station formed a divider between the functioning office and the reception area, and of course there was a small bell above the door that jingled every time someone came in.

Toward the back of this maze of small-scale activity was one luxury that looked just a little too big-town for this place: a glassed-in office for the editor. It was, in fact, a new addition. The new editor/owner was a former big city reporter and having a glassed-in editor's office had been one of his life's dreams.

This new fellow was Marshall Hogan, a strong, big-framed bustler hustler whom his staff—the typesetter, the secretary/reporter/ad girl, the paste-up man, and the reporter/columnist—lovingly referred to as "Attila the Hogan." He had bought the paper a few months ago, and the clash between his big-city polish and their small-town easy-go still roused some confrontations from time to time. Marshall wanted a quality paper, one that ran efficiently and smoothly and made its deadlines, with a place for everything and everything in its place. But the transition from the *New York Times* to the *Ashton Clarion* was like jumping off a speeding train into a wall of half-set jello. Things just didn't click as fast in this little office, and the high-powered efficiency Marshall was used to had to give way to such *Ashton Clarion* quirks as saving all the coffee grounds for the secretary's compost pile, and someone finally turning in a long-awaited human interest story, but with parakeet droppings on it.

On Monday morning the traffic patterns were hectic, with no time for any weekend hangovers. The Tuesday edition was being brought forth in a rush, and the entire staff was feeling the labor pains, dashing back and forth between their desks in front and the paste-up room in the back, squeezing past each other in the narrow passage, carrying rough copy for articles and ads to be typeset, finished typeset galleys, and assorted shapes and sizes of half-tones of photographs that would highlight the news pages.

In the back, amid bright lights, cluttered worktables, and rapidly moving bodies, Marshall and Tom the paste-up man bent over a large, benchlike easel, assembling Tuesday's *Clarion* out of bits and pieces that seemed to be scattered everywhere. This goes here, this can't—so we have to shove it somewhere else, this is too big, what will we use to fill this? Marshall was getting miffed. Every Monday and Thursday he got miffed.

"Edie!" he hollered, and his secretary answered, "Coming," and he told her for the umpteenth time, "The galleys go in the trays over the table, not on the table, not on the floor, not on the—"

"I didn't put any galleys on the floor!" Edie protested as she hurried into the paste-up room with more galleys in her hand. She was a tough little woman of forty with just the right personality to stand up to Marshall's brusqueness. She still knew where to find things around the office better than anyone, especially her new boss. "I've got them right in your cute little trays where you want them."

"So how'd these get here on the floor?"

"Wind, Marshall, and don't make me tell you where *that* came from!"

"All right, Marshall," said Tom, "that takes care of pages three, four, six, seven ... . what about one and two? What are we going to do with all these empty slots?"

"We are going to put in Bernie's coverage of the Festival, with clever writing, dramatic human-interest photos, the whole bit, as soon as she gets her rear in here and gives them to us! Edie!"

"Yo!"

"Bernie's an hour late, for crying out loud! Call her again, will you?"

"Just did. No answer."

"Nuts."

George, the small, retired typesetter who still worked for the fun of it, swiveled his chair away from the typesetting machine and offered, "How about the Ladies Auxiliary Barbecue? I'm just finishing that up, and the photo of Mrs. Marmaselle is spicy enough for a lawsuit."

"Yeah," Marshall groaned, "right on page one. That's all I need, a good impression."

"So what now?" Edie asked.

"Anybody make it to the Festival?"

"Went fishing," said George. "That Festival's too wild for me."

"My wife wouldn't let me," said Tom.

"I caught some of it," said Edie.

"Start writing," said Marshall. "The biggest townbuster of the year, and we've got to have something on it."

The phone rang.

"Saved by the bell?" Edie chirped as she picked up the back-room extension. "Good morning, the *Clarion*." Suddenly she brightened. "Hey, Bernice! Where are you?"

"Where is she?" Marshall demanded at the same time.

Edie listened and her face filled with horror. "Yes . . . well, calm down now . . . sure . . . well don't worry, we'll get you out."

Marshall spouted, "Well, where the heck is she?"

Edie gave him a scolding look and answered, "In jail!"

2

Marshall hurried into the basement of the Ashton Police Station and immediately wished he could disconnect his nose and ears. Beyond the heavily barred gate to the cell block, the crammed jail cells didn't smell or sound much different from the carnival the night before. On his way here he had noticed how quiet the streets were this morning. No wonder—all the noise had moved inside to these half-dozen peeling-painted cells set in cold, echoing concrete. Here were all the dopers, vandals, rowdies, drunks, and no-goods the police could scrape off the face of the town, collected in what amounted to an overcrowded zoo. Some were making a party of it, playing poker for cigarettes with finger-smeared cards and trying to outdo each other's tales of illicit exploits. Toward the end of the cells a gang of young bucks made obscene comments to a cageful of prostitutes with no better place to be locked up. Others just slumped in corners in a drunken stew or a depressed slump or both. The remainder glared at him from behind the bars, made snide remarks, begged for peanuts. He was glad he had left Kate upstairs.

Jimmy Dunlop, the new deputy, was stationed loyally at the guard desk, filling out forms and drinking strong coffee.

"Hey, Mr. Hogan," he said, "you got right down here."

"I couldn't wait . . . and I *won't* wait!" he snapped. He wasn't feeling well. This had been his first Festival, and that was bad enough, but he never expected, never dreamed of such a prolonging of the agony. He towered over the desk, his big frame shifting forward to accentuate his impatience. "Well?" he demanded.

"Hmmm?"

"I'm here to get my reporter out of the can."

"Sure, I know that. Have you got a release?"

"Listen. I just paid off those yo-yos upstairs. They were supposed to call you down here."

"Well . . . I haven't heard a thing, and I have to have authorization."

"Jimmy—"

"Yeah?"

"Your phone's off the hook."

"Oh . . ."

Marshall set the phone down right in front of him with a firmness that made the phone jingle in pain.

"Call 'em."

Marshall straightened up, watched Jimmy dial wrong, dial again, try to get through. He goes well with the rest of the town, Marshall thought, nervously running his fingers through his graying red hair. Aw, it was a nice town, sure. Cute, maybe a little dumb, kind of like a bumbling kid who always got himself into jams. Things weren't really better in the big city, he tried to remind himself.

"Uh, Mr. Hogan," Jimmy asked, his hand over the receiver, "who was it you talked to?"

"Kinney."

"Sergeant Kinney, please."

Marshall was impatient. "Let's have the key for the gate. I'll let her know I'm here."

Jimmy gave him the key. He'd argued with Marshall Hogan before.

A whoop of mock welcome poured out from the cells along with hurled cigarette butts and whistled march tunes as he passed by. He lost no time in finding the cell he wanted.

"All right, Krueger, I know you're in there!"

"Come and get me, Hogan," came the reply from a desperate and somewhat outraged female voice down near the end.

"Well, stick out your arm, wave at me or something!"

A hand stuck out through the bodies and bars and gave him a desperate wave. He got there, gave the palm a slap, and found himself face to face with Bernice Krueger, jailbird, his prize columnist and reporter. She was a young, attractive woman in her midtwenties, with unkempt brown hair and large, wire-rimmed glasses, now smudged. She had obviously had a hard night and was presently keeping company with at least a dozen women, some older, some shockingly younger, mostly trucked-in prostitutes. Marshall didn't know whether to laugh or spit.

"I won't mince words—you look terrible," he said.

"Only in keeping with my vocation. I'm a hooker now."

"Yeah, yeah, one of us," a chunky girl sang out.

Marshall grimaced and shook his head. "What kind of questions were you asking out there?"

"Right now no joke is funny. No anecdote of last night's events is funny. I'm not laughing, I'm seething. The assignment was an insult in the first place."

"Look, *somebody* had to cover the carnival."

"But we were quite right in our prognostication; there was certainly nothing new under the sun, nor the moon, as it were."

"You got arrested," he offered.

"For the sake of grabbing the reader with a scandalous lead. What else was there to write about?"

"So read it to me."

A Spanish girl from the back of the cell offered, "She tried to do business with the wrong trick," at which the whole cell block guffawed and hooted.

"I demand to be released!" Bernice fumed. "And have you stepped in epoxy? Do something!"

"Jimmy's on the phone with Kinney. I paid your bail. We'll get you out of here."

Bernice took a moment to simmer down and then reported, "In answer to your questions, I was carrying on spot interviews, trying to get some good pictures, good quotes, good *anything*. I assume that Nancy and Rosie here"—she looked toward two young ladies who could have been twins, and they smiled at Marshall—"wondered what I was doing, constantly circumnavigating the carnival grounds looking bewildered. They struck up a conversation that really got us nowhere news-wise, but did get us all in trouble when Nancy propositioned an undercover cop and we all got busted together."

"I think she'd be good at it," quipped Nancy as Rosie gave her a playful hit.

Marshall asked, "And you didn't show him your I.D., your press card?"

"He wouldn't give me a chance! I told him who I was."

"Well, did he hear you?" Marshall asked the girls, "Did he hear her?"

They only shrugged, but Bernice shifted her voice into high gear and cried, "Is this voice loud enough for you? I employed it last night while he slapped the cuffs on me!"

"Welcome to Ashton."

"I'll have his badge!"

"It'll only turn your chest green." Hogan held up his hand to halt another outburst. "Hey, listen, it isn't worth the trouble . . ."

"There are different schools of thought!"

"Bernie . . ."

"I have some things I would love to print, four columns wide, all about Supercop and that do-nothing cretin of a chief! Where is he, anyway?"

"Who, you mean Brummel?"

"He has a very handy way of disappearing, you know. *He* knows who I am. Where is he?"

"I don't know. I couldn't reach him this morning."

"And he turned his back last night!"

"What are you talking about?"

Suddenly she clammed up, but Marshall read her face clear as a bell: Make sure you ask me later.

Just then the big gate opened and in came Jimmy Dunlop.

"We'll discuss it later," said Marshall. "All set, Jimmy?"

Jimmy was too intimidated by the yells, demands, hoots, and jeers coming from the cages to answer right away. But he did have the key to the cell in his hand, and that said enough.

"Step away from the door, please," he ordered.

"Hey, when's your voice gonna change?" was characteristic of the answers he got. They did move away from the door. Jimmy opened it, Bernice stepped out quickly, and he slammed it shut again behind her.

"Okay," he said, "you're free to leave on bail. You'll be notified of the date for your arraignment."

"Just return my purse, my press card, my notepad, and my camera!" Bernice hissed, heading for the door.

Kate Hogan, a slender, dignified redhead, had tried to make good use of her time while waiting upstairs in the courthouse lobby. There was much to observe here after the Festival, although it certainly wasn't pleasant: some woeful souls were escorted and/or dragged in, struggling against their cuffs all the way and spouting obscenities; many others were just now being released after spending the night behind bars. It almost looked like a change of shifts at some bizarre factory, the first shift leaving, somewhat sheepishly, their scant belongings still in little paper bags, and the second shift coming in, all bound up and indignant. Most of the police officers were strangers from elsewhere, overtimers sent in to beef up the very small Ashton staff, and they weren't being paid to be kind or courteous.

The heavily jowled lady at the main desk had two cigarettes smoldering in her ashtray, but little time to take a drag between processing papers on every case coming in or going out. From Kate's viewpoint the whole operation looked very hurried and slipshod. There were a few cheap lawyers passing out their cards, but one night in jail seemed to be the extent of punishment any of these people would have to bear, and now they only wanted to get out of town in peace.

Kate unconsciously shook her head. To think of poor Bernice being herded through this place like so much rabble. She must be furious.

She felt a strong but gentle arm around her, and let herself sink into its embrace.

"Mmmmmm," she said, "now there's a pleasant change."

"After what I had to look at downstairs I need some healing up," Marshall told her.

She put her arm around him and pulled him close.

"Is it like this every year?" she asked.

"No, I hear it gets worse each time." Kate shook her head again, and Marshall added, "But the *Clarion* will have something to say about it. Ashton could use a change of direction; they should be able to see that by now."

"How is Bernice?"

"She'll be one heck of an editorialist for a while. She's okay. She'll live."

"Are you going to talk to somebody about this?"

"Alf Brummel's not around. He's smart. But I'll catch him later today and see what I can do. And I wouldn't mind getting my twenty-five dollars back."

"Well, he must be busy. I'd hate to be the police chief on a day like this."

"Oh, he'll hate it even more if I can help it."

Bernice's return from a night of incarceration was marked by an angry countenance and sharp, staccato footsteps on the linoleum. She too was carrying a paper bag, angrily rummaging through it to make sure everything was there.

Kate extended her arms to give Bernice a comforting hug.

"Bernice, how are you?"

"Brummel's name will soon be mud, the mayor's name will be dung, and I won't be able to print what that cop's name will be. I'm indignant, I could be constipated, and I desperately need a bath."

"Well," said Marshall, "take it out on your typewriter, swat some flies. I need that Festival story for Tuesday's edition."

Bernice immediately fumbled through her pockets and retrieved a wad of crinkled toilet paper, giving it to Marshall with forcefulness.

"Your loyal reporter, always on the job," she said. "What else was there to do in there besides watch the paint peel and wait in line for the toilet? I think you'll find the whole write-up very descriptive, and I threw in an on-the-spot interview with some jailed hookers for extra flavor. Who knows? Maybe it'll make this town wonder what it's coming to."

"Any pictures?" Marshall asked.

Bernice handed him a can of film. "You should find something in there you can use. I've got some film still in the camera, but that's of personal interest to me."

Marshall smiled. He was impressed. "Take the day off, on me. Things will look better tomorrow."

"Perhaps by then I will have regained my professional objectivity."

"You'll smell better."

"Marshall!" said Kate.

"It's okay," said Bernice. "He hands me that stuff all the time." By now she had recovered her purse, press card, and camera and threw the wadded paper bag spitefully into a trash can. "So what's the car situation?"

"Kate brought your car," Marshall explained. "If you could take her home, that should work things out best for me. I've got to get things salvaged at the paper and then try to track down Brummel."

Bernice's thoughts snapped into gear. "Brummel, right! I've got to talk to you."

She started pulling Marshall aside before he could say yea or nay, and he could only give Kate an apologetic glance before he and Bernice rounded a corner and stood out of sight near the restrooms.

Bernice spoke in lowered tones. "If you're going to accost Chief Brummel today, I want you to know what I know."

"Besides the obvious?"

"That he's a crumb, a coward, and a cretin? Yes, besides that. It's pieces, disjointed observations, but maybe they'll make sense someday. You always said to have an eye for details. I think I saw your pastor and him together at the carnival last night."

"Pastor Young?"

"Ashton United Christian Church, right? President of the local ministerial, endorses religious tolerance and condemns cruelty to animals."

"Yeah, okay."

"But Brummel doesn't even go to your church, does he?"

"No, he goes to that little dinky one."

"They were off behind the dart throwing booth, in the semidark with three other people, some blond woman, some short, pudgy old fellow and a ghostly-looking black-haired shrew in sunglasses. Sunglasses at *night!*"

Marshall wasn't impressed yet.

She continued as if she was trying to sell him something. "I think I committed a cardinal sin against them: I snapped their picture, and from all appearances they didn't want that. Brummel was quite unnerved and stuttered at me. Young asked me in firm tones to leave: 'This is a private meeting.' The pudgy fellow turned away, the ghostly-looking woman just stared at me with her mouth open."

"Have you considered how this might all appear to you after a good bath and a decent night's sleep?"

"Just let me finish and then we'll find out, all right? Now, right after that little incident was when Nancy and Rosie latched onto me. I mean to say, I did not approach them, they approached me, and soon afterward, I was arrested and my camera confiscated."

She could see she wasn't getting through to him. He was looking around impatiently, shifting his weight back toward the lobby.

"All right, all right, one more thing," she said, trying to hold him in place. "Brummel was there, Marshall. He saw the whole thing."

"What whole thing?"

"My arrest! I was trying to explain who I was to the cop, I was trying to show him my press card, he only took my purse and camera away from me and handcuffed me, and I looked over toward the dart throwing booth again and I saw Brummel watching. He ducked out of sight right away, but I swear I saw him watching the whole thing! Marshall, I went over this all last night, I replayed it and replayed it, and I think . . . well, I don't know what to think, but it has to mean something."

"To continue the scenario," Marshall ventured, "the film is gone from your camera."

Bernice checked. "Oh, it's still in the camera, but that means nothing."

Hogan sighed and thought the thing over. "Okay, so shoot up the rest of the roll, and try to get something we can use, right? Then develop it and we'll see. Can we go now?"

"Have I ever made any impulsive, imprudent, overassuming mistakes like this before?"

"Sure you have."

"Aw, c'mon, now! Extend me a little grace just this once."

"I'll try to close my eyes."

"Your wife's waiting."

"I know, I know."

Marshall didn't quite know what to say to Kate when they rejoined her.

"Sorry about this . . ." he muttered.

"Now then," Kate said, trying to pick up from where they left off, "we were talking about vehicles. Bernice, I had to drive your car here so you could have it to get home. If you drop me off at our house . . ."

"Yes, right, right," said Bernice.

"And, Marshall, I have a lot of things to do this afternoon. Can you pick up Sandy after her psychology class?"

Marshall didn't say a word, but his face showed a resounding no.

Kate took a set of keys from her purse and handed them to Bernice. "Your car is right around the corner, next to ours in the press space. Why don't you bring it around?"

Bernice took her cue and went out the door. Kate held Marshall with a loving arm and searched his face for a moment.

"Hey, c'mon. Try it. Just once."

"But cockfights are illegal in this state."

"If you ask me, she's just a chip off the old block."

"I don't know where I'll start," he said.

"Just being there to pick her up will mean something. Cash in on it."

As they started for the door, Marshall looked around and let his gut senses feel things out.

"Can you figure this town, Kate?" he said finally. "It's like some kind of disease. Everybody's got the same weird disease around here."

A sunny morning always helps make the previous night's problems seem less severe. That is what Hank Busche thought as he pushed open his front screen door and stepped out onto the small concrete stoop. He lived in a low-rent, one-bedroom house not far from the church, a little white box settled in one corner, with beveled siding, small hedged yard and mossy roof. It wasn't much, and often seemed far less, but it was all he could afford on his pastor's salary. Well, he wasn't complaining. He and Mary were comfortable and sheltered, and the morning was beautiful.

This was their day to sleep in, and two quarts of milk waited at the base of the steps. He snatched them up, looking forward to a bowl of milk-sodden Wheaties, a bit of distraction from his trials and tribulations.

He had known trouble before. His father had been a pastor while Hank was growing up, and the two of them had lived through a great many glories and hassles, the kind that come with pioneering churches, pastoring, itinerating. Hank knew from the time he was young that this was the life he wanted for himself, the way he wanted to serve the Lord. For him, the church had always been a very exciting place to work, exciting helping his father out in the earlier years, exciting going through Bible school and seminary and then two years of pastoral internship. It was exciting now too, but it resembled the exhilaration the Texans must have felt at the Alamo. Hank was just twenty-six, and usually full of fire; but this pastorate, his very first, seemed a difficult place to get the fire spread around. Somebody had wetted down all the kindling, and he didn't know what to make of it yet. For some reason he had been voted in as pastor, which meant somebody in the church wanted his kind of ministry, but then there were all the others, the ones who . . . made it exciting. They made it exciting whenever he preached on repentance; they made it exciting whenever he confronted sin in the fellowship; they made it exciting whenever he brought up the cross of Christ and the message of salvation. At this point, it was more Hank's faith and assurance that he was where God wanted him than any other factor that kept him by his guns, standing steadfast while getting shot at. Ah well, Hank thought to himself, at least enjoy the morning. The Lord put it here just for you.

Had he backed into the house again without turning, he would have spared himself an outrage and kept his lightened spirit. But he did turn to go back in, and immediately confronted the huge, black, dripping letters spray-painted on the front of the house: "YOU'RE

DEAD MEAT, _____." The last word was an obscenity. His eyes saw it, then did a slow pan from one side of the house to the other, taking it all in. It was one of those things that take time to register. All he could do was stand there for a moment, first wondering who could have done it, then wondering why, then wondering if it would ever come off. He looked closer, and touched it with his finger. It had to have been done during the night; it was quite dry.

"Honey," came Mary's voice from inside, "you're leaving the door open."

"Mmmmm . . ." was all he said, having no better words. He didn't really want her to know.

He went back inside, closing the door firmly, and joined young, beautiful, long-tressed Mary over a bowl of Wheaties and some hot, buttered toast.

Here was the sunny spot in a cloudy sky for Hank, this playful little wife with the melodic giggle. She was a doll and she had real grit too. Hank often regretted that she had to go through the struggles they were now having—after all, she could have married some stable, boring accountant or insurance salesman—but she was a terrific support for him, always there, always believing God for the best and always believing in Hank too.

"What's wrong?" she asked immediately.

Rats! You do what you can to hide it, you try to act normal, but she *still* picks it up, Hank thought.

"Ummmm . . ." he started to say.

"Still bothered about the board meeting?"

There's your out, Busche. "Sure, a little."

"I didn't even hear you come home. Did the meeting last real late?"

"No. Alf Brummel had to take off for some important meeting he wouldn't talk about and the others just, you know, had their say and went home, just left me to lick my wounds. I stuck around and prayed for a while. I think that worked. I felt okay after that." He brightened just a little. "As a matter of fact, I really felt the Lord comforting me last night."

"I still think they picked a funny time to call a board meeting, right during the Festival," she said.

"And on Sunday night!" he said through his flakes. "I no sooner give the altar call than I get them calling a meeting."

"About the same thing?"

"Aw, I think they're just using Lou as an excuse to make trouble."

"Well, what did you tell them?"

"The same thing, all over again. We did just what the Bible says: I went to Lou, then John and I went to Lou, and then we brought it before the rest of the church, and then we, well, we removed him from fellowship."

"Well, it did seem to be what the congregation decided. But why can't the board go along with it?"

"They can't read. Don't the Ten Commandments have something in there about adultery?"

"I know, I know."

Hank set down his spoon so he could gesture better. "And they were mad at *me* last night! They started giving me all this stuff about judging not lest I be judged—"

"*Who* did?"

"Oh, the same old Alf Brummel camp: Alf, Sam Turner, Gordon Mayer . . . you know, the Old Guard."

"Well, don't just let them push you around!"

"They won't change my mind, anyway. Don't know what kind of job security that gives me."

Now Mary was getting indignant. "Well, what on earth is wrong with Alf Brummel? Has he got something against the Bible or the truth or what? If it weren't this, it would certainly be something else!"

"Jesus loves him, Mary," Hank cautioned. "It's just that he feels under heavy conviction, he's guilty, he's a sinner, he knows it, and guys like us will always bother guys like him. The last pastor preached the Word and Alf didn't like it. Now I'm preaching the Word and he still doesn't like it. He pulls a lot of weight in that church, so I guess he thinks he can dictate what comes across that pulpit."

"Well, he can't!"

"Not in my case, anyway."

"So why doesn't he just go somewhere else?"

Hank pointed his finger dramatically. "That, dear wife, is a good question! There seems to be a method in his madness, like it's his mission in life to destroy pastors."

"It's just the picture they keep painting of you. You're just not like that!"

"Hmmmm . . . yes, painting. Are you ready?"

"Ready for what?"

Hank drew a breath, sighed it out, then looked at her. "We had some visitors last night. They—they painted a slogan on the front of the house."

"What? *Our* house?"

"Well . . . our landlord's house."

She got up. "Where?" She went out the front door, her fuzzy slippers scuffing on the front walk.

"Oh, no!"

Hank joined her, and they drank in the view together. It was still there, real as ever.

"Now that makes me mad!" she declared, but now she was crying. "What'd we ever do to anybody?"

"I think we were just talking about it," Hank suggested.

Mary didn't catch what he said, but she had a theory of her own, the most obvious one. "Maybe the Festival . . . it always brings out the worst in everyone."

Hank had his own theory but said nothing. It had to be someone in the church, he thought. He'd been called a lot of things: a bigot, a heel-dragger, an overly moral troublemaker. He had even been accused of being a homosexual and of beating his wife. Some angry church member could have done this, perhaps a friend of Lou Stanley the adulterer, perhaps Lou himself. He would probably never know, but that was all right. God knew.

3

Just a few miles east of town on Highway 27, a large black limousine raced through the countryside. In the plush backseat, a plump middle-aged man talked business with his secretary, a tall and slender woman with long, jet-black hair and a pale complexion. He talked crisply and succinctly as she took fluid shorthand, laying out some big-scale business deal. Then something occurred to the man.

"That reminds me," he said, and the secretary looked up from her memo pad. "The professor claims she sent me a package some time ago, but I don't recall ever receiving it."

"What kind of package?"

"A small book. A personal item. Why not make a note to yourself to check for it back at the ranch?"

The secretary opened her portfolio and appeared to make a note of it. Actually, she wrote nothing.

It was Marshall's second visit to Courthouse Square in the same day. The first time was to get Bernice bailed out, and now it was to pay a visit to the very man Bernice wanted to string up: Alf Brummel, the chief of police. After the *Clarion* finally got to press, Marshall was about to call Brummel, but Sara, Brummel's secretary, called Marshall first and made an appointment for 2 o'clock that afternoon. That was a good move, Marshall thought. Brummel was calling for a truce before the tanks began to roll.

He pulled his Buick into his reserved parking space in front of the new courthouse complex and paused beside his car to look up and down the street, surveying the aftermath of the Festival's final Sunday night death throes. Main Street was trying to be the same old Main

Street again, but to Marshall's discerning eye the whole town seemed to be walking with a limp, sort of tired, sore, and sluggish. The usual little gaggles of half-hurried pedestrians were doing a lot of pausing, looking, headshaking, regretting. For generations Ashton had taken pride in its grass-roots warmth and dignity and had striven to be a good place for its children to grow up. But now there were inner turmoils, anxieties, fears, as if some kind of cancer was eating away at the town and invisibly destroying it. On the exterior, there were the store windows now replaced with unsightly plywood, the many parking meters broken off, the litter and broken glass up and down the street. But even as the store owners and businessmen swept up the debris, there seemed to be an unspoken sureness that the inner problems would remain, the troubles would continue. Crime was up, especially among the youth; simple, common trust in one's neighbor was diminishing; never had the town been so full of rumors, scandals, and malicious gossip. In the shadow of fear and suspicion, life here was gradually losing its joy and simplicity, and no one seemed to know why or how.

Marshall headed into Courthouse Square. The square consisted of two buildings, tastefully garnished with willows and shrubs, facing a common parking lot. On one side was the classy two-story brick courthouse, which also housed the town's police department and that somewhat decadent basement cell block; one of the town's three squad cars was parked outside. On the other side was the two-story, glass-fronted town hall, housing the mayor's office, the town council, and other decision-makers. Marshall headed for the courthouse.

He went through the unimposing, plain doorway marked "Police" and found the small reception area empty. He could hear voices from down the hall and behind some of the closed doors, but Sara, the secretary, seemed temporarily out of the room.

No—behind the receptionist's formica-topped counter a huge file was slowly rocking back and forth, and grunts and groans were coming up from below. Marshall leaned over the counter to see a comical sight. Sara, on her knees, dress or no dress, was in the middle of a blue-streak struggle with a jammed file drawer that had entangled itself with her desk. Apparently the score was File Drawers 3, Sara's Shins 0, and Sara was a poor loser. So were her pantyhose.

She let out an ill-timed curse just as her eye caught him standing there, and by then it was too late to rebuild her usual poised image.

"Oh, hi, Marshall . . ."

"Wear your Marine boots next time. They're better for kicking things in."

At least they knew each other, and Sara was glad for that. Marshall had been in this place often enough to become well-acquainted with most of the staff.

"These," she said with the tone of an articulate tour guide, "are the infamous file cabinets of Mr. Alf Brummel, Chief of Police. He just got some fancy new cabinets, so now I've inherited these! Why I have to have them in my office is beyond me, but upon his express orders, here they must stay!"

"They're too ugly to go in *his* office."

"But khaki . . . it's *him*, you know? Oh well, maybe a little decoupage would cheer them up. If they must move in here, the least they can do is smile."

Just then the intercom buzzed. She pressed the button and answered.

"Yes sir?"

Brummel's voice squawked out of the little box, "Hey, my security alarm is flashing . . ."

"Sorry, that was me. I was trying to get one of your file drawers shut."

"Yeah, right. Well, try to rearrange things, will you?"

"Marshall Hogan is here to see you."

"Oh, right. Send him in."

She looked up at Marshall and only shook her head pathetically. "Got an opening for a secretary?" she muttered. Marshall smiled. She explained, "He's got these files right next to the silent alarm button. Every time I open a drawer the building's surrounded."

With a good-bye wave, Marshall went to the nearest office door and let himself into Brummel's office. Alf Brummel stood and extended his hand, his face exploding in a wide, ivory smile.

"Hey, there's the man!"

"Hey, Alf."

They shook hands as Brummel ushered Marshall in and closed the door. Brummel was a man somewhere in his thirties, single, a one-time hotshot city cop with a big buck lifestyle that belied his policeman's salary. He always came on like a likable guy, but Marshall never really trusted him. Come to think of it, he didn't like him that much either. Too much teeth showing for no reason.

"Well," Brummel grinned, "have a seat, have a seat." He was talking again before either man's cushion could compress. "Looks like we made a laughable mistake this weekend."

Marshall recalled the sight of his reporter sharing a cell with prostitutes. "Bernice didn't laugh the whole night, and I'm out twenty-five dollars."

"Well," said Brummel, reaching into his top desk drawer, "that's why we're having this meeting, to clear this whole thing up. Here." He produced a check and handed it to Marshall. "This is your refund on that bail money, and I want you to know that Bernice will be receiving an official signed apology from myself and this office. But, Marshall, please tell me what happened. If I had just been there I could have put a stop to it."

"Bernie says you *were* there."

"I was? Where? I know I was in and out of the station all night, but . . ."

"No, she saw you there at the carnival."

Brummel forced a wider grin. "Well, I don't know who it was she saw in actuality, but I wasn't at the carnival last night. I was busy here."

Marshall had too much momentum by now to back off. "She saw you right at the time she was being arrested."

Brummel didn't seem to hear that statement. "But go on, tell me what happened. I need to get to the bottom of this."

Marshall halted his attack abruptly. He didn't know why. Maybe it was out of courtesy. Maybe it was out of intimidation. Whatever the reason, he began to rattle the story off in neat, almost news-copy form, much the way he heard it from Bernice, but he cautiously left out the implicating details she shared with him. As he talked, his eyes studied Brummel, Brummel's office, and any particular details in decor, layout, agenda. It was mostly reflex. Over the years he had developed the knack of observing and gathering information without looking like he was doing it. Maybe it was because he didn't trust this man, but even if he did, once a reporter, always a reporter. He could see that Brummel's office belonged to a fastidious man, from the highly polished, orderly desk right down to the pencils in the desk caddy, every point honed to perfect sharpness.

Along one wall, where the ugly filing cabinets used to stand, stood a very attractive set of shelves and cabinets of oil-rubbed oak, with glass door panels and brass hardware.

"Say, moving up on the world, huh, Alf?" Marshall quipped, looking toward the cabinets.

"Like them?"

"Love them. What are they?"

"A very attractive replacement for those old filing cabinets. It just goes to show what you can do if you save your pennies. I hated having those file cabinets in here. I think an office should have a little class, right?"

"Eh, yeah, sure. Boy, you have your own copier . . ."

"Yes, and bookshelves, extra storage."

"And another phone?"

"A phone?"

"What's that wire coming out of the wall?"

"Oh, that's for the coffeemaker. But where were we, anyway?"

"Yeah, yeah, what happened to Bernice . . ." and Marshall continued his story. He was well practiced in reading upside down, and while he continued to talk he scanned Brummel's desk calendar. Tuesday afternoons stuck out a little because they were consistently blank, even though they were not Brummel's day off. One Tuesday did have an appointment written down: Rev. Oliver Young, at 2 P.M.

"Oh," he said conversationally, "gonna pay my pastor a visit tomorrow?"

He could tell right away that he had overstepped his bounds; Brummel looked amazed and irritated at the same time.

Brummel forced a toothy grin and said, "Oh yes, Oliver Young is your pastor, isn't he?"

"You two know each other?"

"Well, not really. We have met on an occasional, professional basis, I suppose . . ."

"But don't you go to that other church, that little one?"

"Yes, Ashton Community. But go on, let's hear the rest of what happened."

Marshall was impressed at how easy this guy was to fluster, but he tried not to press his challenge any further. Not yet, anyway. Instead, he picked up his tale where he left off and brought it to a neat finish, including Bernice's outrage. He noticed that Brummel had found some important paperwork to look over, papers that covered up the desk calendar.

Marshall asked, "Say, just who was this turkey cop who wouldn't let Bernice identify herself?"

"An outsider, not even on our force here. If Bernice can get us the name or badge number, I can see that he is confronted with his behavior. You see, we had to bring some auxiliaries down from Windsor to beef things up for the Festival. As for our own men, they all know full well who Bernice Krueger is." Brummel said that last line with a slightly wolfish tone.

"So why isn't she sitting here hearing all this apologizing instead of me?"

Brummel leaned forward and looked rather serious. "I thought it best to talk to you, Marshall, rather than cause her to parade through this office, already somewhat stigmatized. I suppose you know what that girl's been through."

Okay, thought Marshall, I'll ask. "I'm new in town, Alf."

"She hasn't told you?"

"And you'd love to?"

It slipped out, and it stung. Brummel sank back in his chair just a little and studied Marshall's face.

Marshall was just now thinking that he didn't regret what he said. "I'm upset, in case you hadn't noticed."

Brummel started a new paragraph. "Marshall . . . I wanted to see you personally today because I wanted to . . . heal this thing up."

"So let's hear what you have to say about Bernice." Brummel, you'd better choose your words carefully, Marshall thought.

"Well—" Brummel stammered, suddenly put on the spot. "I thought you might want to know about it in case you might find the information helpful in dealing with her. You see, it was several months before you took over the paper that she herself came to Ashton. Just a few weeks before that, her sister, who had been attending the college, committed suicide. Bernice came to Ashton with a fierce vindictiveness, trying to solve the mystery surrounding her sister's death, but . . . we all knew it was just one of those things for which there will never be an answer."

Marshall was silent for a significant amount of time. "I didn't know that."

Brummel's voice was quiet and mournful as he said, "She was positive it had to be some kind of foul play. It was quite an aggressive investigation she had going."

"Well, she does have a reporter's nose."

"Oh, that she does. But you see, Marshall . . . her arrest, it was a mistake, a humiliating one, quite frankly. I really didn't think she would want to see the inside of this building for some time to come. Do you understand now?"

But Marshall wasn't sure he did. He wasn't even sure he'd heard all of it. He suddenly felt very weak, and he couldn't figure out where his anger had gone so quickly. And what about his suspicions? He knew he didn't buy everything this guy was saying—or did he? He knew Brummel had lied about not being at the carnival—or had he?

Or did I just hear him wrong? Or . . . where were we, anyway? C'mon, Hogan, didn't you get enough sleep last night?

"Marshall?"

Marshall looked into Brummel's gazing gray eyes, and he felt a little numb, like he was dreaming.

"Marshall," Brummel said, "I hope you understand. You do understand now, don't you?"

Marshall had to force himself to think, and he found it helped not to look Brummel in the eye for a moment.

"Uh . . ." It was a stupid beginning, but it was the best he could do. "Hey, yeah, Alf, I think I see your point. You did the right thing, I suppose."

"But I do want to heal this whole thing up, particularly between you and me."

"Aw, don't worry about it. It's no big deal." Even as Marshall said it, he was asking himself if he really had.

Brummel's big teeth reappeared. "I'm really glad to hear that, Marshall."

"But, say, listen, you might give her a call at least. She was hurt in a pretty personal way, you know."

"I'll do that, Marshall."

Then Brummel leaned forward with a strange smile on his face, his hands folded tightly on the desk and his gray eyes giving Marshall that same numbing, penetrating, strangely pacifying gaze.

"Marshall, let's talk about you and the rest of this town. You know, we're really glad to have you here to take over the *Clarion*. We knew your fresh approach to journalism would be good for the community. I can be straightforward in saying that the last editor was . . . rather injurious to the mood of this town, especially toward the end."

Marshall felt himself going right along with this pitch, but he could sense something coming.

Brummel continued. "We need your kind of class, Marshall. You wield a great deal of power through the press, and we all know it, but it takes the right man to keep that power guided in the right direction, for the common good. All of us in the offices of public service are here to serve the best interests of the community, of the human race when you get right down to it. But so are you, Marshall. You're here for the sake of the people, just like the rest of us." Brummel combed his hair with his fingers a bit, a nervous gesture, then asked, "Well, do you get what I'm saying?"

"No."

"Well . . ." Brummel groped for a new opener. "I guess it's like you said, you're new in town. Why don't I simply try the direct approach?"

Marshall shrugged a "why not?" and let Brummel continue.

"It's a small town, first of all, and that means that one little problem, even between a handful of people, is going to be felt and worried about by almost everyone else. And you can't hide behind anonymity because there simply is no such thing. Now, the last editor didn't realize that and really caused some problems that affected the whole population. He was a pathological soap-boxer. He destroyed the good faith of the people in their local government, their public servants, each other, and ultimately himself. That hurt. It was a wound in our side, and it's taken time for all of us to heal up from that. I'll cap it off by telling you, for your own information, that that man finally had to leave this town in disgrace. He'd molested a twelve-year-old girl. I tried to get that case settled as quietly as I could. But in this town it was really awkward, difficult. I did what I felt would cause the least amount of trouble and pain for the girl's family and the people at large. I didn't press for any legal proceedings against this man, provided he leave Ashton and never show his face around here again. He was agreeable to that. But I'll never forget the impact it made, and I doubt that the town has ever forgotten it.

"Which brings us to you, and we, the public servants, and also the citizens of this community. One of the greatest reasons I regret this mixup with Bernice is that I really desired a good relationship between this office and the *Clarion*, between myself and you personally. I'd hate to see anything ruin that. We need unity around here, comradeship, a good community spirit." He paused for effect. "Marshall, we'd like to know that you'll be standing with us in working toward that goal."

Then came the pause and the long, expectant gaze. Marshall was on. He shifted around a little in his chair, sorting his thoughts, probing his feelings, almost avoiding those gazing gray eyes. Maybe this guy was on the up and up, or maybe this whole little speech was some sly diplomatic ploy to shy him away from whatever Bernice may have stumbled upon.

But Marshall couldn't think straight, or even *feel* straight. His reporter had been arrested falsely and thrown into a sleazy jail for the night, and he didn't seem to care anymore; this toothy-smiled police chief was making a liar out of her, and Marshall was buying it. *C'mon, Hogan, remember why you came down here?*

But he just felt so tired. He kept recalling why he had moved to Ashton in the first place. It was supposed to be a change of lifestyle for him and his family, a time to quit fighting and scratching the big-city intrigues and just get down to the simpler stories, things like high school paper drives and cats up trees. Maybe it was just force of habit from all those years at the *Times* that made him think he had to take on Brummel like some kind of inquisitor. For what? More hassles? For crying out loud, how about a little peace and quiet for a change?

Suddenly, and contrary to his better instincts, he knew there was nothing at all to worry about; Bernice's film would be just fine, and the pictures would prove that Brummel was right and Bernice was wrong. And Marshall really wanted it to be that way.

But Brummel was still waiting for an answer, still giving him that numbing gaze.

"I . . ." Marshall began, and now he felt stupidly awkward in trying to get started. "Listen, I really am tired of fighting, Alf. Maybe I was raised that way, maybe that's what made me good at my job with the *Times,* but I did decide to move here, and that's got to say something. I'm tired, Alf, and not any younger. I need to heal up. I need to learn what being human and living in a town with other humans is really like."

"Yes," said Brummel, "that's it. That's exactly it."

"So . . . don't worry. I'm here after some peace and quiet just like everybody else. I don't want any fights, I don't want any trouble. You've got nothing to fear from me."

Brummel was ecstatic, and shot out his hand to shake on it. As Marshall took the hand and they shook, he almost felt he had sold part of his soul. Did Marshall Hogan really say all that? *I must* be tired, he thought.

Before he knew it, he was standing outside Brummel's door. Apparently their meeting was over.

After Marshall was gone and the door was safely closed, Alf Brummel sank into his chair with a relieved sigh and just sat there for a while, staring into space, recuperating, building up the nerve for his next difficult assignment. Marshall Hogan was just the warm-up as far as he was concerned. The real test was coming up. He reached for his telephone, pulled it a little closer, stared at it for a moment, and then dialed the number.

Hank was touching up his paint job on the front of the house when the phone rang and Mary called, "Hank, it's Alf Brummel!"

Wow, Hank thought. And here I am with a loaded paintbrush in my hand. I wish he was standing here.

He confessed his sin to the Lord on his way in to answer the phone.

"Hi there," he said.

In his office, Brummel turned his back to the door to make it a private conversation even though he was alone, and spoke in a lowered voice. "Hi, Hank. This is Alf. I thought I should call you this morning and see how you are . . . since last night."

"Oh . . ." said Hank, feeling like a mouse in a cat's mouth. "I'm okay, I guess. Better, maybe."

"So you've given it some thought?"

"Oh, sure. I've thought about it a lot. I've prayed about it, re-checked the Word regarding some questions—"

"Hmmm. Sounds like you haven't changed your mind."

"Well, if the Word of God would change then I'd change, but I guess the Lord won't back down from what He says, and you know where that leaves me."

"Hank, you know the congregational meeting is this Friday."

"I know that."

"Hank, I'd really like to help you. I don't want to see you destroy yourself. You've been good for the church, I think, but—what can I say? The division, the bickering . . . it's all about to tear that church apart."

"Who's bickering?"

"Oh, come on . . ."

"And for that matter, who called that congregational meeting in the first place? You. Sam. Gordon. I have no doubt that Lou is still at work out there, as well as whoever it was that painted on the front of my house."

"We're just concerned, that's all. You're, well, you're fighting against what's best for the church."

"That's funny. I thought I was fighting against *you*. But did you hear me? I said someone painted on the front of my house."

"What? Painted what?"

Hank let him have it all.

Brummel let out a groan. "Aw, Hank, that's sick!"

"And so is Mary, and so am I. Put yourself in our position."

"Hank, if I were in your position, I'd reconsider. Can't you see what's happening? Word's getting around now, and you're setting the whole town against you. That also means the whole town's going to be set against our church before long, and we have to survive in this town, Hank! We're here to help people, to reach out to them, not drive a wedge between ourselves and the community."

"I preach the gospel of Jesus Christ, and there are plenty who appreciate it. Just where is this wedge you're talking about?"

Brummel was getting impatient. "Hank, learn from the last pastor. He made the same mistake. Look what happened to him."

"I did learn from him. I learned that all I have to do is give up, bag it, bury the truth in a drawer somewhere so it won't offend anybody. Then I'll be fine, everybody will like me, and we'll all be one happy family again. Apparently Jesus was misguided. He could have kept a lot of friends by wilting and just playing politics."

"But you want to be crucified!"

"I want to save souls, I want to convict sinners, I want to help newborn believers grow up in the truth. If I don't do that, I'll have a lot more to fear than you and the rest of the board."

"I don't call that love, Hank."

"I love you all, Alf. That's why I give you your medicine, and that goes especially for Lou."

Brummel pulled a big gun. "Hank, have you considered that he could sue you?"

There was a pause at the other end.

Finally Hank answered, "No."

"He could sue you for damages, slander, defamation of character, mental anguish, who knows what else?"

Hank drew a deep breath and called on the Lord for patience and wisdom.

"You see the problem?" he said finally. "Too many people don't know—or don't want to know—what the truth is anymore. We don't stand for something, so we fall for anything, and now guys like Lou get themselves into a fog where they can hurt their own families, start their own gossip, ruin their own reputations, make themselves miserable in their sin . . . and then look for someone else to blame! Just who's doing what to whom?"

Brummel only sighed. "We'll talk it all out Friday night. You *will* be there?"

"Yes, I will. I'll be counseling somebody and then I'll go in for the meeting. Ever done any counseling?"

"No."

"It gives you a real respect for the truth when you have to help clean up lives that have been based on a lie. Think about it."

"Hank, I have other people's wishes to think about."

Brummel hung up loudly and wiped the sweat from his palms.

4

C ould anyone have seen him, the initial impression would not have been so much his reptilian, warted appearance as the way his figure seemed to asborb light and not return it, as if he were more a shadow than an object, a strange, animated hole in space. But this little spirit was invisible to the eyes of men, unseen and immaterial, drifting over the town, banking one way and then the other, guided by will and not wind, his swirling wings quivering in a greyish blur as they propelled him.

He was like a high-strung little gargoyle, his hide a slimy, bottomless black, his body thin and spiderlike: half humanoid, half animal, totally demon. Two huge yellow cat-eyes bulged out of his face, darting to and fro, peering, searching. His breath came in short, sulfurous gasps, visible as glowing yellow vapor.

He was carefully watching and following his charge, the driver of a brown Buick moving through the streets of Ashton far below.

Marshall got out of the *Clarion* office just a little early that day. After all the morning's confusion it was a surprise to find Tuesday's *Clarion* already off to the printer and the staff gearing up for Friday. A small-town paper was just about the right, pace . . . perhaps he *could* get to know his daughter again.

Sandy. Yes sir, a beautiful redhead, their only child. She had nothing but potential, but had spent most of her childhood with an overtime mother and a hardly-there father. Marshall was successful in New York, all right, at just about everything except being the kind of father Sandy needed. She had always let him know about it, too, but as Kate said, the two of them were too much alike; her cries for love and attention always came out like stabs, and Marshall gave her attention all right, like dogs give to cats.

No more fights, he kept telling himself, no more picking and scratching and hurting. Let her talk, let her spill how she feels, and don't be harsh with her. Love her for who she is, let her be herself, don't try to corral her.

It was crazy how his love for her kept coming out like spite, with anger and cutting words. He knew he was only reaching for her, trying to bring her back. It just never worked. Ah well, Hogan, try, try again, and don't blow it this time.

He made a left turn and could see the college ahead. The Whitmore College campus looked like most American campuses—beautiful, with stately old buildings that made you feel learned just to look at them, wide, neatly-lawned plazas with walkways in carefully laid patterns of brick and stone, landscaping with rocks, greenery, statuary. It was everything a good college should be, right down to the fifteen-minute parking spaces. Marshall parked the Buick and set out in search of Stewart Hall, home of the Psychology Department and Sandy's last class for the day.

Whitmore was a privately-endowed college, founded by some landholder as a memorial to himself back in the early twenties. From old photos of the place one could discover that some of the red-brick and white-pillared lecture halls were as old as the college itself: monuments of the past and supposedly guardians of the future.

The summertime campus was relatively quiet.

Marshall got directions from a frisbee-throwing sophomore and turned left down an elm-lined street. At the end of the street he found Stewart Hall, an imposing structure patterned after some European cathedral with towers and archways. He pulled open one of the big double doors and found himself in a spacious, echoing hallway. The close of the big door made such a reverberating thunder off the vaulted ceiling and smooth walls that Marshall thought he had disturbed every class on the floor.

But now he was lost. This place had three floors and some thirty classrooms, and he had no idea which one was Sandy's. He started walking down the hall, trying to keep his heels from tapping too loudly. You couldn't even get away with a burp in this place.

Sandy was a freshman this year. Their move to Ashton had been just a little late, so she was enrolled in summer classes to catch up, but all in all it had been the right point of transition for her. She was an undeclared major for now, feeling her way and taking prerequisites. Where a class in "Psychology of Self" fit into all that Marshall couldn't guess, but he and Kate weren't out to rush her.

From somewhere down the cavernous hall echoed the indistinguishable but well-ordered words of a lecture in progress, a woman's voice. He decided to check it out. He moved past several classroom doors, their little black numbers steadily decreasing, then a drinking fountain, the restrooms, and a ponderously ascending stone and iron staircase. Finally he began to make out the words of the lecture as he drew near Room 101.

". . . so if we settle for a simple ontological formula, 'I think, therefore I am,' that should be the end of the question. But *being* does not presuppose *meaning* . . ."

Yeah, here was more of that college stuff, that funny conglomeration of sixty-four-dollar words which impress people with your academic prowess but can't get you a paying job. Marshall smirked to himself a little bit. Psychology. If all those shrinks could just agree for a change, it would help. First Sandy blamed her snotty attitude on a violent birth experience, and then what was it? Poor potty training? Her new thing was self-knowledge, self-esteem, identity; she already knew how to be hung up on herself—now they were teaching it to her in college.

He peeked in the door and saw a theater arrangement, with rows of seats built in steadily rising levels toward the back of the room, and the small platform in front with the professor lecturing against a massive blackboard backdrop.

". . . and meaning doesn't necessarily come from thinking, for some have said that the Self is not the Mind at all, and that the Mind actually denies the Self and inhibits Self-Knowledge. . . ."

Whoosh! For some reason Marshall had expected an older woman, skinny, her hair in a bun, wearing horn-rimmed glasses with a little beady chain looped around her neck. But this one was a startling surprise, something right out of a lipstick or fashion commercial: long blonde hair, trim figure, deep, dark eyes that twitched a bit but certainly needed no glasses, horn-rimmed or otherwise.

Then Marshall caught the glint of deep red hair, and he saw Sandy sitting toward the front of the hall, listening intently and feverishly scrawling notes. Bingo! That was easy. He decided to slip in quietly and listen to the tail end of the lecture. It might give him some idea of what Sandy was learning and then they'd have something to talk about. He stepped silently through the door, and took one of the empty seats in the back.

Then it happened. Some kind of radar in the professor's head must have clicked on. She homed in on Marshall sitting there and simply would not look away from him. He had no desire to draw any attention to himself—he was rapidly getting too much of that anyway, from the class—so he said nothing. But the professor seemed to examine him, searching his face as if it were familiar to her, as if she were trying to remember someone she had known before. The look that suddenly crossed her face gave Marshall a chill: she gave him a knifelike gaze, like the eyes of a treed cougar. He began to feel a corresponding defense instinct twisting a knot in his stomach.

"Is there something you want?" the professor demanded, and all Marshall could see were her two piercing eyes.

"I'm just waiting for my daughter," he answered and his tone was courteous.

"Would you like to wait outside?" she said, and it wasn't a question.

And he was out in the hall. He leaned against the wall, staring at the linoleum, his mind spinning, his senses scrambled, his heart pounding. He had no understanding of why he was there, but he was out in the hall. Just like that. How? What happened? Come on, Hogan, stop shaking and *think!*

He tried to replay it in his mind, but it came back slowly, stubbornly, like recalling a bad dream. That woman's eyes! The way they looked told him she somehow knew who he was, even though they had never met—and he had never seen or felt such hate. But it wasn't just the eyes; it was also the fear; the steadily rising, face-draining, heart-pounding fear that had crept into him for no reason, with no visible cause. He had been scared half to death . . . by nothing! It made no sense at all. He had never run or backed down from anything in his life. But now, for the first time in his life . . .

For the first time? The image of Alf Brummel's gazing gray eyes flashed across his mind, and the weakness returned. He blinked the image away and took a deep breath. Where was the old Hogan gut strength? Had he left it back in Brummel's office?

But he had no conclusions, no theories, no explanations, only derision for himself. He muttered, "So I gave in again, like a rotted tree," and like a rotted tree he leaned against the wall and waited.

In a few minutes the door to the lecture hall burst open and students began to fan outward like bees from a hive. They ignored him so thoroughly that Marshall felt invisible, but that was fine with him for now.

Then came Sandy. He straightened up, walked toward her, started to say hello . . . and she walked right by! She didn't pause, smile, return his greeting, anything! He stood there dumbly for a moment, watching her walk down the hall toward the exit.

Then he followed. He wasn't limping, but for some reason he felt like he was. He wasn't really dragging his feet, but they felt like lead weights. He saw his daughter go out the door without looking back. The clunk of the big door's closing echoed through the huge hall with a ponderous, condemning finality, like the crash of a huge gate dividing him forever from the one he loved. He stopped there in the broad hall, numb, helpless, even tottering a little, his big frame looking very small.

Unseen by Marshall, small wisps of sulfurous breath crept along the floor like slow water, along with an unheard scraping and scratching over the tiles.

Like a slimy black leech, the little demon clung to him, its taloned fingers entwining Marshall's legs like parasitic tendrils, holding him back, poisoning his spirit. The yellow eyes bulged out of the gnarled face, watching him, boring into him.

Marshall was feeling a deep and growing pain, and the little spirit knew it. This man was getting hard to hold down. As Marshall stood there in the big empty hall, the hurt, the love, the desperation began to build inside him; he could feel the tiniest remaining ember of *fight* still burning. He started for the door.

Move, Hogan, move! That's your daughter!

With each determined step, the demon was dragged along the floor behind him, its hands still clinging to him, a deeper rage and fury rising in its eyes and the sulfurous vapors chugging out of its nostrils.

The wings spread in search of an anchor, any way to hold Marshall back, but they found none.

Sandy, Marshall thought, give your old man a break.

By the time he reached the end of the hall he was nearly into a run. His big hands hit the crash bar on the door and the door flung open, slamming into the doorstop on the outside steps. He ran down the stairs and out onto the pedestrian walkway shaded by the elms. He looked up the street, across the lawn in front of Stewart Hall, down the other way, but she was gone.

The demon gripped him tighter and began to climb and slither upward. Marshall felt the first pangs of despair as he stood there alone.

"I'm over here, Daddy."

Immediately the demon lost its grip and fell free, snorting with indignation. Marshall spun around and saw Sandy, standing just beside the door he had just burst through, apparently trying to hide from her classmates among the camelia bushes and looking very much like she was about to take him to task. Well, anything was better than losing her, Marshall thought.

"Well," he said before he considered, "pardon me, but I get the distinct impression you disowned me in there."

Sandy tried to stand straight, to face him in her hurt and anger, but she still could not look him squarely in the eye.

"It was—it was just too painful."

"What was?"

"You know . . . that whole thing in there."

"Well, I like coming on with a real splash, you know. Something people will remember . . ."

"Daddy!"

"So who stole all the 'No Parents Allowed' signs? How was I to know she didn't want me in there? And just what's so all-fired precious and secret that she doesn't want any outsiders to hear it?"

Now Sandy's anger rose above her hurt, and she could look at him squarely. "Nothing! Nothing at all. It was just a lecture."

"So just what is her problem?"

Sandy groped for an explanation. "I don't know. I guess she must know who you are."

"No way. I've never even seen her before." And then a question automatically popped into Marshall's mind, "What do you mean, she must know who I am?"

Sandy looked cornered. "I mean . . . oh, c'mon. Maybe she knows you're the editor of the paper. Maybe she doesn't want reporters snooping around."

"Well, I hope I can tell you I wasn't snooping. I was just looking for you."

Sandy wanted to end the discussion. "All right, Daddy, all right.

She just read you wrong, okay? I don't know what her problem was. She has the right to choose her audience, I suppose."

"And I don't have the right to know what my daughter is learning?"

Sandy stopped a word halfway up her throat and inferred a few things first. "You *were* snooping!"

Even as it happened, Marshall knew good and well that they were at it again, the old cats-and-dogs, fighting roosters routine. It was crazy. Part of him didn't want it to happen, but the rest of him was too frustrated and angry to stop.

As for the demon, it only cowered nearby, shying from Marshall as if he were red hot. The demon watched, waited, fretted.

"In a pig's eye I was snooping!" Marshall roared. "I'm here because I'm your loving father and I wanted to pick you up after classes. Stewart Hall, that's all I knew. I just happened to find you, and . . ." He tried to brake himself. He deflated a little, covered his eyes with his hand, and sighed.

"And you thought you'd keep an eye on me!" Sandy suggested spitefully.

"Got some law against that?"

"Okay, I'll lay it all out for you. I'm a human being, Daddy, and every human entity—I don't care who he or she is—is ultimately subject to a universal scheme and not to the will of any specific individual. As for Professor Langstrat, if she doesn't want you present at her lecture, it's her prerogative to demand that you leave!"

"And just who's paying her salary, anyway?"

She ignored the question. "And as for me, and what I am learning, and what I am becoming, and where I am going, and what I wish, I say you have no right to infringe on my universe unless I personally grant you that right!"

Marshall's eyesight was getting blurred by visions of Sandy turned over his knee. Enraged, he had to lash out at somebody, but now he was trying to steer his attacks away from Sandy. He pointed back toward Stewart Hall and demanded, "Did—did *she* teach you that?"

"You don't need to know."

"I have a right to know!"

"You waived that right, Daddy, years ago."

That punch sent him into the ropes, and he couldn't fully recover before she took off down the street, escaping him, escaping their miserable, bullish battle. He hollered after her, some stupid-sounding question about how she'd get home, but she didn't even slow down.

The demon grabbed its chance *and* Marshall, and he felt his anger and self-righteousness give way to sinking despair. He'd blown it. The very thing he never wanted to do again, he did. Why in the world was he wired up this way? Why couldn't he just reach her, love her, win her back? She was disappearing from sight even now, becoming smaller and smaller as she hurried across the campus, and she seemed so very far away, farther than any loving arm could ever reach. He had always tried to be strong, to stand tough through life and through struggles, but right now the hurt was so bad he couldn't keep that strength from crumbling away from him in pitiful pieces. As he watched, Sandy disappeared around a distant corner without looking back, and something broke inside him. His soul felt like it would melt, and at this moment there was no person on the face of the earth he hated more than himself.

The strength of his legs seemed to surrender under the load of his sorrow, and he sank to the steps in front of the old building, despondent.

The demon's talons surrounded his heart and he muttered in a quivering voice, "What's the use?"

"YAHAAAAA!" came a thundering cry from the nearby shrubs. A bluish-white light glimmered. The demon released its grip on Marshall and bolted like a terrified fly, landing some distance away in a trembling, defensive stance, its huge yellow eyes nearly popping out of its head and a soot-black, barbed scimitar ready in its quivering hand. But then there came an unexplainable commotion behind those same bushes, some kind of struggle, and the source of the light disappeared around the corner of Stewart Hall.

The demon did not stir, but waited, listened, watched. No sound could be heard except the light breeze. The demon stalked ever so cautiously back to where Marshall still sat, went past him, and peered through the shrubbery and around the corner of the building.

Nothing.

As if held for this entire time, a long, slow breath of yellow vapor curled in lacy wisps from the demon's nostrils. Yes, it knew what it had seen; there was no mistaking it. But why had they fled?

5

A short distance across the campus, but enough distance to be safe, two giant men descended to earth like glimmering, bluish-white comets, held aloft by rushing wings that swirled in a blur and burned like lightning. One of them, a huge, burly, black-bearded bull of a man, was quite angry and indignant, bellowing and making fierce gestures with a long, gleaming sword. The other was a little smaller and kept looking about with great caution, trying to get his associate to calm down.

In a graceful, fiery spiral they drifted down behind one of the college dormitories and came to rest in the cover of some overhanging willows. The moment their feet touched down, the light from their clothes and bodies began to fade and the shimmering wings gently subsided. Save for their towering stature they appeared as two ordinary men, one trim and blond, the other built like a tank, both dressed in what looked like matching tan fatigues. Golden belts had become like dark leather, their scabbards were dull copper, and the glowing, bronze bindings on their feet had become simple leather sandals.

The big fellow was ready for a discussion.

"Triskal!" he growled, but at his friend's desperate gestures he spoke just a little softer. "What are you doing here?"

Triskal kept his hands up to keep his friend quiet.

"Shh, Guilo! The Spirit brought me here, the same as you. I arrived yesterday."

"You know what that was? A demon of complacency and despair if ever I saw one! If your arm hadn't held me I could have struck him, and only once!"

"Oh, yes, Guilo, only once," his friend agreed, "but it's a good thing I saw you and stopped you in time. You've just arrived and you don't understand—"

"What don't I understand?"

Triskal tried to say it in a convincing manner. "We . . . must not fight, Guilo. Not yet. We must not resist."

Guilo was sure his friend was mistaken. He took firm hold of Triskal's shoulder and looked him right in the eye.

"Why should I go anywhere but to fight?" he stated. "Here I was called. Here I will fight."

"Yes," said Triskal, nodding furiously. "Just not yet, that's all."

"Then you must have orders! You *do* have orders?"

Triskal paused for effect, then said, "*Tal's* orders."

Guilo's angry expression at once melted into a mixture of shock and perplexity.

Dusk was settling over Ashton, and the little white church on Morgan Hill was washed with the warm, rusty glow of the evening sun. Outside in the small churchyard, the church's young pastor hurriedly mowed the lawn, hoping to be finished before mealtime. Dogs were barking in the neighborhood, people were arriving back home from work, kids were being called in for supper.

Unseen by these mortals, Guilo and Triskal came hurriedly up the hill on foot, secretive and unglorified but moving like the wind nevertheless. As they arrived in front of the church, Hank Busche came around the corner behind the roaring lawn mower, and Guilo had to pause to look him over.

"Is he the one?" he asked Triskal. "Did the call begin with him?"

"Yes," Triskal answered, "months ago. He's praying even now, and often walks the streets of Ashton interceding for it."

"But . . . this place is so small. Why was I called? No, no, why was *Tal* called?"

Triskal only pulled at his arm. "Hurry inside."

They passed quickly through the walls of the church and into the humble little sanctuary. Inside they found a contingent of warriors already gathered, some sitting in the pews, others standing around the platform, still others acting as sentries, looking cautiously out the stained glass windows. They were all dressed much as Triskal and Guilo, in the same tan tunics and breeches, but Guilo was immediately impressed by the imposing stature of them all; these were the mighty warriors, the powerful warriors, and more than he had ever seen gathered in one place.

He was also struck by the mood of the gathering. This moment could have been a joyful reunion of old friends except that everyone was strangely somber. As he looked around the room he recognized many whom he had fought alongside in times far past:

Nathan, the towering Arabian who fought fiercely and spoke little. It was he who had taken demons by their ankles and used them as warclubs against their fellows.

Armoth, the big African whose war cry and fierce countenance had often been enough to send the enemy fleeing before he even assailed them. Guilo and Armoth had once battled the demon lords of villages in Brazil and personally guarded a family of missionaries on their many long treks through the jungles.

Chimon, the meek European with the golden hair, who bore on his forearms the marks of a fading demon's last blows before Chimon banished him forever into the abyss. Guilo had never met this one, but had heard of his exploits and his ability to take blows simply as a shield for others and then to rally himself to defeat untold numbers alone.

Then came the greeting of the oldest and most cherished friend. "Welcome, Guilo, the Strength of Many!"

Yes, it was indeed Tal, the Captain of the Host. It was so strange to see this mighty warrior standing in this humble little place. Guilo had seen him near the throne room of Heaven itself, in conference with none other than Michael. But here stood the same impressive figure with golden hair and ruddy complexion, intense golden eyes like fire and an unchallengeable air of authority.

Guilo approached his captain and the two of them clasped hands.

"And we are together again," said Guilo as a thousand memories flooded his mind. No warrior Guilo had ever seen could fight as Tal could; no demon could outmaneuver or outspeed him, no sword could parry a blow from the sword of Tal. Side by side, Guilo and his captain had vanquished demonic powers for as long as those rebels had existed, and had been companions in the Lord's service before there had been any rebellion at all. "Greetings, my dear captain!"

Tal said by way of explanation, "It's a serious business that brings us together again."

Guilo searched Tal's face. Yes, there was plenty of confidence there, and no timidity. But there was definitely a strange grimness in the eyes and mouth, and Guilo looked around the room once again. Now he could feel it, that typically silent and ominous prelude to the breaking of grim news. Yes, they all knew something he didn't but were waiting for the appointed person, most likely Tal, to speak it.

Guilo couldn't stand the silence, much less the suspense. "Twenty-three," he counted, "of the very best, the most gallant, the most undefeatable . . . gathered now as though under siege, cowering in a flimsy fortress from a dreaded enemy?" With a dramatic flair, he drew his huge sword and cradled the blade in his free hand. "Captain Tal, who is this enemy?"

Tal answered slowly and clearly, "Rafar, the Prince of Babylon."

All eyes were now on Guilo's face, and his reaction was much like that of every other warrior upon hearing the news: shock, disbelief, an awkward pause to see if anyone would laugh and verify that it was only a mistake. There was no such reprieve from the truth. Everyone in the room continued to look at Guilo with the same deadly serious expression, driving the gravity of the situation home mercilessly.

Guilo looked down at his sword. Was it now shaking in his hands? He made a point of holding it still, but he couldn't help staring for a moment at the blade, still gashed and discolored from the last time Guilo and Tal had confronted this Baal-prince from the ancient times. Guilo and Tal had struggled against him twenty-three days before finally defeating him on the eve of Babylon's fall. Guilo could still remember the darkness, the shrieking and horror, the fierce, terrible grappling while pain seared every inch of his being. The evil of this would-be pagan god seemed to envelop him and everything around him like thick smoke, and half the time the two warriors had to maneuver and strike blindly, each one not even knowing if the other was still in the fight. To this day neither of them even knew which one finally delivered the blow that sent Rafar plummeting into the abyss. All they remembered was his heaven-shaking scream as he fell through a jagged rift in space, and then seeing each other again when the great darkness that surrounded them cleared like a melting fog.

"I know you speak the truth," Guilo said at last, "but . . . would such as Rafar come to this place? He is a prince of nations, not mere hamlets. What *is* this place? What interest could he possibly have in it?"

Tal only shook his head. "We don't know. But it *is* Rafar, there's no question, and the stirrings in the enemy's realm indicate something is in the making. The Spirit wants us here. We must confront whatever it is."

"And we are not to fight, we are not to resist!" Guilo exclaimed. "I will be most fascinated to hear your next order, Tal. We cannot fight?"

"Not yet. We're too few, and there's very little prayer cover. There are to be no skirmishes, no confrontations. We're not to show ourselves in any way as aggressors. As long as we stay out of their way, keep close to this place, and pose no threat to them, our presence here will seem like normal watchcare over a few, struggling saints." Then he added with a very direct tone, "And it will be best if it not be spread that I am here."

Guilo now felt a little out of place still holding his sword, and sheathed it with an air of disgust.

"And," he prodded, "you do have a plan? We were not called here to watch the town fall?"

The lawn mower roared by the windows, and Tal guided their attention to its operator.

"It was Chimon's task to bring him here," he said, "to blind the eyes of his enemies and slip him through ahead of the adversary's choice for the pastor of this flock. Chimon succeeded, Hank was voted in, to the surprise of many, and now he's here in Ashton, praying every hour of every day. We were called here for his sake, for the saints of God and for the Lamb."

"For the saints of God and for the Lamb!" they all echoed.

Tal looked at a tall, dark-haired warrior, the one who had taken him through the town the night of the Festival, and smiled. "And you had him win by just one vote?"

The warrior shrugged. "The Lord wanted him here. Chimon and I had to make sure he won, and not the other man who has no fear of God."

Tal introduced Guilo to this warrior. "Guilo, this is Krioni, watch-carer of our prayer warrior here and of the town of Ashton. Our call began with Hank, but Hank's presence here began with Krioni."

Guilo and Krioni nodded silent greeting to each other.

Tal watched Hank finishing up the lawn and praying out loud at the same time. "So now, as his enemies in the congregation regroup and try to find another way to oust him, he continues to pray for Ashton. He's one of the last."

"If not *the* last!" lamented Krioni.

"No," cautioned Tal, "he's not alone. There's still a Remnant of saints somewhere in this town. There is always a Remnant."

"There is always a Remnant," they all echoed.

"Our conflict begins in this place. We'll make this our location for now, hedge it in and work from here." He spoke to a tall Oriental in the back of the room. "Signa, take as your charge this building, and choose two now to stand with you. This is our rest point. Make it secure. No demon is to approach it."

Signa immediately found two volunteers to work with him. They vanished to their posts.

"Now, Triskal, I'll hear news of Marshall Hogan."

"I followed him up to my encounter with Guilo. Though Krioni has reported a rather eventless situation up to the time of the Festival, ever since then Hogan has been hounded by a demon of complacency and despair."

Tal received that news with great interest. "Hm. Could be he's beginning to stir. They're covering him, trying to hold him in check."

Krioni added, "I never thought I'd see it happen. The Lord wanted him in charge of the *Clarion,* and we took care of that too, but I've never seen a more tired individual."

"Tired, yes, but that will only make him more usable in the Lord's hands. And I perceive that he is indeed waking up, just as the Lord foreknew."

"Though he could awaken only to be destroyed," said Triskal. "They must be watching him. They fear what he could do in his influential position."

"True," replied Tal. "So while they bait our bear, we must be sure they stir him up and no more than that. It's going to be a very critical business."

Now Tal was ready to move. He addressed the whole group. "I expect Rafar to take power here by nightfall; no doubt we'll all feel it when he does. Be sure of this: he will immediately search out the greatest threat to him and try to remove it."

"Ah, Henry Busche," said Guilo.

"Krioni and Triskal, you can be sure that a troop of some kind will be sent to test Hank's spirit. Select for yourselves four warriors and watch over him." Tal touched Krioni's shoulder and added, "Krioni, up until now you've done very well in protecting Hank from any direct onslaughts. I commend you."

"Thank you, captain."

"I ask you now to do a difficult thing. Tonight you must stand by and keep watch. Do not let Hank's life be touched, but aside from that prevent nothing. It will be a test he *must* undergo."

There was a slight moment of surprise and wonderment, but each warrior was ready to trust Tal's judgment.

Tal continued, "As for Marshall Hogan . . . he's the only one I'm not sure about yet. Rafar will give his lackeys incredible license with him, and he could either collapse and retreat, or—as we all hope— rouse himself and fight back. He'll be of special interest to Rafar—and to me—tonight. Guilo, select two warriors for yourself and two for me. We'll watchcare over Marshall tonight and see how he responds. The rest of you will search out the Remnant."

Tal drew his sword and held it high. The others did the same and a forest of shining blades appeared, held aloft in strong arms.

"Rafar," Tal said in a low, musing voice, "we meet again." Then, in the voice of a Captain of the Host: "For the saints of God and for the Lamb!"

"For the saints of God and for the Lamb!" they echoed.

Complacency unfurled his wings and drifted into Stewart Hall, sinking down through the main floor and into the catacombs of the basement level, the area set aside for administration and the private offices of the Psychology Department. In this dismal nether world the ceiling was low and oppressive, and crawling with water pipes and heat ducts that seemed like so many huge snakes waiting to drop. Everything—walls, ceiling, pipes, woodwork—was painted the same dirty beige, and light was scarce, which suited Complacency and his associates just fine. They preferred the darkness, and Complacency noticed that there seemed to be a touch more than usual. The others must have arrived.

He floated down a long burrow of a hallway to a large door at the end marked "Conference Room," and passed through the door into a cauldron of living evil. The room was dark, but the darkness seemed more of a presence than a physical condition; it was a force, an atmosphere that drifted and crept about the room. Out of that darkness glared many pairs of dull yellow cat-eyes belonging to a horrible gallery of grotesque faces. The various shapes of Complacency's fellow workers were outlined and backlit by a sourceless red glow. Yellow vapor slithered in lacy wisps about the room and filled the air with its stench as the many apparitions carried on their hushed, gargling conversations there in the dark.

Complacency could sense their common disdain for him, but the feeling was mutual enough. These belligerent egotists would walk on anyone to exalt themselves, and Complacency just happened to be the smallest, hence the easiest to persecute.

He approached two hulking forms in the middle of some debate, and from their massive, spine-covered arms and poisonous words he could tell they were demons who specialized in hate—planting, aggravating, and spreading it, using their crushing arms and venomous quills to constrict and poison the love out of anyone.

Complacency asked them, "Where is Prince Lucius?"

"Find him yourself, lizard!" one of them growled.

A demon of lust, a slithery creature with darting and shifty eyes and slippery hide, overheard and joined in, snatching Complacency with his long, sharp talons.

"And where have you been sleeping today?" it asked with a sneer.

"I do not sleep!" Complacency retorted. "I cause *people* to sleep."

"To lust and steal innocence is far better."

"But someone must turn away the eyes of others."

Lust thought that over and gave a smirk of approval. He dropped Complacency rudely as those who watched laughed.

Complacency passed Deception, but didn't bother to ask him anything. Deception was the proudest, haughtiest demon of them all, very arrogant in his supposedly superior knowledge of how to control men's minds. His appearance was not even as gruesome as the other demons; he almost looked human. His weapon, he boasted, was always a compelling, persuasive argument with lies ever so subtly woven in.

Many others were there: Murder, his talons still dripping with blood; Lawlessness, his knuckles honed into spikelike protrusions and his hide thick and leathery; Jealousy, as suspicious and difficult a demon to work with as any.

But Complacency finally found Lucius, the Prince of Ashton, the demon who held the highest position of all of them. Lucius was in conference with a tight huddle of other power holders, going over the next strategies for controlling the town.

He was unquestionably the demon in charge. Huge to begin with, he always maintained an imposing posture with his wings wrapped loosely around him to widen his outline, his arms flexed, his fists clenched and ready for blows. Many demons coveted his rank, and he knew it; he had fought and banished many to get where he was, and he had every intention of staying there. He trusted no one and suspected everyone, and his black, gnarled face and hawk-sharp eyes always carried the message that even his associates were his enemies.

Complacency was desperate and enraged enough to violate Lucius's ideas of respect and decorum. He shoved his way through the group and right up to Lucius, who glared at him, surprised by the rude interruption.

"My Prince," Complacency pleaded, "I must have a word with you."

Lucius's eyes narrowed. Who was this little lizard to interrupt him in the middle of a conference, to violate decorum in front of these others?

"Why aren't you with Hogan?" he growled.

"I must speak with you!"

"Dare you speak to me without my first speaking to you?"

"It is vitally important. You're—you're making a mistake. You're bothering Hogan's daughter, and—"

Lucius immediately became a small volcano, spewing forth horrible cursings and wrath. "You accuse your prince of a mistake? You dare to question my actions?"

Complacency cowered, expecting a stinging blow any moment, but he spoke anyway.

"Hogan will do us no harm if you let him alone. But you have only lit a fire within him, and he casts me off!"

The blow came, a walloping swat from the back of Lucius's hand, and as Complacency tumbled across the room he debated whether or not to speak another word. When he came to rest and regathered himself, he looked up to see every eye upon him, and he could feel their mocking disdain.

Lucius walked slowly toward him, and towered over him like a giant tree. "Hogan casts you off? Is it not you who releases him?"

"Do not strike me! Only hear my appeal!"

Lucius's big fists clenched painfully around handfuls of Complacency's flesh and snatched him up so they were eye to eye. "He could stand in our way and I won't have that! You know your duty. Perform it!"

"Well I was, well I was!" Complacency cried. "He was nothing to fear at all, a slug, a lump of clay. I could have held him there forever."

"So do it!"

"Prince Lucius, please hear me! Give him no enemy. Let him have no need to fight."

Lucius dropped him on the floor in a humiliated heap. The prince addressed the others in the room.

"We have given Hogan an enemy?"

They all knew how to answer. "No indeed!"

"Deception," Lucius called, and Deception stepped forward, giving Lucius a formal bow. "Complacency accuses his prince of bothering Hogan's daughter. You would know about that."

"You have ordered no attack on Sandy Hogan, Prince," Deception answered.

Complacency pointed his taloned finger and screamed, "You have followed her! You and your lackeys! You have spoken words to her mind, confused her!"

Deception only raised his eyebrows in mild indignation and answered sedately, "Only upon her own invitation. We have only told her what she prefers to know. That can hardly be called an attack."

Lucius seemed to take on some of Deception's maddening haughtiness as he said, "Sandy Hogan is one case, but certainly her father is quite another. She poses no threat to us. He does. Shall we send someone else to hold him in check?"

Complacency had no answer, but added another note of concern. "I . . . I saw messengers of the living God today!"

That only brought laughter from the group.

Lucius sneered, "Are you becoming that timid, Complacency? We see messengers of the living God every day."

"But they were close! About to attack! They knew my actions, I am sure."

"You look all right to me. Though if I were one of them, I would surely pick you as an easy prey." More laughter from the group spurred Lucius on. "A limp and easy target for mere sport . . . a lame demon with which a weak angel can prove his strength!"

Complacency cowered in shame. Lucius strode about, addressing the group.

"Do we fear the host of heaven?" he asked.

"As you do not, we do not!" they all answered with great polish.

As the demons remained in their basement lair, patting each other's backs and stabbing Complacency's, they took no notice of the strange, unnatural cold front outside. It moved slowly over the town, bringing a harsh wind and chilling rain. Though the evening had promised to be bright and clear, it now grew dark under a low, oppressive shroud, half natural, half spirit.

Atop the little white church, Signa and his two companions continued to stand guard as the darkness descended over Ashton, deeper and colder with each passing moment. All over the nearby neighborhood dogs began to bark and howl. Here and there a quarrel broke out among humans.

"He's here," Signa said.

In the meantime, Lucius's preoccupation with his own glory kept him from noticing the little attention he was now getting from his troops. All the other demons in the room, large or small, were gripped by a steadily rising fear and agitation. They could all feel something horrible coming closer and closer. They began to fidget, their eyes darting about, their faces twisting with apprehension.

Lucius gave Complacency a kick in the side as he walked by and continued his boasting.

"Complacency, you can be sure that we have things very much in control here. No worker from our number has ever had to sneak about for fear of attack. We roam this town freely, doing our work unhampered, and we will succeed in every place until the town is fully ours. You listless, limp, little bungler! To fear is to fail!"

Then it happened, and so very suddenly that none of them could react with anything other than air-piercing shrieks of terror. Lucius had hardly gotten the word "fail" out of his mouth before a violent, boiling cloud crashed and thundered into the room like a tidal wave, a sudden avalanche of force that crushed like iron. The demons were swept across the room like so much debris in a raging tide, tumbling, screaming, wrapping their wings tightly around themselves in terror—all except for Lucius.

As the demons recovered from the initial shock wave of this new presence, they looked up and saw Lucius's body, contorted like a broken toy, in the grip of a huge, black hand. He struggled, choked, gagged, cried for mercy, but the hand only tightened its crushing grip, inflicting punishment without mercy, descending down out of the darkness like a cyclone from a thundercloud. Then the full figure of a spirit appeared, carrying Lucius by the throat and shaking him about like a rag doll. The thing was bigger than any they had ever seen before, a giant demon with a lion-like face, fiery eyes, incredibly muscular body, and leathery wings that filled the room.

The voice gargled up from deep within the demon's torso and sprayed out in clouds of fiery red vapor.

"You who have no fear—are you now afraid?"

The spirit angrily hurled Lucius across the room to join the others, then stood like a mountain in the center of the room, wielding a deadly, S-curved sword the size of a door. His bared fangs glistened like the jeweled chains around his neck and across his chest. Obviously this prince of princes had been greatly honored for past victories. His jet black hair hung like a mane to his shoulders, and on each wrist he wore a gold bracelet studded with sparkling stones; his fingers displayed several rings, and a ruby-red belt and scabbard adorned his waist. The expansive black wings draped down behind him now like the robe of a monarch.

For an eternity he stood there, glaring at them with sinister, smoldering eyes, studying them, and all they could do was remain motionless in their terror like a macabre tableau of frightened goblins.

Finally the big voice echoed off the walls: "Lucius, I feel I was not expected. You will announce me. On your feet!"

The sword moved across the room and the tip snagged Lucius in the hide of his neck, jolting him to his feet.

Lucius knew he was being belittled in the sight of his underlings, but he made every effort to hide his rising bitterness and anger. His fear showed well enough to adequately cover his other feelings.

"Fellow workers . . ." he said, his voice quivering despite every effort. "Ba-al Rafar, the Prince of Babylon!"

Automatically they all leaped to their feet, partly out of fearful respect, mostly out of fear of the tip of Rafar's sword, still waving slowly back and forth, ready to move against any dawdlers.

Rafar gave them all a quick looking over. Then he inflicted another personal blow against Lucius.

"Lucius, you will stand with the others. I have come, and only one prince is needed."

Friction. Everyone could feel it immediately. Lucius refused to move. His body was stiff, his fists clenched as tightly as ever, and though he was visibly trembling, he purposely returned the glaring look of Rafar and stood his ground.

"You . . . have not asked me to yield my place!" he challenged.

The others were not about to intervene or even get close. They backed off, remembering that Rafar's sword could probably sweep a very wide radius.

The sword did move, but so quickly that the very first thing anyone perceived was a scream of pain from Lucius as he coiled into a twisted knot on the floor. Lucius's sword and scabbard lay on the floor, skillfully cut away by one swift slash from Rafar. Again the sword moved, and this time the flat of the blade clamped Lucius to the floor by his hair.

Rafar leaned over him, blood-red breath spewing from his mouth and nostrils as he spoke.

"I perceive you wish to challenge for my position." Lucius said nothing. "ANSWER!"

"No!" Lucius cried. "I yield."

"Up! Get up!"

Lucius struggled to his feet, and Rafar's strong arm stood him with the others. By now Lucius was a most pitiful sight, totally humiliated. Rafar reached down with his sword and with the barbed tip picked up Lucius's sword and scabbard. The sword swung like a huge crane and deposited Lucius's weapons in the deposed demon's hands.

"Listen well, all of you," Rafar addressed them. "Lucius, who fears not the hosts of heaven, has shown fear. He is a liar and a worm and is not to be heeded. I say to you, fear the hosts of heaven. They are your enemies, and they are intent on defeating you. As they are ignored, as they are given place, so they shall overcome you."

Rafar walked with heavy, ponderous steps up and down the line of demons, giving them all a closer look. When he came to Complacency, he drew close and Complacency fell backwards. Rafar caught him around the back of the neck with one finger and pulled him up straight.

"Tell me, little lizard, what did you see today?"

Complacency was suffering from a sudden memory lapse.

Rafar prodded him. "Messengers of the living God, you said?"

Complacency nodded.

"Where?"

"Just outside this building."

"What were they doing?"

"I . . . I . . ."

"Did they attack you?"

"No."

"Was there a flash of light?"

That seemed to register with Complacency. He nodded.

"When a messenger of God attacks, there is always light." Rafar addressed all of them angrily. "And you let it slip by! You laughed! You mocked! A near attack from the enemy and you ignored it!"

Now Rafar returned to grill Lucius some more.

"Tell me, deposed prince, how stands the town of Ashton? Is it ready?"

Lucius was quick to say, "Yes, Ba-al Rafar."

"Oh, then you have taken care of this praying Busche and this sleeping troublemaker Hogan."

Lucius was silent.

"You have not! First you allow them to come into places we reserved for our own special appointments—"

"It was a mistake, Ba-al Rafar!" Lucius blurted. "The *Clarion* editor was eliminated according to our orders, but . . . no one knows where this Hogan came from. He bought the paper before anything could be done."

"And Busche? It was my understanding that he fled from your attacks."

"That . . . that was another man of God. The first one. He did flee."

"And?"

"This younger man sprung up in his place. From nowhere."

A long, foul sigh hissed out through Rafar's fangs.

"The host of heaven," he said. "While you have taken them for granted, they have moved in the Lord's chosen right under your noses! It is no secret that Henry Busche is a man who prays. Do you fear that?"

Lucius nodded. "Yes, of course, more than anything. We have been attacking him, trying to drive him out."

"And how has he responded?"

"He . . . he . . ."

"Speak up!"

"He prays."

Rafar shook his head. "Yes, yes, he is a man of God. And what about Hogan? What have you done about him?"

"We—we have attacked his daughter."

Complacency's ears perked up at that.

"His daughter?"

But Complacency couldn't contain himself. "I told them it wouldn't work! It would only make Hogan more aggressive and wake him from his lethargy!"

Lucius grabbed for Rafar's attention. "If my lord would allow me to explain . . ."

"Explain," Rafar instructed Lucius while warily eyeing Complacency.

Lucius quickly formulated a plan in his mind. "Sometimes a direct attack is not wise, so . . . we found a weakness in his daughter and felt we could divert his energies toward her, perhaps destroy him at home and disintegrate his family. It seemed to work on the former editor. It was at least a start."

"It will fail," cried Complacency. "He was harmless until they tampered with his sense of well-being and comfort. Now I fear I won't be able to hold him back. He is—"

A quick, threatening gesture from Rafar's outstretched hand stifled Complacency's wailings.

"I do not want Hogan held back," Rafar said. "I want him destroyed. Yes, take his daughter. Take anything else that can be corrupted. A risk is best removed, not tolerated."

"But—" cried Complacency, but Rafar quickly took hold of him and spoke with noxious fumings right into his face.

"Discourage him. Surely you can do that."

"Well . . ."

But Rafar was in no mood to wait for an answer. With a powerful spin of his wrist he hurled Complacency out of the room and back to work.

"We will destroy him, assault him on every side until he has no solid ground left from which to fight. As for this new man of God who has sprung up, I'm sure an adequate trap can be laid. But concerning our enemies: how strong are they?"

"Not strong at all," answered Lucius, trying to recover his competency rating.

"But cunning enough to make you think they are weak. A fatal mistake, Lucius." He addressed all of them. "You are to no longer take the enemy for granted. Watch him. Count his numbers. Know his whereabouts, his skill, his name. No mission was ever undertaken that was not challenged by the hosts of heaven, and this mission is nothing small. Our lord has very important plans for this town, he has sent me to fulfill them, and that is enough to draw the very hordes of the enemy down upon our heads. Be fearful of that, and give place nowhere! And as for these two thorns in our hoof, these two implanted barriers . . . tonight we will see what they are made of."

6

It was a dark, rainy night, and the raindrops pelting against the old single-pane windows made sleep difficult for Hank and Mary. She dropped off eventually, but Hank, already troubled in spirit, found it much harder to relax. It had been a lousy day anyway; he had worked on painting that slogan off the front of the house and tried to figure out who in the world would write such a thing against him. His ears were still ringing with the conversation he'd had with Alf Brummel, and his mind was still playing over and over the bitter comments from the board meeting. Now he could add to his apprehensions the congregational meeting on Friday, and he prayed to the Lord in desperate, hushed whispers as he lay there in the dark.

Funny how every lump in the mattress seems so much more lumpy when you're upset. Hank began to worry that he would keep Mary awake with all his tossing and turning. He lay on his back, his side, his other side, put his arms under his pillow, over his pillow; he grabbed a Kleenex and blew his nose. He looked over at the clock: 12:20. They had turned in at 10.

But sleep finally does come, usually in such an unannounced way that you don't even know you're out until you wake up. Sometime that night Hank dozed off.

But after a few hours his dreams began to go sour. They were the usual silly thing at first, like driving a car through his living room and then flying in the car as it turned into an airplane. But then the images began to rush and riot through his head, growing frantic and chaotic. He started running from dangers. He could hear screams; there was the sensation of falling and the sight and taste of blood. Images went from bright and colorful to monochromatic and dismal. He was constantly fighting, struggling for his life; innumerable dangers and enemies surrounded him, closing in. None of it made any sense, but one thing was very definite throughout: stark terror. He wanted desperately to scream but didn't have time between fighting off enemies, monsters, unseen forces.

His pulse began to pound in his ears. The whole world was reeling and throbbing. The horrible conflict rushing in his head began to push its way to the surface of the conscious, everyday Hank. He stirred in the bed, rolled over on his back, drew a deep waking-up breath. His eyes half opened, not focused on anything. He was in that strange state of stupor halfway between sleep and consciousness.

Did he really see it? It was an eerie projection in midair, a glowing painting on black velvet. Right above the bed, so close he could smell sulfurous breath, a hideous mask of a face hovered, contorting in grotesque movements as it spit out vicious words he couldn't understand.

Hank's eyes opened like a sprung trap. He thought he could still see the face, just fading away, but instantly he felt like he'd been struck by a very heavy blow to his chest; his heart began to race and pound like it would burst through his ribs. He could feel his pajamas and the bedsheets sticking to him, drenched in sweat. He lay there panting for breath, waiting for his heart to calm down, for the stark terror to go away, but nothing changed and he couldn't make it change.

You're just having a nightmare, he kept telling himself, but he couldn't seem to wake up. He purposely opened his eyes wide and looked around the darkened room, even though part of him wanted to regress back to childhood and just hide under the covers until the ghosts and monsters and burglars went away.

He saw nothing in the room out of the ordinary. A goblin in the corner was nothing but his shirt hanging on a chair, and the strange halo of light on the wall was only the streetlight reflecting off the crystal of his watch.

But he had been severely frightened, and he was still scared. He could feel himself shaking as he desperately tried to sort hallucination from reality. He watched, listened. Even the silence seemed sinister. He found no comfort in it, only the dread that something evil hid behind it, an intruder or a demon, waiting, watching for the right moment.

What was that? A creak in the house? Footsteps? No, he told himself, just the wind against the windows. The rain had stopped.

Another noise, this time a rustling in the living room. He had never heard that noise at night before. I gotta wake up, I gotta wake up. Come on, heart, quiet down so I can hear.

He forced himself to sit up in bed, even though it made him feel more vulnerable, and he remained there for several minutes, trying to stifle his heart's pounding with his hand over his chest. The pounding finally settled back a little, but the rate remained rapid. Hank could feel the sweat turning cold against his skin. To get up or go back to sleep? Sleep was definitely out. He decided to get up, look around, walk it off.

A clatter this time, in the kitchen. Now Hank started praying.

Marshall had had the same kind of dreams and felt the same heart-pounding fear. Voices. It sure sounded like voices somewhere. Sandy? Maybe a radio.

But who knows? he thought to himself. This town is going crazy anyway, and now the sickies are in my house. He slid stealthily out of bed, put on his slippers, and moved over to the closet to procure a baseball bat. Just like back home, he thought. Now somebody's gonna have mush for brains.

He looked out his bedroom door, up and down the hallway. No lights were on anywhere, no flashlight beams played about. But his guts were doing a square dance under his ribs, and there had to be some reason for it. He reached for the hallway light and flipped the switch. Nuts! The bulb was burnt out. Since when he didn't know, but he stood in the dark and felt his courage deflated just that much more. He gripped the bat more tightly and moved down the hall, staying close to the wall, looking ahead, looking behind, listening. He thought he could hear a quiet rustling somewhere, something moving.

At the archway that led into the living room his eyes caught something, and he pressed himself against the wall for concealment. The front door was open. Now his heart really started pounding, thudding rudely in his ears. In a strange, jungle way he felt better; at least there was indication of a real enemy. It was this lousy fear without any reason that was spooking him. He had already been through that sort of thing once today.

With that thought came a strange idea: That professor lady must be in the house.

He moved down the hall to check Sandy's room and make sure she was all right. He wanted to stay between Kate and Sandy and whatever was out there in the rest of the house. Sandy's bedroom door was open, and that was unusual; it made him all the more cautious. He inched along the wall toward the doorway and then, bat ready in his hands, he peered into the room.

Something was up. Sandy was, at least—her bed was empty and she was gone. He flicked on her bedroom light. The bed had been slept in, but now the covers were thrown back hastily and the room was in disarray.

As Marshall moved cautiously down the darkened hallway, it did occur to him that Sandy might just be up getting a drink, using the bathroom, reading. But such simple logic weakened against the horrible feeling that something was dreadfully wrong. He took deep breaths, trying with his greatest effort to hold himself steady while all the time he felt an insidious, unearthly terror as if he were inches from the crushing teeth of some monster he couldn't see.

The bathroom was cold and dark. He turned on the light, dreading what he thought he might see. He saw nothing out of the ordinary. He left that light on and headed back toward the living room.

He peered like some kind of stalking fugitive through the archway. There was that rustling sound again. He flipped on the lights. Ah. The cold night air was coming in through the front door, rustling the drapes. No, Sandy was nowhere to be seen, not in the living room, not anywhere in or near the kitchen. Perhaps she was right outside.

But he had undeniable qualms about crossing the living room to the front door, walking past all the furniture that could hide an assailant. He gripped the bat tightly, keeping it up and ready. He kept his back to the wall as he made his way around the perimeter of the room, stepping around the sofa after checking behind it, hurriedly maneuvering around the stereo, and finally reaching the door.

He went out onto the porch, into the cool night air, and for some reason suddenly felt safer. The town was still quiet this time of night. Everyone else was certainly asleep right now, not sneaking around their houses with baseball bats. He took a moment to regather himself and then went back inside.

Locking the door behind him was just like shutting himself in a dark closet with a couple of hundred vipers. The fear returned and he tightened his grip on the bat. With his back against the door, he looked around the room again. Why was it so dark? The lights were on, but every bulb seemed so dim, as if there were some kind of brown-out. Hogan, he thought to himself, either you've really lost a screw or you're in big, big trouble. He remained frozen there by the door, motionless, looking and listening. There had to be somebody or something in the house. He couldn't hear them or see them, but he could certainly feel them.

Outside the house, lying low in the evergreens and hedges, Tal and his company watched as demons—at least forty according to Tal's count—played havoc with Marshall's mind and spirit. They swooped like deadly black swallows in and out of the house, through the rooms, around and around Marshall, screaming taunts and blasphemies, and playing with and ever increasing his fears. Tal kept careful watch for the dreaded Rafar, but the Ba-al wasn't among this wild group. There could be no doubt, however, that Rafar had sent them.

Tal and the others agonized, feeling Marshall's pain. One demon, an ugly little imp with bristling, needle-sharp quills all over his body, leaped upon Marshall's shoulders and beat upon his head, screaming, "You're going to die, Hogan! You're going to die! Your daughter is dead and you are going to die!"

Guilo could hardly control himself. His big sword slipped with a metallic ring from its sheath, but Tal's strong arm held him back.

"Please, captain!" Guilo pleaded. "Never before have I only watched this happen!"

"Bridle yourself, dear warrior," Tal cautioned.

"I will strike them only once!"

Guilo could see that even Tal was severely pained by his own order: "Forbear. Forbear. He must go through it."

Hank had the lights on in the house, but he thought his eyes must have been playing tricks on him because the rooms still looked very dark, the shadows deep. Sometimes he couldn't tell if it was himself moving or the shadows in the room; a strange, undulating motion in the light and shadows made the depths in the house shift back and forth like the slow, steady motion of breathing.

Hank stood in the doorway between kitchen and living room,

watching and listening. He thought he could feel a wind moving through the house, but not a cold one from outside. It was like hot, sticky breath laden with repulsive odors, close and oppressive.

He had discovered that the clatter in the kitchen was due to a spatula sliding off the drainboard and onto the floor. That should have calmed his nerves right down, but he still felt terrified.

He knew he would sooner or later have to move into the living room to have a look. He took his first step out of the doorway and into the room.

It was like falling into a bottomless well of blackness and terror. The hairs on his neck bristled as if with static electricity. His lips started spilling out a frantic prayer.

He went down. Before he even knew what was happening, his body pitched forward and slammed into the floor. He became a trapped animal, instinctively struggling, trying to get loose from the unseen crushing weight that held him. His arms and legs were smacking into furniture and knocking things over, but in his terror and shock he felt no pain. He squirmed, twisted, gasped for breath, and lashed out at whatever it was, feeling resistance against the motion of his arms like stroking through water. The room seemed filled with smoke.

Blackness like blindness, a loss of hearing, a loss of contact with the real world, time standing still. He could feel himself dying. An image, a hallucination, a vision or a real sight broke through for an instant: two ghastly yellow eyes full of hate. His throat began to compress, squeezing shut.

"Jesus!" he heard his mind cry out, "help me!"

His next thought, a tiny, instant flash, must have come from the Lord: "Rebuke it! You have the authority."

Hank spoke the words though he couldn't hear the sound of them: "I rebuke you in Jesus' name!"

The crushing weight upon him lifted so quickly Hank felt he would sail upward from the floor. He filled his lungs with air and noticed he was now struggling against nothing. But the terror was still there, the black, sinister presence.

He sat up halfway, drew another breath, and spoke it clearly and loudly. "In the Name of Jesus I command you to get out of this house!"

Mary awoke with a jerk, startled and then terrified by the sound of a multitude screaming in anguish and pain. The cries were deafening at first, but they faded as if moving off into the unseen distance.

"Hank!" she screamed.

Marshall roared like a savage and raised the bat high to strike down his attacker. The attacker screamed also, out of stark terror.

It was Kate. They had unknowingly backed into each other in the dark hallway.

"Marshall!" she exclaimed, and her voice quivered. She was close to tears and angry at the same time. "What on earth are you doing out here!"

"Kate. . . ." Marshall sighed, feeling himself shrink like a punctured inner tube. "What are you trying to do, get yourself killed?"

"What's wrong?" She was looking at the baseball bat and knew something was up. She clung to him in fear. "Is there someone in the house?"

"No . . ." he muttered in a combination of relief and disgust. "Nobody. I looked."

"What happened? Who was it?"

"Nobody, I said."

"But I thought you were talking to someone."

He looked at her with the utmost impatience and said with steadily building volume, "Do I look like I've been having a friendly chat with someone?"

Kate shook her head. "I must have been dreaming. But it was the voices that woke me up."

"What voices?"

"Marshall, it sounded like a New Year's Eve party in there. Come on, who was it?"

"Nobody. There wasn't anybody here. I looked."

Kate was very flustered. "I know I was awake."

"You heard ghosts."

He could feel her hand squeezing the blood out of his arm. "Don't talk like that!"

"Sandy's gone."

"What do you mean, gone? Gone where?"

"She's gone. Her room's empty, she's not in the house. She's poof! Gone!"

Kate hurried down the hall and looked in Sandy's room. Marshall followed her and observed from the doorway as Kate checked the room over, looking through the closet and some of the drawers.

She reported with alarm, "Some of her clothes are gone. Her schoolbooks are missing." She looked at him helplessly. "Marshall— she's left home!"

He looked back at her for a long moment, then around the room, then rested his head against the doorjamb with a quiet thud.

"Nuts," he said.

"I knew she wasn't herself tonight. I should have found out what was wrong."

"We didn't hit it off too well today . . ."

"Well, that was obvious. You came home without her."

"How'd she get home, anyway?"

"Her girlfriend Terry brought her."

"Maybe she went over to Terry's for the night."

"Should we call and find out?"

"I dunno . . ."

"You don't know!?"

Marshall closed his eyes and tried to think. "Naw. It's late. Either she's there or she isn't. If she isn't, we'll be getting them out of bed for nothing, and if she is, well, she's okay anyway."

Kate seemed a little panicked. "I'm going to call."

Marshall held up his hand and leaned his head against the doorjamb again as he said, "Hey, don't get all spooked now, all right? Gimme a minute."

"I just want to see if she's there—"

"All right, all right . . ."

But Kate could see something was very wrong with Marshall. He was pale, weak, shaken.

"What's the matter, Marshall?

"Gimme a minute . . ."

She put her arm around him, concerned. "What is it?"

He had quite a struggle getting it out. "I'm scared." Trembling a bit, his eyes closed, his head resting against the doorjamb, he said again, "I'm really scared and I don't know why."

That scared Kate. "Marshall . . ."

"Don't get upset, will you? Keep it level."

"Can I do anything?"

"Just be tough, that's all."

Kate thought for a moment. "Well, why don't you get your robe on? I'll warm you some milk, okay?"

"Yeah, great."

It was the first time any demons had ever been actually confronted and rebuked by Hank Busche. They had certainly come with an arrogant brashness at first, descending on the house in the dead of night to raid and ravage, screaming and swooping through the rooms and leaping on Hank, trying to terrify him. But as Krioni, Triskal, and the others watched from their hiding place, confused and scattered flocks of demons suddenly came thundering and fluttering out of the house like bats, screaming, indignant, stopping their ears. There must have been close to a hundred, all the usual demonic pranksters and troublemakers Krioni had seen at work all over the town. No doubt the great Ba-al had sent them, and now that they had been routed there was no telling what Rafar's reaction or his next plan would be. But Hank had proven himself very well.

In a moment the coast was clear, the trouble was over, and the warriors came out of hiding, breathing easier. Krioni and Triskal were impressed.

Krioni commented, "Tal was right. He's not so insignificant."

Triskal agreed, "Stern stuff, this Henry Busche."

But as Hank and Mary sat trembling at their kitchen table, she preparing an icepack and he sporting a welt on his forehead and a great many bruises and scrapings on his arms and shins, neither one of them felt entirely stern, powerful, or victorious. Hank was thankful to have escaped with his life, and Mary was still in a mild state of shock and disbelief.

It was awkward, with neither of them wanting to relate his or her experience first for fear that the whole thing was nothing but an excess of pickles and pastrami before bedtime. But Hank's welt kept growing, and he could only tell what he knew. Mary bought every word of it, scared as she was by the screams that had awakened her. As they shared their not-so-pleasant experiences, they were able to accept the fact that the whole night of madness had been very frighteningly real and not some nightmare.

"Demons," Hank concluded.

Mary could only nod.

"But why?" Hank pleaded to know. "What was it for?"

Mary wasn't ready to come up with any answers. She kept waiting for Hank to do that.

He muttered, "Like Lesson Number One in Frontlines Combat. I wasn't a bit ready for it. I think I flunked."

Mary gave him the icepack and he placed it against the welt, wincing at the pressure.

"What makes you think you flunked?" she asked.

"I don't know. I just walked into it, I guess. I let them clobber me." Then he prayed, "Lord God, help me to be ready next time. Give me the wisdom, the sensitivity to know what they're up to."

Mary squeezed his hand, said amen, and then commented, "You know, I might be wrong, but hasn't the Lord already done that? I mean, how are you going to know how to fight Satan's direct attacks unless you just . . . do it?"

That was what Hank needed to hear.

"Wow," he mused. "I'm a veteran!"

"And I don't think you flunked, either. They're gone, aren't they? And you're still here, and you should have heard those screams."

"Are you sure it wasn't me?"

"Quite sure."

Then came a long, troubled silence.

"So what now?" Mary finally asked.

"Uh . . . let's pray." said Hank. For him, that option was always easy to jump to.

And pray they did, clasping hands at the little kitchen table, having a conference with the Lord. They thanked Him for the experience of that night, for protecting them from danger, for showing them a very close glimpse of their enemy. Over an hour passed, and during that time the field of concern continued to grow outward; their own problems began to take a small place in a vastly wider perspective as Hank and Mary prayed for their church, the people in it, the town, the people that ran it, the state, the nation, the world. Through it all came the beautiful assurance that they had indeed connected with the throne of God and had conducted serious business with the Lord. Hank grew more determined to stay in the battle and give Satan a real run for his money. He was sure that was what God wanted.

The warm milk and Kate's company had a soothing effect on Marshall's nerves. With each swallow and each additional minute of normalcy, he gained more and more assurance that the world would still go on, he would live, the sun would rise in the morning. He was amazed at how bleak things had looked just a little while ago.

"Feeling better?" Kate asked, buttering some fresh toast.

"Yeah," he answered, noticing that his heart had retreated back into his chest and returned to its normal, everyday pace. "Boy, I don't know what got into me."

Kate placed the two slices of toast on a plate and set them on the table.

Marshall crunched off a bite of toast and asked, "So she's not at Terry's?"

Kate shook her head. "Do you *want* to talk about Sandy?"

Marshall was ready. "We probably need to talk about a lot of things."

"I don't know how to start—"

"You think it's my fault?"

"Oh, Marshall . . ."

"C'mon, be honest now. I've been getting my behind whipped all day. I'll listen."

Her eyes met his and remained in place, denoting a sincerity and firm love.

"Categorically, no," she said.

"I botched it today."

"I think we've all botched it, and that includes Sandy. She's made some choices too, remember."

"Yeah, but maybe it was because we didn't have anything better to give her."

"What do you think of talking to Pastor Young?"

"Case in point."

"Hmmmm?"

Hogan shook his head despondently. "Maybe . . . maybe Young's just a little too cush, you know? He's into all this family of man stuff, discovering yourself, saving the whales . . ."

Kate was a little surprised. "I thought you liked Pastor Young."

"Well . . . I guess I do. But sometimes—no, a lot of the time, I don't even feel like I'm going to church. I may as well be sitting at a lodge meeting or in one of Sandy's weird classes."

He checked her eyes. They were still steady. She was listening. "Kate, don't you ever get the feeling that God's got to be, you know, a little . . . bigger? Tougher? The God we get at that church, I feel like He isn't even a real person, and if He is, He's dumber than we are. I can't expect Sandy to buy that stuff. I don't even go for it myself."

"I never knew you felt this way, Marshall."

"Well, maybe I never did either. It's just that this thing tonight . . . I've really got to think about it; there's been so much of it going on lately."

"What do you mean? What's been going on?"

I can't tell her, Marshall thought to himself. How could he explain the strange, hypnotic persuasion he was sure he got from Brummel, the spooky feelings he'd gotten from Sandy's professor, the stark terror he'd felt that night? None of it made sense, and now, to top it off, Sandy was gone. All through these situations he had been horrified by his own inability to fight back. He had felt controlled. But he couldn't tell Kate anything like that.

"Aw . . . it's a long story," he said finally. "All I know is, this whole thing—our lifestyle, our schedule, our family, our religion, whatever it is—just isn't working. Something's got to change."

"But you don't think you want to talk to Pastor Young?"

"Aw, he's a turkey . . ."

Just then, 1 A.M. or not, the phone rang.

"Sandy!" Kate exclaimed.

Marshall snatched up the receiver.

"Hello?"

"Hello?" said a female voice. "You're up!"

Marshall recognized the voice, with disappointment. It was Bernice.

"Oh, hi, Bernie," he said, looking at Kate, whose face sank now with frustration.

"Don't hang up! I'm sorry for calling at this late hour, but I had a date and I didn't get home until late, but I wanted to develop that film . . . are you mad?"

"I'll be mad tomorrow. Right now I'm too tired. What have you got?"

"Get this. I know the film in the camera had twelve pictures of the carnival, including the ones of Brummel, Young, and those three unknowns. Today I went home and shot the rest of the roll, twelve more frames—my cat, the neighbor lady with the big mole, the evening news, et cetera. Today's pictures came out."

There was a pause, and Marshall knew he would have to ask. "What about the other ones?"

"The emulsion was blacked out, totally exposed, the film scratched and fingerprinted in a few places. There's nothing wrong with the camera." Marshall said nothing for a long moment. "Marshall . . . hello?"

"That's interesting," he said.

"They're up to something! It's got me all excited. I'm wondering if I can trace those prints." There was another long pause. "Hello?"

"What did the other woman look like, the blonde one?"

"Not too old, long blonde hair . . . kind of mean looking."

"Heavy? Thin? In between?"

"She looked good."

Marshall's forehead crinkled a bit, and his eyes shifted about as he followed his ideas. "I'll see you in the morning."

"Good-bye, and thanks for answering."

Marshall hung up the phone. He stared at the tabletop, drumming his fingers.

"What was that all about?" Kate asked.

"Mmmmmm," he said, still thinking. Then he answered, "Uh, newspaper stuff. No biggie. What was it we were talking about, anyway?"

"Well, if it still matters, we were just talking about whether or not you should talk to Pastor Young about our problem—"

"Young," he said, and almost sounded angry.

"But if you don't want to . . ." Marshall stared at the table while his warm milk got cold. Kate waited, then roused him with, "Would you rather talk about this in the morning?"

"I'll talk to him," Marshall said flatly. "I . . . I want to talk to him. You *bet* I'll talk to him!"

"It couldn't hurt."

"No, it sure couldn't."

"I don't know when he'd be able to see you, but—"

"One o'clock would be nice." He scowled a bit. "One o'clock would be perfect."

"Marshall . . ." Kate started, but she kept it back. There was something happening to her husband, and she picked it up in his voice, in his expression.

She had never really missed that fire in his eyes; perhaps she'd never known it was gone until this moment when, for the first time since they left New York, she saw it again. Some old, unpleasant feelings rose up within her, feelings she had no desire to cope with late at night with her daughter mysteriously missing.

"Marshall," she said, sliding her chair out and picking up the plate of half-eaten toast, "let's get some sleep."

"I may not be able to sleep."

"I know," she said quietly.

All this time, Tal, Guilo, Nathan, and Armoth had stood in the room, carefully observing, and now Guilo began to chuckle in his gruff, quaking way.

Tal said with a smile, "No, Marshall Hogan. You never were much of a sleeper . . . and now Rafar has helped to awaken you again!"

7

On Tuesday morning the sun was shining through the windows and Mary was busy beating the daylights out of some bread dough. Hank found the name and number in the church records: the Reverend James Farrel. He had never met Farrel, and all he knew was the tasteless and malicious gossip going around about the man who had been his predecessor and had since moved far away from Ashton.

It was a whim, a stab in the dark, Hank knew that. But he sat down on the couch, picked up the phone, and dialed the number.

"Hello?" a tired older man's voice answered.

"Hello," said Hank, trying to sound pleasant despite his tight nerves. "James Farrel?"

"Yes. Who is this?"

"This is Hank Busche, pastor of the—" he heard Farrel give a drawn-out, knowledgeable sigh, "—Ashton Community Church. I guess you must know who I am."

"Yes, Pastor Busche. So how are you?"

How do I answer that, Hank wondered. "Uhh . . . okay in some respects."

"And not okay in other respects," Farrel offered, completing Hank's thought.

"Boy, you've really been keeping up on things."

"Well, not actively. I do hear from some of the members from time to time." Then he added quickly, "I'm glad you called. What can I do for you?"

"Uh . . . talk to me, I guess."

Farrel answered, "I'm sure there's a lot I could say to you. I do hear there's a congregational meeting this Friday. Is that true?"

"Yes, it is."

"A vote of confidence, I understand."

"That's right."

"Yes, I went through the same thing, you know. Brummel, Turner, Mayer, and Stanley were in charge of that one, too."

"You gotta be kidding."

"Oh, it's strictly history repeating itself, Hank. Take it from me."

"They drummed you out?"

"They decided they didn't like what I was preaching and the direction of my ministry, so they stirred up the congregation against me and then managed to take it to a vote. I didn't lose by much, but I did lose."

"The same four guys!"

"The same four . . . but now, did I hear right? Did you really put Lou Stanley out of fellowship?"

"Well, yeah."

"Now that is something. I can't imagine Lou letting anyone do that to him."

"Well, the other three made that a pivotal issue; they haven't left me alone about it."

"And how is the congregation leaning?"

"I don't know. They could be pretty evenly divided."

"So how are you standing up under all this?"

Hank could think of no better way to phrase it. He said, "I think I'm under attack—direct, spiritual attack." Silence at the other end. "Hello?"

"Oh, I'm here." Farrel talked slowly, falteringly, as if thinking hard while trying to converse. "What kind of spiritual attack?"

Hank stammered a bit. He could imagine how last night's experience would sound to a stranger. "Well . . . I just think Satan is really involved here . . ."

Farrel was almost demanding, "Hank, what kind of spiritual attack?"

Hank began his account carefully, trying very hard to sound like a sane and responsible individual as he related the major points: the mania Brummel seemed to have for getting rid of him, the church division, the gossip, the angry church board, the slogan painted on his house, and then the spiritual wrestling match he had gone through last night. Farrel interrupted only to ask clarifying questions.

"I know it all sounds crazy . . ." Hank concluded.

All Farrel could do was let out a deep sigh and mutter, "Oh, blast it all!"

"Well, like you say, it's just history repeating itself. No doubt you've encountered things like this, right? Or am *I* the one who has the real problem here?"

Farrel struggled with the words. "I am glad you called. I always struggled with whether or not I should call *you*. I don't know if you're going to like hearing this, but . . ." Farrel paused for new strength, then said, "Hank, are you sure you belong there?"

Uh-oh. Hank felt a defensiveness rising in him. "I do believe firmly in my heart that God called me here, yes."

"Do you know you were chosen as pastor by accident?"

"Well, some are saying that, but—"

"It is true, Hank. You really should consider that. You see, the church ousted me; they had some other minister all picked out and ready to move in, some guy who had a wide and liberal enough religious philosophy to suit them. Hank, I really don't know how you ended up with the job, but it was definitely some kind of organizational fluke. The one thing they did not want in there was another fundamentalist minister, not after they went to such great lengths to get rid of the one they had."

"But they voted me in."

"It was an *accident*. Brummel and the others were definitely not planning on it."

"Well, that's obvious now."

"Okay, good, you can see that. So let me just get right down to some direct advice. Now, after Friday this may all be moot anyway, but if I were you, I'd get packing and start looking for a position elsewhere, no matter how the vote comes out."

Hank deflated a little. This conversation was turning sour; he just couldn't buy it. All he could do was sigh into the phone.

Farrel was forceful. "Hank, I've been there, I've been through it, I know what you're going through, and I know what you have yet to go through. Believe me, it isn't worth it. Let them have that church, let them have the whole town; just don't sacrifice yourself."

"But I can't leave . . ."

"Yeah, right, you have a calling from God. Hank, so did I. I was ready to go into battle, to make a real stand in that town for God. You know, it cost me my home, my reputation, my health, it almost cost me my marriage. I left Ashton literally planning on changing my name. You have no idea of who you're really dealing with. There are forces at work in that town—"

"What kind of forces?"

"Well, political, social . . . spiritual too, of course."

"Oh yeah, you never did answer my question: what about what happened to me last night? What do you think about that?"

Farrel hesitated, then said, "Hank . . . I don't know why, but it's very difficult for me to talk about such things. All I can say to you is get out of that place while you can. Just drop it. The church doesn't want you there, the town doesn't want you there."

"I can't leave, I told you that."

Farrel paused for a long time. Hank was almost afraid he had hung up. But then he said, "All right, Hank. I'll tell you, and you listen. What you went through last night, well, I think I may have had similar experiences, but I can assure you, whatever it was, it was only the beginning."

"Pastor Farrel—"

"I'm not a pastor. Call me Jim."

"That's what the gospel is all about, fighting Satan, shining the light of the gospel into the darkness . . ."

"Hank, all the nice homilies you can dig up won't help you there. Now I don't know how equipped or ready you are, but to be perfectly honest, if you come through it all with even your life I'll be surprised. I'm serious!"

Hank had no other answer he could give. "Jim . . . I'll let you know how it turns out: Maybe I'll win, maybe I won't come out alive. But God didn't tell me I'd come out alive; He just told me to stay and fight. You've made one thing clear to me: Satan does want this town. I can't let him have it."

Hank replaced the receiver and felt he would cry.

"Lord God," he prayed, "Lord God, what shall I do?"

The Lord gave no immediate answer, and Hank sat there on the couch for several minutes trying to regather his strength and confidence. Mary was still busy in the kitchen. That was good. He couldn't talk to her right now; there were too many thoughts and feelings to be sorted out.

Then a verse came to his mind: "Arise, walk through the land in the length of it and in the breadth of it; for I will give it unto thee."

Well, it sure beat sitting home just fussing and fuming and not really doing anything. So on went his sneakers and out the door he went.

Krioni and Triskal were outside waiting for their charge. Invisibly they joined Hank, one on each side, and walked with him down Morgan Hill toward the center of town. Hank was not a man of great stature anyway, but between these two giants he looked even smaller. He did, however, appear very, very safe.

Triskal kept a wary eye open, saying, "What's he up to, anyway?"

Krioni knew Hank pretty well by now. "I don't think he even knows. The Spirit is driving him. He's giving action to a burden in his heart."

"Oh, we'll have action, all right!"

"Just don't be a threat. So far it's the best way to survive in this town."

"So tell that to the little pastor here."

As Hank neared the main business district he paused on a corner to look up and down the street, watching old cars, new cars, vans and four-by-fours, shoppers, walkers, joggers, and bicyclers stream in four and more directions, regarding the orders of the traffic light as mere suggestions.

So where was the evil? How could it be so vivid last night and a distant, dubious memory today? No demons or devils lurked in the office windows or reached out of the storm drains; the people were the same, simple, ordinary folks he had always seen, still ignoring him and passing by.

Yes, this was the town he prayed for night and day with deep groanings of the heart because of a burden he couldn't explain, and now it was taxing his patience, unsettling him.

"Well, are you in trouble or aren't you, or don't you even care?" he said aloud.

Nobody listened. No deep, sinister voices answered back with a threat.

But the Spirit of the Lord inside him wouldn't leave him alone. *Pray, Hank. Pray for these people. Don't let them escape your heart. The pain is there, the fear is there, the danger is there.*

So when do we win, Hank answered the Lord. Do You know how long I've been sweating and praying over this place? Just once I'd like to hear my little pebble make a splash; I'd like to see this dead dog twitch when I poke it.

It was amazing how well the demons could hide, even behind the doubts he sometimes felt about their very existence.

"I know you're out there," he said quietly, gazing carefully over the blankly staring faces of the buildings, the concrete, the brick, the glass, the trash. The spirits were teasing him. They could descend on him in a moment, terrorize and choke him, and then vanish, slipping back into the hiding places behind the facade of the town, snickering, hide-and-seeking, watching him grope about like a blind fool.

He sat down on a sidewalk bench feeling miffed.

"I'm here, Satan," he said. "I can't see you, and maybe you can move faster than I can, but I'm still here, and by the grace of God and the power of the Holy Spirit I intend to be a thorn in your side until one of us has had enough!"

Hank looked across the street at the impressive structure of the Ashton United Christian Church. Hank had known some terrific Christians who belonged to that denomination, but this particular bunch in Ashton were different, liberal, even bizarre. He had met Pastor Oliver Young a few times and could never get very close to him; Young seemed rather cold and aloof, and Hank could never figure out why.

As Hank sat there, watching a brown Buick pull into the church parking lot, Triskal and Krioni stood beside the bench, also watching the car come to a stop. Only the two of them could see the car's special passengers: sitting on the roof were two big warriors, the Arabian and the African, Nathan and Armoth. No swords were visible. They were taking a passive, noncombatant posture according to Tal's orders, just like all the rest.

Marshall had seen Bernice's film. He had seen the minute scratches from some kind of mishandling: he had seen the clumsy fingerprints at regular intervals that could very well have been placed there by a hand pulling the film out of the camera, unrolling it in the light.

Marshall had gotten his appointment with Young for 1 o'clock. He pulled into the vast, blacktop parking lot at 12:45, still downing a deluxe cheeseburger and large coffee.

Ashton United Christian was one of the large, stately-looking edifices around town, constructed in the traditional style with heavy stone, stained glass, towering lines, majestic steeple. The front door fit the motif: large, solid, even a little intimidating, especially when you tried to heave it open all by yourself. The church was located near the center of town, and the carillon in the tower chimed each hour and gave a short concert of hymns at noon. It was a respected establishment, Young was a respected minister, the people who attended the church were respected members of the community. Marshall had often thought that respect and status just might be a prerequisite for membership.

He engaged the big front door in a short Indian arm wrestle and finally got inside. No, this congregation had never spared the expense, that was for sure. The floors of the foyer, stairs, and sanctuary were covered with thick red carpeting, the woodwork was all deep finished oak and walnut. On top of that was all the brass: brass door handles, coat hooks, stairway railing, window latches. The windows, of course, were stained glass; and all the ceilings were lofty, with great hanging chandeliers and delicate scrollwork.

Marshall entered the sanctuary through another ponderous door and walked down the long center aisle toward the front. This room was a cross between an opera house and a cavern: the platform was big, the pulpit was big, the choir loft was big. Of course the choir was big, too.

Pastor Young's big office, just to the side of the sanctuary, afforded a very visible access to the platform and pulpit, and Pastor Young's entrance through the big oak door each Sunday morning was a traditional part of the ceremonies.

Marshall pushed that big door open and stepped into the reception office. The pretty secretary greeted him, but didn't know who he was. He told her, she checked the appointment book and verified it.

Marshall checked the book too, reading upside down again. The 2 o'clock hour was marked A. Brummel.

"Well, Marshall," Young said with a cordial, businesslike smile and handshake, "come in, come in."

Marshall followed Young into his plush office. Young, a large-framed man in his sixties with a roundish face, wire-rimmed glasses, and thin, well-oiled hair, seemed to enjoy his position both in the church and in the community. His dark-paneled walls sported many plaques from community and charitable organizations. Along with those were several framed photographs of him posing with the governor, a few popular evangelists, some authors, and a senator.

Behind his impressive desk Young created a perfect picture of the successful professional. The high-backed leather chair became a throne, and his own reflection in the desk top made him all the more scenic and impressive, like a mountain reflected in an alpine lake.

He motioned Marshall to a chair, and Marshall sat down, noticing that he sank to an eye level quite below Young's. He began to feel a familiar tinge of intimidation; this whole office seemed designed for it.

"Nice office," he commented.

"Thank you very much," said Young with a smile that shoved his cheeks into piles against his ears. He leaned back in his chair, his fingers interlaced and wiggling on the edge of his desk. "I enjoy it, am thankful for it, and I rather appreciate the warmth, the atmosphere of the place. It sets one at ease."

Sets *you* at ease, thought Marshall. "Yeah . . . yeah."

"So how is the *Clarion* these days?"

"Oh, pulling itself together. Did you get today's?"

"Yes, it was very good. Very neat, stylish. You've brought some of that big-city class here with you, I see."

"Mm-hmmm." Marshall suddenly didn't feel too talkative.

"I'm glad you're with us, Marshall. We're looking forward to a very good relationship."

"Well yeah, thanks."

"So what's on your mind?"

Marshall fidgeted just a little, then jumped to his feet; that chair made him feel too much like a microbe under a microscope. Next time I'll bring my own big desk, he thought. He walked around the office, trying to look casual.

"We've got a lot to cover in an hour," he began.

"We can always have more meetings."

"Yeah, sure. Well, first of all, Sandy—that's my daughter—ran off last night. We haven't heard anything, we don't know where she is . . ." He gave Young a quick synopsis of the problem and its history, and Young listened intently with no interruptions.

"So," Young finally asked, "you think she has turned her back on your traditional values and that disturbs you?"

"Hey, I'm not a deeply religious person, you know what I mean? But some things have to be right, and some things have to be wrong, and I have trouble with Sandy just—just jumping over the fence from one to the other like she does."

Young rose majestically from his desk and walked toward Marshall with the air of an understanding father. He put his hand on Marshall's shoulder and said, "Do you think she's happy, Marshall?"

"I never see her happy, but that's probably because she's around me every time I see her."

"And that could be because you find it hard to understand the direction she's now choosing for her life. Obviously you project a definite displeasure toward her philosophies . . ."

"Yeah, and toward that professor lady who dumps all those philosophies on her. You ever met that, what's her name, Professor Langstrat, out at the college?"

Young thought, then shook his head.

"I think Sandy's taken a couple of courses from her now, and every quarter I find my daughter more out of touch with reality."

Young chuckled a bit. "Marshall, it sounds like she's just exploring, just trying to find out about the world, about the universe she lives in. Don't you remember growing up? So many things just weren't true until you could prove them yourself. That's probably the way it is right now with Sandy. She's a very bright girl. I'm sure she just needs to explore, to find herself."

"Well, whenever she finds out where she is I hope she calls."

"Marshall, I'm sure she would feel much more free to call if she could find understanding hearts at home. It's not for us to determine what another person must do with himself, or think about his place in the cosmos. Each person must find his own way, his own truth. If we're ever going to get along like any kind of civilized family on this earth, we're going to have to learn to respect the other man's right to his own views."

Marshall felt a flash of *déjà vu,* as if a recording from Sandy's brain had been plugged into Young's. He couldn't help but ask, "You *sure* you never met Professor Langstrat?"

"Quite sure," Young answered with a smile.

"How about Alf Brummel?"

"Who?"

"Alf Brummel, the police chief."

Marshall watched his face. Was he struggling for an answer?

Young finally said, "I *may* have met him on occasion . . . I was just trying to match the name with the face."

"Well, he thinks the way you do. Talks a lot about getting along and being peaceful. How he got to be a cop, I'll never know."

"But weren't we talking about Sandy?"

"Yeah, okay. Speak on."

Young spoke on. "All the questions you're struggling with, the matters of right and wrong, or what truth is, or our different views of these issues . . . so many of these things are unknowable, save in the heart. We all feel the truth, like a common heartbeat in each of us. Every human has the natural capacity for good, for love, for expecting and striving for the best interests of himself and his neighbor."

"I guess you weren't here for the Festival."

Young chuckled. "I'll admit we humans can certainly misdirect our better inclinations."

"Say, *did* you make the Festival, by the way?"

"Yes, some parts of it. Most of it was of little interest to me, I'm afraid."

"So you didn't drop by the carnival, eh?"

"Certainly not. It's a waste of money. But about Sandy . . ."

"Yeah, we were talking about what's true, and everyone's view . . . like the whole subject of God, for example. She can't seem to find Him, I'm just trying to pin Him down, we can't agree on our religion, and so far you haven't helped much."

Young smiled thoughtfully. Marshall could feel a very lofty homily coming.

"Your God," said Young, "is where you find Him, and to find Him, we need only to open our eyes and realize that He is truly within all of us. We've never been without Him at all, Marshall; it's just that we've been blinded by our ignorance, and that has kept us from the love, security, and meaning that we all desire. Jesus revealed our problem on the cross, remember? He said, 'Father, forgive them, for they know not . . .' So His example to us is to search for knowledge, wherever we may find it. That's what you are doing, and I'm convinced that's what Sandy is doing. The source of your problem is a narrow perspective, Marshall. You must be open-minded. You must search, and Sandy must search."

"So," Marshall said thoughtfully, "you're saying it's all a matter of how we look at things?"

"That would be part of it, yes."

"And if I might perceive something a certain way, that doesn't mean everybody's going to see it that way, right?"

"Yes, that's right!" Young seemed very pleased with his student.

"So . . . let me see if I've got this right. If my reporter, Bernice Krueger, perceived that you, Brummel, and three other people were having some kind of little meeting behind the dart throwing booth at the carnival . . . well, that was just *her* perception of reality?"

Young smiled with an odd what-are-you-trying-to-pull grin, and answered, "I suppose so, Marshall. I guess that would be a case in point. I was nowhere near the carnival, and I told you that. I abhor that kind of event."

"You weren't there with Alf Brummel?"

"No, not at all. So you see, Ms. Krueger had quite an incorrect perception of someone else."

"Of *both* of you, I suppose."

Young smiled and shrugged.

Marshall pressed a little. "What do you suppose the odds are of that happening?"

Young kept smiling, but his face got a little red. "Marshall, what do you wish me to do? Argue with you? Certainly you didn't come here for that sort of thing."

Marshall took a real stab at whatever it might catch. "She even took some pictures of you."

Young sighed and looked for a moment at the floor. Then he said coolly, "Then why don't you bring those photographs next time, and then we can discuss it?"

The little smile on Young's face hit Marshall like spittle.

"Okay," Marshall muttered, not dropping his eyes.

"Marge will set another appointment for you."

"Thanks a lot."

Marshall checked his watch, went to the door, and opened it. "Come on in, Alf."

Alf Brummel had been sitting in the reception area. At the sight of Marshall he jumped awkwardly to his feet. He looked the way one might a split second before being hit by a train.

Marshall grabbed Alf by the hand and shook that hand excitedly. "Hey, buddy! Say, seeing as how the two of you don't seem to know each other very well, let me introduce you. Alf Brummel, this is Reverend Oliver Young. Reverend Young, Alf Brummel, chief of police!"

Brummel didn't seem to appreciate Marshall's cordiality at all, but Young did. He stepped forward, grabbed Brummel's hand, shook it, and then pulled Brummel quickly into his office saying over his shoulder, "Marge, make another appointment for Mr. Hogan."

But Mr. Hogan had left.

8

Sandy Hogan sat dismally at a small lunch table in a campus plaza shaded by an expansive grape arbor. She was staring at a slowly cooling, microwaved, packaged hamburger and a slowly warming half-pint carton of milk. She had made her classes that morning, but they had all slipped by her, mostly unabsorbed. Her mind was too much on herself, her family, and her belligerent father. Besides, it had been a horrible way to spend the night, walking clear across town and sitting all night in the Ashton bus depot reading from her psychology textbook. After her last class of the day she tried to take a nap out on the lawn in the sculpture garden and had managed to doze for a short time. When she awoke, her world was no better and she had only two impressions: hunger and loneliness.

Now, sitting at this little table with a machine-vended lunch, her loneliness was stealing away her hunger and she was on the brink of tears.

"Why, Daddy?" she whispered in very soft tones, dabbling her straw in her carton of milk. "Why can't you just love me for what I am?"

How could he have so much against her when he hardly even knew her? How could he be so adamant against her thoughts and philosophies when he couldn't even understand them? They were living in two different worlds, and each disdained the other's.

Last night she and her father had not said a word to each other the whole evening, and Sandy had gone to bed depressed and angry. Even as she lay there listening to her folks turning out the lights, brushing their teeth, and turning in for the night, they seemed half a world away. She wanted to call them into her room and reach out to them, but she knew it wouldn't work; Daddy would make demands and place conditions on their relationship instead of loving her, just loving her.

She still didn't know what had terrified her in the pit of the night. All she could remember was waking up plagued by every fear she had ever known—fear of dying, fear of failure, fear of loneliness. She had to get out of the house. She knew, even as she hastily dressed and ran out the door, that it was foolish and pointless, but the feelings were greater than any common sense she could muster.

Now she felt very much like some poor animal shot into space with no means of returning, floating listlessly, waiting for nothing in particular and with nothing to look forward to.

"Oh, Daddy," she whimpered, and then she began to cry.

She let her red hair fall down like soft blinds on either side of her face and the tears dropped one by one to the tabletop. She could hear people passing , but they chose to live in their own world and left her alone in hers. She tried to cry softly, which was hard to do when her emotions wanted to rush out of her like the cascade from a broken dam.

"Uh . . ." came a soft and hesitant voice, "Excuse me—"

Sandy looked up and saw a young man, blond, slightly thin, with big brown eyes full of compassion.

The young man said, "Please forgive me for intruding . . . but . . . is there anything I can do to help?"

It was dark in the living room of Professor Juleen Langstrat's apartment, and very, very quiet. One candle on the coffee table cast a dull yellow light on the ceiling-high bookcases, the strange oriental masks, the neatly arranged furniture, and the faces of two people who sat opposite each other, the candle between them. One of the people was the professor, her head resting against the back of her chair, her eyes closed, her arms outstretched in front of her, her hands making gentle sweeping motions as if she were treading water.

The man sitting opposite her was Brummel, also with eyes closed, but not mirroring Langstrat's expression and actions very well. He looked stiff and uncomfortable. At short intervals, and for a split second, he would crack his eyes open just enough to see what Langstrat was doing.

Then she began to moan and her face registered pain and displeasure. She opened her eyes and sat upright. Brummel looked back at her.

"You don't feel well today, do you?" she asked.

He shrugged and looked at the floor. "Ehhh, I'm okay. Just tired."

She shook her head, not satisfied with his answer. "No, no, it's the energy I feel from you. You're very disturbed."

Brummel had no answer.

"Did you talk to Oliver today?" she probed.

He hesitated, and finally said, "Yeah, sure."

"And you went to talk to him about our relationship."

That got a reaction. "No! That's—"

"Don't lie to me."

He wilted a little and let out a frustrated sigh. "Yeah, sure, we talked about it. We talked about other things too, though."

Langstrat probed him with her eyes as if doing some kind of X-ray scan. Her hands opened and began to wave in the air just slightly. Brummel tried to sink out of sight into his chair.

"Hey, listen," he said shakily, "it's no big deal—"

She began to speak as if reading off a note pinned on his chest. "You're . . . frightened, you feel cornered, you went to tell Oliver . . . you also feel controlled . . ." She looked at his face. "Controlled? By whom?"

"I don't feel controlled!"

She laughed a little to put him at ease. "Well, of course you do. I just read it."

Brummel looked for a split second toward the telephone on the end table. "Did Young call you?"

She smiled with amusement. "There was no need to. Oliver is very close to the Universal Mind. I'm beginning to meld with his thoughts now." Her expression hardened. "Alf, I really wish you were doing as well."

Brummel sighed again, hid his face behind his hands, then finally blurted, "Hey, listen, I can't tackle everything at once! There's just too much to learn!"

She put her hand on his comfortingly. "Well then, let's deal with

these things one at a time. Alf?" He looked up at her. "You're frightened, aren't you? What are you frightened of?"

"You tell me," and it was almost a dare.

"I'm giving you a chance to speak first."

"Well then, I'm not frightened."

At least not until this very second, when Langstrat's eyes narrowed
and began to bore into him.

"You are indeed frightened," she said sternly. "You are frightened
because we were photographed the other night by that reporter from
the *Clarion*. Isn't that right?"

Brummel pointed his finger at her angrily. "See, now that's exactly
one of the things Young and I talked about! He called you! He had to
have called you!"

She nodded, unabashed. "Yes, of course he called me. He withholds nothing from me. None of us withholds truth from all the
others, you know that."

Brummel knew he might as well open up. "I'm concerned about
the Plan. We're getting too big, too big to hide anymore; we're risking
exposure in too many places. I think we were careless to meet out in
public like that."

"But it's all been taken care of. There's nothing to worry about."

"Oh no? Hogan's on our scent! I suppose you know he was asking
Oliver some very delicate questions?"

"Oliver can handle himself."

"So how do we handle Hogan?"

"The same way we handle anyone else. Are you aware that he
talked to Oliver about problems he's having with his daughter? You
should find that interesting."

"What kind of problems?"

"She's run away from home . . . and yet she still had the desire to
be in my class today. I like the sound of that."

"So how do we use it?"

She smiled her cunning smile. "All in good time, Alf. We can't rush
things."

Brummel got up and began to pace. "With Hogan I'm not so sure.
He may not be the pushover that Harmel was. Maybe having Krueger
arrested was the wrong thing to do."

"But you got access to the film; you had it destroyed."

He turned to face her. "And what did that get us? Before that they
weren't asking any questions, and now they are! Come on, I know
what I'd think if I got my camera back and the film was ruined. Hogan
and Krueger just aren't that gullible."

Langstrat spoke soothingly, putting her arms around him like the
tendrils of a vine. "Ah, but they are vulnerable, first to you, and
ultimately to me."

"Just like everybody," he muttered.

He should have expected her reaction. She grew very cold and frightening and looked right into his eyes.

"And that," she said, "is another topic you discussed with Oliver today."

"He tells you everything!"

"The Masters would tell me even if he didn't."

Brummel tried to turn his eyes away from her. He couldn't stand whatever it was that made such beauty so immensely hideous.

"Look at me!" she insisted, and Brummel obeyed. "If you are not happy with our relationship, I can always have it terminated."

He looked down, stuttered a bit. "It's—it's okay . . ."

"What?"

"I mean I'm happy with our relationship."

"Truly happy?"

He felt desperate to appease her, to get her to let go of him. "I . . . I just don't want things to get out of control . . ."

She gave him a slow, vampirish kiss. "You are the one who needs more control. Haven't I always taught you that?"

She was cutting him to pieces and he knew it, but she had him. He belonged to her.

He still had a concern he couldn't shake. "But how many adversaries can we continue to remove? It seems like every time we get rid of one, bingo, another pops up in his place. Harmel went out, in came Hogan . . ."

She completed the thought for him. "You took care of Farrel, and in came Henry Busche."

"It can't go on. The odds are against us."

"Busche is as good as gone. Isn't there a confidence vote this Friday?"

"The congregation is getting good and upset. But . . ."

"Yes?"

"You know he removed Lou Stanley from the church for adultery?"

"Ah, yes. That should help the congregation decide."

"A lot of them agreed with that move!"

She backed away in order to gaze at him better, freezing his blood with her eyes. "Are you afraid of Henry Busche?"

"Listen, he still has a lot of support in the church, more than I thought he did."

"You *are* afraid of him!"

"Somebody's on his side, I don't know who. And what if he finds out about the Plan?"

"He will never find out anything!" If she had fangs, they would have been showing. "He will be destroyed as a minister long before then. You will see to that, won't you?"

"I'm working on it."

"Do not bow to this Henry Busche! He bows to you, and you bow to me!"

"I'm working on it, I said!"

She relaxed and smiled. "Next Tuesday, then?"

"Ehh . . ."

"We'll celebrate Busche's Friday demise. You can tell me all about it."

"What about Hogan?"

"Hogan is a limp and weakened fool. Don't worry about him. He's not your responsibility."

Before Brummel knew it, he was standing outside her back door.

Langstrat watched him through her window until he drove off, taking the usual alley route where he would not be seen. She opened the drapes to let some light in, extinguished the candle on the coffee table, then took a folder from her desk drawer.

Soon she had arranged in neat piles the life histories, personality profiles, and current photographs of Marshall, Kate, and Sandy Hogan. When her eyes fell on the photograph of Sandy, they glinted maliciously.

Hovering invisibly over Langstrat's shoulder was a huge black hand adorned with jeweled rings and bracelets of gold. A deep and seductive voice spoke thoughts to her mind.

Tuesday afternoon at the *Clarion* resembled a battlefield after everyone is either dead or retreated. The place was deathly quiet. George, the typesetter, usually took the day after publishing off to recover from the wild deadline race. Tom, the paste-up man, was out covering a local story.

As for Edie, the secretary/reporter/ad girl, she had resigned and walked off the job last night. Marshall had not known that she once was happily married, but gradually became unhappily married, and finally got a little thing going with a trucker that resulted in a very recent blow-up at home, with pieces of marriage flying everywhere and spouses fleeing abruptly in opposite directions. Now she was gone, and Marshall could feel the sudden void.

Bernice and he sat alone in the glass-enclosed office at the back of the little newsroom/ad room/front office. From his secondhand, ten-dollar desk Marshall could look through the glass and survey the three desks, two typewriters, two wastebaskets, two telephones, and one coffeemaker. Everything looked cluttered and busy, with papers and copy lying everywhere, but absolutely nothing was happening.

"I don't suppose you know where everything is?" he asked Bernice.

Bernice was sitting up on the worktable adjacent to Marshall's desk, her back against the wall, stirring a personalized mug of hot chocolate.

"Aw, we'll find it all," she answered. "I know where she kept the books, and I'm sure her Rolodex has all the addresses and phone numbers."

"What about the cord to the coffeemaker?"

"Why do you think I'm drinking hot chocolate?"

"Nuts. I wish somebody would've told me."

"I don't think anybody really knew."

"We'd better get an ad in for a new secretary this week. Edie carried more than her weight around here."

"I guess it was a bad blow-up. She's leaving town for good, before her husband's black eyes heal up and he can see to find her."

"Affairs. Nothing good ever comes of 'em."

"So have you heard the latest about Alf Brummel?"

Marshall looked up at her. She perched on the worktable like some coy bird, trying to look more interested in her hot chocolate than in the spicy news.

"Under the circumstances," he said, "I'm dying to hear it."

"I had lunch with Sara, his secretary, today. Guess he's gone for several hours every Tuesday afternoon and never says where, but Sara knows. Guess our friend Alf has a special girlfriend."

"Yeah, Juleen Langstrat, psychology prof out at the college."

That ruined it for Bernice. "How did you know?"

"The blonde woman you saw that night, remember? The day after one of my reporters gets busted for taking the wrong pictures at the carnival, Langstrat kicks me out of her class. Add to that Oliver Young's ears getting all red when he told me he didn't know her."

"You're brilliant, Hogan."

"Just a good guesser."

"She and Brummel do have *something* going. He calls it therapy, but I think he enjoys it, if you get my drift."

"So what's Young's connection to either of them?"

Bernice didn't hear his question. "Too bad Brummel isn't already married. I could have done more with it."

"Hey, reset your frequency, will you? We've got a little club here, and all *three* of these people are members."

"Sorry."

"What we're really after is whatever it is they don't want us to know, especially if—and I mean IF— it's worth trumping up a false arrest to cover up."

"*And* destroying my film."

"I wonder if any of those fingerprints on the film would tell us something?"

"Not much. They're not on file."

Marshall twisted in his chair to face her more directly. "All right, who do you know?"

Bernice was smug. "I have an uncle who's very close to Justin Parker's office."

"The county prosecutor?"

"Sure. He does just about anything for me."

"Hey, don't bring them into this, not yet . . ."

Bernice raised her hands as if he were pointing a gun at her and assured him, "Not yet, not yet."

"But I'm not saying they won't come in handy."

"Don't think I haven't thought of that."

"So tell me this: did Brummel ever apologize?"

"After you bowed to him the way you did, are you kidding?"

"No official, signed apology from him and his office?"

"Is that what he told you?"

Marshall had to sneer. "Aw, both Brummel and Young told me all kinds of things—how they hardly knew each other, how they were never anywhere near the carnival . . . boy, I just wish we had those pictures."

Bernice was offended. "Hey, you *can* believe me, Hogan. You really can!"

Marshall looked into space for a second or two, musing. "Brummel and Langstrat. Therapy. I guess that makes sense now . . ."

"C'mon, let's get all the pieces out on the table."

What pieces? Marshall thought. How do you lay out vague feelings, strange experiences, vibes?

He finally said, "Uh . . . this Brummel and Langstrat . . . they're both into the same kind of thing. I can tell."

"*What* kind of thing?"

Marshall felt cornered. "How about . . . whammies?"

Bernice looked puzzled. Oh c'mon, Krueger, don't make me have to explain it.

She said, "You'll have to explain that to me."

Oh boy, here we go, Marshall thought. "Well . . . now it's gonna sound crazy, but when I talked to each of them—and you ought to try it sometime—each of them had this weird, gooney-eyed thing they did . . . kind of like they were hypnotizing me or something . . ."

Bernice started to crack up.

"Ehhh, go ahead, laugh."

"What are you saying? That they're all into some kind of Svengali trip?"

"I don't know how to label it yet, but yeah. Brummel's not nearly as good at it as Langstrat. He smiles too much. Young might be into it too, but he uses words. Lots of words."

Bernice studied his face for just the slightest moment and then said, "I think you need a good, stiff drink. Would a hot chocolate do?"

"Sure, get me one. Please."

Bernice returned with another personalized mug—Edie's—full of hot chocolate. "Hope it's strong enough," she said, and hopped back onto the table.

"So why do those three try to look unconnected . . ." Marshall mused. "And what about the other two unknowns, Pudgy and the Ghost? You've never seen them before?"

"Never. They could have been out-of-towners."

Marshall sighed. "It's a dead end."

"Maybe not yet. Brummel does go to that little white church, Ashton Community, and I heard somebody just got kicked out of there for shacking up or something . . ."

"Bernice, that's gossip!"

"What would you say, then, to my talking to a friend on the Whitmore faculty who might be able to tell me something about this mysterious professor lady?"

Marshall looked doubtful. "Please don't make any more problems for me. I have enough as it is."

"Sandy?"

Back to the really tough subjects. "We haven't heard a thing yet, but we're still calling around, checking with relatives and friends. We're sure she'll come home sooner or later."

"Isn't she in Langstrat's class?"

Marshall answered with some bitterness, "She's been in *several* of Langstrat's classes—" Then he paused. "Don't you think we might be blurring the line between unbiased journalism and . . . personal vengeance?"

Bernice shrugged. "I'll only find what's really there, and it'll be news or it won't be. In the meantime, I thought perhaps you'd appreciate a little background."

Marshall couldn't shake off the memory of his encounter with the fiery Juleen Langstrat, and he hurt more deeply every time he recalled the professor's ideas coming at him through the mouth of his own daughter.

"If it's a stone, turn it over," he said finally.

"On my time or the *Clarion's*?"

"Just turn it over," he said, and started pounding his typewriter.

9

That evening Marshall and Kate set three places at the dinner table. It was an act of faith, trusting that Sandy would be there just as she always had been. They had called everyone they knew, but no one had seen Sandy anywhere. The police hadn't turned up anything. They had called the college to check whether or not Sandy had been to her classes that day, but so far none of her professors or teaching assistants could be reached for a definite answer.

Marshall sat at the table, staring at Sandy's empty chair. Kate sat across from him, silent, waiting for the rice to steam.

"Marshall," she said, "don't torture yourself."

"I blew it. I'm a wash-out!"

"Oh, stop it!"

"And the problem is, now that I know I blew it, there isn't much chance of a retake."

Kate reached across the table and took his hand. "There certainly is. She'll come back. She's old enough to be reasonable and take care of herself. I mean, just look at how much she took with her. She can't be planning on being gone indefinitely."

Just then the doorbell rang. They both jumped a little.

"Yeah," said Marshall, "go ahead, be the mailman, or a Girl Scout selling cookies, or a Jehovah's Witness. . . !"

"Well, Sandy wouldn't ring the doorbell anyway."

Kate got up to answer the door, but Marshall hurried ahead of her. They both reached the door at about the same time and Marshall opened it.

Neither of them expected a young man, blond and neat, college material. He carried no leaflets or religious propaganda and seemed shy.

"Mr. Hogan?" he asked.

"Yeah," said Marshall. "Who are you?"

The young man was quiet but assertive enough to do business. "My name is Shawn Ormsby. I'm a junior at Whitmore and a friend of your daughter Sandy."

Kate started to say, "Well, please come in," but Marshall interrupted with, "Do you know where she is?"

Shawn paused, then answered carefully, "Yes. Yes, I do."

"Well?" said Marshall.

"May I come in?" he asked politely.

Kate nodded graciously, stepping aside and almost pushing Marshall aside. "Yes, please do."

They showed him into the living room and let him have a seat. Kate held Marshall's hand just long enough to get him into a chair and silently remind him to control himself.

"Thank you very much for coming," Kate said. "We've been very concerned."

Marshall's voice was controlled as he said, "What've you got?"

Shawn was visibly uncomfortable.

"I . . . I met her on campus yesterday."

"She went to *school* yesterday?" Marshall blurted, startled.

"Let him talk, Marshall," Kate reminded him.

"Well," said Shawn, "yes. Yes, she did. But I met her in Jones Plaza, an outdoor eating area. She was by herself and so visibly upset that, well, I just felt I had to get involved."

Marshall was sitting on pins and needles. "What do you mean, visibly upset? Is she okay?"

"Oh, yes! She's perfectly all right. That is, she hasn't come to any harm. But . . . I'm here on her behalf." This time both parents were listening without interrupting, so Shawn continued. "We talked for quite a while and she told me her side of the story. She really does want to come home; I should tell you that first."

"But?" Marshall prompted.

"Well, Mr. Hogan, that's the first thing I tried to persuade her to do, but . . . if you can accept this, she feels afraid to come back, and I think a little ashamed."

"Because of me?"

Shawn was walking on some very thin ice. "Can you . . . are you able to accept that?"

Marshall was ready to be tough on himself. "Yeah, I can accept that, all right. I've been asking for it for years. I had it coming."

Shawn looked relieved. "Well, that's what I'm trying, in my own weak, limited way, to accomplish. I'm no professional—my major's geology—but I'd just like to see this family together again."

Kate said humbly, "We would too."

"Yeah," said Marshall, "we really want to work on it. Listen, Shawn, you get to know me and you'll realize I came out of a pretty bent mold and I'm really tough to straighten out . . ."

"No, you didn't!" Kate protested.

"Yeah, yeah, I did. But I'm learning all the time. I want to keep on learning." He leaned forward in his chair. "Say . . . I take it Sandy sent you here to see us?"

Shawn looked out the window. "She's out in the car right now."

Kate was on her feet immediately. Marshall grabbed her hand and settled her back into her seat.

"Hey," he said, "who's being overanxious now?" He turned to Shawn. "How is she? Is she still afraid? Does she think I'm going to jump on her?"

Shawn nodded meekly.

"Well," said Marshall, feeling emotions he really didn't want any-one to see, "listen, tell her I won't jump on her. I won't yell, I won't accuse, I won't get sly or nasty. I just . . . well, I . . ."

"He loves her," Kate said for him. "He really does."

"Do you, sir?" Shawn asked.

Marshall nodded.

"Tell me." said Shawn. "Say it."

Marshall looked right in his eyes. "I love her, Shawn. She's my kid, my daughter. I love her and I want her back."

Shawn smiled and rose from his seat. "I'll bring her in."

That evening there were four place settings at the table.

The Friday edition of the *Clarion* was on the streets, and the usual postpublication lull around the office gave Bernice the chance she needed to do some hoofing. She had been waiting eagerly for a chance to get over to Whitmore College to talk to some people. A few phone calls had landed her an important lunch appointment.

The North Campus Cafeteria was a new addition, a modern red-brick structure with floor-to-ceiling blue-tinted windows and carefully kept flower gardens. One could eat inside at a small two- or-four-person table, or sit on the patio in the sunshine. The format was buffet, and the food wasn't bad.

Bernice stepped onto the patio carrying a tray with coffee and a light salad. Alongside her was Ruth Williams, a cheerful middle-aged professor in economics, carrying a taco salad.

They chose a secluded table in the semishade. For the first half of their meal they indulged in small talk and general catching up.

But Williams knew Bernice pretty well by now.

"Bernice," she said at last, "I can tell you have something on your mind."

Bernice was able to be honest with her friend. "Ruth, it's something unprofessional and distasteful."

"Do you mean to say you've uncovered something new?"

"Oh, no, not about Pat. No, that subject's been dormant for quite some time. You can be sure it will reawaken if anything new comes up, though." Bernice looked at Williams for a long moment. "You don't think I'll ever find anything, do you?"

"Bernice, you know that I support you in your efforts one hundred percent, but with that support I must add my sincere doubts that your efforts will ever uncover anything. It was just so . . . futile. So tragic."

Bernice shrugged. "Well, that's why I'm trying to focus my efforts only where they'll do some good. Which brings me to the uncomfortable subject for the day. Did you know I was arrested and jailed Sunday night?"

Williams was, of course, incredulous. "Jailed? Whatever for?"

"Soliciting an undercover cop for an act of prostitution."

That brought the right response from Williams. Bernice went on to tell her as much of the indignities as she could remember.

"I can't believe it!" Williams kept saying. "That is disgusting! I can't believe it!"

"Well, anyway," Bernice said, bringing in the punch line, "I feel I have good cause to question Mr. Brummel's motives. Mind you, I only have theory and speculation, but I want to chase these things to their end to see if anything really lies behind them."

"Well, I can understand that. And what could I possibly know that would help you?"

"Have you ever met Professor Juleen Langstrat, over in the Psychology Department?"

"Oh . . . once or twice. We shared a table at a faculty luncheon."

Bernice caught a glint of distaste in Williams's expression. "Hmmmm. Something wrong with her?"

"Well, to each his own," said Williams, stirring her salad absent-mindedly with her fork. "But I found her very difficult to relate to. It was next to impossible to start any coherent conversation."

"How does she carry herself? Is she forceful, retiring, assertive, obnoxious . . . ?"

"Aloof, for one thing, and I guess mysterious, although I use that word for lack of one better. I get the impression that people are nothing but a bore to her. Her academic interests are very esoteric and metaphysical, and she seems to prefer them to bland reality."

"What kind of company does she keep?"

"I wouldn't know. I'd almost be surprised to find her consorting with anyone at all."

"So you've never seen her in the company of Alf Brummel?"

"Oh, and this must be the ultimate goal of your questions. No, never at all."

"But I guess you don't see her much anyway."

"She's not very social, so no. But listen, I really try to mind my own business, if you catch my meaning. I would definitely like to help you in any way I can to satisfy yourself concerning Pat's death, but what you're after this time is—"

"Unprofessional and distasteful."

"Yes, you were certainly right on that score. But, accompanied with my own advice to disengage yourself from this thing, let me, as a friend, refer you to someone who might know more. Have your pencil ready? His name is Albert Darr, and he's in the Psychology Department. From what I've heard, mostly from him, he rubs shoulders with Langstrat every day, doesn't like her at all, and loves to gossip. I'll even go so far as to call him for you."

Albert Darr, a baby-faced young professor with stylish clothes and a certain penchant for ladies, just happened to be in his office grading papers. He had time to talk, especially to the lovely reporter from the *Clarion*.

"Well, hello, hello," he said as Bernice came in the door.

"Well, hello hello yourself," she responded. "Bernice Krueger, the friend of Ruth Williams."

"Uh . . ." He looked to and fro for an empty chair, and finally moved a pile of reference books. "Have a seat. Pardon the mess." He sat down on another pile of books and papers that might have had a chair under it. "What can I do for you?"

"Well, this isn't really an official visit, Professor Darr—"

"Albert."

"Thank you. Albert. I'm actually here on a personal matter, but if my theories are right, it could be important in a newsworthy sense." She paused to indicate a new paragraph and a difficult question. "Now, Ruth tells me you know Juleen Langstrat—"

Darr suddenly smiled broadly, leaned back in his piled-up chair, and rested his hands behind his neck. This was going to be an enjoyable subject for him, it seemed.

"Ahhhh," he said gleefully, "so you dare to infringe on sacred ground!" Darr looked around the room in mock suspicion, searching for imaginary eavesdroppers, then leaned forward and said in a lowered voice, "Listen, there are certain things no one is supposed to know, not even myself." Then he brightened up again and said, "But our dear professor has had many an occasion to hurt and slight me and therefore I feel indebted to her not in the least. I'm dying to answer your questions."

Evidently Bernice could just dive right in; this guy didn't seem to need formalities.

"Okay, to begin with," she said, readying her pen and pad, "I'm really trying to find out about Alf Brummel, the chief of police. I've been informed that he and Langstrat see a lot of each other. Can you verify that?"

"Oh, definitely."

"So . . . they do have something going?"

"What do you mean, 'something'?"

"You fill in the blank."

"If you mean a romantic fling . . ." He smiled and shook his head. "Oh dear. I don't know if you'll like this answer, but no, I don't think anything like that is going on."

"But he does see her quite regularly."

"Oh yes, but a lot of people do. She gives consultations in her off hours. Tell me now, doesn't Brummel see her on a weekly basis?"

With ebbing spirit Bernice answered, "Yes, every Tuesday. On the dot."

"Well, there, you see? He goes to her for regular weekly sessions."

"But why won't he tell anybody? He's very secretive about it."

He leaned forward and lowered his voice. "Everything Langstrat does is a deep, dark secret! The Inner Circle, Bernice. No one is even supposed to know about these so-called consultations, no one but the privileged, the elite, the powerful, the many special patrons that go to her. That's the way she is."

"But what's she up to?"

"Mind you now," he said with a mischievous glint in his eye, "this is privileged information, and I might also caution you that it is not entirely reliable. I know very little of this from direct observation; most of it I've just managed to pick up around the department here. Fortunately, Professor Langstrat has made enough enemies that few of the staff feel any commitment or loyalty to her." He repositioned himself into an eye-to-eye posture. "Bernice, Professor Langstrat is, how should I say it? Not a . . . ground level person. Her areas of study go beyond anything the rest of us have had any desire to tamper with: the Source, the Universal Mind, the Ascended Planes . . ."

"I'm afraid I don't know what you're talking about."

"Oh, none of us know what she's talking about either. Some of us are very concerned; we don't know if she's very brilliant and making some real breakthroughs, or if she's somewhat deranged."

"Well, what is all this stuff, this Source, and this Mind?"

"All right. Uh . . . as nearly as we can tell, she derives it from the Eastern religions, the old mystic cults and writings, things I know nothing about and don't want to know anything about. As far as I'm concerned, her studies in these areas have caused her to lose all contact with reality. As a matter of fact, I may even be mocked and maligned among my peers for saying this, but I don't see Langstrat's advances in these areas as anything other than foolish, neo-pagan witchcraft. I think she's desperately confused!"

Bernice now recalled to mind Marshall's strange descriptions of Langstrat. "I've heard she does strange things to people—"

"Foolishness. Sheer foolishness. I think she believes she can read my mind, control me, put spells on me, whatever. I simply dismiss it and try very hard to be elsewhere."

"But does any of it have credence?"

"Absolutely not. The only people she can control or affect are the poor dupes in the Inner Circle who are stupid and gullible enough to—"

"The Inner Circle . . . you used that term before . . ."

He held up his hand to caution her. "No facts, no facts. I coined that title myself. All I have is a two here and a two there, which make a very persuasive four. I've heard her admit that she counsels these people who come to her, and I've noticed that some of them are quite important. But how could a counselor with such warped ideas possibly straighten out anyone else? Then again . . ."

"Yes?"

"I would expect her to . . . claim a special advantage in such a situation. Who knows, maybe she holds seances and mind-reading sessions. Maybe she cooks slug tails and newt's eyes and serves them with breaded spider legs to evoke some answer from the supernatural . . . but now I'm getting facetious."

"But you do see this as a possibility?"

"Well not nearly as bizarre as I've described, but yes, something along those lines, in keeping with her occult interests."

"And these people in the Inner Circle see her regularly?"

"As far as I know. I really have no idea how it's set up or why people even go. What on earth could they be getting out of it?"

"Can you give me some for-instances?"

"Well . . ." He thought for a moment. "Of course, we've already mentioned and verified your Mr. Brummel. Oh, and you might know of Ted Harmel?"

Bernice just about dropped her pen. *"Ted?"*

"Yes, the former editor of the *Clarion.*"

"I worked for him, before he left and Hogan bought the paper."

"Uh, the way I understand it, Mr. Harmel didn't just 'leave.' "

"No, he fled. But who else?"

"Mrs. Pinckston, a trustee on the board of regents."

"Ah, so it's not just men."

"Oh, certainly not."

Bernice kept writing. "Go on, go on."

"Oh dear, who else? Uh, I think Dwight Brandon . . ."

"Who's Dwight Brandon?"

Darr looked at her condescendingly. "He only owns the property the college is built on."

"Ohhhh . . ." She wrote the name down with a bold lettered explanation.

"Oh, and then there's Eugene Baylor. He's general treasurer, a very influential man on the board of regents, I understand. It seems he's been needled just a little about whatever it is he and the professor do in their sessions together, but he remains self-righteous and steadfast in his convictions."

"Hmm."

"Ah, and there's also that reverend fellow, that . . . uh . . ."

"Oliver Young."

"How did *you* know?"

Bernice only smiled. "A lucky guess. Carry on."

10

On Friday evening Hank couldn't get the upcoming business meeting off his mind, which was probably to his advantage considering the young lady sitting across from him in his little office corner of the house. He had asked Mary to stick closely around and act very loving and wifely. This young lady—Carmen was the only name she gave—was quite a case load. The way she dressed and carried herself, Hank made sure that it was Mary who answered her knock at the door and let her in. But as far as Hank could tell, Carmen wasn't trying to put on a facade; she seemed real enough, just sincerely overdone. And as for her reasons for wanting counseling . . .

"I think," she began, "I think I'm just very lonely, and that's why I keep hearing voices . . ."

Immediately she examined their faces for their reaction. But after their recent experiences nothing sounded too far out to Hank and Mary.

Hank asked, "What kind of voices? What kind of things do they say?"

She thought for a moment, searching the ceiling with big, overly innocent blue eyes.

"What I'm experiencing is legitimate," she said. "I'm not crazy."

"No problem there," Hank said. "But tell us about these voices. When do they talk to you?"

"When I'm alone, especially. Like last night, I was lying in bed and . . ." she related the words the voice spoke to her, and it could have been a perfect script for an obscene phone call.

Mary didn't know what to say; this was becoming heavy. To Hank it sounded kind of familiar, and though he felt very cautious about Carmen and her motives, he still remained open to the possibility that she was encountering some of the same demonic forces he'd been dealing with.

"Carmen," he asked, "do these voices ever say who they are?"

She thought for a moment. "I think one of them was Spanish or Italian. He had an accent, and his name was Amano, or Amanzo, or something like that. He always spoke very soothingly and always said he wanted to make love to me . . ."

Just then the phone rang. Mary quickly got up to answer it.

"Hurry back," said Hank.

She hurried away, that was for sure. Hank was watching her go when he felt Carmen touching his hand.

"You don't think I'm crazy, do you?" she asked with pleading eyes.

"Uh . . ." Hank withdrew his hand to scratch a nonexistent itch. "No, Carmen, I'm not—I mean I don't. But I do want to know where these voices came from. When did you first start hearing them?"

"When I came to Ashton. My husband left me and I came here to start over, but . . . I get so lonely."

"You first started hearing them when you came to Ashton?"

"I think it was because I was lonely. And I still am lonely."

"What was it they said at first? How did they introduce themselves?"

"I was alone, and lonely, I'd just moved here, and I thought I heard Jim's voice. You know, my husband . . ."

"Go on."

"I really thought it was him. I didn't even think about how he could talk to me without being there, but I talked back and he told me how much he missed me, and how he thought it would be better this way, and he spent the rest of the night with me." She began to shed some tears. "It was beautiful."

Hank didn't know what to make of this. "Incredible," was all he could say.

She looked at him with those big pleading eyes again and said through her tears, "I knew you'd believe me. I've heard about you. They say you're a very compassionate man, and very understanding . . ."

Depends on who you listen to, Hank thought, but then her hand was touching his again. Time to call a recess, Hank thought.

"Uh," he said, trying to be comforting, sincere, and nonjudgmental. "Listen, I think it's been a fruitful hour . . ."

"Oh, yes!"

"Would you like to come again, next week sometime?"

"Oh, I'd love to!" she exclaimed, as if Hank had asked her for a date. "I've so much more to tell you!"

"Well, okay, I think next Friday will be fine for me if it's fine for you."

Oh, it was, it was, and Hank stood up to give her the hint that the session was over for now. They hadn't covered much ground, but as far as Hank was concerned, boy, was it enough.

"Now let's both take some time to think about these things. After a week they may be a little clearer to us. They might make more sense." Where, oh where was Mary?

Ah, she came back into the room. "Oh, leaving so soon?"

"It was wonderful!" Carmen sighed, but at least she had let go of Hank's hand.

Getting Carmen out the door was easier than Hank had expected. Good old Mary. What a lifesaver.

Hank closed the door and leaned against it.

"Whew!" was all he could say.

"Hank," Mary said in a very hushed voice, "I don't think I like this!"

"She's . . . she's a real hot one, she is."

"What do you think of what she said?"

"Ehhhhh, I'll wait and see. Who was that on the phone?"

"Just wait until you hear this! It was some lady from the *Clarion* wanting to know if it was Alf Brummel we disfellowshipped from the church!"

Hank suddenly looked like an inflatable toy that had sprung a leak.

A little disappointed, Bernice walked into Marshall's office.

Marshall was at his desk, going over some new advertising copy for Tuesday's edition.

"So what'd they say?" he asked her without looking up.

"Nope, it isn't Brummel, and I guess it wasn't a very tactful question. I talked to the pastor's wife, and by her tone of voice I can infer that the whole subject is very touchy."

"Yeah, I've heard talk at the barbershop. Some guy was saying they're going to vote the pastor out tonight."

"Ah, so they do have troubles."

"But totally unrelated to ours, and I'm glad. It's gone far enough." Marshall looked again at the list of names Bernice had gotten from Albert Darr. "How am I supposed to get any work done around here with this kind of stuff hanging around unresolved? Bernie, you're getting to be a lot of trouble, you know that?"

She took it as a compliment. "And have you looked over that flyer of elective courses Langstrat is teaching?"

Marshall picked it up from his desk and could only shake his head incredulously. "What in blazes is all this stuff? 'Introduction to God and Goddess Consciousness and the Craft: the divinity of man, witch, warlock, the Sacred Medicine Wheel, how do spells and rituals work?' You gotta be kidding!"

"Read on, boss!"

" 'Pathways to Your Inner Light: meet your own spiritual guides, discover the light within . . . harmonize your mental, physical, emotional, and spiritual levels of being through hypnosis and meditation.' " Marshall read a little further and then exclaimed, "What? 'How to Enjoy the Present by Experiencing Past and Future Lives.' "

"I like that one near the bottom there: 'In the Beginning Was the Goddess'. Langstrat, perhaps?"

"Why hasn't anyone heard about all this before?"

"For some reason it was never advertised in the school paper or in the public list of classes. Albert Darr gave me the flyer himself and said it was a somewhat exclusive pass-around item among the interested students."

"And my little Sandy is sitting in this woman's class . . ."

"And in a way so are all those people on the list."

Marshall set down the flyer and picked up the list. He shook his head again; it was all he could think of to do.

Bernice added, "I guess I don't mind it too much if a bunch of dupes want to be taken in by this Langstrat, but they're all too important! Just look at that: Two of the college regents, the owner of the college land, the county comptroller, the district judge!"

"And Young! Respected, revered, influential, community-involved Oliver Young!" Marshall let some memory tapes play in his head. "Yeah, it fits, it makes sense now, all that vague, noncommittal stuff he was handing me in his office. Young's got a religion all his own. He's no hard-shell Baptist, I'll tell you that!"

"Religion I don't care about. Lies and cover-ups I do!"

"Well, he most certainly denied knowing Langstrat. I asked him directly, right to his face, and he told me he didn't know her."

"Somebody's lying," Bernice sing-songed.

"But I just wish we had some more corroboration."

"Yeah, we've only just met Darr."

"What about Ted Harmel? How well did you know him?"

"Well enough, I suppose. You heard why he left?"

Marshall sneered just a bit. "Brummel said there was some kind of scandal, but who can you believe these days?"

"Ted denied it."

"Aw, everybody's saying everything and everybody's denying everything."

"Well, call him anyway. I have the number. He's living up near Windsor now. I think he's trying to be a hermit."

Marshall looked at all the advertising copy still on his desk, awaiting his time and attention. "How am I going to get any of this stuff done around here?"

"Hey, it's no biggie. If I could do some independent hoofing, the least you can do is give Ted a call. Do it tomorrow . . . Saturday, your day off. Reporter to reporter, newsman to newsman. You might hit it off with him."

Marshall sighed. "Let's have the number."

Mary finished the dinner dishes, put up the towel, and made her way through the little house to the back bedroom. There, in the dark, Hank knelt beside the bed in prayer. She knelt down beside him, took his hand, and together they placed themselves in the hands of the Lord. God's will would be done this night, and they would accept it, whatever it was.

Alf Brummel had a key to the church and was already there, switching on the lights and turning up the thermostat. He wasn't feeling well at all. They'd just better vote right this time, he kept thinking.

Outside, even though it was still a half hour before the meeting, cars began to arrive, more than were usually there on Sundays. Sam Turner, Brummel's chief cohort, drove up in his big Cadillac and helped his wife Helen from the car. He was a rancher of sorts, not a land baron, but he acted like one. Tonight he was grim and determined, as was his wife. In another car came John Coleman and his wife Patricia, a quiet couple who came to Ashton Community after leaving a large church elsewhere in town. They really liked Hank and made no effort to hide it. They knew well that Alf Brummel would not be happy to see them there.

Others arrived and quickly coagulated into little clusters of similar sentiment, speaking in quick syllables and hushed tones and keeping their eyes to themselves, except for a few rubbernecking nose-counters trying to foresee the final tally.

Several dark shadows kept a wary eye on everything from their perch atop the church roof, their stations around the building, or their appointed posts in the sanctuary.

Lucius, more nervous than ever, paced and hovered about. Ba-al Rafar, still wanting a very low profile, had entrusted this task to him, and for this night at least Lucius was back in his old glory.

What worried Lucius the most were the other spirits standing around, the enemies of the cause, the host of heaven. They were held at bay by Lucius's forces, to be sure, but there were some new ones he had never seen before.

Nearby, but not too near, Signa and his two warriors kept watch. Upon Tal's orders they allowed demons access to the building, but monitored the demons' activities and kept an eye out for Rafar. So far their very presence, as well as the presence of so many other warriors, had had a taming effect on the demonic hosts. There had been no incidents, and for now that was all Tal wanted.

When Lucius saw the Colemans come in the front door, he was agitated. In the past, they had never been very strong against the defeats and discouragements Lucius had ordered, and their marriage had just about dissolved. Then they aligned themselves with Praying Busche, hearing his words and becoming stronger all the time. Before long they and others like them would be a real threat.

But their arrival didn't cause Lucius as much agitation as the huge, blond-haired messenger of God who accompanied them. Lucius knew for sure he'd never seen this one before. As the Colemans found a seat, Lucius swooped down and accosted this new intruder.

"I've not seen you before!" he said gruffly, and all the other spirits focused their attention on him and the stranger. "From where do you come?"

The stranger, Chimon of Europe, said nothing. He only riveted his eyes on those of Lucius and stood firm.

"I'll have your name!" Lucius demanded.

The stranger said not a word.

Lucius smiled slyly and nodded. "You are deaf, yes? And dumb? And as mindless as you are silent?" The other demons guffawed. They loved this kind of game. "Tell me, are you a good fighter?"

Silence.

Lucius drew a scimitar that flashed blood-red and droned metallically. On cue, all the other demons did the same. The clatter and ring of burnished blades filled the room as crimson crescents of reflected light danced about the walls. The other messengers of God were barred from intervening by an armed ring of demons as Lucius continued to toy with this one single newcomer.

Lucius peered at his solid, unmoving opponent with a burning hatred that made his yellow eyes bulge and his sulfurous breath chug out through widely flared nostrils. He toyed with his sword, waved it in small circles in the stranger's face, watched for the stranger to make the slightest move.

The stranger only watched him, not moving at all.

With an intense cry Lucius swept his sword across the front of the stranger, slashing his garment. Cheers and laughter came from the crowd of demons. Lucius poised for a fight, held his sword with both hands, crouched, his wings flared.

Before him stood a statue with a slashed tunic.

"Fight, you listless spirit!" Lucius challenged.

The stranger did not respond, and Lucius cut his face. Another cheer from the demons.

"Shall I remove an ear? Or two? Shall I cut out your tongue if you have one?" Lucius taunted.

"I think it's time we got started," said Alf Brummel from the pulpit. The people in the room stopped their hushed conversations, and the place began to quiet down.

Lucius leered at the stranger, and motioned with his sword. "Go stand with the other cowards."

The newcomer stepped back, then took his place with the other messengers of God behind the demonic barricade.

Eleven angels had managed to get into the church without raising too much ire from the demons: Triskal and Krioni had already entered with Hank and Mary. They had often been seen with the pastor and his wife, so they were not paid much attention other than the usual threatening expressions and postures. Guilo was there, as big and threatening as ever, but apparently no demons were the slightest bit interested in asking him any questions.

A newcomer, a burly Polynesian, made his way over to Chimon and tended the wound in Chimon's face while Chimon repaired the slash in his tunic.

"Mota, called here from Polynesia," came the introduction.

"Chimon of Europe. Welcome to our numbers."

"Can you continue?" Mota asked.

"I will continue," Chimon answered, skillfully reweaving his tunic with his fingers. "Where is Tal?"

"Not here yet."

"A demon of fever tried to stop the Colemans. No doubt Tal has encountered an attack on Duster."

"I don't know how he'll ward it off without making himself visible."

"He'll do it." Chimon looked about. "I don't see the Ba-al Prince anywhere."

"We may never."

"And may he never see Tal."

Brummel brought the meeting to order, standing behind the pulpit and looking out over the nearly fifty people who had gathered. From this vantage point even he couldn't help but try to guess the final tally. Some of the people were definitely going to give Hank the ax, some were definitely not going to, and then there was that frustrating and unpredictable group he couldn't be sure about.

"I want to thank you all for coming tonight," he said. "This is a painful matter for us to decide. I'd always hoped that this night would never come, but we all want God's will to be done and we want what will be best for His people. So, let us open with a word of prayer and commit the rest of the evening to His care and guidance."

With that Brummel began a very pious prayer, appealing to the Lord for grace and mercy in words to bring a tear to the driest eye.

In the front corner of the sanctuary, Guilo sulked, wishing an angel could spit on a human.

Triskal asked Chimon, "Getting any strength?"

Chimon answered, "Why? Is somebody else going to pray?"

Brummel finished his prayer, the roomful muttered a few Amens, and then he went on with his introduction to the proceedings.

"The purpose of this meeting is to openly discuss our feelings regarding Pastor Hank, to put an end once and for all to all the backbiting and murmuring that's been going on, and to end our meeting with a final vote of confidence. I would hope that we would all have the mind of the Lord in these matters.

"If you have something you wish to say to the group, we would ask that you limit your time to three minutes. I'll be letting you know when your time is up, so keep that in mind." Brummel looked at Hank and Mary. "I think it would be good to let the pastor have the first say. Afterwards he'll leave us alone so we can talk freely."

Mary squeezed Hank's hand as he got up. He went to the pulpit and stood behind it, gripping its sides. For the longest time he couldn't

say a word, but only looked into every eye of every face. He suddenly
realized how much he truly loved these people, all of them. He could
see the hardness in some of the faces, but he couldn't help seeing past
that to the pain and bondage these people were under, deluded, led
astray by sin, by greed, by bitterness and rebellion. In many other faces
he could read the pain they were feeling for him; he could tell that
some were silently praying for God's mercy and intervention.

Hank let a quick prayer course through his thoughts as he began.
"I have always counted it a privilege to stand behind this sacred desk,
to preach the Word and speak the truth." He surveyed their faces again
for just a moment and then continued, "And even tonight I feel I
cannot stray from God's commission to me and the purpose for which
I have ever stood before you. I am not here to defend myself or my
ministry. Jesus is my advocate, and I rest the course of my life on His
grace, guidance, and mercy. So tonight, since I am standing behind this
pulpit once again, let me share with you what I have received from
God."

Hank opened his Bible and read from Second Timothy, chapter 4.
" 'I solemnly charge you in the presence of God and of Christ Jesus,
who is to judge the living and the dead, and by His appearing and His
kingdom: preach the Word, be ready in season and out of season,
reprove, rebuke, exhort, with great patience and instruction. For the
time will come when they will not endure sound doctrine, but wanting
to have their ears tickled, they will accumulate for themselves teachers
in accordance to their own desires; and will turn away their ears from
the truth, and will turn aside to myths.

" 'But you, be sober in all things, endure hardship, do the work of
an evangelist, fulfill your ministry.' " Hank closed his Bible, looked
about the room, and spoke firmly. "Let each one of us apply God's
Word where it may apply. Tonight I will speak only for myself. I have
my call from God; I just read it. Some of you, I know, have really
gotten the impression that Hank Busche is obsessed with the gospel,
that it's all he ever thinks about. Well, that's true. Sometimes I even
wonder why I remain in such a difficult position, such an uphill effort
. . . but for me, God's call on my life is an inescapable commission, and
as Paul said, 'Woe is me if I do not preach the gospel.' I understand
that sometimes the truth of God's Word can become a divider, an
irritation, a stone of stumbling. But that's only because it remains
unchanged, uncompromising, and steadfast. And what better reason
could there be to build our lives on such an immovable foundation? To
violate the Word of God is only to destroy ourselves, our joy, our
peace, our happiness.

"I want to be fair with you, and so I'll be truthful in letting you
know exactly what you may expect from me. I intend to love all of
you, no matter what. I intend to shepherd and feed you for as long as

you'll have me. I will not discredit, compromise, or turn my back on what I believe the Word of God teaches, and that means that there may be times when you'll feel my shepherd's crook around your neck, not to judge or malign you, but to help you move in the right direction, to protect you, to heal you. I intend to preach the gospel of Jesus Christ, for that is my calling. I have a burden for this town; sometimes I feel that burden so strongly I have to ask myself why, but it's still there and I can't turn my back on it or try to deny it. Until the Lord tells me otherwise, I intend to remain in Ashton to answer that burden.

"If that is the kind of pastor you want, then you can let me know tonight. If you do not want that kind of pastor . . . well, I really need to know that too.

"I love all of you. I want the very best God has to give you. And I guess that's all I have to say."

Hank stepped down from the platform, took Mary's hand, and the two of them walked down the aisle to the door. Hank tried to catch the eyes of as many people as he could. Some gave looks of love and encouragement; some looked away.

Krioni and Triskal left with Hank and Mary. Lucius watched with mocking disdain.

Guilo muttered to his fellows, "While the cat's away the mice will play."

"Where is Tal?" Chimon asked again.

Brummel stood before the group. "We'll now hear statements from the congregation. Just raise your hand to be recognized. Yeah, Sam, why don't you go first."

Sam Turner stood, and walked to the front of the sanctuary.

"Thanks, Alf," he said. "Well, I've no doubt you all know me and my wife Helen. We've been citizens of this community for over thirty years, and we've supported this church through thick and through thin. Now I don't have a lot to say tonight. You all know what kind of man I am, how I believe in loving one's neighbor and living a good life. I've tried to do right and be a good example of what a Christian should be.

"And I'm angry tonight. I'm angry for my friend, Lou Stanley. You may have noticed Lou isn't here tonight, and I'm sure I know why. It used to be he could show his face in this church and be a part of it, and we all loved him and he loved us, and I think we all still do. But this Busche fellow, who thinks he's God's gift to this earth, thought he had a right to judge Lou and kick him out of the church. Now, friends, let me tell you one thing: nobody kicks Lou Stanley out of anything if Lou doesn't feel like it, and the very fact that Lou went along with this whole smear on his character only shows the goodness of his heart. He could have sued Busche by now, or he could have settled the matter like I've seen him settle other matters. He's not afraid of anything. But I just think Lou's so ashamed of the horrible things that have been said about him and so hurt by what he thinks we must think of him that he decided he'd better just stay away.

"Now we have this self-righteous, Bible-pounding gossip-monger to blame for these troubles. Forgive me if I sound a bit harsh, but listen, I can remember when this church was like a family. How long now since it's been that way? Look what's happened: here we are, having a big bicker meeting, and why? Because we let Hank Busche come in here and stir us all up. Ashton used to be a peaceful town, this church used to be a peaceful church, and I say we do what's necessary to get it that way again."

Turner took his seat as a few nearby nodded their silent encouragement and approval.

John Coleman was recognized next. A shy person, he was very nervous about speaking in front of everyone, but concerned enough to do it anyway.

"Well," he said, nervously handling his Bible and looking at the floor a lot, "I don't usually say much, and I'm scared to death to be standing up here, but . . . I think Hank Busche is a real man of God, a good pastor, and I'd really hate to see him go. The church Pat and I came from, well, it just wasn't meeting our needs, and we were getting hungry: hungry for the Word, for the presence of God. We thought we'd found those things here, and we were really looking forward to being involved and growing in the Lord under Hank's ministry, and I know a lot of other folks feel that way too. As far as this stuff about Lou is concerned, that was not just Hank's doing. *All* of us were involved in that decision, including me, and I know Hank's not trying to hurt anybody."

As John sat down, Patricia patted his arm and said, "You did fine." John was not sure.

Brummel addressed the group. "I think it might be a good idea for us to hear what the church secretary, Gordon Mayer, has to say."

Gordon Mayer went to the front with some of the church records and minutes in his hand. He was a tense man with a tight expression and gruff voice.

"I have two items I'd like to address before this group," he said. "First of all, from the business side, you all need to be aware that the offerings have been decreasing over the past several months, but our bills have been staying steady if not going up. In other words, we're running out of money, and I personally have no doubts why. There are differences among us we really need to get resolved, and withholding your giving is not the way to do it. If you have a gripe against the pastor, then do whatever you have to tonight, but let's not bring the whole church down over this one man."

"Secondly, for whatever it's worth, let me tell you that the original pulpit committee was considering *another* man for the job. I was on that committee, and I can assure you that they had no intention of recommending Busche for the office. I'm convinced the whole thing was a fluke, a grave mistake. We voted in the wrong man, and now we're paying for it.

"So let me close with this: Sure, we've made a mistake, but I have faith in the group here, and I think we can turn the whole thing around and start doing things right for a change. I say let's do it."

And so the evening went for the better part of two hours, as both sides took turns in crucifying and praising Hank Busche. Nerves got raw, bottoms got numb, backs got sticky, and the opposing views became more and more vehement in their convictions. After two hours, a common sentiment began to mutter its way around the room: "C'mon, let's have the vote . . ."

Brummel had taken his jacket off, loosened his tie, and rolled up his sleeves. He was gathering a pile of small squares of paper, the ballots.

"Okay, this will be by secret ballot," he said, handing the slips of paper to two quickly appointed ushers who passed them out. "Let's just keep it simple. If you want to keep the pastor, say yes, and if you want to find someone else, say no."

Mota nudged Chimon. "Will Hank have enough votes?"

Chimon only shook his head. "We're not sure."

"You mean he could lose?"

"Let us hope someone is praying."

"Where, oh where is Tal?"

Writing a simple yes or no didn't take long, so almost immediately the ushers were passing the offering plates among the people.

Guilo stood still in his corner, glaring at as many demons as would look at him. Some of the smaller, harassing spirits flitted about the sanctuary trying to see what people were marking on their ballots, and grinning, scowling, cheering, or cursing accordingly. Guilo could envision three or four of their wiry little necks in his fists. Someday soon, little demons, someday soon.

Brummel took charge again. "All right, in the interest of fairness, let's have representatives from the two different . . . uh . . . viewpoints come up and do the counting."

After a bit of nervous chuckling John Coleman was selected by the yeas and Gordon Mayer by the nays to count the ballots. The two men took the offering plates full of ballots to a back pew. A flock of flapping, hissing demons converged on the scene, wanting to see the outcome.

Guilo stepped out too. It was only fair, he thought. Lucius swooped down from the ceiling in an instant and hissed, "Get back in your corner!"

"I wish to see the outcome."

"Oh, don't you now?" Lucius sneered. "And what if I decide to cut you open as I did your friend?"

Something about the way Guilo answered, "Try it," may have caused Lucius to reconsider.

Guilo's approach sent the little demons fluttering away like a flock of chickens. He bent over the two men to have a look. Gordon Mayer was counting first, silently, then handing the ballots to John Coleman. But he stealthily hid a few yea ballots in his palm. Guilo checked to see how closely the demons were watching, then made a stealthy move himself, touching the back of Mayer's hand.

A demon saw it and struck Guilo's hand with bared talons. Guilo jerked his hand away and came infinitely close to tearing the demon to shreds, but he caught himself and honored Tal's orders.

"What is your name?" Guilo wanted to know.

"Cheating," the demon answered.

"Cheating," Guilo rehearsed as he went back to his corner. "Cheating."

But Guilo's move had succeeded in foiling Mayer's effort. The ballots dropped out of Mayer's hand and John Coleman saw them.

"You dropped something there," he said very sweetly.

Mayer couldn't say anything. He just handed the ballots over.

The count was finished, but Mayer wanted to count again. They counted the ballots again. The count came out the same: a tie.

The two reported the result to Brummel, who told the congregation, which moaned quietly.

Alf Brummel could feel his hands getting very damp; he tried drying them on his handkerchief.

"Well, listen," he said, "there may not be much chance that any of you will reconsider, but I'm sure none of us wants to prolong this thing past tonight. I tell you what, why don't we take a short break and give some of you a chance to get up, stretch, use the restroom. Then we'll regather and vote again."

As Brummel spoke, the two demons posted around the church saw something very unsettling. Just about a block up the street were two old women, hobbling toward the church. One walked with the assistance of a cane and a helping hand from her friend. She did not look well at all, but her jaw was set and her eyes bright and determined. Her cane clacked out a syncopated rhythm with her footsteps. Her friend, in better health and stronger, kept up with her, holding her arm to support her and talking gently to her.

"The one with the cane is Duster," said one demon.

"What went wrong?" the other wondered. "I thought she'd been taken care of."

"Oh, she's ill, all right, but she's come anyway."

"And who is the old woman with her?"

"Edith Duster has many friends. We should have known."

The two ladies made their way up the church steps, each step a major task in itself, first one foot, then the other, then the cane placed on the next step, until they were finally up to the front door.

"There, look at that now!" cackled the stronger one. "I knew you could do it. The Lord's gotten you this far, He'll take care of you the rest of the way."

"What Edith Duster needs is a stroke," murmured a sickness demon, drawing his sword.

Perhaps it was simply luck, or incredible coincidence, but just as the demon lunged forward with great speed to slash at the arteries in Edith Duster's brain, the other woman moved to open the door and stepped right in the way. The tip of the demon's sword struck the woman in the shoulder, which could have been concrete; the sword stopped short. Sickness did not, but catapulted over the two women and fluttered like a fractured kite into the church yard as Edith Duster moved inside.

Sickness gathered himself up off the ground and screamed, "The host of heaven!"

The other demon guard stared at him blankly.

Brummel saw Edith Duster come in, alone. He cursed silently. This would be the vote to break the tie, but she would most certainly vote for Busche. The people were gathering again.

The messengers of God were elated. "Looks like Tal succeeded," said Mota.

Chimon was concerned, however. "With such a heavy cover of the enemy, he most certainly had to show himself."

Guilo chuckled. "Oh, I'm sure our captain was very discreet."

A few of the demons were in fact wondering what had happened to Edith Duster's companion between the front door and the sanctuary. Sickness continued insisting it had been a heavenly warrior, but where was she now?

Tal, Captain of the Host, joined Signa and the other sentries at their concealed position.

"You had *me* fooled, captain," said Signa.

"You just might attempt it yourself sometime," Tal replied.

On the platform, Brummel mentally groped for a trump card. He could just see the burning eyes of Langstrat if this vote went the wrong way.

"Well," he said, "why don't we come to order now and get ready for another vote?" The people settled in and quieted down. The yea side was more than ready.

"Now that we've prayed and talked about it, maybe some of us will feel differently about the future of the church here. I . . . umm . . ." Come on, Alf, say something, but don't make a fool of yourself. "I guess I could say a few words; I haven't really shared my feelings. You know, Hank Busche *is* a little young . . ."

A middle-aged plumber on the yea side piped up, "Hey now, if you're going to put in some negative input we've got to have equal time for some positive!"

The yeas all murmured in agreement while the nays sat in cold silence.

"No, listen," Brummel stammered, his face bright red, "I had no intention of trying to sway the vote. I was just—"

"Let's have the vote!" someone said.

"Yes, vote, and quick!" Mota whispered.

Just then the door opened. Oh no, thought Brummel, who's coming in this time?

The silence fell like a shroud of death over the whole group. Lou Stanley had just come in. He grimly nodded greeting to them all and took a seat in a back pew. He looked old.

Gordon Mayer piped up, "Let's have the vote!"

The ushers passed out the ballots while Brummel tried to plan a good escape route in case he had to throw up—his nerves were just about shot. He caught Lou Stanley's attention. Lou looked at him and seemed to laugh nervously.

"Make sure Lou back there gets a ballot," Brummel told one of the ushers. The usher made sure.

Chimon whispered to Guilo, "I think we're ready for any tricks Lucius might have."

"Any tie breakers, you mean," Guilo answered.

"We may be in for a long night," said Mota.

The ballots were collected, and Lucius kept his demons tightly around each offering plate and his eyes on every heavenly warrior.

Mayer and Coleman counted again as the tension in the air tightened. The demons watched. The angels watched. The people watched.

Mayer and Coleman kept a close eye on each other, silently mouthing as they counted. Mayer finished counting, waited for Coleman to finish. Coleman finished, looked at Mayer and asked him if he wanted to count again. They counted again.

Then Mayer took his pen, wrote the result on a slip of paper, and carried it up to Brummel. Mayer and Coleman took their seats as Brummel unfolded the paper.

Visibly shaken, Brummel took a few moments to put on his relaxed, businesslike, public image.

"Well . . ." he began, trying to control the tone of his voice, "all right, then. The . . . pastor has been retained."

One side of the room loosened up, tittered, and smiled. The other side gathered up coats and belongings to leave.

"Alf, what was the vote?" someone wanted to know.

"Uh . . . it doesn't say."

"Twenty-eight to twenty-six!" Gordon Mayer said accusingly, looking back toward Lou Stanley.

But Lou Stanley had left.

11

Tal, Signa, and the other sentries could see the explosion from where they stood. With cries and wails of rage, demons scattered everywhere, erupting through the roof and sides of the church like shrapnel and fanning out in all directions over the town. Their cries became a loud, echoing drone of savage fury that rang over the whole town like a thousand melancholy factory whistles, sirens, and horns.

"They will wreak havoc tonight," said Tal.

Mota, Chimon, and Guilo were there to report.

"By two votes," said Mota.

Tal smiled and said, "Very well, then."

"But Lou Stanley!" Chimon exclaimed. "Was that really Lou Stanley?"

Tal caught the implication. "Yes, that was Mr. Stanley. I've been standing right here ever since I delivered Edith Duster."

"I see the Spirit has been working!" Guilo chuckled.

"Let's get Edith home safely and get a guard around her. Everyone to your posts. There will be angry spirits over the town tonight."

That night the police were busy. Fights broke out in the local taverns, slogans were spray-painted on the courthouse, some cars were stolen and joy-ridden through the lawn and flowers in the park.

Late into the night, Juleen Langstrat hovered in an inescapable trance, halfway between a tormented life on earth and the licking, searing flames of hell. She lay on her bed, tumbled to the floor, clawed her way up the wall to stand on her feet, staggered about the room, and fell to the floor again. Threatening voices, monsters, flames, and blood exploded and pounded with unimaginable force in her head; she thought her skull would burst. She could feel claws tearing at her throat, creatures squirming and biting inside her, chains around her arms and legs. She could hear the voices of spirits, see their eyes and fangs, smell their sulfurous breath.

The Masters were angry! "Failed, failed, failed, failed" pounded in her brain and paraded before her eyes. "Brummel has failed, you have failed, he will die, you will die . . ."

Did she really hold a knife in her hand, or was this too a vision from the higher planes? She could feel a yearning, a terribly strong impulse to be free of the torment, to break loose from the bodily shell, the prison of flesh that bound her.

"Join us, join us, join us," said the voices. She felt the edge of the blade, and blood trickled down her finger.

The telephone rang. Time froze. The bedroom registered on her retinas. The telephone rang. She was in her bedroom. There was blood on the floor. The telephone rang. The knife fell from her hands. She could hear voices, angry voices. The telephone rang.

She was on her knees on the floor of her bedroom. She had cut her finger. The phone was still ringing. She called out hello, but it still rang.

"I won't fail you," she said to her visitors. "Leave me. I won't fail you."

The telephone rang.

Alf Brummel sat in his home, listening to the phone ringing on the other end. Juleen must not be home. He hung up, relieved, if only for the moment. She would not be happy about the vote. Another delay, still another delay in the Plan. He knew he could not avoid her, that she would find out, that he would be confronted and berated by the others.

He flopped down on his bed and contemplated resigning, escape, suicide.

Saturday morning. The sun was out, and lawn mowers called to each other across fences, hedges, and cul-de-sacs; kids were playing, hoses were spraying dirty cars.

Marshall sat in the kitchen, at the table filled with advertising copy and a list of new and old accounts; the *Clarion* still lacked a secretary.

The front door opened and in came Kate. "I need a hand!"

Yes, the inevitable unloading of groceries.

"Sandy," Marshall hollered out the back door, "let's get going!" Over the years the family had developed a pretty good system of grocery separating, handling, and stashing.

"Marshall," said Kate, passing vegetables from a sack to him at the refrigerator, "are you still working on that copy? It's Saturday!"

"Almost finished. I hate to have stuff stack up on me. How's Joe and the gang?"

Kate stopped a bunch of celery in midtransfer and said, "You know what? Joe's gone. He sold the store and moved away, and I didn't even hear about it."

"Brother. Things happen fast around here. So where'd he move?"

"I don't know. Nobody would tell me. As a matter of fact, I don't think I like that new owner."

"What's this cleaner here?"

"Oh, put that under the sink." It went under the sink. "I asked that guy about Joe and Angelina and why they sold the store and why they moved and where they moved and he wouldn't tell me anything, just said he didn't know."

"That's the owner of the store? What's his name?"

"I don't know. He wouldn't tell me that either."

"Well, does he talk? Does he know English?"

"Enough to ring up your groceries and take your money, and that's about it. Now could we get all this stuff off the table?"

Marshall started gathering up all his papers before the oncoming invasion of cans and produce.

Kate continued, "I guess I'll get used to it, but for a while I thought I'd gone into the wrong store. I didn't recognize anybody. They might even have all new people working there."

Sandy spoke for the first time. "Something weird's going on in this town."

Marshall asked, "Oh yeah?"

Sandy didn't elaborate.

Marshall tried to draw it out of her. "Well, what do you think it is?"

"Aw, nothing, really. It's just a feeling I get. People around here are starting to act weird. I think we're being invaded by aliens."

Marshall let it go.

The groceries were all put away, Sandy went back to her studies, and Kate got ready to work in the garden. Marshall had a phone call to make. Talk about weird aliens invading the town jarred his memory and also his reporter's nose. Maybe Langstrat wasn't an alien, but she was certainly weird.

He sat on the couch in the living room and took the slip of paper with Ted Harmel's phone number from his wallet. A sunny Saturday morning would be a strange time to find someone home and indoors, but Marshall figured he'd try.

The phone on the other end rang several times and then a man's voice answered. "Hello?"

"Hello, Ted Harmel?"

"Yes, who's this?"

"This is Marshall Hogan, the new *Clarion* editor."

"Oh, uh-huh . . ." Harmel waited for Marshall to go on.

"Well, anyway, you know Bernice Krueger, right? I have her working for me."

"Oh, she's still there, eh? Has she found out anything about her sister?"

"Mm, I don't know much about that, she's never told me."

"Oh. So how's the paper doing?"

They talked for a few minutes about the *Clarion,* the office, circulation, whatever may have happened to the cord to the coffee-maker. Harmel seemed particularly concerned to hear that Edie had left.

"Her marriage broke up," Marshall told him. "Hey, it was a complete surprise to me. I came in too late to know what was going on."

"Hmmm . . . yeah . . ." Harmel was doing some thinking on the other end.

Keep it flowing, Hogan. "Yeah, well, I've got a daughter who's a freshman at the college."

"Is that right."

"Yeah, doing her prerequisites, jumping through the hoop. She likes it."

"Well, more power to her."

Harmel was certainly being patient.

"You know, Sandy has a psychology professor I thought was an interesting gal."

"Langstrat."

Bingo. "Yeah, yeah. A lot of unusual ideas."

"I bet."

"Do you know anything about her?"

Harmel paused, sighed, and then asked, "Well, what is it you want to know?"

"Where's she coming from, anyway? Sandy's bringing home some weird ideas . . ."

Harmel had trouble coming up with an answer. "It's . . . uh . . . Eastern mysticism, ancient religious craft. She's just into, you know, meditation, higher consciousness . . . uh . . . the oneness of the universe. I don't know if any of that makes sense to you."

"Not much. But she seems to spread it around a lot, doesn't she?"

"What do you mean?"

"You know, she meets with people on a regular basis; Alf Brummel, and, uh, who else? Pinckston . . ."

"Delores Pinckston?"

"Right, on the board of regents. Dwight Brandon, Eugene Baylor—"

Harmel cut in abruptly. "What is it you want to know?"

"Well, I understand you were pretty close to the situation—"

"No, that's wrong."

"Didn't you have sessions with her yourself?"

There was a long pause. "Who told you that?"

"Oh, we . . . just found out."

Another long pause. Harmel sighed through his nose. "Listen," he asked, "what else do you know?"

"Not much. It just smells like there might be a story in it. You know what that's like."

Harmel was struggling, fuming, groping for words. "Yes, I know what it's like. But you're wrong this time, you're really wrong!" Another pause, another struggle. "Oh, brother, I wish you hadn't called me."

"Hey, listen, we're both newspapermen—"

"No! You're the newspaperman! I'm out. I'm sure you know all about me."

"I know your name, your number, and that you used to own the *Clarion*."

"All right, let's leave it at that. I still have respect for the vocation. I don't want to see you ruined."

Marshall tried not to lose a big fish. "Say, don't leave me in the dark!"

"I'm not trying to leave you in the dark. There are some things I just can't talk about."

"Sure, I understand. No problem."

"No, you *don't* understand. Now listen to me! I don't know what you've found out, but whatever it is, bury it. Do something else. Cover the Kiwanis tree planting, anything innocuous, but just keep your nose clean."

"What are you talking about?"

"And quit pumping me for information! What I'm giving you is all you're going to get, and you'd better make good use of it. I'm telling you, forget Langstrat, forget anything you may have heard about her. Now I know you're a reporter, and so I know you're going to go out and do just the opposite of what I'm telling you, but let me give you fair warning: Don't." Hogan didn't answer. "Hogan, you hear me?"

"How can I possibly leave it alone now?"

"You have a wife, a daughter? Think of them. Think of yourself. Otherwise you'll be out on your ear like everybody else."

"What do you mean, everybody else?"

"I don't know anything, I don't know Langstrat, I don't know you, I don't live there anymore. Period."

"Ted, are you in trouble?"

"Leave it alone!"

He hung up. Marshall slammed the receiver down and let his mind race as he sat there. Leave it alone, Harmel said. Leave it alone.

In a pig's eye.

Edith Duster—wise old matron of the church, former missionary to China, a widow of some thirty years—lived in the Willow Terrace Apartments, a small retirement complex not far from the church. She was in her eighties, subsisted meagerly on Social Security and a minister's pension from her denomination, and loved to have company, especially since it was difficult for her to get out and around these days.

Hank and Mary sat at her little dinette near the large window overlooking the building's courtyard. Grandma Duster poured tea from a very old, very charming teapot into equally charming teacups. She was dressed nicely, almost formally, as always when she received guests.

"No," she said as she sat down at last, the morning tea table properly set, the pastries in place. "I don't believe God's purposes are ever thwarted for long. He has His own ways of working His people through difficulties."

Hank agreed, but weakly, "I imagine so . . ." Mary held his hand.

Grandma was firm. "I *know* so, Henry Busche. Your being here is *not* a mistake; I strongly disagree with that notion. If you were not supposed to be here, the Lord would not have accomplished the things He has through your ministry."

Mary volunteered some information. "He feels a bit down about the vote."

Grandma smiled lovingly and looked into Hank's eyes. "I think the Lord is forcing a revival upon that church, but its like the turning of the tide: before the tide can come back in, it first has to stop all its going out. Give the church time to turn around. Expect opposition, even expect to lose a few people, but the direction will change after the lull. Just give it time.

"But I do know one thing: there was nothing that could keep me away from that meeting last night. I was dreadfully sick, Satan's attack, I suppose, but it was the Lord who got me out. Right about the time of the meeting I could just feel His arms bearing me up and I got my coat on and got down there, and just in time, too. I don't know if I'd even go that far to get groceries. It was the Lord, I know it. I'm just sorry I only had one vote."

"So who do you suppose the other vote came from?" Hank asked.

Mary quickly added, "It couldn't have been Lou Stanley."

Grandma smiled, "Oh, now don't say that. You never know what the Lord might do. But you are curious, aren't you?"

"I'm *really* curious," said Hank, and now he smiled too.

"Well, you might find out, and maybe you never will. But it's all in the Lord's hands, and so are you. Let me warm up your tea."

"That church can't possibly survive if half the congregation removes its support, and I can't imagine them supporting a pastor they don't want."

"Oh, but I've had dreams of angels lately." Grandma was always very matter-of-fact about such things. "I don't usually, but I've seen angels before, and always when there was great headway to be made for the kingdom of God. I just have a feeling in my spirit that something is really stirring here. Haven't you felt that way?"

Hank and Mary looked at each other to see which of them should speak first. Then Hank told Grandma all about the battle of the other night and the burden he had felt lately for the town. Mary slipped in her remembrances whenever they came to her. Grandma listened with great fascination, responding at key moments with "Oh dear," "Well, praise the Lord," and "Well . . . !"

"Yes," she said finally, "yes, that makes a lot of sense to me. You know, I had an experience just the other night, standing right by that window." She pointed to the front window overlooking the courtyard. "I was getting the place straightened up, getting ready for bed, and I walked by that window and looked out at the rooftops and the streetlight and all of a sudden I got really dizzy. I had to sit down or I'd fall down. And I never get dizzy. The only time that ever happened before was in China. My husband and I were visiting a woman's home there, and she was a medium, a spiritist, and I knew she hated us and I think she was trying to put a curse on us. But just outside her door I had the same dizzy sensation, and I'll never forget it. What I felt the other night was just like that time in China."

"What did you do?" Mary asked.

"Oh, I prayed. I just said, 'Demon, be gone in the name of Jesus!' and it went away, just like that."

Hank asked, "So you think it was a demon?"

"Oh yes. God is moving and Satan doesn't like it. I do think there are evil spirits out there."

"But don't you feel like there are more than usual? I mean, I've been a Christian all my life and I've never come up against anything that felt like this."

Her face grew pensive. " 'This kind goeth not out but by prayer and fasting.' We need to pray, and we need to get other people praying. That's just what the angels keep telling me."

Mary was intrigued. "The angels in your dreams?" Grandma nodded. "What did they look like?"

"Oh, people, but different from anybody else. They're big, very handsome, bright clothes, big swords at their sides, very large, bright wings. One of them last night reminded me of my son; he was tall, blond, he looked Scandinavian." She looked at Hank. "He was telling me to pray for you, and you were in the dream too. I could see you up behind that pulpit preaching, and he was standing there behind you with his wings stretched out over you like a big canopy, and he looked back at me and said, 'Pray for this man.' "

"I never knew you were praying for me," said Hank.

"Well, it's time somebody else was praying too. I believe the tide is turning, Hank, and now you need true believers, true visionaries who can stand with you to pray for this town. We need to pray that the Lord will gather them in."

It was so natural then to join hands in praise to the Lord and thanksgiving for the first real encouragement to come along in quite some time. Hank prayed a prayer of thanks and could hardly get through it as his emotions welled up inside him. Mary was grateful, not only for the encouragement but for Hank's revived spirits.

Then Edith Duster, who'd fought in spiritual wars before, who'd won victories on foreign soils, tightly grasped the hands of this young ministering couple and prayed.

"Lord God," she said, and the warmth of the Holy Spirit flowed through them, "I build now a hedge around this young couple, and I bind the spirits in Jesus' name. Satan, whatever your plans for this town, I rebuke you in Jesus' name, and I bind you, and I cast you out!"

CLUNK!

Rafar's eyes darted toward the sound that had interrupted his talking and saw two swords fallen from their owners' hands. The two demons, formidable warriors, were nonplussed. They both stooped hurriedly to gather up their weapons, bowing, apologizing, begging for pardon.

Slam! Rafar's foot fell on one sword, his own huge sword clamped the other down. The two warriors, startled and terrified, backed away.

"Please pardon, my prince!" said one.

"Yes, please pardon!" said the other. "This has never happened before . . ."

"Silence, you two!" Rafar bellowed.

The two warriors braced themselves for a terrible punishment; their frightened yellow eyes peered out from behind black wings unfurled for protection, as if there was any protection from Ba-al Rafar's wrath.

But Rafar did not lash out at them. Not yet. He seemed more interested in the fallen swords; he stared at them, his brow furrowed and his big yellow eyes narrowing. He walked slowly around the swords, strangely bothered in a way the warriors had never seen before.

"Uhnnnnnnnhhh . . ." A low, gurgling growl came from deep in his throat as his nostrils belched forth yellow vapor.

He slowly went down on one knee and picked up one sword in his hand. In his huge fist it looked like a toy. He looked at the sword, looked at the demon who had dropped it, then off into space, his gnarled face registering a burning hatred that slowly rose from deep within.

"Tal," he whispered.

Then, like a slowly swelling volcano, he rose to his feet, the anger building until suddenly, with a roar that shook the room and terrified all those present, he exploded and hurled the sword through the basement wall, through the earth around Stewart Hall, through the air, through several other buildings on the college campus, and up into the sky where it tumbled end over end in a long arc of several miles.

His initial explosion released, he grabbed the sword's owner and with the order, "Go after it!" flung the demon like a spear along the same trajectory.

He grabbed up the other sword and flung it at the other demon, who sidestepped just in time to save himself. Then that demon too went sailing after his sword.

To some in the room the word "Tal" meant nothing, but they could see by the faces and deflating postures of others that it had to mean something dreadful.

Rafar began to storm about the room, growling indiscernible phrases and waving his sword at invisible enemies. The others gave him time to vent himself before daring to ask any question. Lucius finally stepped forward and bowed low, much as he hated to do so.

"We are at your service, Ba-al Rafar. Can you tell us, who is this Tal?"

Rafar spun around in fury, his wings unfurling like a clap of thunder and his eyes like hot coals.

"Who is this Tal?" he screamed, and every demon present fell on his face. "Who is this Tal, this warrior, this Captain of the Hosts of Heaven, this sneaking, conniving rival of rivals? Who is this Tal?"

Complacency happened to be within grabbing distance. With a huge fist around Complacency's scrawny neck, Rafar plucked him up like a frail weed and held him high.

"You," Rafar growled with a cloud of sulfur and steam, "have failed because of this Tal!" Complacency could only tremble, speechless with terror. "Hogan has become a hound, sniffing and barking after our scent, and I have had my fill of you and your whining excuses!"

The huge sword flashed in a wide, crimson arc, cutting a gash in space which became a bottomless abyss into which all light seemed to drain like water.

Complacency's eyes swelled in stark terror, and he screamed his last scream upon the earth. "No, Ba-al, noooooo!"

With a mighty thrust of his arm, Rafar cast Complacency headlong into the abyss. The small demon tumbled, fell, and kept falling, his screams becoming fainter until they vanished altogether. Rafar wiped the rift in space shut with the flat of his blade, and the room was just as it was before.

Just then the two warriors returned with their swords. He grabbed both of them by their wings and jerked them together in front of him.

"On your feet, all of you!" he hollered at the others. They complied instantly. Now he held the two demons aloft as an exhibit. "Who is this Tal? He is a strategist who can make warriors drop their swords!" With that, he hurled the two into the group, causing several to go sprawling. They picked themselves up as quickly as they could. "Who is this Tal? He is a subtle warrior who knows his limitations, who never enters a battle he cannot win, who knows all too well the power of the saints of God, a lesson you could all stand to learn!"

Rafar held his sword in a fist that trembled with rage, waving it about to give extra force to his words. "I knew all too well to expect him. Michael would never have sent anyone less to pit against me. Now Hogan is revived, and it is clear why he was even brought to Ashton to begin with; now Henry Busche is still retained and the Ashton Community Church has not fallen, but stands as a bastion against us; now the warriors are dropping their swords like clumsy fools!

"And all because of this . . . Tal! This is Tal's manner. His strength is not in his own sword, but in the saints of God. Somewhere somebody is praying!"

Those words brought a chill over the group.

Rafar kept pacing and thinking and growling. "Yes, yes, Busche and Hogan were handpicked; Tal's plan must revolve around them. If they fall, Tal's plan falls. There isn't much time."

Rafar selected a slimy-looking demon and asked, "Have you laid a trap for Busche?"

"Oh, yes, Ba-al Rafar," said the demon, and he couldn't help laughing with delight at his own cleverness.

"Be sure it is subtle. Remember, no frontal assault will work."

"Leave it to me."

"And what has been done to destroy Marshall Hogan?"

Strife stepped forward. "We seek to destroy his family. He derives a great amount of strength from his wife. If that support were ripped away . . ."

"Do it, any way you can."

"Yes, my prince."

"And let us not neglect some other avenues. Hogan could be lethal, and Krueger the same, but they could be manipulated to compromise each other . . ." Rafar appointed some demons to look into that possibility. "And what about Hogan's daughter?"

Deception stepped forward. "She is already within our hands."

12

The leaves were green, that fresh, new-growth kind of green they wear in the early months of summer. From their small table on the red brick plaza below, Sandy and Shawn could look up and see the glowing leaves, backlit by the sun, and watch the birds flit about in the branches between their regular scavengings for bread crumbs and french fries. This spot on campus was Sandy's favorite. It was so peaceful here, almost a world away from the strife, questions, and disputes at home.

Shawn enjoyed watching the brown sparrows cheeping and scrambling for every bread crumb he tossed onto the bricks.

"I love the way the universe all fits together," he said. "The tree grew here to give us shade, we sit here and eat and give food to the birds that live in the tree. It all works together."

Sandy was fascinated by the concept. On the surface it seemed very simple, almost storybookish, but part of her was so thirsty for this kind of peace.

"What happens when the universe doesn't fit together?" she asked.

Shawn smiled. "The universe always fits together. The problem is only when people don't realize it."

"So how do you explain the problems I'm having with my folks?"

"None of your minds are tuned in right. It's just like an FM station on your radio. If the signal is fuzzy and the voices hiss and sputter, don't blame the broadcasting station—adjust your radio. Sandy, the universe is perfect. It is unified, harmonious. The peace, the unity, the wholeness are really there, and all of us are a part of the universe; we're made of the same stuff, so there's no reason why we shouldn't just fit into the whole scheme of things. If we don't, we just took a wrong turn somewhere. We're out of touch with true reality."

"Boy, I guess so," Sandy muttered. "But that's what gets me! My folks and I are supposed to be Christians and loving each other and close to God and everything, but all we ever do is argue about who's right and who's wrong."

Shawn laughed and nodded his head. "Yeah, yeah, I know all about that. I've been there too."

"Okay, so how did you solve it?"

"I could only solve it for myself. I can't change other people's minds, only my own. It's a little hard to explain, but if you're in tune with the universe, a few little quirks in it that aren't in tune won't bother you much. That kind of thing is only an illusion of the mind anyway. Once you stop listening to the lies your mind's been telling you, you'll see very clearly that God is big enough for everybody and *in* everybody. Nobody can put Him in a jar and keep Him all to themselves, according to their own whims and ideas."

"I just wish I could find Him, for real."

Shawn looked at her comfortingly and touched her hand. "Hey, He's no trouble to find. We're all a part of Him."

"What do you mean?"

"Well, it's like I said, the whole universe all fits together; it's made of the same essence, the same spirit, the same . . . energy. Right?" Sandy shrugged and nodded. "Well, whatever our individual concept of God might be, we all know that there is something there: a force, a principle, an energy, that holds everything together. If that force is part of the universe, then it must be a part of us."

Sandy wasn't grasping this. "This is pretty foreign to me. I'm from the old Judeo-Christian school of thought, you know."

"So all you've ever learned is religion, right?"

She thought for a moment, then conceded. "Right."

"Well, you see, the problem with religion—any religion—is that it's basically a limited perspective, only a partial view of the whole truth."

"Now you sound like Langstrat."

"Oh, she's right on, I think. When you think about it long enough, it makes a lot of sense. It's just like that classic old story about the blind men who encountered the elephant."

"Yeah, yeah, I heard her tell that story too."

"Well, see? Each man's perspective of the elephant was limited to the part that he touched, so since they all touched different parts, they couldn't agree on what an elephant was really like. They got in a fight over it, just like religionists throughout history have done, and all they needed to realize was that the elephant was only one elephant. It wasn't the elephant's fault that they couldn't agree with each other. They weren't tuned in to each other and to the whole elephant."

"So we're all just like blind men . . ."

Shawn gave a strong, affirmative nod. "We're just like a bunch of bugs crawling around on the ground, never looking up. If an ant could talk, you could ask him if he knew what a tree was, and if he'd never come out of the grass and actually climbed a tree, he'd probably argue with you that the tree didn't exist. But who's wrong? Who's really blind? We're just like that. We've allowed ourselves to be fooled by our own limited perceptions. Are you into Plato at all?"

Sandy laughed a little and shook her head. "I studied that last quarter, and I don't think I got that either."

"Hey, he was into the same enlightenment. He figured there had to be a higher reality, an ideal, a perfect existence of which all we see is a copy. It's kind of like what we see with our limited senses *is* so limited, so imperfect, so broken up into pieces, we can't perceive the way the universe really is, all perfect, running smoothly, everything fitting together, all the same essence. You could even say that reality as we know it is just an illusion, a trick of our ego, our mind, our selfish desires."

"This all sounds very far-out to me."

"Oh, but it's great once you really get into it. It answers a lot of questions and solves a lot of problems."

"Yeah, if you can ever get into it."

Shawn leaned forward. "*You* don't get into *it*, Sandy. *It's* already in *you*. Think about that for a minute."

"I don't feel anything in me . . ."

"And why not? Guess!"

She twisted an invisible radio dial with her fingers. "I'm not tuned in?"

Shawn laughed with delight. "Right! Right! Listen. The universe doesn't change, but we can; if we're not lined up with it, not tuned in, we're the ones who are blind, who are living in an illusion. Say, if your life is messed up, it's really a matter of how you look at things."

Sandy scoffed, "Come on, now. You're not going to tell me that it's all in my head!"

Shawn put up hands of caution. "Hey, don't knock it until you try it." He looked again at the sunshine, the green trees, the busy birds. "Just listen for a moment."

"Listen to what?"

"The breeze. The birds. Watch those leaves waving in the wind up there."

For a moment they were silent.

Shawn spoke quietly, almost in a whisper. "Now be honest. Haven't you ever felt a sort of . . . kinship with the trees, and with the birds, with just about everything? Wouldn't you miss them if they weren't there? Have you ever talked to a houseplant?"

Sandy nodded. Shawn had a point there.

"Now don't resist that, because what you're experiencing there is just a glimpse of the real universe; you're feeling the oneness of everything. Everything is fitted together, interwoven, interlocked. Now you've felt that before, haven't you?"

She nodded.

"So that's what I'm trying to show you; the truth is already within you. You're a part of it. You're a part of God. You just never knew it. You wouldn't *let* yourself know it."

Sandy could hear the birds clearly now, and the wind seemed almost melodic as it shifted in pitch and intensity through the branches of the trees. The sun was warm, benevolent. Suddenly she felt so strongly that she had been in this place before, had known these trees and these birds before. They were trying to reach out to her, to talk to her.

Then she noticed that, for the first time in many months, she felt peace inside. Her heart was at rest. It wasn't an all-pervading peace, and she didn't know if it would last, but she could feel it and she knew she wanted more.

"I think maybe I'm tuning in a little bit," she said.

Shawn smiled and squeezed her hand encouragingly.

Meanwhile, with very gentle, very subtle combing motions of his talons, Deception stood behind Sandy, stroking her red hair and speaking sweet words of comfort to her mind.

Tal and his troops gathered once again in the little church, and the mood was better this time. They had tasted the first promises of battle; a victory, even though a small one, had been won the night before. Most of all, there were more of them. The original twenty-three had grown to forty-seven as more mighty warriors had gathered, called in by the prayers of . . .

"The Remnant!" said Tal with a note of anticipation as he looked over a preliminary list presented to him.

Scion, a red-haired, freckled fighter from the British Isles, explained the progress of the search. "They're out there, Cap, and there's plenty o' them, but these are the ones we'll be bringin' in for sure."

Tal read the names. "John and Patricia Coleman—"

Scion explained, "They were here last night and spoke up for the preacher. Now they're all the more for him, and they drop to their knees easy as droppin' a hat. We've got them workin'."

"Andy and June Forsythe."

"Lost sheep, you could say. Left the United Christian here in Ashton out of sheer hunger. We'll bring them to church tomorrow. They have a son, Ron, who's searchin' for the Lord. A bit wayward now, but reachin' his fill o' his ways."

"And plenty more, I see," said Tal with a smile. He handed the list to Guilo. "Assign some of our newcomers to this list. Gather these people in. I want them praying."

Guilo took the list and conferred with several new warriors.

"And what about relatives, friends elsewhere?" Tal asked Scion.

"Plenty o' them are redeemed and ready for prayer. Shall I send emissaries to burden them?"

Tal shook his head. "I can't let any warriors be gone for long. Instead, have messengers carry word to the watchcarers over these people's towns and cities, and let the watchcarers see that these people are burdened with prayer for their loved ones here."

"Done."

Scion set right to work, assigning messengers who immediately vanished to their missions.

Guilo had sent his warriors also and was excited to see the campaign in motion. "I like the feel of this, captain."

"It is a good beginning," Tal said.

"And what of Rafar? Do you suppose he knows of your presence here?"

"The two of us know each other all too well."

"Then he will be expecting a fight, and soon."

"Which is why we won't fight, not yet. Not until the prayer cover is sufficient and we know why Rafar is here. He's not a prince of small towns but of empires, and he would never be here for any task below his pride. What we've seen is far less than the enemy has planned. How's Mr. Hogan?"

"I hear little Complacency has been banished for failure and the Ba-al is in a rage."

Tal chuckled. "Hogan has come to life like a dormant seed. Nathan! Armoth!" They were there immediately. "You have more warriors now. Take as many as you need to surround Marshall Hogan. Greater numbers may intimidate where swords cannot."

Guilo was visibly indignant and looked longingly at his sheathed sword.

Tal cautioned, "Not yet, brave Guilo. Not yet."

Right after Marshall's call to Harmel, Bernice's phone nearly jumped off the wall. Marshall didn't ask her, he told her, "Be at the office tonight at 7, we've got work to do."

Now, at 7:10, the rest of the *Clarion* office was deserted and dark. Marshall and Bernice were in the back room, digging old issues of the *Clarion* out of the archives. Ted Harmel had been quite fastidious; most of the past issues were neatly kept in huge binders.

"So when did Harmel get run out of town?" Marshall asked as he flipped through several old pages of a back issue.

"About a year ago," Bernice answered, bringing more binders up to the big worktable. "The paper operated on a skeleton crew for several months before you bought it. Edie, Tom, myself and some of the college journalism majors kept it going. Some of the issues were okay, some of them were a lot like a college paper."

"Like this one here?"

Bernice looked at the old issue from the previous August. "I'd appreciate it if you wouldn't look too closely."

Marshall flipped the pages backward. "I want to see the issues up to the time Harmel left."

"Okay. Ted left in late July. Here's June . . . May . . . April. Just what are you looking for?"

"The reason why he got run out."

"You know the story, of course."

"Brummel says he molested some girl."

"Yes, Brummel says a lot of things."

"Well, did he or didn't he?"

"The girl said he did. She was about twelve, I guess, a daughter of one of the college regents."

"*Which* one?"

Bernice probed her brain, finally forcing the memory out. "Jarred. Adam Jarred. I think he's still there."

"Is he on that list you got from Darr?"

"No. But perhaps he should be. Ted knew Jarred pretty well. The two of them used to go fishing together. He did know the daughter, had frequent access to her, and that helped the case against him."

"So why wasn't he prosecuted?"

"I don't think it ever went that far. He was arraigned before the district judge—"

"Baker?"

"Yes, the one on the list. The case went into the judge's chambers and apparently they struck some kind of deal. Ted was gone just a few days after that."

Marshall gave the worktable an angry slap. "Boy, I wish I hadn't let that guy get away. You didn't tell me I'd be putting my fist through a beehive."

"I didn't know that much about it."

Marshall kept scanning the pages in front of him; Bernice was going through the previous month.

"You say this all blew up in July?"

"Mid to late July."

"The paper's pretty quiet about it."

"Oh sure. Ted wasn't going to print anything against himself, obviously. Besides, he didn't have to; his reputation was shot to pieces anyway. Our circulation dropped critically. Several weeks went by without any paychecks."

"Oh-oh. What's this?"

The two of them zeroed in on a letter to the editor in a Friday issue from early July.

Marshall scanned, muttered as he read, " 'I must express my indignation at the unfair treatment this board of regents has received from the local press. . . . The recent articles published in the *Ashton Clarion* amount to nothing less than blatant malfeasance of journalism, and we hope our local editor will be professional enough to check his facts from now on before printing any more groundless innuendoes . . .' "

"Yes!" Bernice brightened with recollection. "This was a letter from Eugene Baylor." And then she slapped her hands to either side of her face and exclaimed, "Oh. . . ! *Those* articles!" Bernice started flipping hurriedly through the June binder. "Yes, here's one."

The headline read, "STRACHAN CALLS FOR AUDIT." Marshall read the lead: " 'Despite continuing opposition from the Whitmore College board of regents, College Dean Eldon Strachan today called for an audit of all Whitmore College accounts and investments, still voicing his concern over recent allegations of mishandling of funds.' "

Bernice's eyes rolled up and scanned the heavens as she said, "Hoo-boy, this may be more than just a beehive!"

Marshall read a little further: " 'Strachan has asserted that there is "more than adequate evidence" to justify such an audit even though it would be costly and premature, as the board of regents still maintains.' "

Bernice explained, "You see, I never paid that much attention when all this was going on. Ted was an aggressive sort, he'd gotten on the bad side of people before, and this just sounded like another mundane political thing. I was just a reporter on the innocuous human interest staff . . . what did I care about all this?"

"So," said Marshall, "the college dean got himself in hot water with the regents. Sounds like a real feud."

"Ted was a good friend of Eldon Strachan. He took sides and the regents didn't like it. Here's another one, just the week after."

Marshall read, " 'REGENT MAULS STRACHAN. Whitmore College Regent Eugene Baylor, the college general treasurer, today accused Dean Eldon Strachan of "malicious political hatcheting," asserting that Strachan is using "deplorable and unethical methods" to further his own dynasty within the college administration.' Heh. Not exactly a harmless little tiff between friends."

"Oh, I understand it got bitter, really bitter. And Ted probably stuck his nose out a little too far. He started catching the crossfire."

"Hence Eugene Baylor's angry letter."

"Along with political pressure, I'm sure. Strachan and Ted had many meetings and Ted was finding out a lot, maybe too much."

"But you have no details . . ."

Bernice only threw up her hands and shook her head. "We have these articles and Ted's phone number, and the list."

"Yeah," Marshall mused, "the list. A lot of college regents on it."

"Plus the chief of police and the district judge who cooked Ted's goose."

"So what became of Strachan?"

"Fired."

Bernice flipped through some more old *Clarions*. A loose page fluttered out and dropped to the floor. Marshall picked it up. Something on the page caught his eye and he perused it until Bernice found what she was looking for, an article from late June.

"Yes, here's the write-up," she said. " 'STRACHAN FIRED. Citing conflicts of interest and professional incompetency as their reasons, the Whitmore College board of regents today unanimously called for Dean Eldon Strachan's resignation.' "

"Not a very long article," Marshall commented.

"Ted put it in because he had to, but it's obvious he held back any damaging details. He firmly believed Strachan's cause was just."

Marshall kept flipping through the pages. "Ehhh, what's this one here? 'WHITMORE COULD BE MILLIONS IN ARREARS, SAYS STRACHAN'." Marshall read that one carefully. "Wait a minute here, he's saying the college could be in big trouble, but he isn't saying how he knows."

"It kept coming out in bits and pieces. We just never got all of them before Strachan and Ted were silenced."

"But millions . . . you're talking real money here."

"But you see all the connections?"

"Yeah. The regents, the judge, the police chief, Young, the comptroller, and who knows who else, all connected to Langstrat and very quiet about it."

"And don't forget Ted Harmel."

"Yeah, he's quiet about it too. I mean, *real* quiet. The guy's scared out of his socks. But he wasn't a very loyal member of the group if he sided with Strachan against the regents."

"So they rubbed him out, so to speak, along with Strachan."

"Maybe. So far we have just a theory, and it's foggy."

"But we do have a theory, and my being in jail fits the pattern."

"Too nicely just yet," Marshall thought aloud. "We need to realize what we're saying here. We're talking political corruption, abuse of process, racketeering, who knows what else? We'd better be really sure of ourselves."

"What was that page there that dropped?"

"Huh?"

"The one you picked up."

"Mm. It was out of order. It's dated clear back in January."

Bernice reached for the proper binder on the archive shelf. "I don't want the archives all mixed up after—hey, what'd you fold it all up for?"

Marshall shrugged a little, gave her a very gentle look, and unfolded the page.

"There's an article about your sister," he said.

She took the page from him and looked at the news story. The headline read "KRUEGER DEATH RULED SUICIDE." She put the page down quickly.

"I figured you wouldn't want to be reminded," he said.

"I've seen it before," she said abruptly. "I have a copy at home."

"I read the article just now."

"I know."

She pulled out another binder, opening it on the worktable.

"Marshall," she said, "you may as well know everything about it. It might come up again. The case is not resolved in my mind, and it's been a very difficult battle for me."

Marshall only sighed and said, "You started this, remember that now."

Bernice kept her lips tight and her body straight. She was trying to be a detached machine.

She pointed to the first story, dated mid-January: "BRUTAL DEATH ON CAMPUS."

Marshall read silently. He wasn't prepared for the horrible details.

"The story isn't entirely accurate," Bernice commented in a very guarded tone of voice. "They didn't find Pat in her own dorm room; she was down the hall in an unoccupied room. I guess some of the girls used that room to study by themselves if it got too noisy on the floor. No one knew where she was until someone spotted the blood running out under the door . . ." Her voice cracked, and she shut her mouth tightly.

Patricia Elizabeth Krueger, age nineteen, had been found in a dorm room, naked and very dead, her throat slashed. There was no sign of a struggle, the entire college was in a state of shock, there were no witnesses.

Bernice flipped to another page and another headline, "NO CLUES TO KRUEGER DEATH." Marshall read it quickly, feeling more and more like he was invading a very sensitive area where he had no business to be. The article stated that no witnesses had come forth, no one had heard or seen anything, there was no clue to who the assailant might be.

"And you read the last one," Bernice said. "They finally ruled it was a suicide. They decided that my sister had stripped herself and cut her own throat."

Marshall was incredulous. "And that was that?"

"That was that."

Marshall closed the binder quietly. He had never seen Bernice looking so vulnerable. The feisty little reporter who could hold her own in a jail cell full of hookers had one part of her still laid bare and wounded beyond healing. He put his hands gently on her shoulders.

"I'm sorry," he said.

"It's why I came here, you know." She wiped her eyes with her fingers, reached for a nearby tissue to wipe her nose. "I . . . I just couldn't leave it at that. I knew Pat. I knew her better than anyone. She just wasn't the type to do such a thing. She was happy, well-adjusted, she liked college. She sounded just fine in her letters."

"Why . . . why don't we just pack it up for the night?"

Bernice didn't acknowledge his suggestion. "I checked the dorm layout, the room where she died, the roster for the names of every girl living in that building; I talked to all of them. I checked the police reports, the coroner's report, I went through all of Pat's personal effects. I tried to track down Pat's roommate, but she'd left. I still can't remember her name. I only met her once when I was here for a visit.

"I finally decided just to stick around, get a job, wait and see. I had some newspaper background, the job here was easy enough to land."

Marshall put his arm around her shoulders. "Well, listen. I'll help you out, any way I can. You don't have to carry this whole thing by yourself."

She relaxed a bit, leaning into him just enough to acknowledge his embracing arm. "I don't want to bother you."

"You're not bothering me. Listen, as soon as you're ready, we can go over it, recheck everything. There might still be some leads somewhere."

Bernice shook her two fists and whimpered, "If I could just be more objective about it!"

Marshall gave her a gentle, comforting chuckle and a friendly squeeze. "Well, maybe I can handle that end of it. You're doing a good job, Bernie. Just hang in there."

She was a nice kid, Marshall thought, and as far as he could remember this was the first time he'd ever touched her.

13

For obvious reasons the congregation of Ashton Community Church was much smaller and fragmented this Sunday morning, but Hank had to admit that the whole atmosphere was more peaceful. As he stood behind the old pulpit to open the service, he could see the smiling faces of his supporters peppered throughout the small crowd: yes, there were the Colemans sitting in their usual spot. Grandma Duster was there too, in much better health, praise the Lord, and there were the Coopers, the Harrises, and Ben Squires, the mailman. Alf Brummel hadn't made it, but Gordon Mayer and his wife were there, and so were Sam and Helen Turner. Some of the not-so-actives were there for their usual once-a-month drop-in, and Hank gave them special glances and smiles to let them know they were noticed.

As Mary banged out "All Hail the Power of Jesus' Name" on the piano and Hank led the singing, another couple came in the back door and took a seat near the rear, as new folks usually did. Hank didn't recognize them at all.

Scion remained near the back door, watching Andy and June Forsythe take their seats. Then he looked up toward the platform and gave Krioni and Triskal a friendly salute. They smiled and saluted back. A few demons had come in with the humans, and they were not happy to see this new heavenly stranger even lurking about, let alone bringing new people into the church. But Scion backed nonthreateningly out the door.

Hank couldn't explain why he felt as joyful as he did this morning. Maybe it was having Grandma Duster there, and the Colemans, and the new couple. And then there was that other new fellow, the big blond guy sitting in the back. He had to be a football lineman or something.

Hank kept remembering what Grandma had said to him, "We need to pray that the Lord will gather them in . . ."

He got to the sermon and opened his Bible to Isaiah 55.

" 'Seek the Lord while He may be found; call upon Him while He is near. Let the wicked forsake his way, and the unrighteous man his thoughts; and let him return to the Lord, and He will have compassion on him; and to our God, for He will abundantly pardon . . . For my thoughts are not your thoughts, neither are your ways My ways, declares the Lord. For as the heavens are higher than the earth, so are my ways higher than your ways, and my thoughts than your thoughts. For as the rain and the snow come down from heaven, and do not return there without watering the earth, and making it bear and sprout, and furnishing seed to the sower and bread to the eater; so shall my word be which goes forth from my mouth; it shall not return to Me empty, without accomplishing what I desire, and without succeeding in the matter for which I sent it. For you will go out with joy, and be led forth with peace; the mountains and the hills will break forth into shouts of joy before you, and all the trees of the field will clap their hands.' "

Hank loved that passage, and he couldn't help smiling as he began to explain it. Some people simply stared at him, listening out of obligation. But others even leaned forward in their seats, hanging on every word. The new couple sitting in the back kept nodding their heads with very intent expressions. The big blond man smiled, nodded his head, even shouted out an "Amen!"

The words kept coming to Hank's heart and mind. It had to be the Lord's anointing. He stopped by the pulpit from time to time to look at his notes, but most of the time he was all over the platform, feeling like he was somewhere between heaven and earth, speaking forth the Word of God.

The few little demons lurking about could only cower and sneer. Some did manage to stop the ears of the people they owned, but the onslaught this morning was particularly severe and painful. To them, Hank's preaching had all the soothing effect of a buzz saw.

On top of the church, Signa and his warriors refused to bend or back down. Lucius dropped by with a sizeable flock of demons just in time for the service, but Signa would not step aside.

"You know better than to tamper with me!" Lucius threatened.

Signa was sickeningly polite. "I'm sorry, we cannot allow any more demons into the church this morning."

Lucius must have had more important things for his demons to do that morning than try to hack their way through a wall of obstinate angels. He delivered a few choice insults and then the whole bunch roared off into the air, bound for some other mischief.

When the service ended, some people made a beeline for the door. Others made a beeline for Hank.

"Pastor, my name is Andy Forsythe, and this is my wife June."

"Hello, hello," Hank said, and he could feel a wide smile stretching his face.

"That was great," Andy said, shaking his head in amazement and still shaking Hank's hand. "It was . . . boy, it was really great!"

They made small talk for a few minutes, finding out about each other. Andy owned and ran the lumberyard just on the outskirts of town; June was a legal secretary. They had a son, Ron, who was in trouble with drugs and needed the Lord.

"Well," said Andy, "We haven't been saved too long ourselves. We used to go to the Ashton United Christian . . ." His voice trailed off.

June was less inhibited. "We were starving there. We couldn't wait to get out."

Andy cut back in, "Yeah, that's right. We heard about this church; well, actually we heard about you; we heard you were in a bit of trouble for being such a stickler with the Word of God, and we just thought to ourselves, 'We ought to check that guy out.' Now I'm glad we did.

"Pastor," he continued, "I want you to know there are a lot of hungry people out there. We have some friends who love the Lord and have no place to go. It's been really strange the last few years. One by one the churches around here have kind of died. Oh, they're still there, all right, and they have the people and the bucks, but . . . you know what I mean."

Hank wasn't sure that he did. "What *do* you mean?"

Andy shook his head. "Satan's really playing games with this town, I guess. Ashton never used to be this way, with so much weird stuff going on. Hey, you may have trouble believing this, but we have friends who have dropped out of three, no, *four* of the local churches."

June exchanged glances with Andy as she went through a mental list of names. "Greg and Eva Smith, the Bartons, the Jennings, Clint Neal . . ."

"Yeah, right, right," said Andy. "Like I said, there are a lot of hungry people out there, sheep without a shepherd. The churches around here just don't cut it. They don't preach the gospel."

Just then Mary walked up, all smiles. Hank happily introduced her.

Then Mary said, "Hank, I'd like you to meet—" and she turned toward the empty room. Whoever was supposed to be there wasn't. "Well . . . he's gone!"

"Who was it?" Hank asked.

"Oh, you remember that big guy sitting in the back?"

"The big blond guy?"

"Yes. I got a chance to talk to him. He told me to tell you that," Mary deepened her voice to mimic him, " 'the Lord is with you, keep praying and keep listening.' "

"Well, that was nice. Did you get his name?"

"Uh . . . no, I don't think he ever told me."

Andy asked, "Who was this?"

"Oh," said Hank, "you know, that big guy in the back. He was sitting right next to you."

Andy looked at June, and her eyes got wide. Andy started smiling, then he started laughing, and then he started clapping his hands and practically dancing.

"Praise the Lord!" he exclaimed, and Hank hadn't seen such enthusiasm in a long time. "Praise the Lord, there was nobody there. Pastor, we didn't see a soul!"

Mary's mouth dropped open, and she covered it with her fingers.

Oliver Young was a real showman; he could work an audience right down to each tear or titter and time it so well that they became just so many puppets on a string. He would stand behind the pulpit with incredible dignity and poise, and his words were so well-chosen that whatever he was saying had to be right. The vast congregation certainly seemed to think so; they had packed the place out. Many of them were professionals: doctors, teachers, lawyers, self-proclaimed philosophers and poets; a very large segment was from or connected in some way with the college. They took fastidious notes on Young's message, as if it were a lecture.

Marshall had heard a lot of this little song and dance before, so on this particular Sunday he mulled over the questions he couldn't wait to spring on Young after the service was over.

Young continued. "Did not God say, 'Let us make man in our image, according to our likeness'? What had remained in the darkness of tradition and ignorance, we find now revealed within ourselves. We discover—no, rather, we rediscover the knowledge we have always had as a race: we are inherently divine in our very essence, and have within ourselves the capacity for good, the potential to become, as it were, gods, made in the exact likeness of Father God, the ultimate source of all that is . . ."

Marshall took a quick and furtive glance sideways. There was Kate, and there was Sandy taking notes like mad, and next to her sat Shawn Ormsby. Sandy and Shawn had hit it off pretty well, and he had a definite positive influence on her life. Today, for example, he had made a deal with Sandy: he would go to church with her if she would go with her folks. Well, it worked.

Marshall had to admit, even though a little reluctantly, that Shawn could communicate with Sandy in ways Marshall never could. There had been several occasions when Shawn had served quite well as a liaison or interpreter between Sandy and Marshall and opened lines of communication neither of them thought could ever materialize. Things were getting peaceful around the house at last. Shawn seemed a gentle sort with a real gift for refereeing.

So what do I do now? Marshall wondered. For the first time in who knows how long, my whole family is sitting together in church, and that's nothing but a miracle, a real miracle. But we sure picked one heck of a church to be sitting together in, and as for that preacher up there . . .

It would be so comfortable and so nice to let everything be, but he was a reporter, and this Young had something to hide. Nuts. Talk about conflict of interests!

So while Pastor Oliver Young was up there trying to get across his ideas on the "infinite divine potential within seemingly finite man," Marshall had his own nagging issues to think about.

The service ended punctually at noon, and the carillon in the tower automatically clicked on and began to play a very traditional, very Christian-sounding accompaniment to all the hand shaking, visiting, and filing out.

Marshall and his family entered the flow of traffic that oozed toward the foyer. Oliver Young was standing by the front door in his usual spot, greeting all his parishioners, shaking hands, cootchy-cooing the babies, being pastorly. Soon Marshall, Kate, Sandy, and Shawn had their turn with him.

"Well, Marshall, good to see you," Young gushed, shaking Marshall's hand.

"Have you met Sandy?" Marshall asked, and formally introduced Young to his daughter.

Young was very warm. "Sandy, I'm very glad to see you."

Sandy at least acted glad to be there.

"And Shawn!" Young exclaimed. "Shawn Ormsby!" The two of them shook hands.

"Oh, so you two know each other?" Marshall asked.

"Oh, I've known Shawn since he was just a little shaver. Shawn, don't make yourself so scarce, all right?"

"All right," Shawn answered with a shy smile.

The others moved on, but Marshall lagged behind and came up close on the other side to speak to Young some more.

He waited until Young had finished greeting one little group of people, and then interjected into the pause, "Hey, I just thought you'd like to know that things are going better now with Sandy and me."

Young smiled, shook a few hands, then said sideways to Marshall, "Wonderful! That's really wonderful, Marshall." He offered his hand to someone else: "Nice seeing you here today."

In another space between exiting greetees, Marshall interjected, "Yeah, she really enjoyed your sermon this morning. She said it was very challenging."

"Well, thank you for saying so. Yes, Mr. Beaumont, how are you?"

"You know, it even seemed to be along the same lines as what Sandy's getting in school, in Juleen Langstrat's classes."

Young didn't answer that, but directed all his attention to a young couple with a baby. "Oh my, she's getting so big."

Marshall continued, "You're going to have to meet Professor Langstrat sometime. There's a very interesting parallel between what she teaches and what you preach." There was no response from Young. "I understand, as a matter of fact, that Langstrat's pretty deeply involved in occultism and Eastern mysticism . . ."

"Well," Young finally responded, "I wouldn't know anything about that, Marshall."

"And you definitely don't know this Professor Langstrat?"

"No, I told you that."

"Haven't you attended several private sessions with her on a regular basis, and not only you, but also Alf Brummel, Ted Harmel, Delores Pinckston, Eugene Baylor, and even Judge Baker?"

Young turned just a little red, paused, then grimaced with embarrassed recollection.

"Oh, for goodness sake!" he laughed. "Where in the world has my mind been? You know, all this time I've been thinking of someone else!"

"So you do know her?"

"Well, yes, of course. Many of us do."

Young turned aside to greet some more people. When those people had gone, Marshall was still standing there.

Marshall pressed, "So what about these private sessions? Does she really have a clientele including community leaders, elected officials, regents at the college . . ."

Young looked directly at Marshall, and his eyes were a little cold. "Marshall, just what is your specific concern here?"

"Just doing my job. Whatever this is, it seems to be something the people of Ashton should know about, especially because it involves so many of the influential people who are shaping this town."

"Well, if you are concerned about it, I'm not the person to talk to. You should go and ask Professor Langstrat herself."

"Oh, I intend to. I just wanted to give you the chance to give me some honest answers, something I feel you're not quite doing."

Young's voice got a bit strained. "Marshall, if I seem to be elusive it is because what you are trying to pry into is protected by professional ethics. It is privileged information. I was simply hoping you would figure that out without my having to tell you."

Kate was calling from the sidewalk. "Marshall, we're all waiting for you."

Marshall stepped away from the conversation, and it was just as well. It could only have gotten hotter from that point, and it was getting him nowhere anyway. Young was cool, very tough, and very slippery.

A few states away, in a deep, secluded, and steep-sided valley rimmed by high mountains and carpeted with thick green ground cover and moss-tufted rock, a small but well-constructed cluster of buildings nestled like a lonely outpost in the center of the valley floor, accessible only by one rough and meandering gravel road.

That little cluster of buildings, once a dismal and dilapidated old ranch, had been expanded into a complex of stone and brick buildings which now housed a small dormitory, an office complex, a dining hall, a maintenance building, a clinic, and several private dwellings. There were no signs, however, no labels anywhere, nothing to indicate where or what anything was.

Drawing a charcoal streak across the sky, a sinister black object flew over the mountaintops and began to drop into the valley, piercing through the paper-thin layers of mist that hung in the air. Cloaked by oppressive spiritual darkness and silent as a black cloud, Ba-al Rafar, the Prince of Babylon, floated along. He stayed close to the contour of the mountainside, maneuvering on a course that weaved this way and that among the dead snags and rocky crags. The canopy of darkness followed him like a cast shadow, like a tiny circle of night upon the landscape; a faint streak of red and yellow vapor trailed from his nostrils and hung in the air behind him like a long, slowly settling ribbon.

Below, the ranch looked like a huge hive of hideous black insects. Several layers of ruthless warriors hovered almost stationary in a vast dome of defense over the complex, swords drawn, yellow eyes peering across the valley. Deep within this shell, demons of all shapes, sizes, and strengths darted about in a boiling mass of activity. As Rafar dropped closer, he noted a concentration of black spirits around a large multistoried stone house on the fringe of the cluster. The Strongman is there, he thought, so he banked gently to one side, changing his course for that building.

The outer sentinels saw him approaching and gave an eerie, siren-like wail. Immediately the defenders radiated outward from Rafar's flight path, opening a channel through the defense layers. Rafar swooped skillfully through the channel as demons on all sides saluted him with upheld swords, their glowing eyes like thousands of paired yellow stars on black velvet. He ignored them and passed quickly through. The channel closed again behind him like a living gate.

He floated slowly down through the roof of the house, through the attic, past rafters, walls, plaster, through an upstairs bedroom, through a thick, beam-supported floor and down into a spacious living room below.

The evil in the room was thick and confining, the darkness like black liquid that swirled about with any motion of the limbs. The room was crowded.

"Ba-al Rafar, the Prince of Babylon!" a demon announced from somewhere, and monstrous demons all around the perimeter of the room bowed in respect.

Rafar folded his wings in regal, capelike fashion and stood with an intimidating air of royalty and might, his jewels flashing impressively. His big yellow eyes studied carefully the orderly ranks of demons lined up all around him. A horrible gathering. These were spirits from the principality levels, princes themselves of their own nations, peoples, tribes. Some were from Africa, some were from the Orient, several were from Europe. All were invincible. Rafar noted their tremendous size and formidable appearance; they all matched him for size and ferocity, and he doubted he would ever venture to challenge any of them. To receive a bow from them was a great honor, a compliment indeed.

"Hail, Rafar," said a gargling voice from the end of the room.

The Strongman. It was forbidden to speak his name. He was one of the few majesties intimate with Lucifer himself—a vicious global tyrant responsible over the centuries for resisting the plans of the living God and establishing Lucifer's kingdom on the earth. Rafar and his kind controlled nations; those such as the Strongman controlled Rafar and his kind.

The Strongman rose from his place, and his huge form filled that part of the room. The evil that emanated from him could be felt everywhere, almost like an extension of his body. He was grotesque, hulking, his black hide hanging like sacks and curtains from his limbs and torso, his face a macabre landscape of bony prominences and deep, folded furrows. His jewels flashed brilliantly from his neck, chest, arms; his big black wings draped his body like a royal robe and trailed along the floor.

Rafar bowed low in homage, feeling the Strongman's presence from clear across the room. "Hail, my lord."

The Strongman never wasted words. "Shall we be detained again?"

"The errors of Prince Lucius are being corrected. The new resistance is failing, my lord. Soon the town will be ready."

"And what of the host of heaven?"

"Limited."

The Strongman did not like Rafar's answer—Rafar could feel that distinctly. He spoke slowly. "We have received reports of a strong Captain of the Host being sent to Ashton. I believe you know him."

"I have reason to believe Tal has been sent, but I have anticipated him."

The big, velvet-draped eyes burned with fury. "Is it not this Tal who vanquished you at the fall of Babylon?"

Rafar knew he must answer, and quickly. "It is this Tal."

"Then the delays have cost us our advantage. You have now been matched strength for strength."

"My lord, you will see what your servant can do."

"Bold words, Rafar, but your strengths can only succeed with immediacy; the strengths of our enemies grow with time."

"All will be ready."

"And what of the man of God and the newspaper man?"

"Does my lord even give them his attention?"

"Your lord wishes you to give them yours!"

"They are powerless, my lord, and will soon be removed."

"But only if Tal is removed," the Strongman said derisively. "Let me see it happen before you bother me in boasting about it. Until then, we remain confined here. Rafar, I will not wait long!"

"Nor shall you need to."

The Strongman only smirked. "You have your orders. Begone!"

Rafar bowed low, and with an unfurling of his wings he quietly rose through the house until he was outside.

Then, with a furious burst of rage, he swooped upward, sending unexpecting demons tumbling out of the way. He picked up speed, his wings rushing in a blinding blur, and the defenders could barely get a channel opened before he burst through it trailing a hot stream of sulfurous breath. They closed up the channel again, giving each other curious looks as they watched him soar away.

Rafar roared like a rocket up the side of the mountains and then out over the craggy peaks and back toward the little town of Ashton. In his rage he cared not who saw him, he cared not about stealth or even decorum. Let the whole world see him, and let it tremble! He was Rafar, the Prince of Babylon! Let all the world bow before him or be decimated under the edge of his sword!

Tal! The very name was bitterness itself on his tongue. The lords of

Lucifer would never let him forget that defeat so long ago. Never—until the day when Rafar redeemed his honor.

And indeed he would. Rafar could see his sword gutting Tal and scattering him in shreds and pieces across the sky; he could feel the impact in his arms, he could hear the ripping sound of it. It was only a matter of time.

Among the jagged rocks on one mountain's summit, a silver-haired man came out of hiding to watch Rafar quickly shrink into the distance, etching a long black trail across the sky until he vanished over the horizon. The man took one more look at the demon-swarmed cluster of buildings in the valley, looked again toward the horizon, then vanished down the other side of the mountain in a flash of light and a flurry of wings.

14

Well, thought Marshall, sooner or later I have to get around to it. On Thursday afternoon, when things were quiet, he closed himself in his office and made some phone calls trying to track down Professor Juleen Langstrat. He called the college, got the number of the Psychology Department, and went through two receptionists in two different offices before he finally found out that Langstrat was not in today and had an unlisted home number. Then Marshall thought of the very cooperative Albert Darr, and gave his office a ring. Professor Darr was teaching, but would return his call if he would leave a message. Marshall left a message. Two hours later, Albert Darr returned Marshall's call, and he did have the unlisted number for Juleen Langstrat's apartment.

Marshall called the number.

It was busy.

The living room of Juleen Langstrat's apartment was dimly lit by one small lamp on the mantel. The room was quiet, warm, and comfortable. The shades were drawn to block out distractions, bright light, and any other disturbances. The phone was off the hook.

Juleen Langstrat sat in her chair, speaking quietly to her counselee who sat opposite her.

"You hear only the sound of my voice . . ." she said, then repeated the sentence several times quietly and clearly. "You hear only the sound of my voice . . ."

This went on for several minutes until her subject was in a deep, hypnotic trance.

"You are descending . . . descending deep within yourself . . ."

Langstrat watched the face of her subject carefully. She then extended her hands palms out, fingers spread, and began to move her hands up and down just inches away from the subject's body, as if feeling for something. "Release your true self . . . let it go . . . it is infinite . . . at unity with all existence . . . Yes! I can feel it! Can you read my energy returning to you?"

The subject murmured, "Yes . . ."

"You are free from your body now . . . your body is an illusion . . . you feel the bounds of your body dissolving away . . ."

Langstrat leaned in close, still using her hands.

"You are free now . . ."

"Yes . . . yes, I am free . . ."

"I can feel your life force expanding."

"Yes, I can feel it."

"That's enough. You may stop there." Langstrat was intent, closely observing everything. "Go back . . . go back . . . Yes, I can feel you receding. In a moment you will feel me slipping from you; don't be alarmed, I'm still here."

In the next several minutes, she brought her subject slowly back out of the trance, step by step, suggestion by suggestion.

Finally she said, "All right, when I count to three, you will awake. One, two, three."

Sandy Hogan opened her eyes, rolled them about dizzily, then took a deep breath, coming fully around.

"Wow!" she responded.

The three of them laughed together.

"Wasn't that something?" asked Shawn, sitting next to Langstrat.

"Wow," was all Sandy could say.

This was a real first for Sandy. It had been Shawn's idea and, though she hesitated at first, now she was very glad that she had gone along with it.

The apartment shades were opened, and Sandy and Shawn prepared to go back to their afternoon classes.

"Well, thank you for coming," said the professor at the door.

" Thank *you*," Sandy piped.

"And thank you for bringing her," Langstrat told Shawn. Then she said to the two of them, "Now remember, I wouldn't advise speaking to anyone about this. It's a very personal and intimate experience that we should all respect."

"Yeah, right, right," said Sandy.

Shawn drove her back to campus.

It was Friday again, and Hank sat at home in his little corner office looking anxiously at the clock. Mary was usually very reliable. She had said she would be back before Carmen got there for her afternoon counseling appointment. Hank had no idea if there were any spies watching the house, but he could never be sure. All he needed was for someone to figure out that Carmen was dropping in to see him while Mary went grocery shopping. Hank's fearful side could envision all kinds of plots his enemies might be forming against him, such as sending some strange and seductive woman to compromise and ruin him.

Well, he knew one thing: If Carmen didn't show a genuine responsiveness to the counseling and begin to apply real solutions to a real problem, that would be the end of it as far as he was concerned.

Oh-oh. There was the doorbell. He sneaked a look out the window. Carmen's red Fiat was parked out front. Yes, she was standing at the door, in broad daylight, in full view of ten or fifteen houses. The way she was dressed today made Hank figure he'd better let her in quickly, if only to get her out of sight.

Where, oh where, was Mary?

Mary was not sure she liked the new owners of what used to be Joe's Market. Oh, it wasn't their service or the way they ran the store, or whether or not they were friendly; they were okay in most of those departments, and Mary also figured it would take time for them to know everyone and vice versa. What bothered Mary was how obviously secretive they became any time she asked them whatever became of Joe Carlucci and his family. As far as Mary could find out, Joe, Angelina, and their children left Ashton abruptly and didn't tell anyone, and so far no one could be found who even knew where they went.

Oh well. She hurried out of the store and toward her car, a young box boy pushing a cart of groceries along behind her. She opened the trunk and watched the boy load the groceries in.

And then she felt it, suddenly, without any apparent reason: an unexplainable tinge of emotion, an odd mixture of fear and depression. She felt cold, nervous, a little shaky, and could think of nothing but getting out of that place and hurrying home.

Triskal had been accompanying her, guarding her, and he felt it too. With a metallic ring and a flash of light, his sword was instantly in his hand.

Too late! From somewhere behind him came a stunning blow on the back of his neck. He toppled forward. His wings shot out to steady him, but an incredible weight came down on his back like a pile driver and pinned him down.

He could see their feet, like the clawed feet of hideous reptiles, and the red flicker of their blades; he could hear their sulfurous hissing. He looked up. At least a dozen demonic warriors surrounded him. They were towering, fierce, with glowing yellow eyes and dripping fangs, and they were sneering and gargling with laughter.

Triskal looked to see if Mary was all right. He knew her safety would soon be threatened if he didn't act. But what could he do?

What was that? He suddenly felt an intense wave of evil rolling over him.

"Pick him up," said a voice like thunder.

A viselike hand curled around his neck and jerked him up as if he were a toy. Now he was looking at all these spirits eye to eye. They were newcomers to Ashton. He had never seen such size, strength, and brazenness. Their bodies were covered with thick, ironlike scales, their arms rippled with power, their faces were mocking, their sulfurous breath choked him.

They turned him around and held him tightly, and he found himself face to face with a vision of sheer horror.

Flanked by no less than ten more huge demonic warriors, a gargantuan spirit stood with an S-curved sword in his monstrous black hand.

Rafar! The thought coursed through Triskal's mind like a death sentence; every inch of his being tightened with the anticipation of blows, defeat, unbearable pain.

The big, fanged mouth broke into a mocking and hideous grin; amber saliva dripped from the fangs, and sulfur chugged forth in rancid clouds as the giant warlord chuckled mockingly.

"Are you so surprised?" Rafar asked. "You should feel privileged. You, little angel, are the first to look upon me."

"And how are you today?" Hank asked as he showed Carmen to a comfortable chair in his office area.

She sank into the chair with a coo and a sigh, and Hank began to wonder where he left his tape recorder. He knew he was innocent of wrongdoing here, but some proof would be nice.

"I'm much better," she answered, and her voice was pleasant and even. "You know, maybe you can tell me why, but I haven't heard any voices talking to me all week."

"Oh . . . um . . . yeah," said Hank, finally getting his counselor's thoughts in gear. "That was what we were talking about, wasn't it?"

Triskal looked toward Mary. She was thanking the box boy and closing her trunk.

Rafar watched Triskal, amused. "Oh, I see. You are here to protect her. From what? Did you expect to swat mere flies?" Triskal had no answer. Rafar's tone became cruel and cutting. "No, you are mistaken, little angel. It is a much greater power with whom you have to do."

Rafar tapped the ground with his sword, and Triskal immediately felt the iron hands of two demons clamping his arms from behind. He looked toward Mary. She was looking for the key to the car door. She was getting into the car. Another demon stretched out his sword and pierced the hood of the car. Mary tried to start the engine. Nothing happened.

Rafar looked toward the nearby laundromat that faced the parking lot. A young, greasy-looking character stood in front of it, leaning against a post. Triskal could tell the man was possessed by one of Rafar's henchmen—as a matter of fact, several of them. At Rafar's nod, the demons went into action and the man started walking toward Mary's car.

Mary checked her lights. No, she had not left them on. She turned the key on and turned on the radio. It played. The horn honked. What on earth was the matter? She saw the young character coming her way from the direction of the laundromat. Oh, great.

As Triskal watched helplessly, the demons guided the man up to the car window.

"Hey, cutie," he said, "having some trouble here?"

Mary looked out at him. He was skinny, dirty, and dressed in black leather and chrome chains.

She called through the window, "Uh . . . no thanks. I'm all right."

He only smirked, eyeing her up and down as he said, "Why don't you open up and let me see what I can do?"

Hank didn't feel right about any of this. Where was Mary? At least Carmen was making a little more sense this time. She seemed to be dealing with her problems intelligently and with a genuine desire to change things. Maybe it would be different this time, but Hank wasn't counting on it.

"So," he asked, "what do you suppose became of those amorous voices in the night?"

"I don't listen to them anymore," she answered. "There's one thing you helped me to realize, just by talking about it: Those voices aren't real. I've only been fooling myself."

Hank was very gentle when he agreed, "Yes, I think you're right."

She heaved a deep sigh and looked at him with those big blue eyes. "I was trying to cope with my loneliness, that's all. I think that was it. Pastor, you're just so strong. I wish I could be that way."

"Well, the Bible says, 'I can do all things through Christ who strengthens me.'"

"Uh-huh. Where's your wife?"

"Getting groceries. She should be back any minute."

"Well . . ." Carmen leaned forward and smiled ever so sweetly. "I'm really drawing strength from your company. I want you to know that."

Mary could feel her heart pounding. What would this guy do next?

The man leaned against the window and his breath fogged the glass as he said, "Say, sweetheart, why don't you tell me your name?"

Rafar grabbed Triskal by the hair and jerked his head around. Triskal thought his head would snap off.

Rafar breathed sulfur right into Triskal's face as he said, "And now, little angel, I will have words with you." The tip of the long sword came up to Triskal's throat. "Where is your captain?"

Triskal did not answer.

Rafar yanked his head around and let him look toward Mary.

The man tried the latch on Mary's door. She was terrified. She groped for every lock button in the car, pushing each one down only seconds before the man could grab the outside latch. He tried all the doors, a leering smile on his face. Mary tried the horn again. A demon had already taken care of that—it didn't work. Rafar twisted Triskal's head back again, and the cold blade pressed against Triskal's face.

"I will ask you again: Where is your captain?"

Carmen was still telling Hank how much good this counseling was doing her, how he reminded her of her former husband, and how she was looking for a man with his qualities. Hank had to put a lid on this stuff.

"Well," he finally cut in, "do you have any other people in your life that you feel are significant as far as strength, support, friendship, those kinds of things?"

She looked at him just a little mournfully. "Sort of. I have friends who hang out at the tavern. But nothing ever lasts." She let her thoughts brew for a moment, then asked, "Do you think I'm attractive?"

The man in black leather leaned close to Mary's window, threatened her with horrible obscenities, then started banging on the glass with a large metal buckle.

Rafar nodded to a warrior whose hand passed through Mary's window and grasped the lock button, ready to pull it up at Rafar's order. The demons in the young man were drooling and ready. His hand was on the latch.

Rafar made sure Triskal could see it all, and then said, "Your answer?"

Triskal finally spoke, moaning, "The brake . . ."

Rafar held him tighter, leaning closer. "I didn't hear you."

Triskal repeated it. "The brake."

Mary had a flash. The car was parked on an incline. It wasn't much, but it might be enough to get the car moving. She released the parking brake and the car started to roll. The creep wasn't expecting that; he banged on the window, tried to get around in front of the car to stop it, but it began to roll at a steady clip and he soon realized that his efforts to stop it were becoming a little too obvious to other shoppers.

A husky contractor standing by his big four-wheeler finally saw what was going on and hollered, "Hey, creep, whaddaya doin'?"

Rafar watched it happen, his rising anger coursing through his big iron fist, making it tighten more and more around Triskal. Triskal thought his neck would crack any moment.

But then Rafar seemed to give in.

"Desist!" he ordered the demons. They backed off; the man gave up the chase and tried to saunter nonchalantly away. The big contractor started after him, and he fled.

The car kept rolling. There was an exit from the parking lot that emptied onto a backstreet with a fairly good grade. Mary steered for it, hoping no other cars or pedestrians would get in her way.

Triskal saw that she would make it.

So did Rafar. The cold steel of his blade pressed against Triskal's throat. "Well done, little angel. You have spared your charge until a more opportune time. I will leave you with only a message for today. Pay careful attention."

With that, Rafar released Triskal into the hands of his henchmen. One huge, warty demon pounded his iron fist into Triskal's torso and sent him spinning into the air where another demon intercepted him with a swat of his sword, carving a deep gash in his back. Triskal fluttered and tumbled down in a daze, into the clutches of two more demons who pummeled his limp body with iron fists and tore at him with taloned feet. For several horrible minutes the demons made violent sport with him as Rafar coldly watched. Finally the great Ba-al gave a growled command, and the warriors let Triskal go. He flopped to the ground, and Rafar's big taloned foot stomped down on his neck. The huge sword swung down and waved in small circles before Triskal's eyes as the demon master spoke.

"You will tell your captain that Rafar, the Prince of Babylon, is looking for him." The big foot pressed harder. "You will *tell* him!"

Suddenly Triskal was alone, a limp, ragged wreck. He struggled to his feet again. All he could think of now was Mary.

Hank gently took hold of Carmen's hand, lifted it off his own, and placed it courteously in her lap. He held it there for just a moment and looked into her eyes with compassion and yet firmness. He let go of it and then leaned back in his chair to a safe distance.

"Carmen," he said with a soft and understanding voice. "I'm very flattered that you're so impressed with my masculine qualities . . . and really, I have no doubts that a woman of your particular qualities will have no trouble finding a good man with whom to build a lasting and meaningful relationship. But listen—I don't mean to sound abrupt, but I have to emphasize one thing right here and now: I am not that man. I'm here as a minister and counselor, and we have to keep this relationship strictly limited to that of a counselor and his client."

Carmen seemed very disturbed, and very offended. "What are you saying to me?"

"I'm saying that we really can't continue these appointments. They're causing emotional conflicts for you. I think you'll be better off going to someone else."

Hank couldn't explain why, but even as he said that, he felt like he had just won some kind of battle. From the icy look in Carmen's eyes, he figured she had lost.

Mary was crying, wiping the tears from her face with her sleeve and praying a mile a minute. "Father God, dear Jesus, save me, save me, save me!" The hill was beginning to flatten out; the car slowed down, fifteen, ten, five miles an hour. She looked behind and saw no one following, but she was too scared by now to be comforted. She just wanted to get home.

Then, up the street behind her and about ten feet above the ground, Triskal flew, his clothes flashing with white-hot light and his wings rushing. His flight path was wobbly and the rhythm of his wings out of sync, but he was determined nevertheless. His face was etched with deep concern for her welfare. He spread his tattered, fluttering wings like a large canopy and let them brake him to a stop as he settled down onto the roof of the car. By now it was barely rolling and Mary just kept crying and wailing, jerking her body in futile attempts to urge the car onward.

Triskal reached down through the roof and gently placed his hand on Mary's shoulder. "Shhh . . . be calm, it's all right now. You're safe."

She looked behind her again and began to quiet down a little.

Triskal spoke to her heart. "The Lord has saved you. He won't let you go. You're all right."

The car was almost to a complete stop now. Mary pulled it over to the side of the street and parked it while she still had the momentum to do so. She pulled on the parking brake and sat there for several minutes just to compose herself.

"That's it," said Triskal, comforting her in her spirit. "Rest in the Lord. He's here."

Triskal slid off the roof of the car and reached his arm down through the hood, probing around. He found whatever it was he was looking for.

"Mary," he said, "why don't you try again?"

Mary sat in the car thinking to herself that the stupid thing would never start and what horrible timing it had, to die and leave her in such a fix.

"C'mon," Triskal prodded. "Take a step of faith. Trust God. You never know what He might do."

Mary decided to take one more stab at starting the car, even though she had little faith that anything would happen. She twisted the key. The engine cranked over, then sputtered, then started. She gave it several powerful revs just to make sure it stayed awake. Then, still in a very great hurry to get home to Hank's protecting arms, she pulled out into the street and hot-rodded for home with Triskal riding on the roof.

Hank was very relieved to hear the slam of the car door outside. "Oh, that must be Mary!"

Carmen got up. "I guess I'd better go."

Now that Mary was here, Hank added, "Oh, listen, you don't have to. You can stay for a while."

"No, no, I'll just leave. Maybe I ought to go out the back, even."

"No, don't be silly. Here. I'll see you to the door. I need to help Mary with those groceries anyway."

But Mary had forgotten about the groceries and only wanted to get inside the house. Triskal ran beside her. He was battered and limping, his clothing was torn, and he could still feel the fiery wound in his back.

Hank opened the door. "Hi, hon. Boy, I was getting worried about you." Then he saw her tear-filled eyes. "Hey, what—"

Carmen screamed. It was a sudden, heart-piercing scream that halted every thought and stifled any words. Hank spun around, not knowing what to expect.

"NOOOO!" Carmen shrieked, her arms guarding her face. "Are you mad? Get away from me, you hear? Get away!"

As Hank and Mary both looked on in horror, Carmen backed into the room, waving her arms as if trying to shield herself from some invisible attacker; she stumbled around the room, she tumbled over the furniture, she cursed and spewed horrible obscenities. She was terrified and enraged at the same time, her eyes wide and glassy, her face contorted.

Krioni tried to grab Triskal and hold him back. Triskal had glorified and was a shimmering white; his tattered wings filled the room and glimmered like a thousand rainbows. He held a gleaming sword in his hand, and the sword flashed and sang in blinding arcs as he engaged in a frenzied battle with Lust, a hideous demon with a black-scaled, slippery body like a lizard and a red tongue that lashed about his face like the tail of a snake. Lust was first defending himself, then lashing back with his glowing red sword, the crescent blade cutting crimson arcs through the air. The swords clashed with explosions of fire and light.

"Let me be, I tell you!" Lust screamed, his wings propelling him like a trapped hornet about the room.

"Let him be!" shouted Krioni, trying to hold Triskal back while staying out of the path of that infinitely sharp blade. "Do you hear my order? Let him be!"

At last Triskal withdrew, but held his sword steady and kept it raised in front of him, the light from the blade illuminating his raging face, his burning eyes.

Carmen calmed down, rubbed her eyes, and looked about the room with a frightened expression. Hank and Mary went to her immediately and tried to comfort her.

"What's wrong, Carmen?" Mary asked, wide-eyed and concerned. "It's just me, Mary. Did I do something? I didn't mean to scare you."

"No . . . no . . ." moaned Carmen. "It wasn't you. It was somebody else . . ."

"Who? What?"

Lust backed off, his sword still held high.

Krioni told him, "We will give place to you no longer today. Begone, and don't come here again!"

Lust folded his wings and circled carefully around the two heavenly warriors and over to the door.

"I was leaving anyway," the demon hissed.

"I was leaving anyway," said Carmen, composing herself. "There's . . . there's bad energy in this place. Good-bye."

She bolted out the door. Mary tried to call after her, but Hank touched Mary's arm and let her know that silence would be best for now.

Krioni held Triskal until the light around him faded and he replaced his sword. Triskal was shaking.

"Triskal," Krioni scolded, "you know Tal's orders! I was with Hank the whole time; he did just fine. There was no need—" Then Krioni saw Triskal's many injuries and the deep wound in his back. "Triskal, what happened?"

"I . . . I could not let myself be assailed by still another," Triskal gasped. "Krioni, we are more than matched."

Mary finally remembered that she was about to cry. She picked up where she had left off.

"Mary, what in the world is going on here?" Hank asked, putting his arms around her.

"Just close the door, honey!" she cried. "Just close the door and hold me. Please!"

15

Kate grabbed a kitchen towel and hurriedly wiped her hands so she could pick up the phone.

"Hello?"

"Hi there." It was Marshall.

Kate knew what was coming; it had been happening a lot the last two weeks. "Marshall, I am cooking dinner and I am cooking enough for all four of us . . ."

"Yeah, well . . ." Marshall had the tone of voice he always used when he was about to weasel out of something.

"Marshall!" Then Kate turned her back toward the living room where Sandy and Shawn were studying and talking, but mostly talking; she didn't want them to see the distress in her face. She lowered her voice. "I want you home for dinner. You've been out late all this week, you've been so busy and so preoccupied I hardly have a husband anymore—"

"Kate!" Marshall broke in. "It won't be as bad as you thought: I'm just calling to say I'll be a little late, not that I won't be there."

"How late?"

"Oh brother . . ." Marshall wasn't sure at all. "How about an hour?"

Kate couldn't think of what to say. She only sighed in disgust and anger.

Marshall tried to appease her. "Listen, I'll get there as soon as I can."

Kate decided to say it over the phone; she might never get the chance any other time. "Marshall, I'm concerned about Sandy."

"What's wrong with her now?"

Oh, she could just punch him for that tone of voice! "Marshall, if you'd just be around here once in a while you'd know! She's . . . I don't know. She just isn't the same old Sandy anymore. I'm afraid of what Shawn is doing to her."

"What *Shawn* is doing to her?"

"I can't talk about it over the phone."

Now Marshall sighed. "All right, all right. We'll talk about it."

"When, Marshall?"

"Oh, tonight, when I get home."

"We can't talk right in front of them—"

"I mean . . . oh, you know what I mean!" Marshall was tiring of this conversation.

"Well, just get home, Marshall, *please!*"

"All right, all right!"

Marshall hung up the phone with hardly a loving gentleness. For a split second he regretted the act and thought about how it must have made Kate feel, but he forced his thoughts onward to the next, very pressing project: interviewing Professor Juleen Langstrat.

Friday evening. She should be home now. He dialed the number, and this time it rang. And rang. And rang one more time.

Click. "Hello?"

"Hello, this is Marshall Hogan, editor of the *Ashton Clarion*. Am I speaking with Professor Juleen Langstrat?"

"Yes, you are. What can I do for you, Mr. Hogan?"

"My daughter Sandy has been in some of your classes."

She seemed pleased to hear that. "Oh, very good!"

"At any rate, I was wondering if we might set up a date for an interview."

"Well, you'd have to speak with one of my teacher assistants. They are the ones responsible for checking the progress and problems of the students. The classes are large, you understand."

"Oh, well, no, that's not exactly what I had in mind. I was thinking I would like to interview *you*."

"Pertaining to your daughter? I'm afraid I don't know her. I wouldn't be able to tell you much . . ."

"Well, we could talk a little about the class, of course, but I was also curious about the other interests you're pursuing there on the campus, the elective classes you've been teaching at night . . ."

"Oohh," she said, with a down note at the end that didn't sound promising. "Well, that was part of an experimental college idea we were trying. If you wish to check that out, the registrar might have some old flyers available. But I should inform you that I am very uncomfortable with the idea of granting any interview to the press, and I really cannot do so."

"So you're not willing to discuss the very influential people you have among your circle of friends?"

"I don't understand the question," and it sounded like she didn't appreciate it either.

"Alf Brummel, chief of police, Reverend Oliver Young, Delores Pinckston, Dwight Brandon, Eugene Baylor, Judge John Baker . . ."

"I have no comment," she said sharply, "and I really have some other things that are very pressing. Is there anything else I can help you with?"

"Well . . ." Marshall thought he'd go ahead and try for it. "I guess the only other thing I could ask you about is why you ejected me from your class."

Now she was getting indignant. "I don't know what you're talking about."

"Your class on Monday afternoon two weeks ago. 'The Psychology of Self,' I think it was. I'm the big guy you told to leave."

She began to laugh incredulously. "I haven't the slightest idea what you're talking about! You must have the wrong person."

"You don't remember telling me to wait outside?"

"I am convinced you have me mixed up with someone else."

"Well, do you have long blonde hair?"

She said simply, "Good night, Mr. Hogan," and hung up.

Marshall stood there a moment, then asked himself, "C'mon, Hogan, what did you expect?"

He dropped the receiver into the cradle and went out into the front office where a question from Bernice grabbed his attention.

"So I'd like to know how you're finally going to corner Langstrat," she quipped, flipping through some papers at her desk.

Marshall felt like his face must be awfully red.

"Boy, your face is sure red," Bernice confirmed.

"Talking to too many temperamental women in one night," he explained. "Langstrat was one of them. Boy, I thought Harmel was bad!"

Bernice turned around, excited. "You got Langstrat on the phone?"

"For all of thirty-two seconds. She had absolutely nothing to say to me, and she didn't remember kicking me out of her class."

Bernice made a screwy face. "Isn't it funny how no one seems to remember having any encounters with us? Marshall, we must be invisible!"

"How about very undesirable and very inconvenient?"

"Well," Bernice said, going back to her paperwork, "Professor Langstrat probably has been very busy, too busy to talk to nosy reporters . . ."

A wad of paper bounced off her head. She turned around and saw Marshall looking over some lists. He looked like he couldn't possibly have tossed that little projectile.

He said, "Boy, I wonder if I could contact Harmel again? But *he* won't talk either."

The same wad of paper bounced off his ear. He looked at Bernice and she was dead serious, all business.

"Well, it's obvious he knew too much. It's my guess that both he and former Dean Strachan are running good and scared."

"Yeah." Marshall had a memory come to the surface. "Harmel talked that way, warning *me*. He said something like, I'd be out on my ear like everybody else."

"So who's everybody else?"

"Yeah, who else do we know who could have been removed?"

Bernice looked over some of her notes. "Well, you know, now that I look over this list, none of these people have really been in their position for a very long time."

The wad of paper ricocheted off her head and skittered across her desk.

"So who did they replace?" Marshall asked.

Bernice solemnly picked up the wad of paper as she said, "We can check that out. In the meantime, the most obvious thing to do is call Strachan and see what—" she hurled the wad at Marshall "—he has to say!"

Marshall grabbed the wad in midflight and quickly crumpled another one to add to his arsenal, sending them both back in Bernice's direction. Bernice began to prepare an adequate counterattack.

"All right," Marshall said, starting to crack up with laughter, "I'll give him a ring." He was suddenly in the middle of a blizzard of paper wads. "But I think we'd better get out of here, my wife's waiting."

Bernice was not finished with the war yet, so they finished it and then had to clean up before they could leave.

Rafar paced up and down the dark basement room, chugging out hot breath that became a layer of cloud obscuring him from the shoulders up. He pounded his fists together, he tore invisible enemies in his outstretched talons, he cursed and fumed.

Lucius stood with the other warriors, waiting for Rafar to calm down and give the reason for calling this meeting. Lucius rather enjoyed the little scene before him. Obviously Rafar, the great braggart, had been cut down to size in his meeting with the Strongman! Lucius could hardly keep a hideous smirk off his face.

"Wouldn't the little angel tell you where you could find this . . . what was that name again?" Lucius asked, knowing full well Tal's name.

"TAL!" Rafar roared, and Lucius could detect Rafar's humiliation at the very sound of the name.

"The little angel, the helpless little angel, told you nothing?"

Rafar's immediate response was a monstrous black fist clamped instantly around Lucius's throat. "Do you mock me, little imp?"

Lucius had learned the right tone of groveling to please this tyrant. "Oh, be not offended, great one. I only seek your pleasure."

"Then seek this Tal!" Rafar growled. He released Lucius and turned to all the other demons present. "All of you, seek this Tal! I want him in my hands to shred him at my pleasure. This battle could be settled easily between the two of us. Find him! Bring me word!"

Lucius tried to hide his words behind a whimpering tone, but they were specially selected for another purpose. "Indeed we shall, great one! But surely this Tal must be a formidable foe to have routed you at the fall of Babylon! Whatever will you do, should we find him? Will you dare to assail him again?"

Rafar grinned, his fangs shining. "You will see what your Ba-al can do!"

"And may we not see what this *Tal* can do!"

Rafar drew close to Lucius and stared him down with fiery yellow orbs. "When I have vanquished this Tal and hurled his little pieces across the skies as my victory banner, I will most certainly give you your chance to better me. I will relish every moment of it."

Rafar turned away, and for an instant the whole room was filled with his black wings before he shot upward through the building and into the sky.

For hours afterwards as angels all over Ashton watched from their hiding places, the Ba-al flew slowly over the town like a sinister vulture, his sword visible and challenging. Up, down, back and forth he flew, weaving in among the downtown buildings, then soaring high above the town in graceful arcs.

Down below, through the window of an obscure store basement, Scion watched as Rafar passed overhead again. He turned to his captain, who sat nearby on some appliance crates with Guilo, Triskal, and Mota. Triskal, with the help of others, was getting himself patched up and back together again.

"I don't understand," said Scion. "What's he think he's doin'?"

Tal looked up from Triskal's wounds and said matter-of-factly, "He's trying to draw me out."

Mota added, "He wants the captain. Apparently he has offered great honors to whatever demon can find Captain Tal and report his whereabouts."

Guilo said gruffly, "The devils are crawling all over the church with no other aim. It was the first place they looked."

Tal anticipated Scion's next question and answered it. "Signa and the others are still there at the church. We've tried to keep our guard there looking as it usually does."

Scion watched Rafar circle over the far side of the town and come back for another pass. "I'd have trouble bein' taunted by such as *him!*"

Tal spoke the truth, without shame. "If I were to meet him now I would most certainly lose, and he knows it. Our prayer cover is insufficient—while he has all the backing he needs."

They could all hear the rushing of Rafar's huge, leathery wings and see his shadow fall over the building for an instant as he passed overhead.

"We will all have to be very, very careful."

Hank was walking through the town again, up and down the streets and storefronts, driven by the Lord and praying with every step he took. He had a feeling that God had some particular purpose for this little jaunt, but he couldn't begin to guess what it was.

Krioni and Triskal walked on either side of him; they had gotten some extra reserves to stay at the house and watch over Mary. They were wary and alert, and Triskal, still recovering from his recent encounter with Rafar, felt especially edgy when he considered where they were leading Hank.

Hank took a turn he had never taken before, down a street he had never looked at before, and finally stopped outside a business establishment he had only heard bad stories about but could never find. He stood outside the door, staring, amazed at the number of kids going in and out like bees. Finally he stepped inside.

Krioni and Triskal tried their very best to look meek and non-threatening as they followed him.

The Cave was aptly named: the power it took to run the rows upon rows of flickering, beeping video games was made up for by the total absence of any other lights, except a little blue globe here and there in the black ceiling with an occasional watt meandering through it. There was more sound than light; heavy metal rock music pounded from speakers all around the room and clashed painfully with the myriads of electronic sounds tumbling out of the machines. One lone proprietor sat behind his little cash register in the corner, reading a girlie magazine whenever he wasn't making change for the game players. Hank had never seen so many quarters in one place.

Here were kids of all ages, with few other places to go, congregating after school and all through the weekends to hang out, hang on, play games, pair up, wander off, do drugs, do sex, do whatever. Hank knew this place was a hell hole; it wasn't the machines, or the decor, or the dimness—it was just the pungent spiritual stench of demons having their heyday. He felt sick to his stomach.

Krioni and Triskal could see hundreds of narrowing yellow eyes peering at them from the corners and dark hiding places of the room. Already they had heard several metallic rings as blades were drawn and made ready.

"Do I look harmless enough?" Triskal quietly asked.

"They do not think you are harmless anymore," Krioni said dryly.

The two looked around at all the eyes looking back at them. They smiled in a trucelike way, raising their empty hands to show no intent of hostility. The demons made no reply, but several blades could be seen glowing in the dark.

"So where is Seth?" Triskal asked.

"On his way, I'm sure."

Triskal tensed. Krioni followed his look to see a surly demon approaching them. The demon's hand was on his sword; he hadn't drawn it, but plenty of other swords were drawn behind him.

The black spirit looked the two angels up and down and hissed, "You are not welcome here! What is your business?"

Krioni answered quickly and politely, "We are watching over the man of God."

The demon took one look at Hank and lost the better portion of his cockiness. "Busche!" he exclaimed nervously while those behind him backed away. "What is he doing here?"

"That's nothing we wish to discuss," said Triskal.

The demon only sneered. "Are you Triskal?"

"I am."

The demon laughed, coughing up puffs of red and yellow. "You enjoy a fight, don't you?" Several demons joined him in laughter.

Triskal had no intention of answering. The demon had no time to demand an answer. Suddenly all the mocking spirits grew tense and agitated. Their eyes darted about, and then like a flock of timid birds they backed away and huddled in the dark corners. At the same time Krioni and Triskal could feel a new strength coursing through them. They looked down at Hank.

He was praying.

"Dear Lord," he said silently, "help us to reach these kids; help us to touch their lives."

Hank was praying at a very good time, considering the commotion just coming in the backdoor. As demons slinked away from the entrance, three of their comrades came into the building wailing, hissing, and drooling, their arms and wings over their heads. They were chased and prodded along by a very tall and quite unshakable angelic warrior.

"Well," said Triskal, "Seth has brought us Ron Forsythe and then some!"

"I was afraid of that," said Krioni.

Triskal was referring to a young man barely visible under the three demons, a very confused and disoriented victim of their destructive influence. They clung to him like leeches, causing him to stagger to and fro as they fought to avoid the goading tip of the big warrior's sword. Seth had them under very tight control, however, and he herded them right toward Hank Busche.

"Hey, Ron," said some guys at a bombardier game.

"Hey. . ." was all Ron answered, giving them a slow, heavy wave of his hand. He did not seem very happy.

Hank heard the name and saw Ron Forsythe coming, and for a moment he didn't know whether to remain where he was or get out of harm's way. Ron was a tall, spindly youth with long, unkempt hair, dirty tee shirt and jeans, and eyes that seemed to be looking into some other universe. He staggered toward Hank, looking over his shoulder as if a flock of birds was chasing him and then forward as if he were one step from a cliff. Hank, watching him approach, decided to remain right where he was. If the Lord wanted the two of them to meet, well, it was about to happen.

Then Ron stopped short and leaned against a road-racing game. This man standing in front of him looked familiar.

The demons clinging to Ron were shaking and whimpering, shooting glances toward Seth behind them and Krioni and Triskal in front of them. As for the other demons in the room, they were itching for a fight. Their yellow eyes shifted about and their red blades clattered, but something held them back—that praying man.

"Hi there," Hank said to the young man. "I'm Hank Busche."

Ron's glassy eyes widened. He stared at Hank and said with slurred speech, "I've seen you around. You're that preacher my folks keep talking about."

Hank was sure enough now to guess. "Ron? Ron Forsythe?"

Ron looked around and fidgeted as if he'd been caught doing something illegal. "Yeah . . ."

Hank stretched out his hand. "Well, God bless you, Ron, I'm glad to meet you."

The three demons snarled at that, but the three warriors shifted their weight forward just a little and kept them under control.

"Divination," said Triskal, identifying one of the demons.

Divination clung to Ron with needle-sharp talons and hissed, "And what is your business with us?"

"The lad," said Krioni.

"You can't tell us what to do!" another demon squawked, its fists stubbornly clenched.

"Rebellion?" Krioni asked.

The demon did not deny it. "He belongs to us."

The spirits in the room were getting braver, moving in closer.

"Let's get him out of here," said Krioni.

Hank touched Ron on the shoulder and said, "Can we step outside where we can visit for a minute?"

Divination and Rebellion spoke together, "What for?"

Ron protested, "What for?"

Hank just led him gently, "Come on," and they went out the backdoor. Triskal remained in the doorway, his hand on his sword.

Only the demons attached to Ron were allowed outside, constantly corralled by Seth and Krioni.

Ron sank onto a nearby bench like a rag doll in slow motion. Hank put his hand on Ron's shoulder and kept looking into those dazed eyes, wondering where to start.

"How are you feeling?" Hank finally asked.

The third demon enclosed Ron's head in his bulky, slimy arms.

The boy's head drooped toward his chest and he almost nodded off, oblivious to Hank's words.

The tip of Seth's sword got the demon's attention.

"What?" it screeched.

"Sorcery?"

The spirit laughed drunkenly. "All the time, more and more. He'll never give it up!"

Ron started to chuckle, feeling drugged and silly.

But Hank could feel something in his spirit, the same horrible presence he had felt that one very frightening night. Evil spirits? In such a young boy? *Lord, what can I do? What can I say?*

The Lord answered, and Hank knew what he had to do. "Ron," he said, whether Ron heard him or not, "can I pray for you?"

Only Ron's eyes turned to look at Hank, and Ron actually pleaded, "Yeah. Pray for me, preacher."

But the demons wanted no part of that. They all cried into Ron's brain with one voice, "No, no, no! You don't need that!"

Ron suddenly stirred, his head rocked back and forth, and he mumbled, "No, no . . . don't pray . . . I don't like that."

Now Hank wondered what Ron really wanted. Or was it even Ron who was speaking?

"I *would* like to pray for you, okay?" Hank asked, just to check.

"No, don't," Ron said, and then pleaded, "Please pray, c'mon . . ."

"Do it," Krioni prompted. "Pray!"

"No!" the demons cried. "You can't make us leave him!"

"Pray," said Krioni.

Hank knew he had better take charge of the situation and pray for this boy. He already had his hand on Ron, so he started praying very gently. "Lord Jesus, I pray for Ron; please touch him, Lord, and get through to his mind, and set him free from these spirits that are hanging on to him."

The spirits clung to Ron like spoiled brats and whined at Hank's prayer. Ron moaned and shook his head some more. He tried to get up, then he sat down again and held Hank's arm.

The Lord spoke to Hank again, and Hank had a name. "Sorcery, let go of him in the name of Jesus."

Ron squirmed on the bench and cried out as if stuck with a knife. Hank thought Ron would squeeze his arm off.

But Sorcery obeyed. He whined and hollered and spit, but he obeyed, fluttering away into the nearby trees.

Ron gave an anguished sigh and looked at Hank with eyes full of pain and desperation. "C'mon, c'mon, you're doing it!"

Hank was amazed. He took hold of Ron's hand just to assure him and kept looking into those eyes. They were clearer now. Hank could see an earnest, pleading soul looking back at him. *What next?* he asked the Lord.

The Lord answered, and Hank had another name. "Divination—"

Ron looked right at Hank, his eyes wild and his voice hoarse. "No, not me, never!"

But Hank didn't stop; he looked right into Ron's eyes and said, "Divination, in Jesus' name, let go."

"No!" Ron protested, but then said just as quickly, "Go on, Divination, get out! I don't want you with me anymore!"

Divination grudgingly obeyed. Thanks to this praying man, oppressing Ron Forsythe wasn't fun anymore.

Ron relaxed again, sniffing back some tears.

Seth poked the last little demon. "How about you, Rebellion?"

Rebellion was having trouble making up his mind.

Ron could feel it. "Spirit, please go. I've had it with you!"

Hank prayed the same thing. "Spirit, go. In the name of Jesus leave Ron alone."

Rebellion considered Ron's words, looked at Seth's sword, looked at the praying man, and finally let go.

Ron twitched as if having a terrible cramp, but then he said, "Yeah, yeah, he's out."

Seth shooed the three demons away, and they fluttered back into The Cave where they would be welcome and unhampered.

Hank hung on to Ron's hand and waited, watching and praying until he knew what else to do. This was all so incredible, so fascinating, so frightening, but so necessary. This must be the Lord's Lesson Number Two in Spiritual Combat; Hank knew he was learning something he would have to know to win this battle.

Ron was changing before Hank's very eyes, relaxing, breathing easier, his eyes returning to a normal, down-to-earth gaze.

Hank finally said a very soft "Amen," and asked, "Are you okay, Ron?"

Ron answered right away, "Yeah, I feel better. Thanks." He looked at Hank and smiled a weak, almost apologetic smile. "It's funny. No, it's neat. It was just today I was thinking I needed somebody to pray for me. I just couldn't go on with all the stuff I've been into."

Hank knew what had happened. "It was the Lord, I think, who set it up."

"Nobody's prayed for me before."

"I know your folks do all the time."

"Well, yeah, *they* do."

"And the rest of us at the church, too. We're all pulling for you."

Ron took his first clear-eyed look at Hank. "So you're my folks' pastor, huh? I thought you were older than that."

"Not too much older," Hank quipped.

"Are the other people at the church like you?"

Hank chuckled. "We're all just people; we have our good points and our bad points, but we all have Jesus, and He gives us a special love for each other."

They talked. They talked about school, the town, Ron's folks, drugs in general and particular, Hank's church, the Christians who were around, and Jesus. Ron began to notice that no matter what the subject or the issue, Hank had a way of bringing Jesus into it. Ron didn't mind. This wasn't like a phony sales pitch; Hank Busche really believed that Jesus was the answer to everything.

So, after talking about everything else with Jesus brought into it, Ron let Hank talk about Jesus, just Jesus. It wasn't dull. Hank could really get excited about Him.

16

Nathan and Armoth flew high above the beautiful summer countryside, following the speeding Buick. Things were definitely quieter out here, away from strife-torn Ashton. Still, neither one felt entirely comfortable about the two passengers in the car below; although the heavenly escorts weren't yet certain, they had a feeling that a covert plot on the part of Rafar and his guerrillas might be underway. Marshall and his good-looking young reporter were too critical a combination for those devils to pass up.

Former college dean Eldon Strachan lived on a quaint and unpretentious ten-acre farm an hour away from Ashton. He was not farming the place, just living there, and as Marshall and Bernice drove up the long gravel driveway they could tell his interests extended no further than the immediate yard of the white farmhouse. The lawn was small and manicured, the fruit trees pruned and bearing, the flower beds soft with freshly turned and weeded soil. Some chickens meandered about, pecking and scratching. A collie greeted their approach with furious barking.

"Wow, a normal human being to interview for once," said Marshall.

"That's why he moved out of Ashton," said Bernice.

Strachan stepped onto his porch as the collie ran and barked beside him.

"Hi there!" he called to Marshall and Bernice as they got out of the car. "Quiet down now, Lady," he added to the collie. Lady never obeyed such commands.

Strachan was a healthy, white-haired fellow who got plenty of exercise on this place, and showed it. He wore work clothes and still carried a pair of garden gloves in his hand.

Marshall extended his hand for a good firm handshake. So did Bernice. They exchanged introductions, and then Strachan invited them around the barking Lady and into the house.

"Doris," Strachan called, "Mr. Hogan and Miss Krueger are here."

Within minutes Doris, a sweet and rotund little grandma type, had set the coffee table with tea, coffee, rolls, and goodies, and they were having a pleasant conversation about the farm, the countryside, the weather, the neighbor's wandering cow. They all knew it was obligatory and besides, the Strachans were very pleasant people to talk and visit with.

Finally Eldon Strachan introduced the transitional sentence: "Yes, I suppose things in Ashton aren't quite this nice."

Bernice got out her notepad as Marshall said, "Yeah, and I kind of hate to drag it all out here with us."

Strachan smiled and said philosophically, "You can run but you can't hide." He looked out the window at the trees backed by endless blue sky and said, "I always have wondered if just leaving it all was the right thing. But what else could I do?"

Marshall doubled-checked his notes. "Let's see now. You told me on the telephone when you left—"

"In late June, about a year ago."

"And Ralph Kuklinski took your place."

"And he's still there, I understand."

"Yes, still there. Was he in on any of this—this 'Inner Circle' stuff? I don't know what else to call it."

Strachan thought for a moment. "I don't know for sure, but I wouldn't be surprised if he was. He really had to be one of the group to be put in as dean."

"So there really is some kind of 'in group,' so to speak?"

"Absolutely. That became pretty obvious after a while. All the regents were becoming like peas in a pod, like clones of each other. They all acted the same, talked the same . . ."

"Except for you?"

Strachan laughed a little. "I guess I just didn't fit into the club very well. As a matter of fact I became a definite outsider, even an enemy, and I think that's why they fired me."

"I suppose you're talking about that fracas over the college funds?"

"Exactly." Strachan had to resift his memory. "I never suspected anything until we started having some unexplained disbursement delays. Our bills were being paid late, our payrolls were behind. It wasn't even my job to be hounding after that sort of thing, but when I started getting some indirect complaints—you know, hearing others talking about it—I asked Baylor what the problem was. He never directly answered my questions, or at least I didn't like the sound of his answers. That's when I asked an independent accountant, a friend of a friend, to look into it and maybe do some quick scanning of what the accounting office was doing. I don't know how he ever got access to the information, but he was a clever character and he found a way."

Bernice was ready with a question. "Can we have his name?"

Strachan answered with a shrug. "Johnson. Ernie Johnson."

"How do we reach him?"

"I'm afraid he's dead."

That was a letdown. Marshall grabbed at a hope. "Did he leave you any records, anything written down?"

Strachan only shook his head. "If he did, those records were lost. Why do you think I've been sitting out here so silently? Listen, I even know Norm Mattily, the state attorney general, pretty well, and I thought of going to him and telling him what was going on. But let's face it, those big folks at the top don't give you the time of day unless you have some really substantial proof. It's tough to get the authorities to stick their necks out. They just won't do it."

"All right . . . so what was it that Ernie Johnson found?"

"He came back horrified. According to his findings, monies from grants and tuitions were being reinvested at an alarming rate, but apparently there were no dividends or returns of any kind from whatever the investments were, as if the money had been poured down a bottomless well somewhere. The figures had been juggled to cover it up, accounts payable had been staggered so that other accounts could be dipped into to pay those due . . . it was just one colossal mess."

"A mess worth millions?"

"At least. The college money had been leaking out in large amounts for years, with no clues as to where it was going. Somewhere out there was a money-hungry monster gobbling up all the college's assets."

"And that's when you called for the audit."

"And Eugene Baylor hit the ceiling. The whole thing went from professional to personal in an instant and we became intense enemies. And that convinced me all the more that the college was in big trouble and that Baylor had a lot to do with it. But of course there's nothing Baylor does that all the others don't know about. I'm sure they're all aware of the problem, and it's my feeling that their unanimous vote for my resignation was a common conspiracy."

"But to what end?" asked Bernice. "Why would they want to undermine the college's financial base?"

Strachan could only shake his head. "I don't know *what* they're trying to do, but unless there's something else hidden somewhere to explain where these funds are going and how the losses are going to be made up, that college is most certainly headed for bankruptcy. Kuklinski must know that. As far as I know, he was in total agreement with the financial policies and with my resignation."

Marshall flipped to some other notes. "So just how does our kind Professor Langstrat figure into all this?"

Strachan had to chuckle. "Ah, the dear professor . . ." He considered the question for a moment. "She was always a definite influence and mentor, to be sure, but . . . I don't think she's the ultimate center of things. It seemed to me that she had a lot to do with controlling the group while someone higher up had a lot to do with controlling her. I think—I think she's answering to someone, some unseen authority."

"But you've no idea who?"

Strachan shook his head.

"So what else do you know about her?"

Strachan searched his memory. "A graduate of UCLA . . . she taught at other universities before she came to Whitmore. She's been on the faculty for at least six years. I do recall that she always had a strong interest in Eastern philosophy and occultism. She was once involved in some kind of neo-pagan religious group in California. But you know, I never realized until maybe three years ago that she was openly declaring her beliefs to her classes, and I was rather surprised to find that her teachings had aroused a lot of interest. Her beliefs and practices were not only spreading among the students, but also among the faculty."

"Who on the faculty?" Marshall asked.

Strachan shook his head in disgust. "It started years before I was aware of it, in the Psychology Department, among Langstrat's associates. Margaret Islander—you may know of her—"

"I believe my friend Ruth Williams does," said Bernice.

"I think she was the first to be initiated into Langstrat's group, but she'd always had an interest in psychics like Edgar Cayce, so she was a natural."

"Anyone else?" Marshall prodded.

Strachan pulled out a hastily scrawled list and let Marshall have a look at it. "I've gone over and over this in the months since I left. Here. Here's a list of most of the Psychology Department . . ." He pointed out a few names. "Trevor Corcoran is new on the staff this year. He even studied in India before he came here to teach. Juanita Janke replaced Kevin Ford . . . well, as a matter of fact, a lot of people were replaced over the past few years. We had a lot of turnover."

Marshall noted another portion of the list. "So who are these people?"

"The Humanities Department, and then the Philosophy Department, and these down here are in the biology and pre-med programs. A lot of them are new as well. We had a lot of turnover."

"That's the second time you've said that," Bernice observed.

Strachan stared at her. "What are you thinking?"

Bernice took the list from Marshall and placed it in front of Strachan again. "Well, tell us now. How many of these people have come on staff during the last six years, during the time Langstrat's been there?"

Strachan took a second, more critical look at the list. "Jones . . . Conrad . . . Witherspoon . . . Epps . . ." An overwhelming percentage of the names were those of new faculty members, who had replaced former members who had resigned or whose contracts had simply not been renewed. "Well, isn't that odd?"

"I would say that's odd," Bernice agreed.

Strachan was visibly shaken. "All the turnover . . . I was getting very concerned about it, but I never even considered . . . This would explain a lot of things. I knew there was some kind of common interest spreading among all these people; they all seemed to have a very unique and undefinable rapport with each other—their own lingo, their own inside secrets, their own ideas of reality—and it seemed no one person could do anything without everyone else knowing about it. I thought it was a fad, a sociological phase—" He looked up from the list with a new awareness in his eyes. "So it was more than that. Our campus was invaded and our faculty displaced by a—a madness!"

For just a moment Marshall had a flashback, a quick, fleeting memory of his daughter Sandy saying, "People around here are starting to act weird. I think we're being invaded by aliens." That memory was immediately followed by Kate's voice over the phone: "I'm concerned about Sandy . . . she just isn't the same old Sandy anymore . . ."

Marshall snapped out of it and began leafing through his materials. He finally found the old list Bernice had gotten from Albert Darr. "All right, what about these classes Langstrat was teaching: 'Introduction to God and Goddess Consciousness and the Craft . . . The Sacred Medicine Wheel . . . Spells and Rituals . . . Pathways to Your Inner Light, Meet Your Own Spiritual Guides'?"

Strachan nodded with recognition. "It all began as part of an alternative education program, purely a voluntary thing for any interested students, paid for by special tuitions. I just thought it was a study of folklore, myths, traditions—"

"But I guess they were taking this stuff pretty seriously."

"Ehh, so it seems, and now we have a great percentage of the staff and the student body . . . bewitched."

"Including the regents?"

Strachan did some fresh thinking. "Get ready for this. I think the same kind of upheaval happened on the board of regents as well. There are twelve regent positions altogether, and five, I think, have been suddenly and abruptly replaced in the last year and a half. How else could the vote for my resignation be unanimous? I used to have some very loyal friends on that board."

"What are their names, and where have they gone?"

Bernice started writing the names down as Strachan recalled them, along with any other information he could provide about each person. Jake Abernathy had died, Morris James had gone bankrupt in a business and moved to another job, Fred Ainsworth, George Olson, and Rita Jacobson had all left Ashton with no word as to where they had gone.

"And that," said Strachan, "takes care of just about everyone. There are none left but initiates into this strange mystical group."

"Including Kuklinski, the new dean," Bernice added.

"And Dwight Brandon, the owner of the land."

"And what about Ted Harmel?" Marshall asked.

Strachan tightened his lips, looked at the floor, and sighed. "Yes. He did try to back out, but by then they'd already entrusted too much information to him. When they found they couldn't control him anymore—he has myself and our friendship to blame for that—they arranged to defame him and chase him out of town with that ridiculous scandal."

"Hmmmm," said Bernice. "A conflict of interest."

"Of course. He kept telling me it was a fascinating new science of the human mind, and he claimed he was only after a story, but he just kept getting more and more wrapped up in it, and they wooed him, I'm sure. I heard him say that they had promised him great success with his newspaper because he had aligned himself with them . . ."

Marshall had another flashback: he saw Brummel looking at him with those numbing gray eyes, saying sweetly, "Marshall, we'd like to know that you'll be standing with us . . ."

Strachan was still talking.

Marshall woke up and said, "Uh, excuse me, what was that again?"

"Oh," said Strachan, "I was just saying that Ted became torn between two loyalties: first and foremost he was loyal to the truth and to his friends, and that included me. His other loyalty was to the Langstrat group and their philosophies and practices. I guess he thought that the truth was inviolable and the press would always be free, but, whatever the reason, he began to print stories about the financial problems. And that was definitely stepping over the line as far as the regents were concerned."

"Yes," Bernice recalled. "Now I remember him saying they were trying to control him and dictate what he printed. He was really mad about it."

"Well of course," said Strachan, "when it came down to principles, regardless of what so-called science or metaphysical philosophies he may have been interested in, Ted was still a newspaperman and would not be intimidated." Strachan sighed and looked at the floor. "So, I'm afraid he got caught in the crossfire of my battle with the college regents. Consequently we both lost our positions, our good standing in the community, everything. I guess you could say I was well content to leave it all behind. It was impossible to fight it."

Marshall disliked that kind of talk. "Are they—is this thing— really that strong?"

Strachan was deadly serious. "I don't think I ever realized how vast and strong it really was, and I guess I'm still finding out. Mr. Hogan, I have no idea what the final goal of these people is, but I'm beginning to see that nothing standing in their way can escape being stamped out, eliminated. Even as we sit here I can look back over the years, and, not even considering our faculty turnover, I'm frightened to think of how many other people around Ashton have just dropped out of sight."

Joe, the supermarket owner, Marshall thought. And what about Edie?

Strachan was looking a little pale now, and asked with obvious worry in his voice, "Just what do you people intend to do with this information?"

Marshall had to be honest. "I don't know yet. There are too many missing pieces, too many assumptions. I don't have anything I can print."

"You do remember what happened to Ted? You are keeping that in mind?"

Marshall didn't want to think about that. He wanted to find out something else. "Ted wouldn't talk to me."

"He's scared."

"Scared of what?"

"Of *them,* of the system that destroyed him. He knows more about their weird goings-on than I do; he knows enough to be a lot more afraid than I am, and I believe his fears are justified. I do believe there's a genuine danger here."

"Well, does he ever talk to you?"

"Sure, about anything besides what you're after."

"But the two of you are in touch?"

"Yes. We fish, we hunt, we meet for lunch. He isn't far from here."

"Could you call him?"

"You mean, call him and put in a plug for you?"

"That's exactly what I mean."

Strachan answered cautiously, "Hey, he may not want to talk, and I can't push him."

"But will you just call him, see if he'll talk to me one more time?"

"I'll . . . I'll think about it, but that's all I can promise you."

"I'd appreciate even that."

"But, Mr. Hogan. . . ." Strachan reached over and grabbed Marshall's arm. He looked at both Marshall and Bernice and said very quietly, "You people watch out for yourselves. You're not invincible. None of the rest of us were, and I believe it's possible to lose everything if you make just one wrong move or take just one wrong step. Please, *please* be sure at every moment you know exactly what you're doing."

At the *Clarion,* Tom, the paste-up man, was getting the usual ads, fillers, and completed galleys into the Tuesday edition when the bell over the front door jingled. He had better things to do than deal with callers, but with Hogan and Bernice out on their mysterious mission of intrigue, he was the only remaining fort-holder-downer. Boy, he wished Edie had stuck around. The paper got to be more of a shambles every day and, whatever wild goose chase Hogan and Bernice were on, it took their attention away from the many tasks piling up around the place.

"Hello?" called a woman's sweet voice.

Tom grabbed a shop cloth to wipe his hands and hollered back, "Hold on, I'm coming."

He scurried up the narrow passage to the front office and saw a very attractive and neatly dressed young woman standing at the counter. She smiled when she saw him. Ah yes, thought Tom, if I were only young again.

"Hello there," he said, still wiping his hands on the shop cloth. "What can I do for you?"

The young lady said, "I read your ad for a secretary and general office manager. I've come to apply."

It had to be an angel, Tom thought. "Boy, if you can cut it, let me tell you, there's sure a job to be had around here!"

"Well, I'm ready to start," she said with a bright smile.

Tom made sure his hand was clean enough and then extended it. "Tom McBride, paste-up man and general worrier."

She shook his hand firmly and said her name, "Carmen."

"Pleased to meet you, Carmen. Uh . . . Carmen who?"

She laughed at her lapse of mind and said, "Oh, Carmen Fraser. I get so used to just going by my first name."

Tom swung the little gate open at the end of the counter and Carmen followed him into the office area.

"Let me show you what the devil's going on here," he said.

17

In the faraway secluded valley, in the little cluster of unlabeled buildings hidden by rocky crags, a hurried transition was in full swing.

In the office complex, sitting at desks and worktables, scurrying up and down the aisles, dashing in and out the doors, running up and down the stairways, over two hundred people of all ages, descriptions, and nationalities were typing letters, going through files, checking records, balancing accounts, chattering on telephones in different languages. Maintenance people in blue coveralls brought in large stacks of boxes and crates on handtrucks, and the office workers meticulously began to fill the boxes with the contents of the file cabinets, with any office paraphernalia not immediately needed, with other books and records.

Outside, trucks were being loaded with the crates as more maintenance people driving little grounds tractors went about the complex, shutting down various hookups and utilities and boarding up any buildings no longer occupied.

Nearby, on the porch of the big stone house at the edge of the grounds, a woman stood watching. She was tall and slender, with long, jet-black hair; she wore black, loose-fitting clothes, and she clutched her shoulder bag close to her side with pale, trembling hands. She looked this way and that, evidently trying to relax herself. She took a few deep breaths. She reached into her bag and brought out a pair of dark sunglasses with which she covered her eyes. Then she stepped down from the porch and started across the plaza toward the office building.

Her steps were firm and deliberate, her eyes remained straight ahead. A few office personnel passed and saluted her, pressing their palms together in front of their chins and bowing slightly. She nodded at them and kept walking.

The office staff saluted her in the same way as she entered and she smiled at them, not speaking a word. Upon receiving her smile, they returned to their feverish work. The office manager, a well-dressed woman with tightly pinned hair, stepped up, gave a slight bow and said, "Good morning. What does the Maidservant require?"

The Maidservant smiled and said, "I'd like to run off some copies."

"I can do it immediately."

"Thank you. I'd like to run them off myself."

"Certainly. I'll warm up the machine for you."

The woman scurried toward a small room off to the side, and the Maidservant followed. Several accountants and filing clerks, some oriental, some East Indian, some European, bowed as she passed and then went back to their consultations with each other.

The office manager had the copier ready in less than a minute.

"Thank you, you may go now," said the Maidservant.

"Certainly," answered the woman. "I am at your disposal if you have any problems or questions."

"Thank you."

The manager left and the Maidservant closed the door behind her, shutting out the rest of the office and any intrusions. Then, quickly, the Maidservant reached into her bag and brought out a small book. She leafed through it, skimming over the handwritten pages until she found what she was looking for. Then, laying the book open and face down on the copier, she started pressing the buttons and copying page after page.

Forty pages later she turned off the machine, folded the copies neatly, and placed them in a compartment of her bag, along with the little book. She left the office directly and went back to the big stone house.

The house was majestic in its size and decor, with a large stone hearth and soaring, rough-beamed ceilings. The Maidservant hurried up the thickly-carpeted staircase to her bedroom and closed the door behind her.

Placing the little book on her stately antique vanity, she opened a drawer and pulled out some brown wrapping paper and twine. The paper already had a name written on it, the addressee: Alexander M. Kaseph. The return address included the name J. Langstrat. She quickly rewrapped the book as if it had never been opened, then bound the package with string.

Elsewhere in the house, in a very large office, a middle-aged, roundly built man dressed in loose trousers and tunic sat Indian fashion on a large cushion. His eyes were closed, his breathing deep. The fine furnishings of a man of great prestige and power surrounded him: souvenirs from around the world, such as swords, war clubs, African artifacts, religious relics, and several rather grotesque idols of the East; a battleship of a desk with built-in computer console, multilined telephone, and an intercom; a long, deep-cushioned couch with matching hand-carved oak chairs and coffee table; hunting trophies of bear, elk, moose, and lion.

Without hearing a knock, the man spoke loftily. "Come in, Susan."

The big oak door opened silently and the Maidservant entered, carrying the brown paper package.

Without opening his eyes, the man said, "Put it on my desk."

The Maidservant did so, and the man began to stir from his motionless position, opening his eyes and stretching his arms as if awakening from sleep.

"So you finally found it," he said with a teasing smile.

"It was there all the time. With all the packing and rearranging it got shoved over in a corner."

The man rose from his cushion, stretched his legs, and walked a few laps around the office. "I really don't know what it is," he said as if answering a question.

"I didn't wonder—" said the Maidservant.

He smiled condescendingly and said, "Oh, maybe not, but it felt like you did." He went up behind her. and placed his hands on her shoulders, speaking in her ear. "Sometimes I can read you so very well, and sometimes you drift away. You've been feeling so troubled lately. Why?"

"Oh, all the moving, I guess, the upheaval."

He put his arms around her waist and held her close as he said, "Don't let it bother you. We're going to a far better place. I have a house all picked out. You'll love it."

"I grew up in that town, you know."

"No. No, not really. It won't be the same town at all, not as you remember it. It will be better. But you don't believe that, do you?"

"As I said, I grew up in Ashton—"

"And all you wanted was to get out of there!"

"So you can understand why my feelings are confused."

He twirled her around and laughed playfully as he looked into her eyes. "Yes, I know! On the one hand, you have no desire at all for the town, and on the other hand, you sneak off to attend the carnival."

She blushed a little and looked at the floor. "I was searching for something from my past, something from which to envision my future."

He held her hand and said, "There is no past. You should have stayed with me. I hold the answers for you now."

"Yes, I can see that. I couldn't before."

He laughed and went behind his desk. "Well, good, good. We don't need any more meetings held in hiding places behind a noisy carnival. You should have seen how embarrassed our friends were to have to meet there."

"But why did you even have to come looking for me? Why did you have to drag them along?"

He sat at the desk and began handling a wicked-looking ceremonial knife with a golden handle and razor-sharp blade.

Looking over the edge of the blade at her, he said, "Because, dear Maidservant, I do not trust you. I love you, I am one in essence with you, but . . ." He held the knife up to the level of his eye and peered down the edge of the blade at her, his eyes as sharply cutting as the knife. "I do not trust you. You are a woman given to many conflicting passions."

"I cannot harm the Plan. I am only one person among myriads."

He rose and came around to the side of the desk where other knives were stuck into the carved head of some pagan idol.

"You, dear Susan, share my life, my secrets, my purposes. I have to protect my interests."

With that, he dropped the knife, point first, and it thudded into the idol's head.

She smiled in acquiescence and sidled up to him, giving him an alluring kiss. "I am, and will always be, yours," she said.

He gave her a sly smile, and the cutting look never left his eyes as he answered, "Yes. Of course you are."

High above the valley, amid the rocks and crevices of the mountaintops, two figures concealed themselves. One, the silver-haired man who had been here before, continually watched the activity below. He was stately and mighty, his piercing eyes full of wisdom.

The other was Tal, the Captain of the Host.

"This is what you're looking for," said the silver-haired man. "Rafar had business there only days ago."

Tal peered down into the valley. The swarms of black demons were too numerous to even estimate.

"The Strongman?" he asked.

"Undoubtedly, with a cloud of guards and warriors all around him. We've been unable to penetrate it yet."

"And she's right in the middle of it!"

"The Spirit has been steadily opening her eyes and calling her. She is close to the Strongman—dangerously close. The prayers of the Remnant have placed a blindness and stupor on the demonic hosts all around her. At present it will buy you time, but little more."

Tal grimaced. "My general, it will take more than a stupor for us to break through to her. We can barely hold the town of Ashton, much less take on the Strongman directly."

"And you can only expect this buildup to worsen. Their numbers increase tenfold each day."

"Yes, they are preparing, that's for certain."

"But, at the same time, her conflicts continue to grow. Soon she won't be able to conceal her true feelings and intentions from her lord down there. Tal, she has learned of the suicide."

Tal looked directly at the general. "I understand she and Patricia were very close."

The general nodded. "It jolted her, which made her more receptive. But her time of safety is limited. Here's your next step. The Universal Consciousness Society is holding a special fund-raising and promotional dinner in New York for its many cohorts and members in the United Nations. Kaseph can't attend because of his present activities here. He will send Susan, however, to represent him. She'll be closely escorted, but this will be the one time she'll be out from under the Strongman's demonic cover. The Spirit knows she plans to get away and make contact with one remaining friend on the outside, who can in turn contact your newspaperman. She'll take that chance, Tal. You must arrange for her to succeed."

Tal's first response was, "Is there prayer cover in New York?"

"You will have it."

Tal looked at the swarms below. "And they must not find out . . ."

"No. They must not suspect anything has happened until you can get Susan out for good. They would destroy her if they knew."

"And who is the friend?"

"His name is Kevin Weed, a former classmate and boyfriend."

"To work, then. I have some more prayer to gather in."

"Godspeed, dear captain!"

Tal climbed behind some large rocks for concealment before he unfurled his wings. Then, with the silence and grace of a drifting cloud, he floated up over the mountaintop. Once he had cleared the summit and could no longer be seen by any of the swarms in the valley, his wings snapped into a rushing pattern and he shot forward like a bullet, trailing a brilliant arc of light across the sky and over the horizon.

Marshall and Bernice drove through the forested countryside in the big brown Buick, talking about themselves, their pasts, their families, and anything else that came to mind. They were getting tired of only talking about business anyway, and finding it enjoyable to share each other's company.

"I grew up Presbyterian," said Marshall. "Now I don't know what I am."

"My folks were Episcopalian," said Bernice. "I don't think I was ever anything. They dragged me along to church every Sunday, and I couldn't wait to get out of there."

"I didn't mind it that much. I had a good Sunday school teacher."

"Yeah, maybe that's where I missed out. I never went to Sunday school."

"Aw, I think a kid needs to know something about God."

"What if God doesn't exist?"

"See what I mean? You never went to Sunday school!"

The Buick came to a crossroads, and a sign indicated the way back to Ashton was to the left. Marshall turned left.

Bernice answered one of Hogan's questions. "Nope, no parents alive anymore. Dad died in '76 and Mom died . . . let's see, two years ago."

"That's too bad."

"And then I lost my only sibling, Patricia."

"Is that right! Boy, I'm sorry."

"It's a lonely world out there sometimes . . ."

"Yeah, I suppose . . . and I wonder who there is to meet in Ashton?"

She only looked at him and said, "I'm not hunting, Marshall."

About a mile ahead of them was a wide spot in the road referred to as Baker, a little town indicated by the smallest possible dot on the map. It was one of those typical roadsides where truckers and four-wheeling hunters drop in for black coffee and cold eggs. Blink just once and you'd miss it.

Above the Buick, whisking just over the tops of the trees, Nathan and Armoth kept a careful eye on the vehicle, their wings rushing in an even pattern and their bodies trailing two streaks of diamond-studded light.

"So this is where it all begins," said Nathan with a playful tone.

"And you have been chosen to strike the blow," responded Armoth.

Nathan smiled. "Child's play."

Armoth teased him a little. "I'm sure Tal could pick someone else who would like the honor—"

Nathan drew his sword, and it flashed like a lightning bolt. "Oh no, dear Armoth! I've waited long enough. I'll take it."

Nathan banked away from Armoth, dropped down over the roadway as it wound through the tall trees, and began to keep pace with the car, flying lazily about thirty feet above it. He kept his eye on the little town of Baker now approaching, made a quick judgment as to the coasting distance the car could travel, and then, at the right moment, he hurled his sword like a fiery spear downward. The sword traveled a perfect trajectory and shot through the hood of the car.

The engine died.

"Nuts!" said Marshall, shifting quickly into neutral.

"What's wrong?" Bernice asked.

"Something's broke."

Marshall tried to restart the engine as the car continued to coast along. No response.

"Probably electrical . . ." he muttered.

"Better pull over at that station."

"Yeah, I know, I know."

The Buick limped into the little filling station in Baker and rolled to a stop right at the front door. Marshall opened the hood.

"I'm going to excuse myself," said Bernice.

"Go for me too, will you?" Marshall said crossly, looking here and there around the engine compartment.

Bernice went to the next little building, The Evergreen Tavern. Age and settling were slowly swallowing it from the bottom up, and one end was badly sunken, the paint on the front door was peeling. The neon beer logo in the window still worked, though, and the juke box inside was twanging some country hit.

Bernice pushed the door open—the bottom scraped a worn arc across the linoleum—and went inside, twisting her nose a little at the blue cigarette smoke that had replaced the air. Just a few men sat in the establishment, probably the first of the logging crews getting off work. They were talking loudly, swapping stories, cussing it up. Bernice looked directly toward the back of the room, trying to find the little Men and Women signs. Yes, there was Restrooms.

One of the men at a nearby table said, "Hey, baby, how's it goin'?"

Bernice wasn't going to even look in his direction, but did just happen to give him a glance and an appropriately dirty look. A little too *much* local color in this place, she thought.

She slowed her walk. Her eyes locked on him. He looked back at her with a boozy, lazy-eyed smile on his bearded face.

Another man said, "Looks like you got her attention, buddy."

Bernice kept looking at him. She approached the table and took an even closer look. The hair was long and tangled, bound into a ponytail with a rubber band. The eyes were glassy and now heavily lined. But she knew this man.

The man's friend said, "Good evening, ma'am. Don't let him bother you, he's just having a good time, right, Weed?"

"Weed?" Bernice asked. "Kevin Weed?"

Kevin Weed just looked up at her, enjoying the view and saying little. Finally he said, "Can I buy you a beer?"

Bernice came closer to him, made sure he could clearly see her face. "Do you remember me? Bernice Krueger?" Weed only looked puzzled. "Do you remember Pat Krueger?"

A light slowly began to dawn in Weed's face. "Pat Krueger. . . ? Who are you?"

"I'm Bernice, Pat's sister. Do you remember me? We met a couple of times. You and Pat's roommate were going together."

Weed brightened and smiled, and then he cursed and excused himself. "Bernice Krueger! Pat's sister!" He cursed again, and excused himself again. "What're you doin' in this place?"

"Just passing through. And I will take a small Coke, thank you."

Weed smiled and looked at his friends. Their eyes and mouths were getting wide, and they were starting to laugh.

Weed said with a leer, "I think it's time you boys found another table . . ."

They gathered up their hard hats and lunch boxes and laughed. "Yeah, you got it, Weed."

"Dan," Weed hollered, "a small Coke for the lady here."

Dan had to stare for a moment at the nice girl who had come into a place like his. He got the Coke and brought it to her.

"So what have you been doing?" Weed asked her.

Bernice had her pen and notebook out. She told him a little about what she had been doing and what she was doing now. Then she said, "I haven't seen you since before Pat's death."

"Hey, I'm really sorry about that."

"Kevin, can you tell me anything about it? What do you know?"

"Nothing much . . . no more than what I read in the papers."

"What about Pat's roommate? Do you hear from her anymore?" Bernice noticed Weed's eyes widen and his mouth drop open the moment she mentioned the girl.

"Man, this world is getting smaller all the time!" he said.

"You saw her?" Bernice couldn't believe her good fortune.

"Well, yeah, sort of."

"When?" Bernice insisted.

"But just for a little while."

"Where? When?" Bernice was having a very difficult time holding herself back.

"I saw her at the carnival."

"In Ashton?"

"Yeah, yeah, in Ashton. I just ran into her. She called my name, and I turned around and there she was."

"What did she say? Did she say where she's living now?"

Weed fidgeted a little. "Man, I don't know. I don't really care. She dumped me, you know, ran off with that other goon. She was even with him that night."

"What was her name again?"

"Susan. Susan Jacobson. She's a real heartbreaker, she is."

"Do you have any idea—did she give you any idea of where I might find her? I have to talk to her about Pat. She might know something."

"Man, I don't know. She didn't talk to me for very long at all. She was in a hurry, had to meet her new boyfriend or something. She wanted my phone number, that was about it."

Bernice couldn't let go of her hope. Not yet. "Are you sure she didn't give you some idea of where she's living now, or any way to get in touch with her?" Weed shrugged drunkenly. "Kevin, I've been trying to find her for ages! I've got to talk to her!"

Weed was bitter. "Talk to her boyfriend, that fat little geezer with all the bucks!"

No, no, that wasn't really a legitimate hunch that ran through Bernice's mind. Or was it?

"Kevin," she said, "what did Susan look like that night?"

He was staring off into space, like a drunken and jilted lover. "Foxy," he said. "Long, black hair, black dress, sexy shades."

Bernice felt her stomach tighten into a knot as she said, "And what about her boyfriend? Did you see him?"

"Yeah, later. Susan acted like she didn't even know me when he came into the picture."

"Well, what did he look like?"

"Like some wimp from Fat City. It had to have been his money, that's why Susan latched on to him."

Bernice picked up her pen in a shaking hand. "What's your phone number?"

He gave it to her.

"Address?"

He mumbled that off too.

"Now, you say she asked you for your phone number?"

"Yeah, I don't know why. Maybe things aren't working out with loverboy."

"Did you give it to her?"

"Yeah. Maybe I'm a sucker, but yeah, I did."

"So she just might be calling you."

He shrugged.

"Kevin . . ." Bernice gave him one of her cards. "Listen carefully to me. Are you listening?"

He looked at her and said yes.

"If she calls, if you hear anything from her at all, please give her my name and number and tell her I want to talk to her. Get *her* number so I can call *her*. Will you do that?"

He took the card and nodded. "Yeah, sure."

She finished her Coke and prepared to leave. He looked at her with his dull, glassy eyes.

"Hey, you doin' anything tonight?"

"If you hear from Susan, call me. We'll have plenty to talk about then."

He looked at her card again. "Yeah, sure."

A few moments later Bernice was back at the filling station just in time to see Marshall start the car up. The old and bent station owner was looking at the engine and shaking his head.

"Hey, that did it!" Marshall shouted from behind the wheel.

"Heck, I didn't do a thing," said the old man.

High above the filling station, Nathan soared skyward to join Armoth, his sword retrieved. "Done," he said.

"And now we'll see how the captain and Guilo succeed in New York."

The Buick started out again, and Nathan and Armoth followed behind and above it like two kites on strings.

18

H ank started the Sunday morning service with a good rousing song, one Mary performed on the piano particularly well. Both were in good spirits and feeling encouraged; in spite of the approaching sounds of battle, they sensed that God in His infinite wisdom was indeed working out a very mighty and effective plan for reestablishing his kingdom in the town of Ashton. Victories large and small were in the making, and Hank knew it had to be the hand of God.

For one thing, this morning he would be ministering to an almost entirely new congregation; at least it sure felt that way. Many of the old dissenters had dropped out of the church and taken their embittering presence with them, and the whole mood and spirit of the place had risen several notches because of their absence. Sure, Alf Brummel, Gordon Mayer, and Sam Turner still hovered around, brooding together like some kind of hit squad, but none of them were in the service this morning and a lot of new, fresh faces were. The Forsythes' example had been followed by their numerous friends and acquaintances, some married couples, some singles, and some students. Grandma Duster was there, as strong and healthy as ever and ready for a spiritual fight; John and Patty Coleman were back, and John couldn't keep from grinning in his joy and excitement.

Of the rest, Hank had only met one. Next to Andy and June, looking a little sheepish, sat Ron Forsythe, along with his girlfriend, a short, very made-up sophomore. Hank had to choke down some very strong emotion when he saw the Forsythes enter accompanied by their son: it was a miracle, a genuine act of grace by the living God. He would have shouted hallelujah right there, but he didn't want to scare the young fellow away; this could be one of those kid-gloves cases.

After the first song, Hank figured he might as well address the situation before him.

"Well," he said informally, "I don't know whether to call all you people visitors or refugees or what."

They all laughed and exchanged glances.

Hank continued, "Why don't we just take a moment here to introduce ourselves? I guess you probably know who I am; I'm Hank Busche, the pastor, and this flower sitting at the piano is my wife, Mary." Mary stood quickly, smiled meekly, then sat down again. "Why don't we go around the room here and tell everybody who we are . . ."

And the first roll call of the Remnant took place as the angels and demons watched: Krioni and Triskal stood at their posts right beside Hank and Mary while Signa and his squad, now numbering ten, kept a hedge about the building.

Again Lucius had carried on a bitter argument with Signa, trying to gain admittance. But he knew better than to push the matter too far—Hank Busche was bad enough, but now he had a whole church full of praying saints. The heavenly warriors were enjoying their first real advantage. Lucius finally ordered his demons to remain outside and hear what they could.

The only demons that had managed to enter had come in with their human hosts, and now they sat here and there in the congregation, brooding over this horrible development. Scion stood near the back like a hen watching over her brood, and Seth stayed near the Forsythes and the group with them.

There was power in this place today, and everyone could feel it grow as each new person stood and introduced himself. To Hank it seemed just like the gathering of a special army.

"Ralph Metzer, sophomore at Whitmore . . ."

"Judy Kemp, sophomore at Whitmore . . ."

"Greg and Eva Smith, friends of the Forsythes."

"Bill and Betty Jones. We run the Whatnot Shop over on Eighth Street . . ."

"Mike Stewart. I live with the Joneses, and I work out at the mill."

"Cal and Ginger Barton. We're still new in town."

"Cecil and Miriam Cooper, and we're sure glad to see you all here . . ."

"Ben Squires. I'm the guy who brings you your mail if you live on the west side . . ."

"Tom Harris, and this is my wife Mabel. Welcome to all of you and praise the Lord!"

"Clint Neal—I work at the filling station."

"Greg and Nancy Jenning. I teach and she's a writer."

"Andy Forsythe, and praise the Lord!"

"June Forsythe, and amen to that."

Ron stood to his feet, put his hands in his pockets, and looked at the floor a lot as he said, "I'm—I'm Ron Forsythe, and this here is Cynthia, and . . . I met the pastor at The Cave, and . . ." His voice cracked with emotion. "I just want to thank you people for praying for me and for caring." He stood there for a moment, looking at the floor while tears welled up in his eyes.

June stood beside him and addressed the group on his behalf. "Ron wants you all to know that he and Cynthia gave their hearts to Jesus last night."

Everyone smiled with delight and murmured encouragement, and that loosened Ron up enough to say, "Yeah, and we flushed all our drugs down the toilet!"

That brought down the house.

With increased joy and fervor, the roll call continued.

Outside, the demons listened with great alarm and hissed exclamations of forboding.

"Rafar must know of this!" one said.

Lucius, his wings half unfurled just to keep his fussing ranks from pestering him, stood still and brooded.

One little demon hovered about his head and cried out, "What shall we do, Master Lucius? Shall we find Rafar?"

"Back to whatever you were doing!" he hissed back. "Let *me* see to informing Ba-al Rafar myself!"

They gathered around him, wanting to hear his next order. Lately it seemed he had spoken so very little.

"What are you all staring at?" he shrieked. "Go, do mischief! Let me worry about these petty little saints!"

They flurried away in all directions, and Lucius stood in his place outside the church window.

Tell Rafar indeed! Let Rafar humble himself enough to *ask*. Lucius would not be his lackey.

In this part of New York City, things were tailored for the elite and discerning; the shops, boutiques, and restaurants were the exclusive kind, the hotels quite lavish. Carefully groomed flowering trees grew in round stucco planters along the sidewalks, and maintenance workers kept the streets and walks spotless.

Among the hurried shoppers and browsers crowding the district were two very large men in tan tunics, strolling the sidewalk and looking here and there.

"The Gibson Hotel," Tal read on the front of an old, distinguished stone building that towered thirty stories above them.

"I see no activity," said Guilo.

"It's early yet. They'll be along. Let's be quick about this."

The two of them slipped through the big front doors and into the hotel lobby. People passed on all sides of them, and sometimes right through them, but that, of course, was of no consequence. Within moments they had checked the schedule at the desk for the hotel's banquet facilities and verified that the Grand Ballroom was reserved that night for the Universal Consciousness Society.

"The general's information was right," Tal commented with pleasure.

They hurried down a long, thickly-carpeted hallway past a barbershop, a beauty salon, a shoeshine nook, and a gift shop, and at length came to two huge oak doors with lavishly wrought brass handles. They passed through and found themselves in the Grand Ballroom, now filled with dining tables adorned with crystal place settings and white linen tablecloths. One lone, long-stemmed rose in a bud vase stood on every table. The hotel caterers were hurriedly making final preparations, setting out the artfully folded napkins and wine glasses. Tal checked the place cards at the head table. One, towards the end, said "Kaseph, Omni Corporation."

They went through a nearby exit door and looked right and left. Down the hall, to the left and toward the back of the hotel, was the ladies' lounge. They went in, passed a few women primping at the mirrors and found what they were after: the very last stall, designated for use by the handicapped. It was built against the rear wall of the hotel, just below a window large enough for a limber human to crawl through. Tal reached up, broke the lock, and tested the window to make sure it would open and close easily. Guilo passed quickly through the wall into the alley where he found a large dumpster and, with incredible ease, moved it several feet so that it was situated below the window. He then arranged some crates and garbage cans in a very handy stair-stepped fashion against the dumpster.

Tal joined him and the two went up the alley to the street. Down one block was a phone booth. Tal picked up the receiver and made sure everything was functioning.

"Here they come!" Guilo warned, and they leaped through the wall of a department store and peered out a window just as a long, black limousine and then another and then another began an ominous parade down the street toward the hotel. Inside the limousines sat dignitaries and other VIPs from many different nations and races, and within and on top were demons, large, black, warty, and fierce, their yellow eyes darting warily in every direction.

Tal and Guilo watched with fascination. In the sky overhead, other demons began flocking to the hotel like swallows, their black winged outlines silhouetted against the reddening sky.

"A significant gathering, captain," said Guilo.

Tal nodded and continued watching. Amid the limousines were many taxis, also carrying a vast cross section of humanity: Orientals, Africans, Europeans, Westerners, Arabians—people of great power, esteem, and dignity from all over the world.

"As written in the Scriptures, the kings of the earth," Tal observed, "being made drunk with the wine of the great harlot's immorality."

"Babylon the Great," said Guilo. "The Great Harlot arising at last."

"Yes, Universal Consciousness. The world religion, the doctrine of demons spreading among all the nations. Babylon revived right before the end of the age."

"Hence the return of the Prince of Babylon, Rafar."

"Of course. And that explains why *we* were called. We were the last to confront him."

Guilo only winced at that. "My captain, our last battle with Rafar is not a pleasant memory."

"Nor a pleasant expectation."

"Do you expect him here?"

"No. This gathering is only a party before the real battle, and the real battle is slated for the town of Ashton."

Tal and Guilo remained where they were, watching the gathering forces of mankind and of Satanic evil converge on the Gibson Hotel. They kept looking for the one key person: Susan Jacobson, Alexander Kaseph's Maidservant.

They finally spotted her in a very fancy Lincoln Continental, probably Kaseph's private vehicle, driven by a hired chauffeur. She was accompanied by two escorts sitting on either side of her.

"She'll be closely watched," said Tal. "Come on, we need a better look."

They stalked quickly through the department store, through walls, displays, and people, then ducked under the street and came up inside the restaurant right across from the hotel's main door. All around them well-dressed people sat at quiet, candlelit tables eating expensive French cuisine. They hurried to a front window right next to an older couple enjoying seafood and wine and watched as the Lincoln carrying Susan pulled up in front of the hotel.

Susan's door was opened by the red-coated doorman. One escort got out and extended his hand to help her disembark; she stepped out and was immediately joined by the other escort. The two tuxedo-clad escorts were very handsome, but also very intimidating. They kept very close to her. Susan wore a very loose-fitting evening gown that draped her body stunningly and cascaded to her feet.

Guilo had to ask, "Are her plans the same as ours?"

Tal answered assuredly, "The general has yet to err."

Guilo only shook his head in apprehension.

"To the alley," said Tal.

They moved along under the cracked cobbled alley and surfaced to a hiding place behind a fire escape. Night had fallen, and it was very dark in the alley. From their vantage point they could count twenty pairs of shifting yellow eyes, evenly spaced along the alley and against the hotel.

"About a hundred sentries are around the place," said Tal.

"Under better circumstances, a mere handful," Guilo muttered.

"You need only concern yourself with these twenty."

Guilo took his sword in his hand. He could feel the prayers of the local saints.

"It will be difficult," he said. "The prayer cover is limited."

"You don't have to defeat them," answered Tal. "Just get them to chase after you. We need the alley clear for just a few moments."

They waited. The air in the alley was still and dank. The demons moved very little, remaining at their posts, mumbling back and forth in different languages, their sulfurous breath forming a strange, meandering ribbon of yellow vapor that hung along the alley like a putrid river floating in midair. Tal and Guilo could feel themselves getting more and more tense, like ever-tightening springs, with each passing second. The banquet must be in progress by now. At any time Susan could excuse herself from the table.

More time passed. Suddenly both Tal and Guilo felt the prompting of the Spirit. Tal looked at Guilo, and Guilo nodded. She was on her way. They watched the window. The light from the ladies' lounge shone brightly through it; they could just barely hear the sound of the door opening and closing as patrons came and went.

The door opened. High heels clicked on the tile floor, moving toward the window. The demons began to stir a little, muttering among themselves. The door to the last stall swung open. Guilo's hand gripped his sword. He began to breathe deeply, his big torso heaving in and out, the power of God coursing through him. Their eyes were riveted on the window. The demons became more alert, their yellow eyes wide open and darting back and forth. They were talking louder.

The shadow of a woman's head suddenly appeared on the window. A woman's hand reached for the latch.

Tal touched Guilo on the shoulder, and Guilo instantly dropped into the ground. Only a fraction of a second passed.

"YAHAAAAA!" came the sudden, deafening war cry from Guilo's powerful lungs, and the whole alley instantly exploded in a blinding flash of white light as Guilo shot up out of the ground, his sword flashing and shimmering, tracing brilliant arcs in the air. The demons jumped, hooting and shrieking in terror, but recovered immediately and drew their swords. The alley echoed with the metallic ringing, and the red glow of their blades danced like comets on the high brick walls.

Guilo stood tall and strong, and he bellowed out a laugh that shook the ground. "Now, you black lizards, I'll test your mettle!"

A big spirit on the end shrieked out an order, and all twenty demons converged on Guilo like starving predators, their swords flashing and their fangs bared. Guilo shot straight up out of their midst like a slippery bar of soap and added an agile spin as he went, throwing light everywhere in colorful spirals. The demons unfurled their wings and shot up after him. As Tal watched, Guilo looped and corkscrewed all over the sky like a loose balloon, laughing, taunting and teasing, staying just out of their reach. The demons were in a blind rage by now.

The alley was empty. The window was opening. Tal was beneath the window in an instant, unglorified and concealed in the darkness. He grabbed Susan the moment her hand came through the window and pulled so hard she practically shot through the window on his strength alone. She was dressed in a simple blouse and jeans, and had small slippers on her feet. From the neck up she was still gorgeous; from the neck down she was ready for running down dark alleys.

Tal helped her find her way down from the dumpster and then prodded her up the alley and out to the street where she hesitated, looked this way and that, and then spotted the phone booth. She ran like the wind, in a terrible and desperate hurry. Tal followed her, trying to stay as concealed as possible. He looked back over his shoulder; Guilo's diversion had worked. For now, Guilo was the main problem for the demons, and their attention was far from this one frantically running woman.

Susan leaped into the booth and slammed the door behind her. She took a pile of coins from her jeans pocket, dialed the operator, and put through a long-distance call.

Somewhere between Ashton and the little roadside of Baker, in a rundown warehouse refashioned into low-rent apartments, Kevin Weed was awakened from an exhausted sleep by the ringing of his phone. He rolled over on his mattress and lifted the receiver.

"Yeah, who's this?" he asked.

"Is this Kevin?" came the desperate voice on the other end.

Kevin perked up a little. It was a woman's voice. "Yeah, that's me. Who's this?"

In the phone booth, Susan looked up and down the street fearfully as she said, "Kevin, this is Susan. Susan Jacobson."

Kevin was beginning to wonder about all this. "Hey, what do you want with me anyway?"

"I need your help, Kevin. I don't have much time. There *isn't* much time."

"Time for what?" he asked very dully.

"Please listen. Write it down if you have to."

"I don't got a pencil."

"Then just listen. Now you know about the *Ashton Clarion?* The newspaper in Ashton?"

"Yeah, yeah, I know about it."

"Bernice Krueger works there. She's the sister of my old roommate, Pat, the one who committed suicide."

"Oh, man . . . what's going on around here?"

"Kevin, will you do something for me? Will you get ahold of Bernice Krueger at the *Clarion* and . . . Kevin?"

"Yeah, I'm listening."

"Kevin, I'm in trouble. I need your help."

"So where's your boyfriend?"

"He's the one I'm afraid of. You know about him. Tell Bernice all about Alexander Kaseph, everything you know."

Kevin was nonplussed. "So what do I know?"

"Tell her what happened, you know, between us, with Kaseph, the whole thing. Tell her what Kaseph's up to."

"I don't get this."

"I don't have time to explain. Just tell her—tell her that Kaseph is taking over the whole town . . . and let her know I have some very important information about her sister Pat. I'll try to reach her, but I'm afraid the *Clarion* phone might be bugged. Kevin, I need you to be there to answer the phone, to . . ." Susan was frustrated, full of emotion, unable to select the right words. She had too much to say and too little time.

"You're not making a whole lot of sense," Kevin muttered. "You *on* something?"

"Just do it, Kevin, please! I'll call you again as soon as I can, or I'll write, or do something, but please call Bernice Krueger and tell her everything you know about Kaseph and about me. Tell her it was me she saw at the carnival."

"How'm I supposed to remember all this stuff?"

"Please do it. Tell me you'll do it!"

"Yeah, okay, I'll do it."

"I've got to go! Good-bye!"

Susan hung up the phone and dashed out of the booth. Tal followed her, ducking inside the buildings as much as he could.

He reached the alley a few moments ahead of her to check it out. Trouble! Four more sentries had moved in to take the place of the original twenty, and they were fully alert. There was no way of knowing where Guilo and the twenty might be. Tal looked behind him. Susan was running full speed for the alley.

Tal dove headfirst through the pavement and penetrated deep under the city, gaining speed, bringing forth his big silver sword. The power of God was increasing now; the saints must be praying somewhere. He could feel it. He only had seconds and he knew it. He checked his bearings, made a wide subterranean sweep away from the hotel and then, over a mile away, he circled back, gaining speed, gaining speed, gaining speed, shining light, building power, faster, faster, faster, his sword a blinding lightning bolt, his eyes like fire, the earth a blur around him, the roar of passing clay, boulders, pipe, and stone like a freight train. He held the sword crossways, the glimmering tip ready for that one infinitesimal moment.

Quicker than a thought, like the explosion of a missile, a brilliant streak of light burst from the ground across the street and seemed to cut space in half as it pierced through the alley and right across the eyes of all four demons. The demons, stunned and blinded, fell to the ground, stumbled about, tried to find each other. The streak of light vanished back into the ground as quickly as it came.

Susan came around the corner and into the alley, heading for the window.

Tal cupped his wings and braked himself. He had to get back to help her through that window before any demons could recover and sound an alarm. He snapped his wings into a violent forward rush and doubled back.

Susan clambered up the crates and cans and onto the dumpster. The demons started to regain their vision and were rubbing their eyes. Tal emerged behind the fire escape, trying to judge the remaining time.

Good! Guilo made it back and dropped like a hawk into the alley, grabbing Susan and thrusting her through the window in an instant, holding her up so she would not tumble to the floor inside. Guilo closed the window himself.

Tal flew out to meet Guilo. "One more time," he shouted.

Nothing more needed to be said. The four sentries had recovered and were pouncing on them, and the other twenty had returned, hot on Guilo's trail. Tal and Guilo shot into the air and streaked away, chased by a flock of frothing demons. The angels flew a course high over the city and kept their speed just slow enough to encourage the demons. They headed west, off into the dark night sky, trailing brilliant white streaks behind them. The demons were tenacious in their pursuit for hundreds of miles, but eventually Tal looked back and found that they had given up the chase and returned to the city. Tal and Guilo picked up speed and headed for Ashton.

In the ladies' room, Susan hurriedly rolled up the legs of her jeans, took her evening gown from its hook in the stall, and quickly resumed her proper appearance for the banquet. She removed the slippers and put them in her handbag, slipped on her dress shoes, then opened the stall door and came out.

A man's voice outside the lounge door called, "Susan, they're waiting for you!"

She checked her appearance in the mirror, combed her hair, and tried to calm her breathing. "Hasty, hasty," she called teasingly.

With ladylike dignity she finally emerged into the hallway and took the arm of the escort. He led her back to the Grand Ballroom, now filled with people, and showed her to her seat at the head table, giving the other escort a reassuring nod.

19

The *Clarion* office was finally recovering the nice, healthy efficiency Marshall liked to see, and the new girl, Carmen, had a lot to do with it. In less than a week she had taken the old bull by the horns and had more than filled Edie's shoes, reestablishing a tight office routine.

It was only Wednesday, and already the paper was in full swing, heading for the Friday edition. Marshall stopped by Carmen's desk on his way to the coffee machine.

She handed him some fresh copy and said, "This is part of Tom's article."

Marshall nodded. "Yeah, the thing on the fire department . . ."

"I've broken it down into three headings—staff, history, and goals—and figured we could run it in three parts. Tom already has it slotted for the next two paste-ups and thinks he can bump something for the third."

Marshall was pleased. "Yeah, go with it, I like it. I'm glad you can read Tom's writing."

Carmen had already proofread the bulk of the material for Friday and was halfway through preparing the copy for George, the typesetter. She had gone through the books and balanced all the accounts. She planned on helping Tom with the paste-up tomorrow. The negatives for the Sportsman's Club layout were ready.

Marshall shook his head with happy amazement. "Glad to have you aboard."

Carmen smiled. "Thank you, sir."

Marshall went to the coffeemaker and poured two cups of coffee. Then it dawned on him: Carmen had found the cord to this fool machine!

He took the two cups back toward his office and gave her a smile of approval as he passed her desk. The location of her desk had been her only request on the job. She had asked if it could be moved to a location right outside Marshall's office door, and Marshall was happy to comply. Now all he had to do was turn and holler, and she would spring into action to do his bidding.

Marshall went into his office, set his cup of coffee on his desk, and offered the other cup to the long-haired, slightly dazed man sitting in the corner. Bernice sat in a chair she had brought in with her own cup of coffee.

"Now where were we?" Marshall asked, sitting at his desk.

Kevin Weed rubbed his face, took a sip of the coffee, and tried to pick up his thoughts again, looking around the floor as if he had dropped them down there somewhere.

Marshall prompted, "Okay, let me at least make sure I've got this straight: Now you used to be the . . . male acquaintance of this Susan, and she used to be the roommate of Pat Krueger, Bernice's sister. Have I got that right?"

Weed nodded. "Yeah, yeah, that's right."

"So what was Susan doing at the carnival?"

"Beats me. Like I said, she just came up behind me and said hi, and I wasn't even looking for her. I couldn't believe it was her, you know?"

"But she got your phone number and then she called you last night . . ."

"Yeah, all tripped out, shook up. It was wild. She didn't make a lot of sense."

Marshall looked at both Weed and Bernice and asked Bernice, "And this is the same ghostly-looking woman you photographed that night?"

Bernice was convinced. "The descriptions Kevin gave me match perfectly the woman I saw, and also that one older man who was with her."

"Yeah, Kaseph." Kevin said the name as if it tasted bad.

"All right," and Marshall made a list in his mind. "So let's talk about this Kaseph first, then we'll talk about Susan, and then we'll talk about Pat."

Bernice had her notepad ready. "What's Kaseph's full name, any idea?"

Weed strained his brain. "Alex—Alan—Alexander . . . something like that."

"But it starts with A."

"Yeah, right."

Marshall asked, "What is he?"

Weed answered, "Susan's new boyfriend, the guy she dumped me for."

"So what does he do? Where does he work?"

Weed shook his head. "I don't know. He's got bucks, though. He's a real wheeler-dealer. When I first heard about him, he was hanging around Ashton and the college and talking about buying property and stuff. Man, the guy was loaded and he liked everybody to know it too." Then he remembered, "Oh, and Susan said he's trying to take over the town . . ."

"What town? *This* one?"

"I guess."

Bernice asked, "So where is he from?"

"Back east, maybe New York. I think he's the big-city type."

Marshall told Bernice, "Make a note for me to call Al Lemley at the *Times*. He might be able to track this guy down if he's in New York." Bernice made the note. Marshall asked Weed, "What else do you know about him?"

"He's weird, man. He's into weird stuff."

Marshall was getting impatient. "C'mon, try harder."

Weed stirred and fidgeted in his chair, trying to get comfortable about talking. "Well, you know, he was like a guru, or a witch doctor, or some kind of far-out ooga-booga man, and he got Susan into all that stuff."

Bernice prodded, "Are you talking about Eastern mysticism?"

"Yeah."

"Pagan religions, meditation?"

"Yeah, yeah, all that stuff. He was into all that stuff, he and that professor lady at the college, what's-her-name—"

Marshall was sick of the name. "Langstrat."

Weed's face brightened with recollection. "Yeah, that was it."

"Were Kaseph and Langstrat associated? Were they friends?"

"Yeah, sure. They were teaching some night classes together, I think, the ones that Susan was going to. Kaseph was a special guest star or something. He really had everybody wowed. I thought he was spooky."

"All right, so Susan was attending these classes—"

"And she got crazy, and I mean *crazy.* Man, she couldn't have been on a higher trip with mescaline. I couldn't even talk to her anymore. She was always way out in space somewhere."

Weed kept talking, starting to roll a little on his own. "That's what really started to get me, how she and the rest of that bunch started keeping secrets and talking in codes and not letting me in on what they were talking about. Susan just kept telling me I wasn't enlightened and wouldn't understand. Man, she just gave it all to that Kaseph guy and he took her, I mean he really took her. He owns her now. She's gone. She's had it."

"And was Langstrat mixed up in all this?"

"Oh yeah, but Kaseph was the real heavy. He was the guru, you know. Langstrat was his puppy dog."

Bernice said, "And now Susan gets your phone number and calls you after all this time."

"And she was scared," said Weed. "She's in trouble. She said I was supposed to get in touch with you guys and tell you what I knew, and she said she had some information on Pat."

Bernice was longing to know. "Did she say what kind of information?"

"No, nothing. But she wants to get ahold of you."

"Well, why doesn't she just call?"

That question helped Weed to remember something. "Oh, yeah, she thinks your phone might be bugged."

Marshall and Bernice were silent for a moment. That was a comment they didn't know how seriously to take.

Weed added, "I guess she called me to be a go-between, to tip you guys off."

Marshall ventured, "Like you're the only one she has left to trust?"
Weed only shrugged.

Bernice asked, "Well, what do you know about Pat? Did Susan
ever tell you anything while you were still going together?"

One of Weed's most painful undertakings was trying to remember
things. "Uh . . . she and Pat were good friends, for a while anyway. But
you know, Susan left us all out in the cold when she started following
after that Kaseph bunch. She kinda pushed me off, and Pat too. They
didn't get along very well after that, and Susan kept saying how Pat
was . . . heh . . . just like me, trying to get in the way, not enlightened,
dragging her feet."

Marshall thought of the question and didn't wait for Bernice to
ask it. "So, would you say that this Kaseph bunch may have regarded
Pat as an enemy?"

"Man . . ." Weed remembered some more. "She did stick her neck
out, I mean, she got in the way. Her and Susan had a real fight once
about the stuff Susan was getting into. Pat didn't trust Kaseph and kept
telling Susan she was brainwashed."

Weed's eyes brightened. "Yeah, I talked to Pat once. We were
sitting at a game, and we talked about what Susan was getting into and
how Kaseph was controlling her, and Pat was really shook up about it,
just like I was. I guess Pat and Susan really had some fights about it
until Susan finally moved out of the dorm and ran off with Kaseph.
Boy, she dropped out of her classes and everything."

"So did Pat make any enemies, I mean *real* enemies?"

Weed kept digging up new things that had been buried under the
years and the alcohol. "Uh, yeah, maybe she did. It was after Susan ran
off with this Kaseph guy. Pat told me she was going to check the whole
thing out once and for all, and I think she may have gone to see that
Professor Langstrat a few times. A while later I ran into her again. She
was sitting in a cafeteria on campus, and she looked like she hadn't
slept in days, and I asked her how she was, and she would hardly even
talk to me. I asked how her investigation was going, you know, her
checking out Kaseph and Langstrat and stuff, and she said she'd quit
doing anything about that, said it was really no big deal. I thought that
was a little weird, she'd been so torn up about it before. I asked her,
'Hey, are they coming after you now?' and she wouldn't talk about it,
she said I wouldn't understand. Then she said something about some
instructor, some guy that was helping her out and that she was doing
okay, and I got the message that she didn't want me butting in, so I just
sort of left her there."

"Did her behavior seem strange to you?" Bernice asked. "Did she
seem like herself?"

"No way. Hey, if she hadn't been so against that whole Kaseph and
Langstrat bunch, I woulda thought she was one of them; she had the
same kind of dopey, lost-in-space look all over her."

"When? Just when was it that you saw her like that?"

Weed knew, but hated to say it. "Just a little while before they found her dead."

"Did she seem afraid? Did she give you any indication of any enemies, anything like that?"

Weed grimaced, trying to remember. "She wouldn't talk to me. But I saw her once after that and tried to ask her about Susan, and she acted like I was some kind of mugger or something . . . she hollered, 'Leave me alone, leave me alone!' and tried to pull away and then she saw it was me, and she looked all around like somebody was following her . . ."

"Who? Did she say who?"

Weed looked at the ceiling. "Oh . . . what was that guy's name?"

Bernice was leaning forward, hanging on his words. "There *was* somebody?"

"Thomas, some guy named Thomas."

"Thomas! Did she ever say his last name?"

"Don't remember any last name. I never met the guy, never saw him, but he sure must have owned her. She acted like he was following her all around, talking to her, maybe threatening her, I don't know. She seemed pretty afraid of him."

"Thomas," Bernice whispered. She said to Weed, "Is there anything else about this Thomas? Anything at all?"

"I never saw him . . . she didn't say who he was or where she would meet him. But it was kinda strange. One minute she'd be talking like he was the greatest thing that ever happened to her, and then the next minute she'd be hiding out and saying he was following her."

Bernice got up and headed for the door. "I think we might have a college roster somewhere." She began rummaging around in the desks and shelves of the front office.

Weed fell silent. He looked tired.

Marshall reassured him, "You're doing fine, Kevin. Hey, it's been a while."

"Uh . . . I don't know if this is important—"

"Consider everything important."

"Well, this stuff about Pat having some new instructor . . . I think some of the Kaseph bunch, maybe it was Susan, they had instructors."

"But I thought Pat didn't want anything to do with that group."

"Yeah. Yeah, that's right."

Marshall shifted directions. "So where did you fit into all these goings-on, besides your relationship with Susan?"

"Hey, nowhere! I didn't want anything to do with it, man."

"Were you going to the school?"

"Yeah, taking accounting. Man, when all this started coming down and then Pat killed herself, hey, I got out of there fast. I didn't want to be next, you know?" He looked at the floor. "My life's been nothing but hell ever since."

"You working?"

"Yeah, logging crew for Gorst Brothers up above Baker." He shook his head. "I didn't think I'd ever see Susan again."

Marshall turned to his desk and searched for some paper. "Well, we'll have to keep in touch. Let me have your number and address, at work and at home."

Weed gave Marshall the information. "And if I'm not there, you can probably find me at The Evergreen Tavern in Baker."

"Okay, listen, if you hear anything else from Susan you let us know, day or night." He gave Weed his card with his home phone number added.

Bernice came back in with the roster.

"Marshall, you have a call. I think it's urgent," she said. Then she turned to Weed. "Kevin, let's you and I step outside and go through this roster. Maybe we'll find that guy's full name."

Weed stepped outside with Bernice as Marshall picked up the phone.

"Hogan," he said.

"Hogan, this is Ted Harmel."

Marshall scrambled for a pencil. "Hi, Ted. Thank you for calling."

"So you talked to Eldon—"

"And Eldon talked to you?"

Harmel sighed and said, "You're in trouble, Hogan. I'll give you one interview. Got a pencil handy?"

"I'm ready. Shoot."

Bernice had just said good-bye to Weed and seen him to the door when Marshall emerged from his office with a scribbled-on piece of paper in his hand.

"Any luck?" he asked.

"Zilch. There are no Thomases of any kind, first or last name."

"It's still a lead though."

"Who was that on the phone?"

Marshall produced the scrap of paper. "Thank God for small favors. That was Ted Harmel." Bernice brightened considerably as Marshall explained, "He wants to see me tomorrow, and here are the directions. It must be way back in the sticks. The guy is still paranoid as all get-out; I'm surprised he didn't make me wear a disguise or something."

"He wouldn't say anything about all this?"

"No, not over the phone. It has to be just the two of us, in private."

Marshall leaned over just a little and said, "He's another one who thinks our phone might be bugged."

"So how do we make sure it isn't?"

"Make that one of your assignments. Now here's the rest of them." Bernice grabbed her notepad off her desk and made her list as Marshall spoke. "Check the New York phone book—"

"I did. No A. Kaseph listed."

"Scratch that one. Next: Check around with the local real estate offices. If Weed's right about Kaseph looking for property around here, some of those people might know something. And I'd look around in the commercial listings as well."

"Mm-hmm."

"And while you're at it, find out what you can about whoever owns Joe's Market."

"It's not Joe?"

"No. The place used to belong to Joe and Angelina Carlucci, c-a-r-l-u-c-c-i. I want to know where they went and who owns the store now. See if you can get some straight answers."

"And you were going to check with your friend at the *Times* . . ."

"Yeah, Lemley." Marshall added a note to his piece of paper.

"That it?"

"That's it for now. In the meantime, let's get back to running this paper."

All the time, all through their meeting with Weed and their following conversation, Carmen sat at her desk busily working and acting like she hadn't heard a word.

The morning had been tight, with the next issue's deadline galloping up on them, but by noon the paste-up was ready to go to the printer and the office had a chance to resume its normal pace.

Marshall put in a call to Lemley, his old comrade-in-arms at the *New York Times*. Lemley got all the information Marshall had on this strange character Kaseph, saying he'd get right on it. Marshall hung up the phone with one hand and grabbed his suit jacket with the other; his next stop was his afternoon appointment with the reclusive Ted Harmel.

Bernice drove off for her appointed stops. She parked her red Toyota in the parking lot of what used to be Joe's Market and was now called the Ashton Mercantile, and went into the store. About a half hour later, she returned to her car and drove away. It had been a wasted trip: no one knew anything, they only worked there, the manager wasn't in, and they had no idea when he would be back. Some had never heard of Joe Carlucci, some had but didn't know whatever happened to him. The assistant manager finally asked her to quit bothering all the employees on company time. So much for getting any straight answers.

Now it was off to the realty offices.

Johnson-Smythe Realty occupied an old house remodeled into an office on the edge of the business part of town; the house still had a very charming front yard, with a redwood tree standing tall in the middle of it and a quaint, log cabin mailbox out front. It was warm and welcoming inside, and quiet. Two desks occupied what used to be the living room; both were empty at the time. On the walls hung bulletin boards with snapshots of house after house, with cards below each photograph describing the building, the property, the view, nearness to shopping and so forth, and—last but not least—the price. Boy, what people would pay these days for a house!

At a third desk in what used to be the dining room a young lady stood and smiled at Bernice.

"Hi, can I help you?" she asked.

Bernice smiled back, introduced herself, and asked, "I need to ask a question that might seem a little odd, but here goes. Are you ready?"

"Ready."

"Have you done any business with anyone by the name of A. Kaseph in the last year or so?"

"How do you spell that?"

Bernice spelled it for her, then explained. "You see, I'm trying to get in touch with him. It's just a personal matter. I was wondering if you might have a phone number or address or anything."

The young lady looked at the name she had just written on a piece of paper and said, "Well, I'm new here, so I sure don't know, but let me ask Rosemary."

"In the meantime, might I have a look through your microfiche?"

"Sure. You know how to run it?"

"Yes."

The lady went toward the back of the house where Rosemary— apparently the boss lady—had her office in a back bedroom. Bernice could hear Rosemary talking on the phone. Getting an answer from her might take a while.

Bernice went to the microfiche reader. Where to start? She looked at a map of Ashton and vicinity on the wall and found the location of Joe's Market. The hundreds of little celluloid plates were arranged by Section, Township, Quarters, and the street numbers. Bernice had to do a lot of looking back and forth to get all the numbers off the map. Finally she thought she might have found the right microfiche to put into the viewer.

"Excuse me," came a voice. It was Rosemary, marching down the hall toward her with a grim expression on her face. "Ms. Krueger, I'm afraid the microfiche is only for the use of our staff. If there's something you'd like me to find for you . . ."

Bernice kept cool and tried to keep things flowing. "Sure, I'm sorry. I was trying to find out the new owner of Joe's Market."

"I wouldn't know."

"Well, I thought it might be on the machine here somewhere."

"No, I don't think so. It's been a while since the files have been updated."

"Well, could we look anyway?"

Rosemary totally ignored the question. "Is there anything else you'd like to know?"

Bernice stood firm and unshaken. "Well, there was my original question. Have you done any business with anyone named Kaseph in the last year or so?"

"No, I've never heard the name."

"Well, perhaps someone else on your staff—"

"They've never heard it either." Bernice was about to question that, but Rosemary interrupted with, "I would know. I know all their accounts."

Bernice thought of one other thing. "You wouldn't have a—a cross-reference file, would you—"

"No, we don't," Rosemary answered very abruptly. "Now is there anything else?"

Bernice was tired of being nice. "Well, Rosemary, even if there was, I'm sure you would not be able or willing to supply it. I'm leaving now, so breathe easy."

She left hurriedly, feeling very lied to.

20

Marshall was beginning to worry about his shock absorbers. This old logging road had more potholes than surface; apparently it wasn't used that much anymore by the logging companies, but was left to hunters and hikers who knew the area well enough to keep from getting lost. Marshall did not. He looked again at the scribbled directions and then at the odometer. Boy, the miles go by slowly on roads like this one!

Marshall bumped his way around a gravelly corner and finally saw a vehicle ahead, parked alongside the road. Yes, an old Valiant. It was Harmel. Marshall pulled up behind the Valiant and got out. Ted Harmel got out of his car, dressed in clothing for the outdoors: wool shirt, faded jeans, work boots, a wool cap. He looked the way he had sounded: exhausted and very scared.

"Hogan?" he asked.

"Yeah," said Marshall, extending his hand.

Harmel shook it and then turned away abruptly. "C'mon with me."

Marshall followed Harmel to a trail off the road and they hiked up among the tall timber, picking their way through logs, rocks, and underbrush. Marshall was wearing a suit and his shoes were definitely the wrong kind for this sort of terrain, but he wasn't about to complain—he'd recaptured the big fish that got away.

At last Harmel seemed satisfied with their seclusion. He went to a huge fallen log, weathered and bleached by years of changing seasons, and sat down on it. Marshall joined him.

"I want to thank you for calling me," Marshall said for an opener.

"We never had this meeting," Harmel said bluntly. "Is that an agreement?"

"You've got it."

"Now what do you know about me?"

"Not much. You used to be the editor of the *Clarion*, Eugene Baylor and the other college regents were on your case, you and Eldon Strachan are friends . . ." Marshall reviewed quickly all he had learned, which was mostly what he and Bernice had gleaned from the old *Clarion* articles.

Harmel nodded. "Yeah, that's all true. Eldon and I are still friends. We went through basically the same thing, so that gives us a sort of comradeship. As far as the molesting of Marla Jarred, Adam Jarred's girl—that was a bizarre set-up. I don't know who coached her, or how, but somebody got that girl to say all the right words to the police. I do find it significant that the whole matter was settled so quietly. What I was supposed to have done is a felony; you don't just settle a thing like that quietly."

"Why did it happen, Ted? What did you do to bring it on yourself?"

"I got too involved. You're right about Juleen and all the others. It's a secret society, a club, a whole network of people. Nobody has any secrets from anybody else. The eyes of the group are everywhere; they watch what you do, what you say, what you think, how you feel. They're working toward what they call a Universal Mind, the concept that sooner or later all the inhabitants of the world will make a giant evolutionary leap and meld into one global brain, one transcending consciousness." Harmel stopped, looked at Marshall. "I'm spilling it as it comes to me. Is it making sense?"

Marshall had to compare Harmel's "spillings" with what he already knew. "Every person affiliated with this exclusive network subscribes to these ideas?"

"Yeah. The whole thing is built around occult ideas, Eastern mysticism, cosmic consciousness. That's why they meditate and do psychic readings and try to meld their minds together . . ."

"Is this what they do in Langstrat's therapy sessions?"

"Yes, exactly. Every person who joins the network goes through a certain initiation process. They meet with Juleen and learn to achieve altered states of consciousness, psychic powers, out-of-body experiences. The sessions could involve just one person, or several, but

Juleen is at the core of it all, like some kind of guru, and we were all her disciples. We all became like one, growing, interdependent organism, trying to become one with the Universal Mind."

"You said something about . . . melding your minds together?"

"ESP, telepathy, whatever. Your thoughts are not your own, and neither is your life. You're only one segment of the whole. Juleen's highly skilled in such things. She—she knew my every thought. She owned me . . ." This part became difficult for Harmel to speak about. He grew tense, and his voice faltered and dropped in volume. "Maybe she still does. Sometimes I still hear her calling to me . . . moving through my brain."

"Does she own all the others as well?"

Harmel nodded. "Yeah, everybody owns everybody, and they won't stop until they own that whole town. I could see it coming. Anybody who gets in their way suddenly drops out of sight. That's why I'm still wondering about Edie. Ever since this whole thing started happening, I've been leery about anyone just dropping out of the picture suddenly . . ."

"What danger would Edie be to them?"

"Maybe she's just one more step toward taking you out. I wouldn't be surprised. They took out Eldon, they took out me, they took out Jefferson . . ."

"Who's Jefferson?"

"The district judge. I don't know how they did it, but suddenly he decided he wouldn't run for reelection. He sold his home, left town, no one's heard from him since."

"And now Baker's in—"

"He's part of the network. He's owned."

"So did you know this at the time you had your little crime settled so quietly?"

Harmel nodded. "He told me he could make it really rough for me, turn me over to the county prosecutor and then it would be out of his hands. He knew good and well it was a frame-up! He had me checkmated, so I took him up on it. I got out of town."

Marshall took out a pad and pen. "Who else do you know that belongs to this bunch?"

Harmel looked away. "If I tell you too much, they'll trace it back to me. You'll have to find out for yourself. All I can do is point you in the right direction. Check the mayor's office and the town council; see who's new there and who they replaced. They've had a lot of turnover lately." Marshall made a note of it. "You've got Brummel?"

"Yeah, Brummel, Young, Baker."

"Check the county land commissioner, and the president at the Independent Bank, and . . ." Harmel kept probing his memory. "The county comptroller."

"I've got him on the list."

"The board of regents at the college?"

"Yeah. Say, wasn't it the tiff with them that got you run out of town?"

"That was only part of it. I wasn't controllable anymore. I got in the way. The network took care of me before I could hurt them. But there's no way I can prove it. It doesn't matter anyway. The whole thing's too big; it's like a huge organism, a cancer that just keeps spreading. You can't go after just one part of it like the regents and expect to kill the whole thing. It's everywhere, at every level. Are you religious?"

"In a limited sense, I suppose."

"Well you're going to need *something* to fight it. It's spiritual, Hogan. It doesn't listen to reason, or to the law, or to any set of morals but its own. They don't believe in any God—*they* are God." Harmel paused to calm down and then took off on a different note. "I first got involved with Juleen when I wanted to do a story on some of the so-called research she was doing. I was intrigued by it all—the parapsychology, the strange phenomena she was documenting. I started having these *counseling* sessions with her myself. I let her read and photograph my aura and my energy field. I let her probe my mind and meld our thoughts. I went into it after a novelty story, actually, but I got hooked. I couldn't tear myself away from it. After a while I started picking up on some of the same things she was heavily involved in: I'd leave my body, go out into space, talk to my instructors—" Harmel caught himself. "Oh man, that's right: you're never going to believe any of this stuff!"

Marshall was firm—and maybe he did believe it. "Tell me anyway."

Harmel gritted his teeth and looked skyward. He fumbled, he stammered, his face went pale. "I don't know. I don't think I can tell you. They'll find out."

"Who'll find out?"

"The network."

"We're out in the middle of nowhere, Ted!"

"It doesn't matter . . ."

"You used the word *instructors*. Who are they?"

Harmel only sat there, trembling, terror etched in his face. "Hogan," he said finally, "you just can't cross them. I can't tell you! They'll know about it!"

"But who are they? Can you at least tell me that?"

"I don't even know if they're real," Harmel muttered. "They're just . . . there, that's all. Inner teachers, spirit guides, ascended masters . . . they're called all kinds of things. But anyone who follows Juleen's teachings for very long invariably gets mixed up with them. They come from nowhere, they speak to you, sometimes they appear to you when you're meditating. Sometimes you visualize them yourself, but then they take on a life and personality of their own . . . it's not just your imagination anymore."

"But what are they?"

"Beings . . . entities. Sometimes they're just like real people, sometimes you only hear a voice, sometimes you only feel them—like spirits, I suppose. Juleen works for them, or maybe they work for her, I don't know which way it goes. But you can't hide from them, you can't run, you can't get away with anything. They're part of the network, and the network knows everything, controls everything. Juleen controlled me. She even came between me and Gail. I lost my wife over this whole thing. I started to do everything Juleen told me . . . she'd call me in the middle of the night and tell me to come over, and I'd come over. She'd tell me not to print a certain story, I wouldn't print it. She'd tell me what kind of news to cover and I'd print it, just like she said.

"She owned me, Hogan. She could have told me to take a gun and shoot myself, and maybe I would have done it. You gotta know her to understand what I'm saying."

Marshall remembered standing in the hallway outside Langstrat's class wondering how he got there. "I think I understand."

"But Eldon found out about the college finances, and we both checked into it, and he was right. The college was headed for the rocks, and I'm sure it still is. Eldon tried to stop it, to get the whole mess straightened out. I tried to help him. Juleen came after me right away and made all kinds of threats. I ended up going in two directions, following two different loyalties. It was like being torn apart inside. Maybe that's what snapped me out of it; I made up my mind I wasn't going to be controlled anymore, not by the network, not by anyone. I was a newspaperman; I had to print it the way I saw it."

"And they took care of you."

"And it came as a total surprise. Well, maybe not total. When the police came to the paper and arrested me, I almost knew what it was about. It was something I could have predicted from the way Juleen and the others were threatening me. They've done that sort of thing before."

"For instance?"

"I can't help thinking the real estate offices, the tax rolls, any information you can get on the properties around the town, might show something. I couldn't follow it up when I was still there, but all the recent real estate deals didn't feel quite right to me."

The real estate business wasn't feeling quite right to Bernice either. Just as she pulled up in front of Tyler and Sons Realty, she saw the owner, Albert Tyler, locking up the place and getting ready to leave.

She rolled down her car window and asked him, "Say, aren't you supposed to be open until 5?"

Tyler only smiled and shrugged. "Not on Thursdays."

Bernice could read the hours on the front door. "But your hours say Monday through Friday, 10-5."

Tyler got just a little cross. "Not on Thursdays, I said!"

Bernice noticed Tyler's son Calvin driving his Volkswagen out from behind the building. She got out of her car and waved him down. Unwillingly, he paused and rolled down his window.

"Yeah?" he said.

"Aren't you people usually open on Thursday until 5?"

Calvin only shrugged and made a face. "What do I know? The old man says go home, we all go home."

He drove off. "Old man" Tyler was getting into his Plymouth. Bernice ran up to the car and waved to get his attention.

He was really miffed by now. He rolled down his window and said gruffly, "Lady, we're closed and I have to get home!"

"I just wanted to look through your microfiche. I need some information on some property."

He shook his head. "Hey, I can't help you anyway. Our microfiche is broken down."

"Wha. . . ?"

But Tyler rolled up his window and pulled away, screeching his tires a little.

Bernice shouted angrily after him, "Did Rosemary tip you off?"

She hurried to her car. There was still the Top of the Town Realty. She knew the owner regularly helped out with youth baseball on Thursday afternoons. Maybe the other gal who worked there wouldn't know who she was.

Harmel looked grim and haggard as he said, "They'll do you in, Hogan. They have the clout and the connections to do it. Look at me: I lost all I owned, lost my wife and family . . . they cleaned me out. They'll do the same to you."

Marshall wanted answers, not doomsaying. "What do you know about some guy named Kaseph?"

Harmel grimaced with fresh disgust. "Go after that. He might be the source of all the trouble. Juleen worshiped that guy. Everybody did Juleen's bidding, but she did his."

"Do you know whether or not he was looking for any real estate around Ashton?"

"He was drooling over the college, I know that."

Marshall was taken aback. "The college? Keep going."

"I never got the chance to dig after it, but there might be something there. Talk around the Network said that the college would be taken over entirely by some Network higher-ups, and Eugene Baylor seemed to be spending a lot of time talking money with Kaseph or his reps."

"Kaseph was trying to buy the college?"

"He hasn't *yet*. But he did end up buying everything else around town."

"Like what?"

"A lot of homes, I know, but I couldn't find out very much. Like I said, check the tax rolls or the real estate offices to see if he's been buying up anything else. I know he had the bucks to do it." Harmel pulled a ragged manila envelope from under his jacket. "And take this off my hands, will you?"

Marshall took the envelope. "What is it?"

"A curse, that's what. Something happens to everyone who has it. Eldon's accountant friend, Ernie Johnson, gave it to me, and I hope Eldon told you what happened to *him!*"

"He told me."

"It's Johnson's findings from the college accounting office."

Marshall couldn't believe his luck. "You gotta be kidding! Did Eldon know about this?"

"No, I just came across them myself, but don't start dancing yet. You'd better get some accountant friend of your own to try to decipher it for you. It doesn't make much sense to me . . . I think there's still a whole other half of it missing."

"It's a start. Thanks."

"If you want to play with theories, try this out: Kaseph comes to Ashton and wants to buy everything he can get his hands on. The college is not even thinking of selling. Next thing you know, thanks to Baylor, the college gets itself in such deep financial trouble that selling may be the only way to get out of it. Suddenly Kaseph's offer isn't so far-fetched, and by now the board of regents is stacked with yea-sayers."

Marshall opened the envelope and leafed through the pages and pages of photocopied columns and figures. "And you couldn't find any leads in all this?"

"More leads you don't need, not as much as proof. What you really need to see is who's on the other end of all those transactions."

"Kaseph's books, perhaps?"

"With all the friends and confederates he has at that college, I wouldn't be surprised if Kaseph was coming back to buy the college with its own money!"

"That's some theory. But what would a man like that even want with a little town, or with a whole college?"

"Hogan, a guy with the power and bucks that guy seems to have could take a town like Ashton and do anything he wanted with it. I think he already has to a great extent."

"How do you know?"

"Just check it out."

21

Bernice was in a hurry. She was in the back room of the Top of the Town Realty, going through their microfiche files. Carla, the girl out in front, was new enough to the job and the town that she bought Bernice's little talk about being a historian from the college looking for background on Ashton. It didn't take long for Carla to give Bernice a tour of the files and a short course on how to run the viewer. When Carla left her alone, Bernice went straight for the criss-cross file. This was certainly a wonderful stroke of luck: the other real estate offices had files that told you what land was owned by whom if you knew where the property was; the criss-cross file told you what various people owned if you knew the names of the people.

Kaseph. Bernice flipped through the microfiche holder to the *Ks*. She slipped the celluloid into the viewer and began scanning up and down, across, zigzag, the myriads of microscopic letters and figures streaking in a blur across the viewscreen as she looked for the right column. There. Kw . . . Kh . . . Ke . . . Ka . . . across to the next column. Hurry it up, Bernice!

She found no listing under Kaseph.

"How're you doing?" asked Carla from up front.

"Oh, just fine," Bernice answered. "I'm not finding much yet, but I know where to look."

Well, there was still Joe's Market. She went back to the regular file and pulled out the microfiche for the Section, Township, and Quarter for that address. Into the viewer the celluloid went, and again Bernice raced the myriads of listings up and down, looking for the listing. There! The legal description of what used to be Joe's Market, now the Ashton Mercantile. It was tax assessed at $105,900, and owned by Omni Corporation. That was all it said.

Bernice went back to the crisscross file. Into the viewer went the Ok–Om celluloid. Up, down, across. Olson . . . Omer . . . Omni. Omni. Omni. Omni. Omni. Omni. The listings under Omni Corporation went down, down, down the column; there could have been over a hundred. Bernice got her pen and pad and started writing furiously. The many addresses and legal descriptions meant little to her; many of them weren't even decipherable, but she kept scribbling as fast as she could, hoping she would be able to read her own writing when she looked at it later. She abbreviated, filling page after page in her notepad.

Out front, the telephone rang, as it had been doing; but this time Carla's conversation didn't sound too happy. Her voice was hushed and serious, and she sounded very apologetic. The jig might be up, kid, keep writing!

In a moment Carla appeared. "Are you Bernice Krueger, from the *Clarion?*" she asked directly.

"Who's asking?" Bernice said. That was dumb, but she didn't want to come right out with the truth either.

Carla looked very disturbed. "Listen, you're going to have to leave right away," she said.

"That was your boss on the phone, right?"

"Yes it was, and I'd appreciate it if you wouldn't tell him I let you back here. I don't know what this is all about, and I don't know why you lied to me, but would you please just leave? He's coming over here to lock the place up, and I told him you hadn't come by . . ."

"You're a doll!"

"Well, I lied for you, now you please lie for me."

Bernice scrambled to gather up all her notes and replace the celluloids. "I was never here."

"I appreciate it," said Carla as Bernice raced out the door. "Wow, you just about got me fired."

Andy and June Forsythe had a very nice home, a modern log house on the outskirts of town, not far from Forsythe Lumber. Tonight Hank and Mary had gathered there for a dinner fellowship along with many others of the Remnant, as Krioni, Triskal, Seth, Chimon, and Mota sat up in the lofty rafters looking on. The angels could feel the growing power of this little cluster of praying people. The Joneses were there, as were the Colemans, the Coopers, the Harrises, some of the college students; Ron Forsythe was there along with his girlfriend Cynthia. A few more brand-new Christians were with him, just now getting introduced to the rest of the group. Other latecomers were continually trickling in.

After dinner the people gathered and settled around the big stone hearth in the living room, while Hank took his place on the hearth with Mary beside him. Each person began to share his background.

Bill and Betty Jones had been churchgoers all their lives, but only made a serious commitment to Jesus Christ a year ago. The Lord had spoken to their hearts, and they searched Him out.

John and Patty Coleman had been to another church in town, but never knew much about the Bible or about Christ until coming to this church.

Cecil and Miriam Cooper had always known the Lord, and they were glad to see a new flock gathering to replace the old one. "It feels a lot like replacing a flat tire," Cecil quipped.

As others shared, their various backgrounds were brought out; there were different traditions and different doctrinal backgrounds, but any differences were not very important right now. All of them had one main concern: the town of Ashton.

"Oh, it's a war, all right," said Andy Forsythe. "You can't go out on those streets and not feel it. Sometimes I feel like I'm running through a shower of spears, you know?"

A new couple, friends of the Coopers, Dan and Jean Corsi, spoke up.

Jean said, "I really think it's Satan out there, just like the Bible says, just like a roaring lion trying to devour everyone."

Dan commented, "The problem is that we've all just sat to the side and let it happen. It's time we got concerned and scared and on our knees to see that the Lord does something about it."

Jean added, "Some of you know our son is having some real problems right now. We really wish you'd pray for him."

"What's his name?" someone asked.

"Bobby," Jean answered. She swallowed and went on to say, "He enrolled at the college this year and something's really happened to him . . ." She had to stop, choked with emotion.

Dan picked it up, and his tone was bitter. "Seems like something happens to any kid who goes off to that college. I never knew what kind of weird stuff they were really teaching over there. The rest of you should find out about it and make sure you don't let your kids get involved."

Ron Forsythe, silent up to this time, piped up, "I know what you're talking about, man. It's in the high school, too. The kids are messing around with Satanic stuff like you wouldn't believe. We used to trip out on drugs; now it's demons."

Jean ventured through her tears, "I know this sounds awful, but I really wonder if Bobby isn't possessed."

"I was," said Ron. "I know I was. Man, I heard voices talking to me, telling me to get some drugs, or steal something, all kinds of horrible things. I never let my folks know where I was, I never came home, I'd end up sleeping in the weirdest places . . . and with the weirdest people."

Dan muttered, "Yeah, that's Bobby. We haven't seen him in about a week."

Jean wanted to know, "But how did you get started in such things?"

Ron shrugged. "Hey, I was already going the wrong way. I'm not sure I'm even all the way straightened out yet. But I'll tell you when I think I got into the Satanic Stuff: it's when I had my fortune told. Hey, that's when I caught it, no doubt." Someone asked if the fortune-teller was a certain woman. "No, it was somebody else. It was at the carnival three years ago."

"Aw, they're all over the place," someone else moaned.

"Well that just goes to show how far off-base this town has gotten!" Cecil Cooper protested. "There are more witches and fortune-tellers around here than Sunday school teachers!"

"Well, we'll just see what we can do about that!" said John Coleman.

Ron picked it up again. "It's all heavy duty, man. I mean, I saw some pretty weird things when I was into that stuff: I've seen things just float around by themselves, I've read people's minds, I even left my body once and floated around town. You'd just better all be good and prayed up!"

Jean Corsi began to cry. "Bobby's possessed . . . I just know it!"

Hank could see it was time to take control. "Okay, people, now I have a real burden to pray for this town, and I know you do too, so I think that's where the answer lies. That's the first thing we need to do."

They were all ready. Many felt awkward praying out loud for the first time; some knew how to pray loudly and confidently; some prayed in phrases they'd learned from certain liturgies; all meant every word, however they managed to express it. The fervency slowly began to rise; the prayers became more and more earnest. Someone started a simple song of worship and those who knew it sang, while those who didn't know it learned it.

In the rafters the angels sang along, their voices smooth and flowing like cellos and basses in a symphony. Triskal looked at Krioni, smiled broadly, and flexed his arms. Krioni smiled and flexed back. Chimon took his sword and made it dance from the pivot of his wrist, tracing streaks and curls of shimmering light in the air as the blade sang with a beautiful resonance. Mota just looked toward heaven, his silken wings spreading, his arms upraised, caught up in the rapture of the song.

Kate quietly set her kitchen table with one plate, one cup, and a saucer. That evening she ate by herself, hardly able to get anything down because of the emotions tightening her throat and twisting her stomach. Oh well, it was leftovers anyway—leftovers from those many other meals Marshall never showed up for. It was happening again.

Maybe the place had nothing to do with how busy a newsman could be. Perhaps, even though Marshall had moved to a small, supposedly dull town, he still had that cursed nose for news that led him on his wild hunts into all hours of the night, making a story where one didn't even exist before. Perhaps this was, after all, his first love, more than his wife, more than his daughter.

Sandy. Where was she tonight? Hadn't they made this move for her sake? Now she was further away from them than ever, even though she still lived in the same house. Shawn had grown into her life like a cancer, not a friend, and Kate and Marshall never did talk about it like he had promised. His mind had been totally preoccupied. He was married to that newspaper, maybe enamored by that young, attractive reporter.

Kate shoved her plate away and tried to keep from crying. She couldn't start fussing and shedding tears now, not when she had to think clearly. Undoubtedly there would be decisions to make, and she would have to make them alone.

On the outskirts of Ashton, next to the railroad yard, Tal conferred with his warriors inside an old, unused water tower.

Nathan was pacing back and forth, his voice echoing off the walls of the huge tank. "I could feel it coming, captain! The enemy is luring Hogan into a trap. There has been a dangerous shift in affection toward Krueger. His family is in grave danger."

Tal nodded his head and remained deep in thought. "Exactly as one might expect. Rafar knows no frontal attack will work; he's trying his evil hand at subtlety, at moral compromise."

"And succeeding, I say!"

"Yes, I agree."

"But what can we do? If Hogan loses his family, he'll be destroyed!"

"No. Not destroyed. Knocked down, perhaps. Decimated, perhaps. But it's all because of the dross in his own soul, which the Spirit of God has yet to convict him of. We can do nothing but wait and let all things take their course."

Nathan could only shake his head in frustration. Guilo stood nearby, pondering Tal's words. Of course what Tal said was true. Men will sin if men will.

"Captain," Guilo said, "what if Hogan falls?"

Tal leaned back against the dank metal wall and said, "We can't be concerned with the question of 'if.' The question we must deal with is 'when.' Both Hogan and Busche are now laying the foundation we need for this battle. Once that's done, Hogan as well as Busche *must* fall. Only their clear defeat will coax the Strongman out of hiding."

Guilo and Nathan both looked at Tal with consternation.

"You—you would *sacrifice* these men?" Nathan asked.

"Only for a season," Tal answered.

Marshall brought out Ernie Johnson's large packet of pirated records from the Whitmore College accounting office and handed them across the *Clarion*'s reception counter to Harvey Cole. Cole was a CPA Marshall knew well enough to trust.

"I don't know what you'll be able to make of all this," said Marshall, "but see if you can find whatever Johnson found, and see if it looks crooked."

"Wow!" said Harvey. "This is going to cost you!"

"I'll swap you some free advertising. How about that?"

Harvey smiled. "Sounds fine. Okay, I'll get to it and get back to you."

"A.S.A.P."

Harvey went out the door and Marshall returned to his office, rejoining Bernice in their evening, after-hours project.

They were working amid a flurry of notes, papers, phone books, and any other public records they could get their hands on. In the middle of it all, a consolidated list of names, addresses, jobs, and tax records was forming piece by piece.

Marshall looked over his notes from his interview with Harmel. "Okay, what about that judge, what's-his-name, Jefferson?"

"Anthony C.," Bernice replied, flipping through last year's phone book. "Yeah, Anthony C. Jefferson, 221 Alder Street." She immediately went to her scrawled notes from the Top of the Town Realty. "221 Alder . . ." Her eyes scanned one sheet in her notebook, then another, until finally, "Bingo!"

"Another one!"

"So check me out on this: Jefferson was bumped by the Network and Omni came in and bought his house?"

Marshall scribbled some reminder notes to himself on a yellow legal pad. "I'd like to know why Jefferson moved and how much he sold that house for. I'd also like to know who's living there now."

Bernice shrugged. "We'll just have to go down the list and check all these Network people's addresses. I'll lay you odds it's one of them."

"What about Baker, the judge who replaced Jefferson?"

Bernice looked at another list. "No, Baker's over in the house that used to belong to the high school principal, uh, Waller, George Waller."

"Oh yeah, he's the one who lost his house in the sheriff sale."

"Oh, there are a lot of those, and I'll bet we might find more if we knew where to look."

"We'll have to snoop around the County Finance Office. Somehow, some way, those people's property taxes never got to where they were supposed to go. I can't believe this many people would be delinquent on their taxes."

"Someone diverted the money so the taxes were never paid. It's dirty, Hogan, just plain dirty."

"It wasn't Lew Gregory, the old comptroller. Look at this. He had to resign because of some conflict of interest rap. Now Irving Pierce is in, and he's Omni-owned, right?"

"You got it."

"And what was that you had on Mayor Steen?"

Bernice consulted her notes, but shook her head. "He just recently bought his house; the deal looks legitimate except for the previous owner being the former police chief who left town for no apparent reason. It might mean something, it might not. It's what happened to all those other people that has me wondering."

"Yeah, and why none of them ever squawked or made a fuss about it. Hey, I wouldn't let the county just come in and auction off my house right out from under me, not without asking at least a few questions. There's something else about this that we don't know."

"Well, think about the Carluccis. Did you know their house sold to Omni for $5,000? That's ridiculous!"

"And the Carluccis went poof! Gone, just like that!"

"So I wonder who's living in their house now?"

"Maybe the new high school principal, or the new fire marshal, or a new city councilman, or a *new* this or a *new* that!"

"Or one of the *new* college regents."

Marshall scrambled for some more papers. "Boy, what a mess!" He finally found the list he was looking for. "Let's go through those regents and see what we come up with."

Bernice flipped through a few pages in her notebook. "I know for sure that Pinckston's place is owned by Omni. Some kind of trust arrangement."

"What about Eugene Baylor?"

"Don't you have that somewhere?"

"One of us does, but now I can't remember who."

They both fumbled through their notes, papers, lists. Marshall finally found it among his scattered leaves.

"Here it is. Eugene Baylor, 1024 SW 147th."

"Oh, I think I saw that here somewhere." Bernice perused her notes. "Yes, Omni owns that too."

"Sheesh! Deeding everything over to Omni Corporation must be a requirement for membership."

"Well, that makes Young and Brummel card-carrying members. It makes sense, though. If they all want to meld into one Universal Mind, they have to do away with individuality, and that means no private ownership."

One by one, Marshall read off the names of the college regents, and Bernice researched their addresses. Of the twelve regents, eight were living in homes owned by Omni Corporation. The others rented apartments; one of the apartment buildings was owned by Omni. Bernice had no information on the other apartment buildings.

"I think we've ruled out coincidence," said Marshall.

"And now I can't wait to hear what your friend Lemley has to say."

"Sure, that Kaseph and Omni Corporation are linked. That's obvious." Marshall took just a moment to ponder. "But you know what really scares me? So far, everything we see here is legal. I'm sure they've been crooked somewhere to get where they are, but you can see they're working within the system, or at least doing a very good job of looking like it."

"But come on, Marshall! He's taking over a whole town, for crying out loud!"

"*And* he's doing it legally. Don't forget that."

"But he must leave some tracks somewhere. We've been able to sniff him out at least this far."

Marshall took a deep breath and then sighed it out. "Well, we can try to track down every person who sold out and left town, try to find out why it happened. We can check into what positions they held before they left and who holds that position now. Whoever holds the position now can be asked what connection he or she has with Omni Corporation or with this Universal Consciousness mind-tripping group. We can ask each and every one of them what they might know about the elusive Mr. Kaseph. We can do some more research on the Omni Corporation itself, find out where it's based, what it deals in, what else it owns. We have our work cut out for us. And then I guess it'll be time to go directly to our friends with what we know and get a response from them."

Bernice could feel something coming across in Marshall's manner. "What's bothering you, Marshall?"

Marshall tossed his notes on the desk and leaned back in his chair to ponder. "Bernie, we'd be fools to think we're immune to any of this."

Bernice gave a resigned nod. "Yeah, I've been wondering about it, wondering what they might try."

"I think they already have my daughter." It was a blunt statement. Marshall himself was shocked at the sound of it.

"You don't know that for sure."

"If I don't know that, I don't know *anything*."

"But what kind of real power could they wield except economic and political? I don't buy all this cosmic, spiritual stuff; it's nothing but a mind trip."

"That's easy for you to say, you're not religious."

"You'll find it's a lot easier."

"So what if we end up like—like Harmel, no family left, just hiding in the bushes and talking about . . . spooks?"

"I wouldn't mind ending up like Strachan. He seems comfortable enough just being out of this whole thing."

"Well, Bernie, even so, we'd better see it coming before it gets here." He grabbed her hand in earnest and said to her, "I hope we both know what we're getting ourselves into. We may be in too deep already. We could quit, I suppose . . ."

"You know we can't do that."

"I know *I* can't. I'm not putting any expectations on you. You can get out now, go somewhere else, work for some ladies' journal or something. I won't mind."

She smiled at him and held his hand tightly. "Die all, die merrily."

Marshall only shook his head and smiled in return.

22

In another state, in a low-income section of another town, a little panel truck weaved its way down a kid-cluttered street through a housing project. All the little duplexes, except for different color schemes, came from the same mold. As the truck pulled to a stop at the end of an aging asphalt cul-de-sac, "Princess Cleaners" could be seen printed on its side.

The driver, a young lady in blue overalls, her hair in a red scarf, got out. She opened the side door and pulled out a large laundry bundle and some bag-draped dresses on hangers. Rechecking the address, she made her way up one walk to one particular door and rang the bell.

First the curtain of the front window pulled to the side for a moment, and then there were footsteps toward the door. The door opened.

"Hi, got some cleaning here," said the young lady.

Oh, yes . . ." said the man who answered the door. "Just bring it in."

He opened the door wider so she could make her way into the house as three children tried to keep out of her path despite their great curiosity.

The man called to his wife, "Honey, the cleaning lady is here."

She came in from the small kitchen, looking tense and nervous. "You children go outside and play," she ordered.

They whined a bit, but she herded them out the door, closed it, then drew shut the one window that still remained open.

"Where'd you get all this laundry?" the man asked.

"It was in the truck. I don't know who it belongs to."

The man, a heavyset Italian with graying curly hair, offered his hand. "Joe Carlucci."

The young lady set down the laundry and shook his hand. "Bernice Krueger from the *Clarion*."

He showed her to a chair and then said, "They told me I was never to talk to you or Mr. Hogan . . ."

"For the sake of our children, they said," Mrs. Carlucci added.

"This is Angelina. It was for her sake, for the children's sake, that we—we moved away, we left it all, we said nothing."

"Can you help us?" asked Angelina.

Bernice got her pad ready. "Okay, just take your time. We'll start at the beginning."

At what Al Lemley called "the halfway point" between Ashton and New York, Marshall pulled the Buick into the parking lot of a little insurance office in Taylor, a small town at the crossing of two major highways with no other real reason for being there. He stepped into the little office and was immediately recognized by the lady at the desk.

"Mr. Hogan?" she asked.

"Yes, good morning."

"Mr. Lemley is already here. He's waiting for you."

She showed him to another door which led to a back office that no one was using at the time. "Now there's coffee out here on the counter, and the bathroom is right through this door and to the right."

"Thank you."

"You're welcome."

Marshall closed the door, and only then did Al Lemley stand up and give him a warm handshake.

"Marshall," he said, "it's great to see you. Just great!"

He was a smaller man, bald, with a hooked nose and sharp blue eyes. He had spunk and sparkle, and Marshall had always known him as a priceless associate, a friend who could come through with almost any much-needed favor.

Al sat behind the desk, and Marshall pulled a chair up beside him so they could both look over the materials Al had brought. For a little while they talked old times. Al was pretty much filling the vacancy that

Marshall had left in the City Room at the *Times,* and he was beginning to have a real appreciation for Marshall's ability to handle the job.

"But I don't think I want to trade places with you now, buddy!" he said. "I thought you moved to Ashton to get away from it all!"

"I guess it followed me there," he said.

"Eh . . . in a few weeks New York may be a lot safer."

"What've you got?"

Al pulled an 8 x 10 glossy photo from a file folder and let it slide across the desk under Marshall's nose. "Is this your boy?"

Marshall looked at the picture. He'd never seen Alexander M. Kaseph before, but from all the descriptions he knew, "This has to be him."

"Oh, it's him, all right. He's known and then he's not known, if you catch my drift. The general public never heard of the guy, but start asking investors on Wall Street, or government people, or foreign diplomats, or anyone else in any way connected with international wheeling and dealing and politics and you'll get a response. He is the president of Omni Corporation, yes; they are definitely connected."

"Surprise, surprise. So what do you know about Omni Corporation?"

Al shoved a stack of materials toward Marshall, a stack several inches thick. "Thank goodness for computers. Omni was just a little nontypical in tracking down. They have no central headquarters, no main address; they're scattered into local offices all over the world and keep a very low profile. From what I understand, Kaseph keeps his own immediate staff with him and likes to be as invisible as possible, running the whole operation from no one knows where. It's weirdly subterranean. They're not on the New York or American Stock Exchanges, not by their name, at least. The stocks are all diversified among, oh, maybe a hundred different front corporations. Omni is the owner and controller of retail chain stores, banks, mortgage companies, fast food chains, soft drink bottlers, you name it."

Al continued talking as he thumbed through the stack of materials. "I had some of my staff digging into this stuff. Omni doesn't come right out and print anything about itself. First you have to find out what the front corporation is, then you sort of sneak in the back door and find out what interest the Big Mother Company has in it. Take this one here . . ." Al produced a stockholder's annual report from an Idaho mining company. "You don't know what you're really reading about until you get down here to the end . . . see? 'A subsidiary of Omni International.' "

"International—"

"*Very* international. You wouldn't believe how influential they are in Arab oil, the Common Market, the World Bank, international terrorism—"

"*What?*"

"Don't expect to find any stockholder's reports on the latest car bombing or mass murder, but for every documented aboveboard item here there are a couple hundred pieces of under-the-table scuttlebutt that no one can prove but everyone seems to know."

"And such is life."

"And such is your man Kaseph. I want to tell you, Marshall, he knows how to spill blood if he has to and sometimes when he doesn't have to. I'd say this guy is a perfect cross between the ultimate guru and Adolf Hitler, and he makes Al Capone look like a Boy Scout. Word has it that even the Mafia is afraid of him!"

Angelina Carlucci tended to spill words more from emotions than from objective recall, which made her story travel in agonizing circles. Bernice had to keep asking questions to get things clear.

"Getting back to your son Carl—"

"They broke his hands!" she wept.

"*Who* broke his hands?"

Joe intervened to help his wife. "It was after we said we would not sell the store. They had asked us . . . well, they didn't ask, they told us we'd better . . . but they talked to us about it a few times and we wouldn't sell . . ."

"And that's when they started threatening you?"

"They *never* threaten!" Angelina said angrily. "They say they *never* threatened us!"

Joe tried to explain. "They—they threaten you without sounding like they are. It's hard to explain. But they talk the deal over with you, and they let you know how very wise you will be to go along with the deal, and you know, you just know that you should go along with it if you don't want anything evil to befall you."

"So just who was it that you talked to?"

"Two gentlemen who were—well, they said they were friends of the new people who own the store now. I just thought at first that they were realtors or something. I had no idea . . ."

Bernice looked over her notes again. "All right, so it was after you turned them down the third time that Carl had his hands broken?"

"Yes, at school."

"Well, who did it?"

Angelina and Joe looked at each other. Angelina answered, "No one saw it. It was during recess at school, and no one saw it!"

"Carl must have seen it."

Joe only shook his head and waved his hand at Bernice to stop short. "You cannot ask Carl about it. He is still tormented, he has bad dreams."

Angelina leaned forward and whispered, "Evil spirits, Miss Krueger! Carl thinks it was evil spirits!"

Bernice kept waiting for these two responsible adults to explain the strange perceptions of their young son. She had trouble phrasing a question. "Well, what does—why—what do you . . . Well, surely you must know what really happened, or at least have some idea." The two of them only stared at each other blankly, at a loss for words. "There were no teachers on the grounds who assisted him after it happened?"

Joe tried to explain. "He was playing baseball with some other boys. The ball rolled into the woods and he went after it. When he came back, he was—he was crazy, screaming, he'd wet himself . . . his hands were broken."

"And he never said who did it?"

Joe Carlucci's eyes were glazed with terror. He whispered, "Big black things . . ."

"Men?"

"*Things*. Carl says they were spirits, monsters."

Don't knock it, Bernice told herself. It was clear these poor deluded people really believed something of this nature was attacking them. They were very devout Catholics, but also very superstitious. Perhaps that explained the many crucifixes on every door, the pictures of Jesus and the figurines of the Virgin Mary everywhere, on every table, over every doorway, in every window.

Marshall had perused the materials on the Omni Corporation. He still hadn't read about one thing.

"What about any kind of religious affiliation?"

"Yeah," said Al, reaching for another folder. "You were right on that. Omni is just one of several underwriters for the Universal Consciousness Society, and that's a whole other ball of financial and political wax, and perhaps the main motivation behind the company, even more than money. Omni owns or backs—oh brother, there must be hundreds of them—Society-owned businesses, from cottage-level enterprises clear up to banks, retail stores, schools, colleges—"

"Colleges?"

"Yeah, and law firms too, according to this news clipping. They have a major lobbying task force in Washington, they've been regularly pushing their own special interest legislation . . . it's usually anti-Jewish and anti-Christian, if that's of any interest to you."

"How about towns? Does this Society like to buy towns?"

"I know Kaseph's done it, or other things similar to that. Listen, I got in touch with Chuck Anderson, one of our foreign correspondents, and he's heard all kinds of interesting things besides seeing a lot of it himself. It seems these Universal Consciousness people are a worldwide

club. We've located Society chapters in ninety-three different countries. They just seem to pop up everywhere, no matter what part of the
world, and yes, they have acquired full control of towns, villages,
hospitals, some ships, some corporations. Sometimes they buy their
way in, sometimes they vote their way in, sometimes they just crowd
their way in."

"Like an invasion without guns."

"Yes, usually quite legally, but that's probably out of sheer cleverness, not any integrity, and remember you're also looking at a lot of
power and pull here. You're standing right in the path of Big Daddy
himself, and from what I gather, he doesn't slow, stop, or even go
around."

"Nuts . . ."

"I'd . . . well, I'd cool it, buddy. Call the feds, let somebody bigger
handle it if they want. You still have a job back at the *Times* if you ever
want it. At least cover the story from a distance. You're a class-A
reporter, but you're too close, you have too much to lose."

All Marshall could think was, Why me?

Bernice had stumbled too far into a touchy situation. The Carluccis were getting more unsettled and terrified the more she questioned
them.

"Maybe this wasn't a good idea," Joe finally said. "If they ever find
out we talked to you . . ."

Bernice was about to scream if she heard that word again. "Joe,
who do you mean by 'they'? You keep saying *they* and *them*, but you
never say who."

"I—I can't tell you," he said with great difficulty.

"Well, let me at least clear this much up: Are they people, I mean
real people?"

He and Angelina thought for a moment, then he answered, "Yes,
they are real people."

"So they are real, flesh-and-blood people?"

"And maybe spirits too."

"I'm talking about the real people now," Bernice insisted. "Was it
real people who audited your taxes?"

Reluctantly, they nodded.

"And it was a real, flesh-and-blood man who posted the auction
notice on your door?"

"We didn't see him," Angelina said.

"But it was a real piece of paper, right?"

"But nobody told us it would happen!" Joe protested. "We always
paid our taxes, I have the canceled checks to prove it! The people at the
County Office wouldn't listen to us!"

Angelina was angry now. "We had no money to pay the taxes they wanted. We already paid them, we couldn't pay them again."

"They said they would take our store, take all our inventory, and business was bad, very bad. Half our customers left and wouldn't come in anymore."

"And I know what kept them away!" said Angelina defiantly. "We could all feel it. I tell you, windows don't break by themselves, and groceries don't fly off the shelves by themselves. It was the Devil himself in our store!"

Bernice had to reassure them. "All right, I'm not arguing with that. You saw what you saw, I don't doubt you—"

"But don't you see, Miss Krueger?" Joe asked with tears in his eyes. "We knew we could not stay. What would they do next? Our store was failing, our home was sold out from under us, our children were being tormented by evil people, spirits, whatever. We knew it would be best not to fight. It was God's will. We sold the store. They gave us a good price . . ."

Bernice knew that wasn't so. "You didn't get half of what that store was worth."

Joe broke down and cried as he said, "But we are free . . . We are free!"

Bernice had to wonder.

Then came the blitz, a die-all-die-merrily push for information accompanied by mixed feelings of determination and foreboding, by conflicts between initial impulses and second thoughts. Every Tuesday and Friday for two weeks the *Ashton Clarion* still appeared on the newsstands and in all the mailboxes of subscribers, but its editor and chief reporter were very hard to contact or even catch a glimpse of. Marshall's phone messages stacked up unreturned, Bernice was simply never home; there were several nights when Marshall never went home at all, but slept here and there, now and then in the office, waiting for special calls, making other calls, working at keeping the paper afloat with one hand while going over lists of contacts, tax records, business reports, interviews, and leads with the other.

The people who had left their positions, and usually Ashton, and the people who replaced them were definitely two separate groups of widely different persuasions; after a while, Marshall and Bernice could just about predict what their responses were going to be.

Bernice called Adam Jarred, the college regent whose daughter was allegedly molested by Ted Harmel.

"No," said Jarred, "I really don't know anything about any special . . . what did you call it?"

"A society. The Universal Consciousness Society."

"No, afraid not."

Marshall spoke with Eugene Baylor.

"No," Baylor replied somewhat impatiently, "I've never even heard the name Kaseph, and I really don't understand what you're driving at."

"I'm trying to chase down some claims that the college might be negotiating a sale of its property with Alexander Kaseph of the Omni Corporation."

Baylor laughed and said, "You must have heard about another college. There's nothing like that happening here."

"And what about the information we've received that the college is in heavy financial trouble?"

Baylor didn't like that question at all. "Listen, the last editor of the *Clarion* tried that one too, and it was the dumbest move he ever made. Why don't you just run your paper and leave the running of the college to us?"

The former regents had a different tune.

Morris James, now a business consultant in Chicago, had nothing but bad memories of his last year with the college.

"They really taught me what it must be like to be a leper," he told Bernice. "I felt I could be a good voice on the board, you know, a stabilizing factor, but they simply would tolerate no dissent. I thought it was highly unprofessional."

Bernice asked him, "And what about Eugene Baylor's handling of the college finances?"

"Well, I left before any of this really serious trouble arose, this trouble you've described to me, but I could foresee it. I did try to block some decisions the board made regarding the granting of special powers and privileges to Baylor. I thought it was giving too much unauthorized control to one man without the oversight of the other regents. Needless to say, my opinion was very unpopular."

Bernice asked a very pointed question. "Mr. James, what finally precipitated your resigning from the board and leaving Ashton?"

"Well . . . that's a tough one to answer," he began reluctantly. His answer took about fifteen minutes, but the bottom line came down to, "My wholesale business was so harassed and so sabotaged by . . . unseen mobsters, I guess I would call it . . . that I became too great an insurance risk. I couldn't fill my orders, clientele dropped way off, and I just couldn't stay above water anymore. The business folded, I took the hint, and I got out of there. I've been doing fine ever since. You can't keep a good man down, you know."

Marshall managed to track down Rita Jacobson, now living in New Orleans. She was not happy to hear from someone in Ashton.

"Let the Devil have that town!" she said bitterly. "If he wants it so bad, let him have it."

Marshall asked her about Juleen Langstrat.

"She's a witch. I mean a real, live witch!"

He asked her about Alexander Kaseph.

"A warlock and a gangster rolled into one. Stay out of his way. He'll bury you before you even feel it."

He tried to ask her some other questions, but she finally said, "Please don't ever call this number again," and hung up.

Marshall tracked down as many former members of the city council as he could by telephone and found out that one had simply retired, but all the others stepped down because of some form of hardship: Allan Bates fell ill of cancer, Shirley Davidson went through a divorce and ran off with a new lover, Carl Frohm was "set up," as he called it, with a phony tax scam, Jules Bennington's business was "strong-armed" out of town by a bunch of mobsters whom he knew better than to identify. By cross-checking Marshall found that, in every case, the deposed city councilman or councilwoman was replaced by a new person connected in some way with either the Universal Consciousness Society or Omni Corporation or both; and in every case the deposed person thought that he or she was the only one who had left. Now, out of fear, out of self-interest, out of that typical reluctance to get involved, all of them remained far away, out of touch, out of the picture, saying nothing. Some were cooperative in answering Marshall's questions, and some felt very threatened. All in all, though, Marshall got what he was after.

As for those who used to own businesses now run by this mysterious incognito corporation, very few of them had planned on selling out, moving out, or giving up their peaceful lives in Ashton or their successful businesses. But the reasons for leaving were consistently along the same lines: tax bunglings, harassments, boycotts, personal problems, marriage dissolutions, perhaps a disease or a nervous breakdown here and there, with an occasional macabre tale of strange, maybe-supernatural occurrences.

Former Ashton District Judge Anthony C. Jefferson's story was ominously typical. "Word started circulating around the courthouse and the legal community that I was on the take, receiving bribes for fixing sentences and letting people off. Some false witnesses even confronted me and made accusations, but it never happened—I swear it with all that I have in me!"

"Then can you tell me the truth about why you left Ashton?" Marshall asked, almost knowing what kind of answer to expect.

"Personal reasons as well as professional. Some of these reasons remain with me even now and are still viable enough to restrict what I can share with you. I can say, however, that my wife and I were needing a change. We were both feeling the pressure, she more than I. My health was failing. We at length thought it best to get out of Ashton altogether."

"May I ask, sir, if there were any . . . unfavorable outside influences . . . that brought about your decision to step down from the bench?"

He thought for a moment, and then, with some bitterness in his voice, said, "I cannot tell you who they were—I have my reasons—but I can say yes, some very highly unfavorable influences."

Marshall's last question was, "And you really can't tell me anything about who they might be?"

Jefferson gave a sardonic chuckle and said, "Just keep going the way you are, and you'll find out soon enough yourself."

Jefferson's words were beginning to haunt both Marshall and Bernice; they had heard many similar warnings as they went along, and both of them were growing more aware of something out there around them, building, coming closer, growing more and more malevolent. Bernice tried to shrug it off, Marshall found himself resorting more and more to quickly blurted prayers; but the feeling was still there, that disturbing sense that you are nothing but a sand castle on the beach and a twenty-foot wave is about to crash down on you.

On top of all this, Marshall had to wonder how Kate was holding up through all of this, and how he would ever patch things up between them when this was finally over. She was talking about being a widow again, a newspaper widow, and had even made some very embarrassing suggestions about Bernice. Man, this thing just had to get over with; much more of it and he wouldn't have much of a marriage to come home to.

And then of course there was Sandy, whom Marshall hadn't seen in weeks. But when this was all over, when it was really finally over, things would be different.

For now, the investigation he and Bernice were doing was incredibly urgent, a top priority, something that grew more ominous with every new stone they turned.

23

When things around the office were in their usual quiet, post-Tuesday state, Marshall had Carmen search out a good-sized cardboard box and some file folders and he began to organize the piles of papers, records, documents, scattered notes, and other information he and Bernice had compiled in their investigation into an orderly file. As he went through it all, he also compiled a list of questions on a legal pad on his desk—questions he intended to use in his interview with the first of the real principals in this plot: Alf Brummel.

That afternoon, after Carmen had left for a dentist appointment, Marshall made a call to Alf Brummel's office.

"Police Department," said Sara's voice.

"Hi, Sara, this is Marshall Hogan. Can I have a word with Alf?"

"He's out of the office right now . . ." Sara let out a long sigh and then added in a very strange, very quiet tone of voice, "Marshall—Alf Brummel does not want to talk to you."

Marshall had to think for a moment before he said, "Sara, are you caught in the middle?"

Sara sounded miffed. "Maybe I am, I don't know, but Alf told me in no uncertain terms that I was not to put through any calls from you and that I was to let him know whatever your intentions were."

"Huh . . ."

"Look, I don't know where friendships end and professional ethics begin, but I sure wish I knew what was going on around here."

"What *is* going on around there?"

"What'll you trade me for it?"

Marshall knew he was taking a chance. "I think I can find something of equal value if I look hard enough."

Sara hesitated for just a moment. "From all appearances, you've become his worst enemy. Every once in a while I hear your name coming through that office door of his, and he never says it nicely."

"Who's he talking to when he says it?"

"Uh-uh. It's your turn."

"All right. Well, we talk about him too. We talk about him a lot, and if everything we've uncovered checks out, yeah, I just might be his worst enemy. Now who's he talking to?"

"Some of them I've seen before, some of them I haven't. He's put several calls through to Juleen Langstrat, his whatever-she-is."

"Anyone else?"

"Judge Baker was one, and several members of the city council . . ."

"Malone?"

"Yes."

"Everett?"

"Yes."

"Uh—Preston?"

"No."

"Goldtree?"

"Yes, plus some other VIPs from out of town, and then Spence Nelson from the Windsor Police Department, the same department that supplied our extra manpower for the Festival. I mean, he's been talking to a lot of people, far more than usual. Something's up. What is it?"

Marshall had to be careful. "It might involve me and the *Clarion,* it might not."

"I don't know if I'll accept that or not."

"I don't know if I can trust you or not. Whose side are you on?"

"That depends on who the bad guy is. I know Alf is shady. Are you?"

Marshall had to smile at her spunk. "I'll have to let you be the judge of that. I do try to run an honest paper, and we have been carrying on a very intensive investigation of not only your boss, but just about every other bigwig in this town—"

"He knows it. They all do."

"Well, I've talked to just about all of them. Alf was next on my list."

"I think he knew that too. He told me just this morning that he did not want to talk to you. But he's sure talking up a storm with everybody else, and he just left here with a pile of papers under his arm, heading for another hush-hush meeting with someone."

"Any idea of what they're going to do about me?"

"Oh, you can be sure they *will* do something, and I get the feeling they're loading for bear. Consider yourself warned."

"And I'd advise you to be the sweet, ignorant angel who knows nothing and says nothing. Things could get messy."

"If they do, Marshall, can I come to you for answers, or at least a ticket out of town?"

"We'll be able to deal."

"I'll give you anything I can find if you'll keep me safe."

Marshall caught it in her voice: this gal was scared. "Hey now, remember, I didn't ask you to get involved."

"I didn't ask to be involved. I just am. I know Alf Brummel. I'd better pick you for my friend."

"I'll keep you posted. Now hang up and act normal."

She did.

Alf Brummel was in Juleen Langstrat's office, and the two of them were looking over a very thick portfolio of information Brummel had brought.

"Hogan now has enough to fill a front page!" Brummel said quite unhappily. "You've berated me for being slow in taking care of Busche, but as far as I can see, you've given Hogan nothing but a clear freeway since the beginning."

"Calm down, Alf," Langstrat said soothingly. "Just calm down."

"He's going to be coming after me for an interview any day now, just like he's gone after all the others. What do you suggest I say to him?"

Langstrat was a little shocked at his stupidity. "Don't say anything, of course!"

Brummel paced the room, exasperated. "I don't have to, Juleen! By this point, nothing I say or don't say will make any difference anyway. He already has everything he needs: he knows about the property sales, he has very good leads on all the sheriff sales of the tax delinquent homes, he knows all about the Corporation and the Society, he has good information on the college embezzlements . . . he even has more than enough evidence to accuse me of false arrest!"

Langstrat smiled with pleasure. "Your spy has done very well."

"She brought me a lot of this material today. He's getting it all organized in a file now. He's about to make his move, I'd say."

Langstrat gathered all the material neatly, placed it back in its portfolio, and leaned back in her chair. "I love it."

Brummel only looked at her in amazement and shook his head. "You could lose at this game someday, you know. We could *all* lose!"

"I love a challenge," she exulted. "I love taking on a strong opponent. The stronger the opponent, the more exhilarating the victory! Most of all, I love winning." She smiled at him, truly pleased. "Alf, I've had my doubts about you, but I think you've come through bountifully. I think you should be there to see Mr. Hogan step into the snare."

"I'll believe it when I see it."

"Oh, you will. You will."

There was a short lull, and it got strangely quiet around the town of Ashton. People weren't in touch. Nothing much was said.

During the day Marshall and Bernice organized their materials and stuck close to the office. Marshall took Kate out to dinner one night. Bernice sat at home and tried to read a novel.

Alf Brummel kept regular hours, but he didn't have much to say to Sara or anyone else about anything. Langstrat fell ill, or so the word was from her office, and her classes were canceled for a few days.

Hank and Mary thought that maybe their phone was out of order, the thing had been so silent. The Colemans visited relatives out of town. The Forsythes took the chance to do some inventory at the lumberyard. The rest of the Remnant all went about their normal business.

There was an odd stillness everywhere. The skies were hazy, the sun a blurred ball of light, the air warm and sticky. It was quiet.

But no one could relax.

High on a hill above the town, in the top of a graying, long-dead snag of an old tree, like an enormous black vulture, Rafar, the Prince of Babylon, sat. Other demons attended him, waiting to hear his next command, but Rafar was silent. Hour upon hour, a tense scowl on his face, he sat and gazed down at the town with his slowly shifting yellow eyes.

On another hill, directly across the town from Rafar's big dead tree, Tal and his warriors concealed themselves in the woods. They also were looking out over the town, and they could feel the lull, the silence, the ominous deadness of the air.

Guilo stood at his captain's side, and he knew this feeling. It had always been the same throughout the centuries.

"It could be any time now. Are we ready?" he asked Tal.

"No," Tal said flatly, looking intensely over the town. "Not all the Remnant are gathered. Those who have gathered are not praying, not enough. We haven't the numbers or the strength."

"And the black cloud of spirits over the Strongman grows a hundredfold each day."

Tal looked up into the sky over Ashton. "They will fill the sky from horizon to horizon."

From their hiding place they could look across the valley, over several miles, and see their hideous opponent sitting in the big dead tree.

"His strength has not waned," said Guilo.

"He is more than ready to do battle," said Tal, "and he can pick his own time, his own place, and the best of his warriors. He could attack on a hundred different fronts at once."

Guilo only shook his head. "You know we can't defend that many."

Just then a messenger rushed toward them, on the wing.

"Captain," he said, alighting next to Tal, "I've brought word from the Strongman's Lair. There is a stirring there. The demons are growing restless."

"It's beginning," said Tal, and this word was passed back through the ranks. "Guilo!"

Guilo stepped up. "Captain!"

Tal took Guilo aside. "I have a plan. I want you to take a small contingent with you and set up watch over that valley—"

Guilo was not one to argue with the captain, but "A *small* contingent? To watch the *Strongman?*"

The two of them continued in conference, Tal mapping out his instructions, Guilo shaking his head dubiously. At length Guilo came back to the group, picked out his warriors, and said, "Let's be off!"

With a rush of wings the two dozen weaved and zigzagged through the forest until they were far enough away to take to the open sky.

Tal summoned a strong warrior. "Replace Signa in guarding the church, and tell him to come to me."

Then he summoned another messenger. "Tell Krioni and Triskal to rouse Hank and get him praying, and all the Remnant."

In a short moment Signa arrived.

"Come with me," said Tal. "Let's talk."

It had been a quiet afternoon for Hank and Mary. Mary spent most of it in the little garden behind the house, while Hank worked to repair a corner of the backyard fence that kids had broken a hole through. As Mary hunted for weeds among her vegetables, she noticed Hank's hammering getting more and more sporadic until finally it stopped altogether. She looked his way and saw him sitting there, the hammer still in his hand, praying.

He seemed very disturbed, so she asked, "Are you all right?"

Hank opened his eyes, and without looking up he shook his head. "I don't feel good at all."

She went over to him. "What is it?"

Hank knew where the feeling came from. "The Lord, I guess. I just feel something's really wrong. Something terrible is about to happen. I'm going to call the Forsythes."

Just then the phone in the house rang. Hank went in and answered it. It was Andy Forsythe.

"Sorry to bother you, Pastor, but I was just wondering if you feel a real burden of prayer right now. I know I sure do."

"Come on over," said Hank.

The fence would have to wait.

On into the evening the angelic host waited, while Hank, the Forsythes, and several others prayed. Rafar continued to sit up in the dead tree, his eyes beginning to glow in the steadily thickening darkness. His taloned fingers continued to drum his knee; his brow stayed crinkled with his intense scowl. Behind him a host of demons began to gather, primed with anticipation and rapt with attention, waiting to hear Rafar's order.

The sun dipped behind the hills on the west side; the sky was washed with red fire.

Rafar sat and waited. The demonic host waited.

In her bedroom Juleen Langstrat sat on her bed, her legs crossed in the lotus position of Eastern meditation, her eyes closed, her head erect, her body perfectly still. Except for one single candle, the room was dark. There, under the shroud of the darkness, she convened her meeting with the Ascended Masters, the Spirit Guides from the higher planes. Deep within her consciousness, far within the depths of her inner being, she spoke with a messenger.

To the eyes of Langstrat's entranced mind the messenger appeared as a young lady, all dressed in white, with flowing blonde hair that reached nearly to the ground and was constantly in motion, wafted by the breeze.

"Where is my master?" Langstrat asked the messenger.

"He waits above the town, watching over it," came the girl's answer. "His armies are ready for your word."

"All is ready. He may await my signal."

"Yes, my lady."

The messenger departed like a beautiful gazelle, leaping gracefully away.

The messenger departed, a filthy black nightmare of a creature borne on membranous wings; he departed to take word to Rafar, who still waited.

Darkness deepened over Ashton; the candle in Langstrat's room dwindled to one round, ebbing flame in a pool of wax, the inky blackness overtaking its weak, orange light. Langstrat stirred, opened her glazed eyes, and arose from the bed. With a very small puff of breath she extinguished the candle and moved in a half daze into the living room where another candle was burning on the coffee table, the wax flowing and hardening into macabre fingers across the photograph of Ted Harmel on which the candle sat.

Langstrat sank to her knees beside the coffee table, her head held high, her eyes half shut, her movements slow and liquid. As if floating in space, her arms rose upward over the candle, stretching out an invisible canopy over the flame, and then, so very quietly, the name of an ancient god began to form itself on her lips again and again. The name, a guttural, harsh sound, spilled forth from her like the spitting of hundreds of invisible pebbles, and with each mention of the name, her trance deepened. Steadily, steadily the name tumbled forth, louder and faster, and Langstrat's eyes widened and remained unblinking and glaring. Her body began to quiver and tremble; her voice became an eerie wailing sound.

Rafar could hear it all from where he sat and waited. His own breathing began to deepen and chug out of his nostrils like putrid yellow steam. His eyes narrowed, his talons flexed.

Langstrat swayed and quivered, calling out the name, calling out the name, her eyes fixed on the candle's flame, calling out the name.

And then she froze.

Rafar looked up, very still, very attentive, listening.

Time stood still. Langstrat remained motionless, her arms extended over the candle.

Rafar listened.

Air began to slowly flow into Langstrat's mouth and nostrils, her lungs began to fill, and then, with one sudden cry from deep within, she brought her hands down like a trap, clapping them on the candle's wick, snuffing out the flame.

"Go!" shouted Rafar, and hundreds of demons shot into the sky like a thunderous flock of bats, rushing along a straight and level trajectory northward.

"Look," said an angelic warrior, and Tal and his host all saw what looked like a black swarm silhouetted against the night sky, an elongated puff of smoke.

"Going north," observed Tal. "Away from Ashton."

Rafar watched the squadron disappear at great speed and let a mocking grin bare his fangs. "I'll keep you guessing, Captain of the Host!"

Tal shouted out his orders. "Cover Hogan and Busche! Awaken the Remnant!"

A hundred angels soared downward into the town.

Tal could still see Rafar sitting in the big dead tree.

"Just what are your plans, Prince of Babylon?" he murmured.

The phone startled Marshall out of a restless sleep. The clock said 3:48 A.M. Kate moaned at being awakened. He grabbed up the receiver and mumbled hello.

For a moment he didn't have the slightest idea who was on the other end or what they were saying. The voice was wild, hysterical, high-pitched.

"Hey, simmer down and slow down or I'll hang up!" Marshall snapped hoarsely. Suddenly he recognized the voice. "Ted? Is this Ted?"

"Hogan . . ." came Ted Harmel's voice, "they're coming for me! They're all over the place!"

Marshall was awake now. He pressed the receiver to his ear, trying to understand what Ted was blubbering about. "I can't hear you! What'd you say?"

"They found out I talked! They're all over the place!"

"Who is?"

Ted started crying and screaming unintelligibly, and the sound of it was enough to make Marshall's insides curl up. He groped around the bedside stand for his pen and pad.

"Ted!" he shouted into the phone, and Kate jerked with a start and turned over to look at him. "Where are you? Are you home?"

Kate could hear the cries and wailings squawking out of the receiver, and it unnerved her. "Marshall, who is it?" she demanded.

Marshall couldn't answer her; he was too occupied trying to get a clear answer from Ted Harmel. "Ted, listen, tell me where you are." Pause. Some more cries. "How do I get there? I said, how do I get there?" Marshall began scribbling hurriedly. "Try getting out of there if you can . . ."

Kate listened, but couldn't make out what the party on the other end was saying.

Marshall told whoever it was, "Listen, it's going to take me at least half an hour to get there, and that's if I can find a station open to get some gas. No, I'll get over there, just hang tight. All right? Ted? All right?"

"Who's Ted?"

"All right," said Marshall into the phone. "Give me time, I'll get out there. Just take it easy. Good-bye."

He hung up the phone and bolted out of bed.

"Who in the world was that?" Kate needed to know.

Marshall grabbed his clothes and began to dress hurriedly. "Ted Harmel, remember, I told you about him . . ."

"You're not going over there tonight, are you?"

"The guy's going crazy or something, I don't know."

"You get back in bed!"

"Kate, I have to go! I can't afford to lose this contact."

"No! I don't believe this! You can't be serious!"

Marshall *was* serious. He kissed Kate good-bye before she could even bring herself to believe he was really going, and then he was gone. She sat there in the bed for a few moments, stunned, then flopped down angrily on her back, staring at the ceiling as she heard the car back down the driveway and speed off into the night.

24

Marshall drove about thirty miles north, through the town of Windsor and a little beyond. He was surprised to find out how close to Ashton Ted Harmel still lived, especially after they both met in the mountains over a hundred miles further up Highway 27. This guy has to be crazy, Marshall thought, and maybe I'm just as crazy to be going along with this whole routine. The guy's paranoid, a real space case.

But he sure sounded convincing over the phone. Besides, it was a chance to reopen communications with him after that one-time-only interview.

Marshall had to do some backtracking and groping around the maze of winding, unmarked backroads in his efforts to make sense of Harmel's directions. When he finally located the little shake-sided house at the end of a long gravel road, a ribbon of pink light was growing on the horizon. He'd taken an hour and a half to get there. Yes, there was the old Valiant, parked in the driveway. Marshall pulled in behind it and got out of the car.

The front door of the house was open. The front window was broken. Marshall crouched just a little behind his car, taking a moment to check out the situation. He didn't like the feelings he was getting at all; his insides had gone through this kind of a dance before, that night when Sandy had run off, and again there seemed no obvious, up-front reason for it. He hated to admit it, but he was afraid to take another step.

"Ted?" he called, not too loudly.

There was no answer.

It didn't look good at all. Marshall forced himself to make his way around his car, up the walk, and onto the front porch very slowly, very carefully. He kept listening, looking, feeling. There was no sound except his own pounding heart. His shoes crunched just a little on the shards of broken glass from the window. The sound seemed deafening.

C'mon, Hogan, get with it. "Ted?" he called through the open door. "Ted Harmel? It's Marshall Hogan."

No answer, but this had to be Ted's place. There was his coat hanging on the rack; on the wall above the dining room table was a framed front page from the *Clarion*.

He ventured inside.

The place was a mess. The dishes that had been in the corner hutch were now shattered all over the floor. In the living room a chair lay broken on the floor just below a large hole in the plaster wall. The bulbs were shattered out of the ceiling light fixture. Books from the shelves were thrown everywhere. The side window was also broken out.

And Marshall could feel it, just as strongly as before: that fierce, gut-wrenching terror he had felt that other night. He tried to shake it off, tried to ignore it, but it was there. His palms were slick with sweat; he felt weak. He looked around for a weapon and grabbed a fireplace poker. Keep your back to the wall, Hogan, keep quiet, look out for blind corners. It was dark in here, the shadows were very black. He tried to take his time, tried to let his eyes get used to the dark. He felt for a light switch somewhere, anywhere.

Behind and above him, a black, leathery wing quietly repositioned. Leering yellow eyes watched his every move. Here, there, over there, all over the room, in the corners of the ceiling, upon the furniture, clinging like insects to the walls, were the demons, some of them letting out little snickers, some of them drooling blood.

Marshall made his way stealthily to the desk in the corner and, using a handkerchief to prevent fingerprints, slid the drawers open. They had not been disturbed. Keeping the poker at the ready, he continued to move through the house.

The bathroom was a mess. The mirror was shattered; the shards were in the sink and all over the floor.

He moved down the hall, staying close to the wall.

Hundreds of pairs of yellow eyes watched his every move. There was an occasional hacking from the throat of a demon, a short burst of vapor from its dripping mouth.

In the bedroom the most loathsome spirits of all awaited him. They watched the bedroom doorway from their positions on the ceiling, on the walls, in every corner, and their breathing sounded like the dragging of chains through gravel-filled mud.

From where he stood, Marshall could see just the corner of the bed through the bedroom door. He approached cautiously, making frequent checks behind and even above him.

When he reached the bedroom door a single image, like a photograph, was instantly engraved on his mind. One second seemed like an eternity as his eyes darted from the blood-spattered bedspread to the bullet-blasted skull of Ted Harmel to the large revolver still dangling from Harmel's limp hand.

Shrieks! Thunder! Fangs bared to bite! The demons exploded from the walls, corners, every nook of the room and like arrows went for Marshall's heart.

A blinding flash! Then another, then another! The whitest hot light traced brilliant fiery arcs, a searing edge that cut through the flock of evil spirits like a scythe. Parts of demons tumbled into nothingness; other demons imploded and vanished in instantaneous billows of red smoke. Waves of spirits still poured down upon the one lone man who stood there in reasonless terror, but suddenly this man was surrounded by four heavenly warriors robed in glorious light, their crystalline wings unfurled like a canopy over their charge, their swords blurring into waving, swirling sheets of brilliance.

The air was filled with the deafening cries of hideous spirits as blades met flanks, necks, torsos, and demon after demon was flung aside in pieces that instantly disintegrated and vanished like vapor. Nathan, Armoth, and two other angels, Senter and Cree, darted, feinted, spun, batted away one spirit and sliced another, thrusting their blades in a myriad of directions. The lightning from their swords flashed against the walls, bright enough to bleach out all colors.

Nathan gutted one demon and sent it spiraling through the roof, leaving a red trail of vapor until it vanished. With his sword he slashed; with his free hand he collected demons by their heels.

Armoth and Senter whirled in a high-powered blur, mowing through demons as through grass. Cree threw himself against Marshall and kept his wings spread to protect the stunned man.

"Push them back!" shouted Nathan, and he began to spin his fistful of demons about his head, feeling the shock of their bodies striking other demons with the rhythm of a stick on a picket fence.

The demons began to shy back; half their numbers were now gone, as was half their zeal. Nathan, Armoth, and Senter started flying a tight spiral around Marshall, their swords knifing through the fading demonic ranks.

One demon shot straight into the sky with a wail of terror. Senter got right after it and quickly dispatched it like a slaughtered gamebird. He remained above the house for a time, containing any fleeing spirits very neatly and abruptly, swatting them out of existence as if they were fast-served tennis balls.

And then, almost as suddenly as it had begun, it was over. No demon remained; none had escaped.

Nathan alighted back in the hallway as his wings folded and the light around him faded. "How's our man?"

Cree was relieved to say, "He's still very shaken, but he's all right. He still has the will to fight."

Armoth came in for a landing and immediately checked Ted Harmel's pitiful frame. Senter dropped through the ceiling and joined him.

Armoth shook his head and sighed. "As Captain Tal said, Rafar can choose any front he wants, at any time."

"They have owned and tormented Ted Harmel for a long time," Senter conceded.

"Is Kevin Weed covered?" Nathan asked.

Armoth answered with a little curiosity, "Tal sent Signa to watchcare Weed."

"Signa? Was he not assigned to guard the church?"

"Tal must have a change in plans."

Nathan got back to the immediate business. "We'd best see to Marshall Hogan."

Marshall got a grip on himself. For a moment he thought he would really panic, and that would have been the very first time in his life. Nuts, I don't need to get involved in this stuff, not now, he thought. He took a few more moments to ease up and think the thing through. Harmel was history. But what about the others?

He went into the dining room and found the phone. Using his handkerchief again and a pen to dial, he called the operator, who put him through to the police department in Windsor, a town closer than Ashton, fortunately. Something told Marshall that Brummel and his cops were definitely not the ones to call on this.

"This is an anonymous call," he said. "There's been a fatal shooting, a suicide . . ." He told the sergeant who answered how to get there and then hung up.

Then he got out of there.

Several miles further north, he pulled the Buick into a filling station and went into a phone booth. He first called Eldon Strachan's number. There was no answer.

He had the operator ring the *Clarion*. Bernice should be there by now. C'mon, girl, answer the phone!

"*Ashton Clarion*." It was Carmen.

"Carmen, this is Marshall. Put Bernice on, will you?"

"Sure thing."

Bernice picked up her extension immediately. "Hogan, are you calling in sick?"

"Act normal, Bernie," Marshall said. "I've got some heavy developments."

"Well, take an aspirin or something."

"Good girl. Brace yourself for this one. I just came from Ted Harmel's place. He just blew his brains out. I got a call from him early this morning and he was talking crazy, talking about somebody coming after him, so I drove to his place and just now found him. It looked like he'd had an all-out fight with *something*. The place was a mess."

"So how are you feeling really?" Bernice said, and Marshall could tell this was the acting job of her career.

"I'm shook up but all right. I called the Windsor police but chose to get out of there. Right now I'm up near Windsor on Highway 38. I'm going to head north and drop by Strachan's place to check up on him. I want you to check on Weed right away. I don't want any more sources dying on me."

"Do you—do you think it's catching?"

"I don't know yet. Harmel was a little crazy; it may be an isolated incident. I do know I've got to talk to Strachan about it, and I don't want you to wait to check on Weed."

"Okay, I'll do that today."

"I should be back this afternoon. Be careful."

"You take care of yourself."

Marshall got back in his car and checked his map for the best way to get to Eldon Strachan's place. It took him another hour to make the drive, but soon he was pulling up the same old driveway to the quaint little farmhouse.

He slammed on the brakes and the Buick lurched to a halt, skidding on the gravel. He opened the car door and had another look from outside his car windows. There was no mistake.

The windows were broken in this house too. Come to think of it, by now that collie would be barking, but the place was dead silent.

Marshall left the car where it was and quietly made his way toward the house. No sounds. The windows on the side of the house were also broken. He noted that the glass was broken inward this time, unlike the Harmel house where the glass was broken out. He passed along the side of the house and checked the parking area in the back. No cars. He began praying that Eldon and Doris were gone and nowhere near whatever was happening.

He went around the other side of the house, completely encircling it, then stepped onto the front porch and tried the front door. It was locked. He looked through the front window—the glass was mostly gone—and saw total chaos inside: the house had been ransacked.

He carefully stepped through the window into the once quaint living room, now a pitiful shambles. The furniture was thrown everywhere, the cushions on the sofa were slashed open, the coffee table had been chopped in several pieces, some floor lamps had been thrown down and broken, everything was out of its place and thrown about.

"Eldon!" Marshall called. "Doris! Anybody home?"

As if I really expected an answer, he thought. But what was that on the mirror over the fireplace? He went for a closer look. Someone had taken red paint . . . or was it blood? Marshall checked closely. With great relief he smelled the unmistakable scent of paint. But someone had scrawled an obscene message of hate on the mirror, a very clear threat.

He knew he would have to check every room in the house, and right at this moment he wondered why he didn't feel the same terror he had felt at Harmel's. Maybe this day was turning him numb. Maybe he just wasn't believing any of it anymore.

He checked the whole house, upstairs and downstairs and even the cellar, but there were no terrible discoveries, and he was very glad. That didn't make him any less concerned, nervous, or perplexed, however. This was too much of a coincidence despite the basic differences. As he took a second look around the living room, he tried to think if there could be a connection. Obviously, both Harmel and Strachan had been sources for Marshall's investigation and could have become targets for intimidation. But Harmel in his terrible fear could have done the damage around his house by himself, fighting off whatever it was, while this damage to Strachan's house was clearly the act of vandals, of malicious characters out to scare him. That was one connection: fear. Both Harmel and Strachan were the brunt of fear tactics, whatever form they took. But why would . . .

"All right! Freeze! Police!"

Marshall stayed still, but he did look out through the broken window. There, on the porch, was a sheriff's officer aiming a gun at him.

"Take it easy," Marshall said very gently, without moving.

"Get both hands in the air, in plain sight!" the officer commanded.

Marshall obeyed. "The name's Marshall Hogan, editor of the *Ashton Clarion*. I'm a friend of the Strachans."

"Just hold steady. I'll have to see some I.D., Mr. Hogan."

Marshall explained everything he did as he did it. "I'm going to reach into my back pocket here, see? Here's my wallet. Now I'm going to toss it to you through the window there."

By now the officer's partner had mounted the porch and also had his gun trained on Marshall. Marshall tossed his wallet through the broken window, and the first policeman picked it up.

The officer checked Marshall's I.D. "What are you doing here, Mr. Hogan?"

"Trying to figure out what in blazes happened to Eldon's house. And I'd also like to know what happened to Eldon and Doris, his wife."

The officer seemed satisfied with Marshall's I.D. and relaxed just a little, but his partner kept a gun trained on Marshall.

The officer tried the front door and then asked, "How'd you get in there?"

"Through that window," Marshall answered.

"Okay, Mr. Hogan, I am going to ask you to step very carefully back through the window, and do it very slowly. Please keep both hands in plain sight."

Marshall obeyed. As soon as he got out on the porch the officer turned him around, his hands against the wall, and frisked him.

Marshall asked, "You guys from Windsor?"

"Windsor Precinct," came the short answer, and with that, the officer grabbed Marshall's wrists one at a time and slapped handcuffs on him. "We're placing you under arrest. You have the right to remain silent . . ."

Marshall could think of all kinds of questions to ask and it was all he could do to keep from disassembling these two, but he knew better than to say a word.

25

Bernice called Kevin Weed right after she got off the phone with Marshall, but there was no answer. He was probably working with the logging crew today. She dug through her file and found the phone number for Gorst Brothers Timber.

They told her Kevin had not been in today, and if she saw him she'd better tell him to show up quick or he'd be out of a job.

"Thanks, Mr. Gorst."

She dialed The Evergreen Tavern in Baker. Dan, the proprietor, answered.

"Sure," he said, "Weed was in here this morning, just like he always is. He was in a gosh-awful mood though. He got in a fight with one of his buddies, and I had to throw them both out."

Bernice left Dan the *Clarion*'s number in case he saw Weed again. Then she hung up and thought for a moment. It wasn't out of the question to drive out to Baker, and besides, orders were orders. She went over her schedule for the day and tried to rearrange her jobs to accommodate the trip.

"Carmen," she said, grabbing her jacket and handbag, "I'll be gone for the day, I think. If Marshall calls, tell him I've gone out to check on a source. He'll know what I mean."

"Righto," said Carmen.

Baker was about seventeen miles north on Highway 27; the apartments where Weed lived were about two miles closer. Bernice found them without too much trouble, a sad complex of dry-rotting cubicles honeycombed into a sun-bleached old warehouse. Bernice's nose told her the septic system was failing.

She went up the plank stairs onto the loading dock which now served as a patio and entranceway. Inside, she was appalled at how dark the building was. She looked down one long corridor and noted many closely spaced doors; these weren't apartments, they were lockers.

She had heard some footsteps on the old planks upstairs, and now they came down the stairway just behind her. She turned her head just enough to see an unpleasant-looking character stepping down, a skinny, pimple-faced apparition in black leather. She immediately decided she had a very pressing appointment at the other end of the hall and started in that direction.

"Hi there," the man called to her. "Looking for someone?"

Make it quick, Bernice. "Just visiting a friend, thank you."

"Have a nice visit," he said, and he kept looking her over as if she were a steak.

She walked quickly down the corridor, hoping it wouldn't be a dead end, and though she didn't look back she could tell he was still watching her. Hogan, I'll get you for this.

She was glad to find another stairway leading upstairs. Weed's apartment had a two hundred number, so up the stairs she went. The stairwell was old weathered planks, illumined with one bare light bulb hanging from a very high rafter. Some thirty years ago someone had tried to paint the walls. She wound her way upward, ignoring the disgusting graffiti everywhere, her shoes making hollow thuds on the worn planks.

She reached the upstairs corridor and doubled back, following the descending numbers on the doors. From behind some of the doors came sounds of soap operas, FM rock stations, marital spats.

She finally found Weed's door and knocked; there was no answer. But her knocking nudged the door, and it drifted slowly open. She helped it quietly on its way.

The place was an absolute mess. Bernice had seen the homes of messy people before, but how could Weed possibly live in a disaster area like this?

"Kevin?" she called.

No answer. She stepped inside and closed the door.

It had to be vandalism; Weed didn't own that much, but what he did own was thrown about, broken, spilled, and shattered. Papers and bric-a-brac were everywhere, the little cot in the corner was overturned, Weed's guitar was facedown on the floor, the back stomped through, the bulbs were broken out of the ceiling fixture, the few secondhand dishes were in shattered pieces all over the floor in the little kitchen cubicle. Then she saw words spray-painted across one whole wall, an incredibly obscene threat.

For the longest time she didn't move. She was afraid. The implications were clear enough—how long would it be before they struck her or Marshall? She wondered what Marshall would find at Strachan's, she wondered what her own home looked like, and she realized there were no police to call; the police were with *them*.

Finally she slipped quietly out the door, wrote Weed a quick note in case he ever came back, and shoved it in the crack just above the doorknob. She looked this way and that and then went along the corridor and back down the stairs again.

Just one flight below the second floor, a wall formed a blind corner between the two flights at the middle landing. Bernice was just thinking how she didn't like blind corners in a place like this, and how the lighting was so poor . . .

A black figure leaped at her from the flight below. Her body slammed into the old shiplap wall as her teeth clapped together.

The man in leather! A rough, dirty hand grabbing a fistful of blouse. A violent, sideways jerk. Tearing cloth, her body reeling. An impact like an explosion in her left ear. A blurred, hate-filled face.

She was falling. Her arms went out against the rough plank corner, they were limp, they buckled, she slid down the wall to the floor. A black boot blotted out her vision, her glasses were driven into her face, her skull thudded against the wall. She went numb. Her body kept jerking about—he was still hitting her.

Step step step step step step step—he was gone.

She was dreaming, her head was reeling, there was blood upon the floor and broken glasses in bent pieces. She slumped against the wall, still feeling the fist in her ear and the boot in her face, and hearing blood dripping from her mouth and her nose. The floor drew her down like a magnet until her head finally thumped on the boards.

She whimpered, a gurgling sound as blood and saliva bubbled over her tongue. She spit it all out, raised her head, and cried out in a sound that was half cry, half moan.

From somewhere up above, the boards began to pound and clatter with a sudden flow of traffic. She heard people shouting, swearing, thundering down the steps. She couldn't move; she kept half-dreaming as light and sound faded in and out, were there, were not there. Hands began to hold her, move her, cradle her. A cloth wiped across her mouth. She felt the new warmth of a blanket. A towel kept dabbing her face. She gurgled again, spit again. She heard someone swear again.

Marshall still wouldn't reply to any questions, although the detective at the Windsor Precinct kept trying.

"We're talking about murder here, bub!" the detective said. "Now we have it from reliable sources that you were there at Harmel's place early this morning, and that's right near the time of death. Do you have anything to say about that?"

This flunky was born yesterday, Marshall thought. Sure, punk, I'll tell you all about it so you can hang me! In a pig's eye it was murder.

But what really bothered Marshall was just who this "reliable source" was, and how that reliable source not only knew he'd been at Harmel's, but also knew these cops could find him at Strachan's. He was still working on the answer to that riddle.

The detective asked, "So you're still not going to say anything?"

Marshall wouldn't even nod or shake his head.

"Well," the detective said with a half shrug, "at least give me the name of your lawyer. You're going to need counsel."

Marshall had no name to give him and couldn't even think of one. It became a waiting game.

"Spence," said a deputy, "you've got a call from Ashton."

The detective picked up the phone at his desk. "Nelson. Oh, hi there, Alf. What's up?"

Alf Brummel?

"Yeah," the detective said, "he's right here. Would you like to talk to him? He sure won't talk to *us*." He offered Marshall the receiver. "Alf Brummel."

Marshall took the receiver. "Yeah, this is Hogan."

Alf Brummel was acting shocked and dismayed. "Marshall, what's going on up there?"

"I can't say."

"They tell me Ted Harmel was murdered and that they have you as a suspect. Is that true?"

"I can't say."

Alf was beginning to catch on. "Marshall . . . listen, I'm calling to see if I can help. Now, I'm sure there's been a mistake and I'm sure we can work something out. What were you doing up at Harmel's place anyway?"

"I can't say."

That flustered him. "Marshall, for crying out loud, will you just forget that I'm a cop? I'm also your friend. I want to help you!"

"Do it."

"I want to. I really want to. Now listen, let me talk to Detective Nelson again. Maybe we can work something out."

Marshall handed the receiver back to Nelson. Nelson and Brummel talked for a while, and it sounded like they knew each other pretty well.

"Well, you might be able to do more with him than I ever will," said Nelson quite pleasantly. "Sure, why not? Huh? Yeah, okay." Nelson looked at Marshall. "He's on another line. Guess he'll vouch for you, and I think he can take jurisdiction over your case, if there is one."

Marshall nodded all too knowingly. Now Brummel would have

Marshall right where he wanted him. If there was a case! If there wasn't one, Brummel would find one. What would it be now, Harmel and Hogan running a child-molesting ring with a gangland-type murder?

Nelson heard Brummel come back on the line. "Yeah, hello. Yeah sure." Nelson handed Marshall the receiver again.

Brummel was upset, or at least he sounded like it. "Marshall, that was the fire district that just called. They've just sent an aid car out toward Baker. It's Bernice; she's been assaulted."

Marshall never thought he'd hope Brummel *was* lying. "Tell me more."

"We won't know more until they get out there. It won't take long. Listen, they're going to release you on personal recognizance under my supervision. You'd better get back to Ashton right away. Can you see me in my office at, say, 3?"

Marshall thought he would have a seizure trying to contain all the cuss words he had for this whole thing. "I'll be there, Alf. Nothing could keep me away."

"Good, I'll see you then."

Marshall returned the receiver to Nelson.

Nelson smiled and said, "We'll take you back to your car."

The man in black leather was back in Ashton, running down the streets and then through the alleys like a man possessed, looking behind him, panting, crying, terrified.

Five cruel spirits rode on his back, ducked in and out of his body, clung to him like huge leeches, their talons deeply embedded in his flesh. But they were not in control. They too were terrified.

Just above the five demons and their running victim, six angelic warriors floated along with their swords drawn, moving this way and that, to the right, to the left, whatever it took to keep the demons herded in the right direction.

The demons hissed and spit and made shooing motions with their sinewy hands.

The young man ran, swatting at invisible bees.

The young man and his demons came to a corner. They tried to go left. The angels blocked their way and prodded them with their swords to the right. With a cry and a terrible wailing, the demons fled to the right.

The demons began to cry for mercy. "No! Let us alone!" they pleaded. "You have no right!"

Just up the street, Hank Busche and Andy Forsythe were walking together, taking some time to share their burdens and pray.

Right alongside them walked Triskal, Krioni, Seth, and Scion. The four warriors all saw what their comrades were herding their way, and they were more than ready.

"Time for an object lesson for the man of God," said Krioni.

Triskal only beckoned to the demons with his finger and said, "Come, come!"

Andy looked down the street and saw the man first. "Well . . .!"

"What?" asked Hank, seeing the dumfounded look on Andy's face.

"Get ready. Here comes Bobby Corsi!"

Hank looked and cringed at the sight of a wild-looking character running toward them, his eyes filled with terror, his arms beating the air as he battled unseen enemies.

Andy cautioned, "Be careful. He could be violent."

"Oh, terrific!"

They stood still and waited to see what Bobby would do.

Bobby saw them and cried out in even more terror, "No, no! Leave us alone!"

Heaven's warriors were bad enough, but the five demons wanted no part of Busche and Forsythe. They twisted Bobby around and tried to run away, but were instantly hemmed in by the angelic six.

Bobby stopped dead in his tracks. He looked at nothing ahead of him, then looked at Hank and Andy, then looked again at his unseen enemies. He screamed, standing still where he was, his hands clawlike and trembling, his eyes bulging and glazed.

Hank and Andy moved forward very slowly.

"Easy, Bobby," Andy said soothingly. "Take it easy now."

"No!" Bobby screamed. "Leave us alone! We want no business with you!"

An angel gave one of the demons a prod with the tip of his sword.

"Awww!" Bobby cried out in pain, collapsing to his knees. "Leave us alone, leave us alone!"

Hank stepped forward quickly and said firmly, "In Jesus' name, be quiet!" Bobby let out one more scream. "Be quiet!"

Bobby grew still and began to weep, kneeling there on the sidewalk.

"Bobby," said Hank, bending down and speaking gently, "Bobby, can you hear me?"

A demon clapped his hands over Bobby's ears. Bobby did not hear Hank's question.

Hank, hearing from the Spirit of God, knew what the demon was doing. "Demon, in the name of Jesus, let go of his ears."

The demon jerked his hands away, a surprised look on his face.

Hank asked again, "Bobby?"

This time Bobby answered, "Yeah, preacher, I hear you."

"Do you want to be free from these spirits?"

Immediately one demon answered, "No, you don't! He belongs to us," and Bobby spit the words in Hank's face, "No, you don't! He belongs to us!"

"Spirit, be quiet. I'm talking to Bobby."

The demon said no more, but backed off sulkingly.

Bobby muttered, "I've just done a horrible thing . . ." He began to weep. "You gotta help me . . . I can't stop from doing this stuff . . ."

Hank spoke quietly aside to Andy. "Let's get him somewhere where we can deal with him, where he can make a scene if he has to."

"The church?"

"Come on, Bobby."

They took him by his arms and helped him up, and the three, and the five, and the six, and the four headed up the street.

Marshall sped through Baker and then made a quick swing by the apartment complex where Weed lived. There seemed to be no activity there, so he drove on into Ashton. When he reached the hospital, the aid car was parked outside.

An emergency medical technician who was securing the stretcher back in the vehicle filled Marshall in. "She's in the emergency room, two doors down."

Marshall burst through the main doors and got to the right room in an instant. He heard a cry of pain from Bernice just as he reached the door.

She was lying on a table, attended by a doctor and two nurses who were washing her face and dressing her cuts. At the sight of her, Marshall could contain himself no longer; all the anger and frustration and terror of this whole day exploded from his lungs in one vehement expletive.

Bernice responded through swollen and bleeding lips, "I guess that about covers it."

He hurried to the side of the table as the doctor and two nurses gave him room. He took her hand in both of his and couldn't believe what had happened to her. Her attacker had been merciless.

"Who did this to you?" he demanded, his blood boiling.

"We went the whole fifteen rounds, boss."

"Don't clown with me, Bernie. Did you see who did it?"

The doctor cautioned him, "Easy now, let's take care of her first . . ."

Bernice whispered something. Marshall couldn't make it out. He leaned closer and she whispered it again, her swollen mouth slurring her words. "He didn't rape me."

"Thank God," Marshall said, straightening up.

She wasn't satisfied with his response. She motioned to him again to lean forward and listen. "All he did was beat me up. That's all he did."

"Aren't you satisfied?" Marshall whispered back rather loudly.

She was handed a glass of water to wash her mouth out. She swirled the water around in her mouth and spit into a bowl.

"Was Strachan's house nice and neat?" she asked.

Marshall held back his answer. He asked the doctor, "When can I talk to her in private?"

The doctor thought about it. "Well, she's going in for X-rays in just a few minutes—"

"Give me thirty seconds," Bernice requested, "just thirty seconds."

"It can't wait?"

"No. Please."

The doctor and the nurses stepped out of the room.

Marshall spoke softly. "Strachan's place was a mess; somebody really went through it. He's gone; I've no idea where he is or how he is."

Bernice reported, "Weed's place was the same way, and there was a threat spray-painted on the wall. He didn't show up for work today, and Dan at The Evergreen Tavern said he was really upset about something. He's gone, too. I didn't find him."

"And now they've got me wrapped up with Ted Harmel's death. They found out I was there this morning. They think I did it."

"Marshall, Susan Jacobson was right: our phone must be bugged. Remember? You called me at the *Clarion* and told me you'd been at Ted's and where you were going next."

"Yeah, yeah, I figured that. But that means the Windsor cops would have to be in on it too. They knew right where and when to find me at Strachan's."

"Brummel and Detective Nelson are like *that*, Marshall," Bernice said, holding two fingers together.

"They must have ears everywhere."

"They knew I'd be at Weed's alone . . . and when . . ." Bernice said, and then something else dawned on her. "Carmen knew it too."

That revelation hit Marshall almost like a death sentence. "Carmen knows a *lot* of things."

"We've been hit, Marshall. I think they're trying to get a message to us."

He straightened up. "Wait'll I find Brummel!"

She grabbed his hand. "Be careful. I mean, *really* be careful!"

He kissed her forehead. "Happy X-rays."

He stormed out of the room like a raging bull, and no one dared get in his way.

26

Marshall was seeing red, and was so angry that he parked crooked-ly across two parking places in the Courthouse Square parking lot. He thought that walking fast across the parking lot to the police department's door might air-cool him a bit, but it didn't. He jerked open the door and went into the reception area. Sara wasn't at her desk. Brummel wasn't in his office. Marshall checked his watch. It was 3 o'clock on the dot.

A woman came around the corner. He'd never seen her before.

"Hello," he said, and then added very abruptly, "Who are you?"

She was quite taken aback by the question, and timidly answered, "Well, I'm . . . I'm Barbara, the receptionist."

"The receptionist? What happened to Sara?"

She was intimidated and a little indignant. "I—I don't know of any Sara, but can *I* help you?"

"Where's Alf Brummel?"

"Are you Mr. Hogan?"

"That's right."

"Chief Brummel is waiting for you in the conference room, right down at the end of the hall."

She hadn't finished her sentence before Marshall was already on his way. If the door latch would have given the slightest resistance, it wouldn't have survived Marshall's entrance. He burst into the room ready to wring the first neck he could get his hands around.

There were many necks to choose from. The room was full of people Marshall had not been expecting, but as he looked around at all the faces, he had no trouble guessing the meeting's agenda. Brummel had friends with him. Big shots. Liars. Schemers.

Alf Brummel sat at the conference table surrounded by his many comrades and smiling that toothy grin. "Hello, Marshall. Please close the door."

Marshall kicked the door shut with his foot without looking away from all these people now gathered, no doubt to have it out with him. Oliver Young was there, as was Judge Baker, County Comptroller Irving Pierce, Fire Marshall Frank Brady, Detective Spence Nelson from Windsor, a few other men Marshall didn't recognize, and finally the mayor of Ashton, David Steen.

"Well, hello there, Mayor Steen," Marshall said coldly. "How interesting to find you here."

The mayor only smiled cordially and silently, like the dumb puppet Marshall always thought he was.

"Have a seat," said Brummel, waving his hand toward an empty chair.

Marshall didn't move. "Alf, is this the meeting you and I were going to have?"

"This is the meeting," said Brummel. "I don't think you know everyone in the room . . ." With overcooked graciousness, Brummel introduced the new or possibly new faces. "I'd like you to meet Tony Sulski, a local attorney, and I believe you've dealt with Ned Wesley, president of the Independent Bank. We understand you've had a conversation at least with Eugene Baylor, college regent. And you of course remember Jimmy Clairborne, from Commercial Printers." Brummel showed his teeth widely, obnoxiously. "Marshall, please have a seat."

Cusswords were going through Marshall's mind as he told Brummel squarely, "Not while I'm outnumbered."

Oliver Young piped up in answer to that. "Marshall, I can assure you that this will be a civil and cordial meeting."

"So which one of you beat the ever-living daylights out of my reporter?" Marshall was hardly feeling civil.

Brummel responded, "Marshall, these things happen to people who aren't careful."

Marshall smeared some descriptions on Brummel like icing from a sewer trap and then told him seethingly, "Brummel, this didn't just happen. She was set up. She was assaulted and injured and your cops haven't done a thing, and we all know why!" He glared at them. "You're all in on this whole thing, and your tricks come real cheap. You vandalize homes, you make threats, you drive people out, you act like some kind of Mafia boys' club!" He aimed an accusing finger at Brummel. "And you, buddy, are a disgrace to your profession. You've used your entrusted powers to silence and intimidate, and to cover up your own dirty work!"

Young tried to interject. "Marshall—"

"And you call yourself a man of God, a pastor, a pious example of what a good Christian should be. You lied to me all along, Young, hiding behind some excuse you call professional ethics, guzzling down all that mystical bull from that Langstrat witch and then acting like you knew nothing about it. How many people who trusted you have you sold out to a lie?"

The men in the room sat silent. Marshall kept unloading. "If you guys are public servants, Hitler was a great humanitarian! You schemed and manipulated and horned your way into this town like mobsters, and you silenced anybody who spoke up or got in your way. You will read about it in the paper, gentlemen! If you want to make any comments or denials I'll be glad to hear them, I'll even print them, but it's press time for all of you whether you like it or not!"

Young raised his hands to get just a short moment to speak. "Marshall, all I can say is, be sure of your facts."

"Don't worry about that. I have my facts, all right. I have innocent people like the Carluccis, the Wrights, the Andersons, the Dombrowskis, over a hundred of them, who were driven out of their homes and businesses by intimidation and trumped up tax delinquencies."

Young piped in, "*Intimidation?* Marshall, it's hardly within our control to prevent fear, foolish superstition, family break-ups. Just what will you print? That the Carluccis, for example, were convinced their store was haunted and that evil spirits, of all things, broke their small son's hands? Come now, Marshall."

Marshall pointed at Young straight from the shoulder. "Hey, Young, that's your specialty. I'll print that you and your bunch preyed on their fears and orchestrated their superstitions, and I'll tell all about the wild practices and philosophies you used to pull it off. I know all about Langstrat and her mind-tripping hocus-pocus, and I know that every one of you is into it.

"I'll print that you set people up with phony raps just to get them removed from their jobs and offices so your own people could move in: you framed Lew Gregory, the former comptroller, with a phony conflict of interest charge; you pushed and pressed for that big turnover on the Whitmore College Board of Regents after Dean Strachan caught Eugene Baylor"—Marshall looked right at Baylor as he said it—"juggling the books! You put Ted Harmel out of town on his ear with that phony child-molesting rap, and I find it interesting that Adam Jarred's poor little victim daughter now has a special fund set up for her college education. If I look far enough, I'll probably find the money came out of your pockets!

"I'll print that my reporter was falsely arrested by Brummel's flunkies because she took a picture she wasn't supposed to, a picture of Brummel, Young, and Langstrat with none other than Alexander M. Kaseph himself, the Big Boy behind a conspiracy to take over the town, aided and abetted by all of you, a bunch of power-hungry, pseudo-spiritualized neo-Fascists!"

Young smiled calmly. "Which means you plan to write about the Omni Corporation."

Marshall couldn't believe he was actually hearing it coming from Young's mouth. "So now it's tell-the-truth time?"

Young continued, very relaxed, very confident. "Well, you have been tracking down everything that Omni has bought and owns, isn't that right?"

"That's right."

Young laughed a little when he asked, "And how many houses would you say were turned over to Omni because of tax delinquency?"

Marshall refused to play games. "You tell me."

Young simply turned to Irving Pierce, the comptroller.

Pierce shuffled through some papers. "Mr. Hogan, I believe your records show that one hundred and twenty three homes were auctioned to Omni for failure to pay taxes . . ."

He knew. Well, so what? "I'll stand by that."

"You were in error."

Let's hear the lie, Pierce.

"The correct number is one hundred and *sixty-three*. All legally, all legitimately, over the past five years."

Marshall hated it, but he couldn't think of a comeback.

Young spoke on. "You *are* correct about Omni owning all these properties, plus many other commercial enterprises as well. But you also should note how these properties have been substantially improved under this new ownership. I would say that Ashton is certainly a better town for it."

Marshall could feel the steam rising in his pipes. "Those people paid their taxes! I've talked to over a hundred of them!"

Pierce was unmoved. "We have substantial evidence to show that they did not."

"In a pig's eye!"

"And in regard to the college . . ." Young looked at Eugene Baylor, giving him his cue.

Baylor stood to speak. "I've really had quite enough of this slander and gossip about the college being in financial arrears. The college is doing just fine, thank you, and this—this smear campaign that Eldon Strachan began must stop or we will sue! Mr. Sulski has been retained for just that eventuality."

"I have records, I have proof, Baylor, that you've embezzled Whitmore College out of millions."

Brummel piped in, "You have no proof, Marshall. You have no records."

Marshall had to smile. "Oh, you ought to just see what I have."

Young said simply, "We have seen it. All of it."

Marshall had the feeling deep inside that he had just stepped off a cliff.

Young continued with a progressively cooling tone. "We've been following your futile attempts from the very beginning. We know you talked to Ted Harmel, we know you've been interviewing Eldon Strachan, Joe Carlucci, Lew Gregory, and hundreds of other quacks, malcontents and doomsayers. We know you've been harassing our people and our businesses. We know that you've been snooping in all our personal records." Young paused for effect, and then said, "That's all going to stop now, Marshall."

"Hence this meeting!" Marshall said with sarcastic flair. "What's in store for me, Young? How about it, Brummel? Got a nice morals rap to pin on me? You gonna send someone to tear up my house too?"

Young stood up, motioning for a chance to speak. "Marshall, you may never understand our true motivations, but at least give me one opportunity to try to clear the matter up for you. There is no predatory thirst for power here among us, as you probably think. We do not seek power as an end."

"No, you just came upon it purely by accident," Marshall said cuttingly.

"Power for us, Marshall, is only necessary as one means toward our real goal for mankind, and that is nothing other than universal peace and prosperity."

"Who's 'we' and 'us'?"

"Oh, you already know that too, all too well. The Society, Marshall, the Society you've been hounding after all this time as if chasing after some mysterious burglar."

"The Universal Consciousness Society. And we have our own little chapter here in Ashton, our own little piece of the Conquer the World Club!"

Young smiled ever so tolerantly. "More than a club, Marshall. Actually, a long-awaited, newly rising force for global change, a worldwide voice that will finally unite mankind."

"Yeah, and such a wonderful, humanitarian movement that you have to sneak in with it, you have to hide it . . ."

"Only from old ideas, Marshall, from the old obstacles of religious bigotry and intolerance. We live in a changing and growing world, and mankind is still evolving, still maturing. Many still lag behind in the maturing process and cannot tolerate the very thing that will be best for them. Marshall, too many of us just don't know what's best. Someday—and we hope it will be soon—everyone will understand, there will be no more religion, and then there will be no more secrets."

"In the meantime, you do what you can to scare people and chase them from their homes and businesses—"

"Only, *only* if they are limited in their perspective and resist the truth; only if they stand in the way of what is truly right and good."

Marshall was getting as sick as he was angry. "Truly right and good? What? All of a sudden, you guys are the new authority on what right and good is? C'mon, Young, where's your theology? Where does God fit into all this?"

Young gave a resigned shrug and said, "*We* are God."

Marshall finally did sink into a chair. "Either you people are crazy or I am."

"I know it's quite beyond anything you've ever considered before. Admittedly, ours are very high and lofty ideals, but what we've come to achieve is inevitable for all men. It is nothing more than the final destination of man's evolution: enlightenment, self-realization. Someday all men, even yourself, must realize their own infinite potential, their own divinity, and become united in one universal mind, one universal consciousness. The alternative is to perish."

Marshall had heard enough. "Young, that is pure, unadulterated horse hockey and you are out of your ever-loving mind!"

Young looked at the others and almost looked sad. "We all hoped you would understand, but in truth, we did expect you to feel this way. You have so far to go, Marshall, so very far to go . . ."

Marshall took a good long look at them all. "You plan to take over the town, don't you? Buy out the college? Make it some kind of hive for your cosmic, mind-blown Society?"

Young looked at him with a very sober face and said, "It's for the very best, Marshall. It has to be this way."

Marshall got up and headed for the door. "I'll see you in the paper."

"You have no paper, Marshall," Young said abruptly.

Marshall only turned and shook his head at Young. "Drop dead."

Ned Wesley, the president of the Independent Bank, spoke on cue from Young. "Marshall, we have to foreclose on you."

Marshall did not believe what he had heard.

Wesley opened his file to the records of Marshall's business loan on the *Clarion*. "You've been delinquent in your payments for eight months now, and we've received no response whatsoever from our many inquiries. We really have no choice but to foreclose."

Marshall was totally prepared to make Wesley eat his phony records, but didn't have time before Irving Pierce, the county comptroller, spoke up.

"As for your taxes, Marshall, I'm afraid those have become quite delinquent as well. I just don't know how you thought you could go on living in that house without meeting your obligations."

Marshall knew he could be a murderer right about now. It would be the easiest thing in the world, except that there were two cops in the room who would love to pin such a rap on him and a judge who would love to lock him away for good.

"You are all crazy," he said slowly. "You'll never get away with it."

Just then Jimmy Clairborne from Commercial Printers put in his two cents. "Marshall, I'm afraid we've been having some trouble with you as well. My records here show that we haven't been paid for the last six runs of the *Clarion*. There's no way we can continue to print the paper for you until these accounts are cleared up."

Detective Nelson added, "These are very serious matters, Marshall, and as far as our investigation of Ted Harmel's murder, these things do not put you in a very good light."

"As for the courts," said Judge Baker, "whatever decisions we ultimately render will depend, I suppose, on your behavior from now on."

"Especially in light of the complaints of sexual misconduct we've just received," added Brummel. "Your daughter must be a very frightened girl to have remained silent for so long."

He felt like bullets were ripping into him. He could feel himself dying, he was sure of it.

The five demons clung tenaciously to Bobby Corsi, hissing their sulfurous oaths and cursings as they cowered in the front of the little sanctuary of the Ashton Community Church. Triskal, Krioni, Seth, and Scion were there along with six other warriors, their swords drawn, surrounding the little prayer group. Hank had his Bible handy and had already gone through a few references in the Gospels to get some idea of how to proceed. He and Andy held Bobby firmly but gently as Bobby sat on the floor in front of the pulpit. John Coleman had come right over to help, and Ron Forsythe wouldn't have missed it.

"Yeah," Ron observed, "he's got it bad. Hey, Bobby. Remember me, Ron Forsythe?"

Bobby looked at Ron with glassy, staring eyes. "Yeah, I remember you . . ."

But the demons also remembered Ron Forsythe and the hold their comrades once had on his life. "Traitor! Traitor!"

Bobby began to scream at Ron, "Traitor! Traitor!" as he struggled to free himself from Hank and Andy. John stepped in to help hold Bobby down.

Hank commanded the demons, "Stop it! Stop it right now!"

The demons spoke through Bobby as Bobby turned and cursed at Hank. "We don't need to listen to you, praying man! You will never defeat us! You will die before you defeat us!" Bobby glared at the four men and screamed, "You will all die!"

Hank prayed aloud so everyone, including Bobby, could hear. "Lord God, we come against these spirits now in Jesus' name, and we bind them!"

The five spirits ducked their heads under their wings as if being pelted by stones, crying and whimpering.

"No . . . no . . ." said Bobby.

Hank continued, "And I pray right now that you will send your angels to help us . . ."

The ten warriors were ready and waiting.

Hank addressed the spirits. "I want to know how many are in there. Speak up!"

One demon, a smaller one, ducked inside Bobby's back and shrieked, "Nooo!"

The scream came belching out of Bobby's throat.

"Which one are you?" Hank asked.

"I won't tell you! You can't make me!"

"By the name of Jesus—"

The demon responded immediately, "Fortune-telling!"

Hank asked, "Fortune-telling, how many of you are in there?"

"Millions!" Triskal jabbed Fortune-telling lightly in the flank. "Awww! Ten! Ten!" Another jab. "Aww! No, we are five, only five!"

Bobby began to twitch and shake as the demons got into a scuffle. Fortune-telling found himself the brunt of some very harsh blows.

"No! No!" Bobby screamed for the demon. "Now see what you've made me do! The others are hitting me!"

"In Jesus' name, leave," said Hank.

Fortune-telling let go of Bobby and floated up over the group. Krioni grabbed him.

"Depart from the region!" he ordered.

Fortune-telling obeyed immediately and soared out of the church, not looking back.

A large and hairy demon shouted after the departed spirit, and Bobby stared at the ceiling shouting, "Traitor! Traitor! We'll get you for that!"

"And who are you?" Hank asked.

The demon shut its mouth, as did Bobby, and glared at the men with eyes full of fire and hatred.

"Spirit, who are you?" Andy demanded.

Bobby remained silent, his entire body strained, his lips tightly together, his eyes bulging out. He was taking frantic, short breaths through his nose. His face was crimson.

"Spirit," said Andy, "I command you to tell us who you are in Jesus' name!"

"Don't you mention that name!" the spirit hissed and then cursed.

"I will mention that name again and again," said Hank. "You know that name has defeated you."

"No . . . No!"

"Who are you?"

"Confusion, Madness, Hatred . . . Ha! I do them all!"

"In the name of Jesus I bind you and command you to come out!"

The demons all made a sudden rushing of their wings together, pulling, tearing at Bobby, trying to get away.

Bobby struggled to get free from the men who held him, and it was all they could do to hold him down. They outweighed him at least four to one, and yet he almost threw them off.

"Come out!" all four commanded.

The second spirit lost his grip on Bobby and jolted upward as Bobby suddenly relaxed. The spirit immediately found himself in the waiting hands of two warriors.

"Depart from this region!" they ordered him.

He looked down at Bobby glaringly, and at his three remaining cohorts, then shot out of the church and streaked away.

The third demon spoke right up, speaking through Bobby's voice. "You'll never get me out! I've been here most of his life!"

"Who are you?"

"Witchcraft! Lots of witchcraft!"

"It's time for you to leave," said Hank.

"Never! We're not alone, you know! There are many of us!"

"Only three by my count."

"Yes, in him, yes. But you'll never get to us all. Go ahead and cast us out of this one; there are still millions in the town. Millions!" The demon laughed uproariously.

Andy ventured a question. "And what are you all doing here?"

"This is our town! We own it! We're going to stay, forever!"

"We're going to cast you out!" said Hank.

Witchcraft only laughed and said, "Go ahead, try it!"

"Come out in Jesus' name!"

The demon held tightly, desperately, to Bobby. Bobby's whole body strained again.

Hank commanded again, "Witchcraft, in Jesus' name, come out!"

The demon spoke through Bobby as Bobby's eyes, wild and bulging, glared at Hank and Andy, and every sinew in his neck strained like piano wire. "I won't! I won't! He's mine!"

Hank, Andy, John, and Ron all began to pray together, pounding at Witchcraft with their prayers. The demon ducked inside Bobby and tried to hide his head under his wings; he drooled from pain and agony, he winced at every mention of Jesus. The praying continued. Witchcraft began to gasp for breath. He cried out.

"Rafar," Bobby cried. "Ba-al Rafar!"

"Say that again?"

The demon continued to cry out through Bobby, "Rafar . . . Rafar . . ."

"Who is Rafar?" Hank asked.

"Rafar . . . is Rafar . . . is Rafar . . . is Rafar . . ." Bobby's body twitched, and he spoke like a sickening broken record.

"And who is Rafar?" Andy asked.

"Rafar rules. He rules. Rafar is Rafar. Rafar is lord."

"Jesus is Lord," John reminded the demon.

"Satan is lord!" the demon argued.

"You said Rafar was lord," Hank said.

"Satan is lord of Rafar."

"What is Rafar lord of?"

"Rafar is lord of Ashton. Rafar rules Ashton."

Andy tried a hunch. "Is he prince over Ashton?"

"Rafar is prince. Prince of Ashton."

"Well, we rebuke him too!" said Ron.

Near the big dead tree, Rafar spun quickly around as if someone had just pricked him, and he eyed several of his demons suspiciously.

The demon continued to spout his boasts, speaking through Bobby, whose face contorted in almost a perfect representation of the demon's expressions.

"We are many, many, many!" the demon boasted.

"And Ashton is your town?" asked Hank.

"Except for you, praying man!"

"Then it's time to start praying," said Andy, and they all did.

The demon grimaced in terrible pain, desperately hiding its head under its wings and hanging onto Bobby with all its rapidly ebbing strength.

"No . . . no . . . no!" it whimpered.

"Let go, Witchcraft," said Hank, "and come out of him."

"Please let me stay. I won't hurt him, I promise!"

A sure sign. Hank and Andy glanced at each other. The thing was about to go.

Hank looked directly into Bobby's eyes and commanded, "Spirit, come out in Jesus' name! Now!"

The demon shrieked as his talons began to slip loose from Bobby. Slowly, inch by inch, they began to withdraw despite the demon's most frantic efforts to keep them driven in. He screamed and cursed, and the sounds came out through Bobby's throat as the very last talon broke loose and the demon fluttered upward. The angels were about to command him to leave the region, but he was already on his way.

"I'm going, I'm going!" he hissed, streaking away.

Bobby relaxed, as did the four men who were ministering to him.

"Okay, Bobby?" Andy asked.

Bobby—the real Bobby—answered, "Yeah . . . there are still some in there, I can feel them."

"We'll rest a minute and then get them all out," said Hank.

"Yeah," said Bobby. "Let's do that."

Ron patted Bobby's knee. "You're doing all right, man!"

Just then, Mary walked into the sanctuary to see if she could help in any way. She had heard they were ministering to someone in here and she didn't feel right staying home.

But then she saw Bobby. The man! The man in leather! She froze in her place.

Bobby looked up and saw her.

So did one of the demons inside him. Suddenly Bobby's face changed from that of an exhausted and frightened young man to that of a leering, lustful, raping spirit.

"Hey there," said the spirit through Bobby, and then the spirit referred to Mary in lascivious, obscene terms.

Hank and the others were shocked, but they knew who was doing the speaking. Hank looked toward Mary, and she was backing away, terrified.

"He's—he's the one who threatened me in the parking lot!" she cried.

The demon spouted more obscenities.

Hank intervened immediately. "Spirit, be quiet!"

The spirit cursed at him. "That's your wife, eh?"

"I bind you in Jesus' name."

Bobby curled and writhed as if in terrible pain; the demon was feeling the sting of their prayers.

"Leave me alone!" it screamed. "I want to—I want to . . ." It went on to describe rape in hideous detail.

Mary recoiled, but then regathered herself and spoke back, "How dare you! I'm a child of God, and I don't have to put up with that kind of talk. You be silent and come out of him!"

Bobby curled like a stuck worm and retched.

"Let him go, Rape!" commanded Andy.

"Let go of him!" said Hank.

Mary stepped closer and said firmly, "I rebuke you, demon! In Jesus' name I rebuke you!"

The demon fell from Bobby as if struck by a wrecking ball and fluttered about on the floor. Krioni scooped him up and flung him out of the church.

The one remaining spirit was quite intimidated but very obnoxious anyway. "I beat up a woman today!"

"We don't want to hear about it," said John. "Just get out of there!"

"I hit her and I kicked her and I beat her up—"

"Be quiet and come out!" Hank ordered.

The demon cursed loudly and left, helped on his way by Krioni.

Bobby slumped to the floor exhausted, but a gentle smile crossed his face and he started to laugh happily. "They're gone! Thank God, they're gone!"

Hank, Andy, John, and Ron moved in to comfort him. Mary stayed back, still unsure of this seedy-looking character.

Andy was clear and direct. "Bobby, you need to have the Holy Spirit in your life. You need Jesus if you want to stay free of those things."

"I'm ready, man, I'm ready!" Bobby said.

Right then and there, Bobby Corsi became a new creation. And his first words as a Christian were, "Guys, this town's in trouble! Wait'll you hear what I've been up to and who I've been working for!"

27

It always took place in Professor Juleen Langstrat's apartment, in the darkened living room, sitting on the warm, comfortable sofa, illumined by the one candle on the coffee table. Langstrat was always the teacher and guide, giving instructions in her calm, clear voice. Shawn was always there as a moral supporter and fellow-participant. Sandy was never alone.

They had been meeting like this regularly now, and each time was a whole new adventure. The quiet, restful excursions into other levels of consciousness were like opening a whole new door to a higher reality, the world of psychic powers and experiences. Sandy was totally enthralled.

The metronome on the coffee table ticked, a slow, restful, steady rhythm, breathing in, breathing out, relax, relax, relax.

Sandy was getting quite skilled at dropping below the upper levels of consciousness, those levels in which all humans normally operate, but which are the most distracted and cluttered by outside stimuli. Somewhere below that were the deeper levels where true psychic ability and experience could be found. To reach these levels took careful, methodical relaxation, meditation, concentration. Langstrat had taught her all the steps.

As Sandy sat very still on the couch and Shawn watched intently, Langstrat counted down slowly, steadily, in cadence with the metronome.

"Twenty-five, twenty-four, twenty-three . . ."

In Sandy's mind she was riding an elevator, descending into the lower levels of her being, relaxing, putting her upper levels of brain activity on hold while she moved through the lower realms.

"Three, two, one, Alpha level," said Langstrat. "Now, open the door."

Sandy visualized herself opening the elevator door and stepping into a beautiful green meadow bordered by trees covered with pink and white blossoms. The air was warm, and a playful breeze wafted across the meadow like gentle caresses. Sandy looked here and there.

"Do you see her?" Langstrat asked gently.

"I'm still looking," Sandy answered. Then her face brightened. "Oh, here she comes! She's beautiful!"

Sandy could see the girl coming toward her, a beautiful young lady with cascading blonde hair, all dressed in shimmering white linen. Her face glowed with happiness. She was extending her hands in greeting.

"Hello!" Sandy called happily.

"Hello," said the girl in the most beautiful and melodic voice Sandy had ever heard.

"Have you come to guide me?"

The blonde girl took Sandy's hands in her own and looked into her eyes with tremendous kindness and compassion. "Yes. My name is Madeline. I will teach you."

Sandy looked at Madeline with amazement. "You look so young! Have you lived before?"

"Yes. Hundreds of times. But each life was simply a step upward. I'll show you the way."

Sandy was ecstatic. "Oh, I want to learn. I want to go with you."

Madeline took Sandy by the hand and began to lead her across the green meadow toward an immaculate golden walkway.

As Sandy sat on the sofa in Langstrat's apartment, her face full of joy and rapture, gleaming talons penetrated her skull as the black and gnarled hands of a hideous demon held her head in a viselike grip. The spirit leaned over her and whispered the words to her mind, "Then come. Come with me. I will introduce you to others who have ascended even before me."

"Love to!" Sandy responded.

Langstrat and Shawn smiled at each other.

Tom McBride, the paste-up man, heard the little bell over the front door ring and could only moan. This day had been the most traumatic he'd ever been through. He scurried to the front just in time to see Marshall come in and make a beeline for his office.

Tom was distraught and full of questions. "Marshall, where have you been, and where's Bernice? The papers haven't come from the printer! I've had nothing but calls all day—I finally had to put the phone on the answering machine—and people have been coming by wondering where today's paper is."

"Where's Carmen?" Marshall asked, and Tom noticed Marshall looked very, very sick.

"Marshall," Tom asked, very worried, "what—what's wrong? What's going on around here?"

Marshall just about bit Tom's head off when he growled, "Where's Carmen?"

"She's not here. She was here, but then Bernice took off, and then she took off, and I've been here alone all day!"

Marshall flung the door to his office open and got inside. He went straight for a file drawer and yanked it out. It was empty. Tom stood at a safe distance and watched. Marshall reached under his desk and pulled out a cardboard box. The box slid out easily and lightly. He saw that it was empty too and dashed it to the floor with a loud oath.

"Is . . . is there anything I can do?" Tom asked.

Marshall flopped into his chair, his face like chalk, his hair disheveled. For a moment he just sat there, leaning his head on his hand, breathing deeply, trying to think, trying to calm down.

"Call the hospital," he finally said in a very weak voice that didn't sound much like Marshall Hogan at all.

"The—the hospital?" Tom didn't like the sound of that at all.

"Ask them how Bernice is doing."

Tom's mouth dropped open. "Bernice! Is she in the hospital? What happened?"

Marshall exploded, "Just do it, Tom!"

Tom scurried to a phone. Marshall got up and went to his door.
"Tom . . ."

Tom looked up, but kept trying to dial the phone.

Marshall leaned on the doorpost. He felt so weak, so helpless.
"Tom, I'm sorry. I'm really sorry. Thanks for making that call. Let me
know what they say."

And with that, Marshall turned and went back into his office,
flopping into his chair and sitting there motionless.

Tom came back with his report. "Uh . . . Bernice had a cracked
rib, and they wrapped it . . . but no other serious injuries. Somebody
brought her car back from Baker, so they released her and she drove
home. That's where she is now."

"Yeah . . . *I* gotta get home . . ."

"What happened to her?"

"She was beat up. Somebody jumped her, clobbered her."

"Marshall . . ." Tom was almost too horrified for words. "That's
. . . well . . . that's terrible."

Marshall worked himself out of the chair and leaned against his
desk.

Tom was still concerned. "Marshall, is there going to be a Friday
edition? We sent paste-ups to the printer . . . I don't understand."

"They didn't print it," Marshall answered blandly.

"What? Why not?"

Marshall let his head fall forward, and he shook it just a little. He
blew out a sigh, then looked at Tom again. "Tom, just go ahead and
take the day off, what's left of it. Let me get squared away here and
then I'll call you, okay?"

"Well . . . okay."

Tom went into the back room for his lunchbox and his coat.

The phone rang, a different line, a number Marshall reserved for
special calls. Marshall picked it up.

"*Clarion*," he said.

"Marshall?"

"Yeah . . ."

"Marshall, this is Eldon Strachan."

Oh, thank God, he's alive! Marshall felt his throat tighten. He
thought he would cry. "Eldon, are you all right?"

"Well, no. We just got back from a trip. Marshall, someone just
tore up my house. The place is a mess!"

"Is Doris all right?"

"Well, she's upset. *I'm* upset."

"We've all been hit, Eldon. They're on to us."

"What's happened?"

Marshall recounted it all to him. The hardest part of all was telling
Eldon Strachan that his friend and fellow outcast, Ted Harmel, was
dead.

Strachan had trouble speaking for quite some time. Several minutes were spent in an awkward, painful silence, interrupted only a few times by either man asking if the other was still on the line.

"Marshall," Strachan finally said, "we'd better run. We'd just better get the heck out of here and not come back."

"Run where?" Marshall asked. "You already ran once, remember? As long as you're alive, Eldon, you're going to be living with this and they're going to know it."

"But what can any of us do anyway?"

"You have friends, for crying out loud! What about the state attorney general?"

"I told you, I can't go to Norm Mattily with nothing but my word; I need more than just our friendship. I need proof, some kind of documentation."

Marshall looked down at the empty cardboard box. "I'll get you something, Eldon. One way or another, I'll get you something to show to anybody who'll listen."

Eldon sighed. "I just don't know how much longer this is going to have to go on . . ."

"As long as we let it, Eldon."

He thought for a moment, then said, "Yeah, yeah, you're right. You get me something solid, and I'll see what I can do."

"We have no choice. Our necks are on the block right now; we've got to save ourselves!"

"Well, I certainly intend to do that. Doris and I are going to disappear, and fast, and I'd advise you to do the same. We sure can't stay around here."

"So where do I reach you?"

"I won't tell you over the phone. Just wait to hear from Norm Mattily's office. It'll mean I got through to him, and that's the only way I'll be any good to you anyway."

"If I'm not here, if I've skipped town or ended up dead, have him contact Al Lemley at the *New York Times*. I'll try to leave word with him."

"I'll see you again sometime."

"Let's pray that you do."

"Oh, I'm starting to pray a lot these days."

Marshall hung up, locked all the doors, and headed for home.

Bernice lay on her couch with an ice bag over her face and an uncomfortable bandage around her rib cage, and she really did want a phone call. She had already thrown up once, her head was throbbing, and she felt miserable, but she wanted a phone call. What was happening out there? She tried calling the *Clarion,* but no one answered. She called Marshall's home, but no one answered there either.

Well, what do you know! The phone rang. She snatched it up like an owl grabbing a mouse.

"Hello?"

"Bernice Krueger?"

"Kevin?"

"Yeah, man . . ." He sounded very nervous and high-strung. "Hey, I'm dying, man, I mean I am really scared!"

"Where are you, Kevin?"

"I'm at home. Hey, somebody came in here and tore the place apart!"

"Is your door closed?"

"Yeah."

"Then why don't you lock it?"

"Yeah, I got it locked. I'm scared, man. They must have a contract out on me."

"Be very careful what you say, Kevin. What we heard about our phones being bugged is probably true. They may have bugged your phone."

Weed didn't say anything for a moment; then he cursed out of sheer fright. "Oh man, I just got a call from you know who! You think they heard us talking?"

"I don't know. We just have to be careful."

"What am I gonna do? It's all going down, man. Susan says she's got the goods, and it's all going down! She's gonna split that place—"

Bernice cut him short. "Kevin, don't say another word. You'd better tell me in person. Let's meet somewhere."

"But won't they know where we're meeting?"

"Hey, if they know they know, but at least we'll have some control over what they hear."

"Well, let's do it quick, and I mean *quick!*"

"How about that bridge a few miles north of Baker, the one over the Judd River?"

"The big green one?"

"Yeah, that one. There's a turn-off right at the north end of it. I can be there by . . ." Bernice looked at her wall clock. ". . . let's say 7."

"I'll be there."

"Okay. Good-bye."

Bernice immediately dialed the *Clarion.* No answer. She dialed Marshall at home.

The telephone in the Hogan kitchen rang and rang, but Marshall and Kate remained silent at the kitchen table, letting it ring until finally it stopped.

Kate, her hands shaking just a little, her breathing consciously controlled, looked at her husband with tear-filled eyes.

"The telephone has a way of bringing consistently bad news," she quipped, her eyes dropping for a moment.

Right now Marshall had as much intestinal fortitude as an empty garbage bag, and for one rare occasion in his life he was at a loss for words.

"When did you get that call?" he finally asked.

"This morning."

"But you don't know who it was?"

Kate took a deep breath, trying to stay on top of her emotions. "Whoever it was, he knew just about everything about you and me, and even Sandy; so he wasn't just a crank in that respect. His . . . credentials were very impressive."

"But he was lying!" Marshall said angrily.

"I know," Kate answered assertively.

"It's just another smear tactic, Kate. They're trying to take away my newspaper, they're trying to take away my home, and now they're trying to destroy my marriage. There isn't now, nor has there ever been any kind of goings-on between Bernice and me. For crying out loud, I'm old enough to be her father!"

"I know," Kate answered again. She took a moment to build up strength to continue. "Marshall, you are my man, and if I were ever to lose you I know I'd never find one better. I also know you're not a man given to just tossing around his passions. I have a prize in you, and I've never forgotten that."

He took her hand. "And you're all the woman I could ever handle."

She squeezed his hand as she said, "I do have confidence that these things will never change. I suppose it's that kind of confidence that's kept me hanging on, waiting . . ."

Her voice trailed off, and there was a moment of silence. Kate had to choke down her emotions, and Marshall couldn't think of anything to say.

"Marshall," she said finally, "there are some other things that haven't changed either, but those things were supposed to change; you and I agreed together that they would. We agreed that things would be different after we moved from New York, that you would take it easy, that you would have more time for your family, that maybe we could all get to know one another again and patch things up." The tears began to flow and it was difficult for her to speak, but she was committed now, so she kept going. "I don't know what it is, whether the ultimate scoop simply tags after you no matter where you go or if you concoct it on your own, time after time. But if I were to ever be jealous or suspicious of another lover, that's what the lover would be.

You do have another love, Marshall, and I just don't know if I can compete with it."

Marshall knew he'd never be able to fully explain everything. "Kate, you've no idea how big this whole thing is."

She shook her head. She didn't want to hear it. "That's not at issue here. As a matter of fact, I'm sure it is big, it is extremely important, it probably does warrant the amount of time and energy you've put into it. But what I am coping with now is the detriment that this whole thing has been to myself, to Sandy, and to this family. Marshall, I don't care about comparisons; no matter where Sandy and I have been placed on your list of priorities, we are still suffering, and that is the direct problem that I'm dealing with. I can't care about anything else."

"Kate . . . that's what they want!"

"They're getting it," she countered abruptly. "But don't you dare blame anyone else for your failure to live up to your promises. No one else is responsible for your promises, Marshall, and I am holding you responsible for the promises you made to your family."

"Kate, I didn't ask for this to come up, I didn't ask for this to happen. When it's all over—"

"It's over now!" That stopped him cold. "And it's not really a matter of choice for me. I have my limitations, Marshall. I know there's only so much I can take. I have to get away."

Marshall was too weak to say a word. He couldn't even think of any words. All he could do was look her in the eye and let her speak, let her do whatever she had to do.

Kate kept going. She had to get it all out before she would be unable to. "I talked to my mom this morning. She was very supportive of both of us, and she's not taking sides at all. As a matter of fact—and you might find this interesting—she's been praying for us, for you in particular. She says she even dreamt about you the other night; she dreamt that you were in trouble and that God would send His angels to help you if she prayed. She took the whole thing pretty seriously, and she's been praying ever since."

Marshall smiled weakly. He appreciated that, but what good was it doing?

Kate came to the bottom line. "I'm going to stay with her for a while. I need time to think. And *you* need time to think. We both need to know for sure just which of your promises you are truly willing to live up to. We need to get it settled once and for all, Marshall, before we go one step further.

"As for Sandy, right now I don't even know where she is. If I can find her I might ask her to come with me, although I doubt she'll want to leave Shawn and everything they're involved in." She drew a deep breath as this new pain took hold of her. "All I can say is, you don't know her anymore, Marshall. *I* don't know her. She's been slipping away and slipping away . . . and you were never here." She couldn't go on. She buried her face in her hands and wept.

Marshall found himself wondering if he should even go to her, comfort her, put his arms around her. Would she accept it? Would she even believe that he cared?

He did care. His own heart was breaking. He went to her and gently put his hand on her shoulder.

"I won't give you any pat answers," he said quietly. "You're right. Everything you've said is right. And I don't dare make any more promises now that I may not be able to keep." The words hurt even as he forced himself to say them. "I do need to think about it. I need to do some real housecleaning. Why don't you go ahead? Go ahead and stay with your mom for a while, get away from all this mess. I'll . . . I'll let you know when it's all over, when I'm settled on what's important. I won't even ask you to come back until then."

"I love you, Marshall," she said as she wept.

"I love you too, Kate."

She rose suddenly and embraced him, giving him a kiss he would remember for a long time, a kiss when she held him desperately tight, when her face was wet with tears, when her body trembled with her weeping. He held her with his strong arms as if he were hanging on to his very life, a priceless treasure he might never have again.

Then she said, "I'd better just go," and gave him one final hug.

He held her for one last moment and then said as comfortingly as he could, "It'll be okay. Good-bye."

Her bags were already packed. She didn't take much. After the front door quietly closed behind her and their little pickup truck eased out of the driveway, Marshall sat alone at the kitchen table for a very long time. He numbly stared at the woodgrain patterns in the tabletop, a thousand memories flooding through his mind. Minutes upon minutes passed without his heed; the world went on without him.

At last his stupor crumbled as all his thoughts and feelings came to rest on her name, "Kate . . ." and he cried and cried.

28

Guilo bit his lower lip and surveyed the valley below, along with his two dozen warriors. From their vantage point halfway down the mountain slopes and in among the rocks, the Strongman's Lair was a boiling, humming caldron of black spirits, their myriads forming a swarming, living haze over the cluster of buildings below. The sound of their wings was a constant, low-pitched drone that echoed back upon itself from the rocky crags all around. The demons were very disturbed right now, like an angry hive of bees.

"They're building up for something," a warrior observed.

"Even so," said Guilo, "something doesn't feel right, and I would venture to say it has to do with *her*."

All around the complex, vans and trailers were packed with everything from the office supplies right down to Alexander M. Kaseph's stuffed trophies. The personnel were now going through their dormitories, packing up their personal belongings and sweeping out the rooms. Everywhere there was a pervading excitement and anticipation, and people clustered here and there, chattering in their native languages.

In the big stone house, secluded from all the activity, Susan Jacobson worked hurriedly in her private room, consolidating a huge box of records, ledgers, documents, printed matter. She was trying to eliminate anything she didn't absolutely need, but almost every item seemed indispensable. Even so, only one suitcase—now sitting on her dresser—would have to contain it all. So far, the load was too bulky to fit in the suitcase and too heavy for Susan to carry even if it did.

With some hastily muttered prayers and some more quick perusals, she eliminated half of the items. She then took what was left and began to carefully arrange it all in the suitcase, a ledger here, some affidavits there, more documents, some photographs, another ledger, a computer printout, a thick ream of photocopies, some undeveloped film.

Footsteps in the hall! She hurriedly closed the suitcase, pressing the lid shut so she could fasten the latches, and then lugged the heavy thing over to the big bed where she quickly slid it underneath. She then threw all the other unpacked items back into the box and concealed the box on a shelf behind some linens in a small closet.

Without knocking, Kaseph came into the room. He wore casual clothes because he too had been packing and taking part in all the activity.

She went to him and threw her arms around him. "Well, hi! How are things on your end?"

He returned her embrace briefly, then dropped his arms and began to look around the room.

"We were wondering whatever became of you," he said. "We are meeting in the dining hall, and we were hoping you would attend." There was something strange and ominous in his tone.

"Well," she said, a little abashed at his demeanor, "of course I'm going to attend. I wouldn't miss it for anything."

"Good, good," he said, still looking around the room. "Susan, may I look through your suitcase?"

She looked at him curiously. "What?"

He would not change or qualify his question. "I want to look in your suitcase."

"Whatever for?"

"Bring it here," he said in a tone not to be argued with.

She went to her closet, brought out a large blue suitcase full of clothes, and laid it on the bed. He opened the latches and threw back the lid, then proceeded to very quickly and very rudely unpack it, throwing its contents here and there.

"Hey," she protested, "what are you doing? It took me hours to get all that in there!"

He thoroughly emptied it, opening every side pocket, unloading and shaking out every garment. When he had finished, she was quite angry.

"Alex, what is the meaning of this?"

He turned to her with a very grim expression, and then his face suddenly broke into a smile. "I'm sure you can pack your suitcase even more efficiently the second time." She knew she didn't dare give him any comeback for that. "But it was necessary for me to check on something. You see, dear Susan, you've been absent from the normal flow of the population and absent from my presence for a considerable time." He began to walk slowly around the room, his eyes darting over every nook and corner of it. "And it seems there are some very important records and files missing, things of a very delicate nature—things that you, my Maidservant, would have access to." He smiled that same old smile that cut like a knife. "Of course, I know that your heart is indeed in union with mine, despite your . . . second thoughts and petty fears of late."

She raised her head high and looked right at him. "Those things are strictly the weakness of my humanity, but something over which I expect to gain a victory."

"The weakness of your humanity. . . ." He thought that over for a moment. "That same little weakness that has always made you so intriguing, because it could make you so very dangerous."

"You are implying, then, that I could betray you?"

He approached her and rested his hands on her shoulders. Susan imagined how his hands would not have to move far to clamp around her neck.

"It is possible," he said, "that someone is trying to betray me, even now. I can read it in the atmosphere." He looked at her very closely, his eyes burrowing into hers. "I might even be reading it in your very own eyes."

She turned her eyes away and said, "I would not betray you."

He leaned closer and said very coolly, "Nor would anyone else . . . if they knew what would be in store for them. It would be a very serious business indeed."

She felt his hands tighten their grip.

A messenger streaked across the sky and then darted, zigzagged, and weaved through the woods above Ashton looking for Tal.

"Captain!" he called, but Tal was not there among the others. "Where is the captain?"

Mota answered, "Carrying out another prayer gathering at Hank Busche's home. Be careful not to attract attention."

The messenger soared down the hillside and floated quietly into the maze of streets and alleys below.

At Hank's house, Tal remained carefully hidden within the walls while some of his warriors carried out his orders, bringing in people ready to pray.

Hank and Andy Forsythe had called a special prayer meeting, but they hadn't expected so many people to show up. More and more cars kept arriving, and more and more people kept filing through the door: the Colemans, Ron Forsythe and Cynthia, newly saved Bobby Corsi, his parents Dan and Jean, the Joneses, the Coopers, the Smiths, the Bartons, some college students and their friends. Hank brought out whatever extra chairs he had. People began to find places on the floor. The room was getting stuffy; the windows were opened.

Tal looked out front and saw an old station wagon pull up. He smiled broadly. This was one arrival Hank would be glad to see.

When the doorbell rang several people hollered, "Come in," but whoever it was didn't come in. Hank stepped over several people to get to the door and opened it.

There stood Lou Stanley, together with his wife Margie. They were holding hands.

Lou smiled timidly and asked, "Hi, Hank. Is this where you're holding the prayer meeting?"

Hank believed again in miracles. Here was the man who had been removed from the church for adultery, now standing before him reunited with his wife and wanting to pray with all the others!

"Wow," said Hank, "it sure is! Come on in!"

Lou and Margie entered the packed living room, where they were greeted with love and acceptance.

Just then there was another knock on the door. Hank was still standing there, so he opened the door and saw an older man and his wife standing outside. He had never seen either one of them before.

But Cecil Cooper knew who they were; he called to them from where he was sitting. "Well, praise the Lord! I don't believe it! James and Diane Farrel!"

Hank looked at Cecil, and then at the couple standing there, and his mouth dropped open. "Reverend Farrel?"

Reverend James Farrel, former pastor of Ashton Community Church, extended his hand. "Pastor Henry Busche?" Hank nodded, taking his hand. "We got word there was a prayer meeting here tonight."

Hank invited them in with outstretched arms.

Meanwhile, the messenger arrived and found Tal. "Captain, Guilo sends word that Susan's time is very short! She is very near discovery. You must come *now!*"

Tal took a quick survey of the prayer cover he had gathered. It had to be enough for tonight's plan to work.

Hank was starting the meeting. "The Lord has impressed on all of us that we need to pray tonight for Ashton. Now we've learned some things this afternoon, and we were sure right about Satan having a grip on this town. We need to pray that God will bind the demons that are trying to take over, and we need to pray for victory for the people of God, and for the angels of God . . ."

Good, good! Tal thought. It might be enough. But if what the messenger said was truly the situation at the Strongman's Lair, they would have to proceed with the plan whether the prayer cover was sufficient or not.

The demonic cloud over the valley continued to thicken and swirl, and from their vantage point Guilo and his warriors could see the glimmer of millions of pairs of yellow eyes.

Guilo could not relax at all, but continually watched over the mountaintops for the one streak of light that would mark Tal's arrival. "Where is Tal?" he muttered. "Where is he? They know. They *know!*"

At this very moment Kaseph's entire staff, the implementing force behind Omni Corporation, was gathered in the dining hall for a make-shift banquet and final get-together before the big move for which they had all prepared. It was an informal buffet affair; everything was casual, and the mood was light. Kaseph himself, usually aloof from his inferiors, mingled freely with them now, and hands often reached out to him as if imploring a special blessing.

Susan remained steadfastly by his side, dressed again in her customary black suit, and hands also reached out to her for a special touch, a special glance or look of blessing. These she freely bestowed on the grateful followers.

As the meal got underway, Kaseph and Susan took their places at the head table. She tried to act normal and enjoy her food, but her master still maintained that smile, that strange, cutting, wicked smile, and it unnerved her. She had to wonder how much he really knew.

Toward the end of the dinner Kaseph stood, and as if on signal everyone in the room immediately became silent.

"As we have done in other regions, in other parts of our rapidly uniting world, so we shall do here," Kaseph said, and the whole room

applauded. "As a decisive and powerful tool of the Universal Consciousness Society, Omni Corporation is about to establish still another
foothold for the coming New World Order and the rule of the New
Age Christ. I have received word from our advance people in Ashton
that the purchase of our new facility can be finalized on Sunday, and I
will personally go before you to close the deal. After that, the town
will be ours."

The room broke into applause and cheers.

But then, with a rather abrupt change of mood, Kaseph let a scowl
come upon his face, to which all those present responded with an
equal sobriety. "Of course, all through this massive effort we have often
been reminded of how serious this business really is in which we are
involved, to which we have vowed our lives and our allegiances. We
have often pondered how dire the results would be to everything we
have worked toward if any one of us should ever turn toward the
wrong and answer the persistent call of greed, temporality, or even,"—
he looked at Susan—"human weakness."

Suddenly the room was dead quiet. Everyone's gaze was upon
Kaseph as his eyes scanned slowly across the whole group.

Susan could feel a terror starting to form deep down inside, a
terror she had always tried to push down, avoid, control. She could
feel the one thing she feared most of all slowly stalking up on her.

Kaseph continued, "Only a few of you are aware that in the course
of transferring the files from the head office we discovered that several
of our most sensitive folders were missing. Apparently someone with
high privilege and inside access thought those files would be of value
. . . some other way." The people began to gasp and murmur. "Oh,
don't be alarmed. I have a happy ending to this story. The missing files
have been found!" They were all relieved, and chuckled amongst themselves. This, they seemed to think, was another one of Kaseph's little
teasers.

Kaseph signaled to some security men toward the back of the
room, and one of them picked up—what was it? Susan rose from her
chair just a little to see.

A cardboard box. No! *The* cardboard box? The one she had
hidden behind the linens? He was bringing it toward the front, toward
the head table.

She remained where she was, but she thought she would faint. Her
whole body trembled with fear. The blood drained from her face; her
insides were riddled with horrible pain. She had been discovered.
There was no way out. It was a nightmare.

The security guard lifted the heavy box onto the table, and Kaseph
flung it open. Yes, there were all the materials she had so painstakingly
sorted out and hidden. He lifted them out, and held them up for all to
see. The whole crowd gasped in astonishment.

Kaseph threw the materials back into the box and let the guard carry it away.

"This box," he announced, "was found hidden in the Maid-servant's linen closet."

All were stunned. Some remained frozen with shock. Some shook their heads.

Susan Jacobson prayed. She prayed furiously.

The messenger arrived back in the valley, and Guilo was voracious for news.

"Yes, speak up!"

"He is gathering the prayer cover for the operation tonight. He should be here any moment."

"Any moment may be too late." Guilo looked toward the buildings below. "Any moment and Susan might be dead."

Tal watched while the gathered people prayed intently as the Holy Spirit led them and empowered them. They were praying specifically for the confounding of the demonic hosts. It just might be enough! He slipped out of the house, shrouded by the darkness. He would pass quickly through the town and then fly to the Strongman's Lair, hopefully in time to save Susan's life.

But no sooner had he stepped into the narrow and rutted alley behind the house than he felt a sharp pain in his leg. His sword flashed into view in an instant, and in one quick movement he beheaded a small spirit that had been clinging to him. It dissolved in a puff of blood-red smoke.

Another spirit clamped onto his back. He swept it away. Another on his back, another on his leg, two more slashing and nipping at his head!

"It is *Tal!*" he heard them squeak and chatter. "It is Captain Tal!"

Much more of this noise and they would bring Rafar! Tal knew he would have to vanquish them all or risk exposure. The demons around his head went quickly enough. He swept his sword up and across his back and dismembered the one clinging there.

But they seemed to multiply. Some of them were quite sizable, and all were greedy for the reward Rafar would give for whoever revealed Tal's whereabouts.

A large, laughing spirit flew in close for a look at Tal, and then shot straight into the sky. Tal followed after him in an explosion of light and power and grabbed his ankles. The spirit screamed and began to claw at him. Tal dropped back to earth like a stone, dragging the spirit down with him, the spirit's wings flapping and fluttering like a torn umbrella. Once under the cover of trees and houses, Tal's sword sent the spirit into the abyss.

But more demons were coming upon him from all directions. The word was spreading.

Two powerful and muscular guards, the same two men who had once been her tuxedoed escorts, dragged and carried Susan between them, hardly letting her use her own feet to carry herself, across the grounds, up onto the porch of the big stone house, inside, up the ornate staircase, and down the upstairs hall to her room. Kaseph followed, cool, collected, perfectly ruthless.

The guards threw Susan down in a chair and held her there with their full weight, preventing her escape. Kaseph took a long, icy look at her.

"Susan," he said, "my dear Susan, I am not really shocked at this. Such problems have happened before, with many others, many times. And every time we've had to deal with it. As you well know, such problems never remain. Never."

He moved in close, so close his words seemed to slap her like little whips. "I never trusted you, Susan, I told you that. So I've kept my eye on you, I've had the others keep their eye on you, and I see now that you have rekindled your friendship with my . . . *rival,* Mr. Weed." He laughed at that.

"I have eyes and ears everywhere, dear Susan. Since the moment your Mr. Weed went to the *Ashton Clarion,* we have made his business, every aspect of it, our business: where he goes, whom he knows, whomever he calls, and whatever he says. And as for the hurried and careless call you made to him today . . ." He laughed loudly. "Susan, did you really think we wouldn't monitor every phone call going out of here? We knew you would make your move sooner or later. All we had to do was wait and be ready. An undertaking such as ours is naturally going to have enemies. We understand that."

He leaned over her, his eyes cold and cunning. "But we most certainly do not tolerate it. No, Susan, we deal with it, harshly and abruptly. I had thought that one little harassment would silence Weed, but now I find that, thanks to you, he knows far too much. Therefore, it will be best if you *and* your Mr. Weed are taken care of."

All she could do was tremble; she could think of nothing to say. She knew it would be useless to beg for mercy.

"You have never been to one of our blood rituals, have you?" Kaseph began to explain it to her as if giving a short lecture. "The ancient worshipers of Isis, or Molech, or Ashtoreth, were not too far afield in their practices. They understood, at least, that the offering of a human life to their so-called gods seemed to bring the gods' favor upon them.

"What they performed in ignorance, we now continue with enlightenment. The life-force that intertwines itself through us and our universe is cyclical, never-ending, self-perpetuating. The birth of the new cannot occur without the death of the old. The birth of good is created by the death of evil. This is karma, dear Susan, your karma."

In other words, he was going to kill her.

A warrior asked Guilo, "What is that? What are they doing?"

They both listened. The cloud, still stirring and swirling slowly about the valley floor, was trickling and babbling now with a strange sound, an indefinable noise that gradually rose in volume and pitch. At first it sounded like the rush of faraway waves, then it grew into the roar of a numberless mob. From this it crescendoed into an eerie wailing of millions of sirens.

Guilo slowly brought his sword out, and the metal of the blade rang.

"What are you doing?" asked the warrior.

"Prepare!" Guilo ordered, and the order was spread among the group. Ring, ring, ring went their blades as each warrior took his sword in his hand.

"They're laughing," said Guilo. "There's nothing we can do but go in."

The warrior was willing, and yet the thought was unthinkable. "Go in? Go into . . . that?"

The demons were strong, brutal, savage . . . and now they were laughing with the smell of approaching death like sweet perfume in their nostrils.

Triskal and Krioni came swooping into the valley, swords blazing and sweeping in lethal arcs of light as demons disintegrated on all sides. Other warriors shot into the sky like flares from a cannon, plucking fleeing demons out of the air, silencing them.

Tal was in a real bind, wishing he could release his fighting power full force and yet needing to remain subdued lest he draw attention to himself. Thus he could not vanquish the spirits now clustering on him like angry bees in one violent attack, but rather had to pluck them off one by one, hacking and chopping with his sword.

Mota entered the scuffle and came in close to Tal, swinging his sword and plucking demons off his captain like bats off a cave wall. "There! There now! And another!"

Then came one infinitesimal moment when Tal was clean of demons. Mota quickly slipped into his place while Tal vanished into the
ground.

The spirits were enraged by the fighting, and at first continued to
flock and circle about the area; but then they realized that Tal had
somehow slipped away and they were only placing themselves in the
hands of heavenly warriors to be destroyed for no reason.

Their numbers quickly dwindled, their cries ebbed away, and soon
they were gone.

Several miles outside of Ashton, Tal shot out of the ground like a
bullet from a rifle, streaking across the sky, a trail of light following
him like the tail of a comet, his sword held straight out in front of him.
Farms, fields, forests, and highways became a blur beneath him; the
clouds became rushing mountains passing by on either side.

He could feel his strength building with the prayers of the saints;
his sword began to burn with power, glowing brilliantly. He almost felt
it was pulling him through the sky.

Faster and faster, the wind screaming, the distance shrinking, his
wings an invisible roar, he flew for the Strongman's Lair.

A very strange-looking, black-robed and beaded, long-haired little
guru from some dark and pagan land stepped into Susan's room at
Kaseph's bidding. He bowed in obeisance to his lord and master,
Kaseph.

"Prepare the altar," said Kaseph. "There will be a special offering
for the success of our endeavor."

The little pagan priest left quickly. Kaseph returned his attention
to Susan.

He took one look at her and then gave her the back of his hand.

"Stop that!" he shouted "Stop that praying!"

The force of the blow nearly knocked her out of the chair, but one
guard held her firmly. Her head sank and she began to sob in very
short, shallow gasps of terror.

Kaseph, like a conqueror, stood above her and boasted over her
limp and trembling form. "You have no God to call upon! With the
nearness of your death you crumble, you fall back upon old myths and
religious nonsense!"

Then he said, almost kindly, "What you don't realize is that I'm
actually doing you a favor. Perhaps in your next life your understanding will be deeper, your frailties will have fallen away. Your sacrificial
gift to us now will build wonderful karma for you in the lives to come.
You'll see."

Then he spoke to the guards. "Bind her!"

They grabbed her wrists and held them behind her; she heard a click and felt the cold steel of the manacles. She heard herself screaming.

Kaseph went to his office, now a bare room except for a few remaining shipping crates and travel cases. He went directly to a small case covered with fine old leather and tucked it under his arm.

Then he went down the big staircase to the lower floor, through an imposing plank door and down another stairway into the deep basement below the house. He turned one corner, passed through another door, and entered a dark, candlelit room of stone. The strange little priest was already there, lighting candles and moaning some strange, unintelligible words over and over. Some of Kaseph's closest confidants were present, waiting quietly. Kaseph handed the little case to the priest, who laid it beside a large, rough-hewn bench at one end of the room. The little priest opened the case and began to set out knives—Kaseph's knives—ornate, jeweled, delicately wrought, razorsharp.

Tal could see the mountains ahead. He would have to stay in close to their rocky sides. He must not be seen.

Guilo and his warriors remained in the darkness, unglorified, stalking step by step downward toward the complex, concealing themselves behind rocks and old snags. Just above them now, boiling and towering like a thunderhead, the cloud of leering, laughing spirits continued to swirl. Guilo was sensing some prayer cover; surely the demons would have noticed them by now, but their eyes were strangely unseeing.

Down below, parked very near the main administration building, was a large van. Guilo found a spot from which he could see the van clearly, then had his warriors fan out, keeping one warrior close by for special instructions.

"Do you see the upper window in the big stone house?" Guilo asked him.

"Yes."

"She is there. On my signal, go alone and get her out."

29

In the strange dark room below the house, Alexander M. Kaseph and his little entourage remained transfixed in deep meditation. Before them, just behind the rough wooden bench, stood the Strongman, flanked by his close guards and assistants. His sagging face was spread now with a hideous, drooling grin that bared his fangs as he chuckled with demonic delight.

"One by one the obstacles are falling," he said. "Yes, yes, your offering will bring you good fortune, and it will please me." The big yellow eyes narrowed with the command. "Bring her!"

Upstairs, sitting helplessly between the two guards, her feet and hands bound with manacles, Susan Jacobson waited and prayed. With all that was within her, she cried out to the one true God, the God whom she did not know but must be there, had to hear her, and was the only one who could help her now.

Tal reached the mountains and soared up their steep face, climbing, climbing, easing back his speed. He continued to slow as he neared the top, and then, just as he crested the summit, he stopped all motion and all sound, and let himself glide down the other side silently, invisibly. He noticed with concern that the cloud had grown even more since he'd been away. He could only hope the prayer cover would at least be sufficient to blind these foul creatures.

Guilo had been watching for the captain, and his sharp eyes saw Tal descending like a silent hawk toward them.

"Get ready," Guilo told the warrior at his side.

The warrior was poised, his eyes on that upstairs window.

Tal dropped down so low he was almost skidding along the ground. He finally came to rest right beside Guilo.

"We have the cover," he said.

"Go!" Guilo commanded the warrior, and the warrior half-flew, half-ran toward the big stone house.

The little priest, his eyes darting about with anticipation, made his way up the big staircase, humming and muttering a mantra to himself.

Kaseph and his people waited downstairs in a hushed silence, Kaseph standing right next to the knives.

Susan Jacobson tried to work the shackles loose, but they were clamped on tightly enough to cut into her even if she didn't struggle. The guards only laughed at her.

"Dear God," she prayed, "if You are truly the ruler of this universe, please have mercy on one who dared to stand for Your sake against a terrible evil . . ."

And then—as if she were no longer in that room, as if she were slowly waking up from a nightmare—the agonizing, heart-twisting fear began to ebb from her mind like a fading thought, like the slow, steady calming of a storm. Her heart was at rest. The room seemed strangely quiet. All she could do was look around with very curious eyes. What had happened? Had she died already? Was she asleep, or dreaming?

But she had felt this way before. The memory of that one night in New York came back to her; she thought of that strange, buoyed-up feeling she had had even as she clambered desperately through that window. There was someone in the room. She could sense it.

"Are you here to help me?" she asked in her heart, and the faintest little spark of hope came to life again somewhere deep inside her.

Clink! Her feet were suddenly released and could swing unbound from the chair. The shackles lay on the floor, opened. She felt something break loose from around her wrists, and she pulled her arms free. The manacles clinked to the floor, just like the shackles that had bound her feet.

She looked at the two guards, but they were just standing there looking at her, still smirking, then looking elsewhere as if nothing had happened.

Then she heard a click, and looked just in time to see the window latch twist loose and the big bedroom window swing open all by itself. The cool night air began to waft into the room.

Whether this was illusion or reality, she accepted it. She jumped up from the chair—the guards did nothing. She ran for that open window. Then she remembered.

Still keeping a wary and unbelieving eye on those guards, she hurried to the bed, reached under it, and pulled out the suitcase that Kaseph and his people had not found, even in such an obvious hiding place! It felt strangely light for all the papers she had loaded in it, but nothing at this moment made much sense anyway, so she simply accepted how easy it was to carry the suitcase to the window and set it on the rooftop outside. She looked behind her. The guards were smiling confidently at an empty chair!

Feeling as if someone was lifting her, she climbed through the window and onto the roof. A thick vine grew up one side of the house. It would make a perfect escape ladder.

Outside the administration building, some security people were talking in hushed tones about the fall of the Maidservant and her imminent fate when suddenly they heard footsteps running across the parking area.

"Hey, look there!" someone shouted.

The security men looked just in time to see a woman dressed in black scurrying for one of the trucks.

"Hey, what are you doing?"

"It's the Maidservant!"

They ran after her, but she had already reached a big moving van and climbed inside. The starter growled, the engine came to life, and with a lurch and a whine the van started rolling away.

Guilo leaped from his hiding place and bellowed, "YA-HAAA!" as his little troop of three and twenty popped into the air like fireworks and trailed after the van. "Cover yourselves, warriors!"

The little priest reached Susan's bedroom, and his bony hand opened the door.

"We are ready," he declared, and suddenly realized that he was talking to a pair of very dedicated guards making very sure an empty chair would not get away.

The little pagan had a first-class fit; the guards had no explanation.

The van sluggishly headed up the winding and precarious road that led out of the valley and over the mountains. Four angels swooped down behind it and started pushing it up the grade, helping it to top sixty. They were making good time, but looking back they could see an oncoming legion of demons in hot pursuit, the glimmer of their fangs and the red flicker of their blades filling the night sky.

From high above, Guilo watched the cloud. It remained where it was, covering the Strongman. Only a small contingent of demonic warriors had been sent after the runaway van.

Roaring up the mountain road in pursuit, four of Kaseph's armed security men gave chase in a high-powered jeep. Even so, they had a surprising amount of trouble catching up.

"I thought that thing had a full load!" said one.

"It does," said the other. "I loaded it myself."

"How many horses does that thing *have?*"

By now Kaseph had gotten word of Susan's escape. He ordered eight more armed men in two more vehicles to join the chase. They leaped into another jeep and a V-8 powered sports car and squealed out of the parking lot.

Demons and angels converged on the van, still chugging up the steep grade at more than sixty miles an hour, its tires growling and often skidding sideways across the winding, reeling gravel road. The four angels kept pushing it from behind while the other nineteen did their best to encircle it and ward off demonic attack. Demons dove down from above, their red swords gleaming, and engaged the heavenly warriors in fierce dogfights, the blades singing, droning, and clashing metallically with bursts of sparks.

The van came to the summit and picked up more speed. The pursuing vehicles topped the summit only seconds behind it. As the van accelerated more and more, the bumps and curves in the roadway became one death-dealing jolt or one frame-bending wrench after another, and the van rocked, dancing on two and three wheels as it careened down the steep grade. The road went straight, then turned abruptly, then twisted back the other direction, then took a dip. The van wrestled the road as the rocks and guardrails blurred by. With each sharp curve it groaned and leaned heavily toward the outside, the big frame bottoming out the springs, the tires screeching in protest.

A very sharp left turn! The van's heavy back end fishtailed into the guardrail with a loud grinding and a fiery shower of sparks. Down the road, another dip, the springs bottoming out, the frame crunching down on the axles, groaning and creaking.

The jeeps and the sports car followed behind, doing much better at negotiating the treacherous curves but getting the ride of their lives all the same. Two men in the lead jeep had high-powered rifles ready, but it was impossible to get any clear shot. They fired a few rounds anyway, if only to scare the Maidservant.

The van was headed right for a hairpin turn, with yellow signs everywhere screaming at it to slow down and be cautious. The four angels who had been behind the van pushing were now pressed up against its sides, trying to keep it on the road. Guilo himself swooped down, his sword flashing, hacking his way through demon interceptors until he could work his way to the van. It was only a fraction of a second from the guardrail and the sheer drop beyond it when Guilo slammed forcefully into its side, jolting the front wheels to the left with a sharp jerk. The van made the turn and rolled on. The pursuers in the other vehicles had to slow down or go right through the guardrail.

But the heavenly warriors trying to encircle the van were being steadily cut away. Guilo looked just in time to see one huge spirit pounce with bared talons on top of a warrior like a hawk on a sparrow, knocking the angel senseless, making it flutter down into the deep canyon below. Another dogfight high above and to the left ended in a cry of pain from another warrior who went into a crazy spin, one wing shredded, and disappeared inside the wall of a mountain. The ringing clashes of blades echoed all around. There went a demon, disappearing in a trail of red smoke. Another angel fell toward the canyon floor, still holding his sword but listless and stunned, his demon pursuer right behind him.

The hideous warriors of hell finally began to break through and reach the van. One reached the warrior right behind Guilo and knocked him away. Guilo didn't have time to think another thought before his own sword went up to fend off the incredibly powerful blow of a spirit at least equal to himself. Guilo returned the blow, their swords locked for a moment, arm against arm, and then Guilo made good use of his foot to cave in the demon's face and sent it tumbling out over the canyon.

The van began to swerve wildly, the tires tiptoeing on the very edge of the chasm. Guilo pushed with all his might to get it back on course. The van lurched again and he realized a band of demons must be on the other side, pushing against him. He looked around for help and saw more fangs and yellow eyes than friends. A huge blade swept downward over his shoulder, and he parried it off. Another one thrust toward his midsection, and he struck that away. The van veered toward the cliff. He tried to push back, parry a blow, look for help, strike another demon, kick a face, push the van, cut a flank, parry a blow, guide the van . . .

A blow! He didn't see it coming and had no idea who had struck it, but it stunned him. He lost his grip on the van, saw the canyon floor spinning far below, saw the earth, the sky, the earth, the sky. He was falling. He spread his wings and floated downward like a torn and fallen leaf. From up above he heard a bloodcurdling howl. He looked up. This must be the one who had struck him, a very large, bulb-eyed nightmare with reptilian skin and serrated wings.

"Come, come," Guilo muttered, waiting for the thing to pounce.

It dove straight at him, its jaws gaping, its fangs glimmering, a wide, flat blade with keen edge flashing. Guilo waited. The thing raised its sword high and brought it down with a *woosh!* Guilo was suddenly three feet away from where he had been, and the blade continued on its way without their having met, the demon somersault- ing wildly after it. Guilo made a blinding sweep with his own sword and dewinged the demon, then finished it.

The boiling trail of red smoke cleared away from Guilo's eyes just in time for him to see the van crash through a guardrail and sail out over the precipice. The fall was so far, so very long and extended, that the van seemed to float for an eternity before folding and crushing on the rocks below, twisting, turning, bouncing like a pop can as chairs, desks, and cabinets tumbled out the back and papers upon papers fluttered through the air like snowflakes. About thirty demons ho- vered high above or roosted on the remaining guardrail to watch their work come to completion. After turning and rolling over and over, the van, no longer recognizable as anything, finally came to rest in a heap of scrap and glass at the base of the mountain. The three pursuing vehicles pulled to a stop, and the twelve security men got out to take a satisfied look.

Guilo rested on a rocky crag, setting his sword down and looking skyward. High above he could make out minute streaks of light head- ing in several different directions, each one followed by two or three streaks of red-accented black. His warriors—what was left of them— were scattering in all directions. Guilo thought it best to remain where he was until the skies cleared. He, Tal, and their warriors would all regroup in Ashton soon enough.

Rafar still sat in his big dead tree, watching over the town of Ashton as a master at chess would sit and look over a gameboard. He enjoyed watching the many pieces and pawns make their moves against each other.

When a demon messenger brought the welcome news from the Strongman's Lair that the Maidservant, that traitorous wench, had come to a miserable end and the heavenly host had been routed, Rafar gloated and laughed. He had taken his opponent's queen!

"And so shall it be for the rest," Rafar said with diabolical glee. "The Strongman entrusted the preparation of the town to me. When he comes, he will find it unoccupied, swept, and put in order!"

He called some of his warriors. "It's time to clean house. While the heavenly host are weak and cannot stand against us, we should take care of the final obstacles. I would like Hogan and Busche put away like vanquished kings! Make use of the woman Carmen, and see to it that they are bound and helpless, a byword and a mockery! As for Kevin Weed . . ." The demon warlord's eyes narrowed with disdain. "He could never be a worthy prize for such as myself. See that he is killed, any way you wish; then bring me word." The warriors departed to carry out his orders.

Rafar heaved a deep, half-mocking sigh. "Ah, dear Captain of the Host, perhaps I will see my battle won with no more than a raised finger, a casual order, the poison of my subtlety; your sky-rending trump of battle will be displaced by a pitiful whimper, and my victory will be won without my ever having seen your face, or your sword." He looked over the town and broke into his fiendish grin, clicking his thumb talon across his other four.

"But do be sure of this: We shall meet, Tal! Do not think to hide behind your praying saints, for we can both see they have failed you. You and I shall meet!"

Bernice knew it would be difficult, even dangerous, to drive without her glasses, but Marshall never answered his phone, so the meeting with Kevin Weed was entirely up to her and certainly worth the risk. So far, as she drove up Highway 27, the daylight was sufficient to make out the center line and the oncoming blobs, so she pressed on toward the big green bridge north of Baker.

Kevin Weed also had that bridge in mind as he sat at the bar at The Evergreen Tavern with his hands around a beer and his eyes on the big Lucky Lager clock. Somehow he felt safer here than at home by himself. He had buddies around, lots of noise, the ball game on television, the shuffleboard game going on behind him. His hands still shook, though, every time he let go of his beer mug; so most of the time he hung on to it and tried to act normal. The front door kept scraping the linoleum as more people came in.

The place was warming up, which was just fine. The more the merrier. Several loggers had beers to buy and stories to tell. There were bets going around on the shuffleboard game—tonight a long-standing rivalry would be settled once and for all. Kevin took time to smile and greet his friends and exchange a little jaw time. That helped him loosen up.

Two loggers came in. They were new, he figured; he'd never seen them before. But they fit right in with the rest of the bunch and were quick to get everyone caught up on where they were working and for how long and how the weather had been good, bad, or indifferent.

They even came up and sat with him at the bar.

"Hey," said one, extending his hand, "Mark Hansen."

"Kevin Weed," he said, shaking Mark's hand.

Mark introduced Kevin to the other guy, Steve Drake. They hit it off fine, talking logging, baseball, deer hunts, and booze, and Kevin's hands quit shaking. He even finished his beer.

"Want another beer?" Mark asked.

"Yeah, sure, thanks."

Dan brought the beers, and the conversation kept rattling on.

A loud cheer went up from the shuffleboard championship-for-all-time, and the three of them spun around in their seats to see the winner shaking hands with the loser.

Mark was quick. When no one was looking, he emptied a small vial into Kevin's beer.

The shuffleboard crowd began to congregate at the bar. Kevin checked the clock. It was time to go anyway. In all the hubbub and chatter he managed to say so long to his two new acquaintances, down his beer, and head for the door. Mark and Steve gave him a friendly wave as he went.

Kevin climbed in his old pickup and drove off. He figured he would even get to the bridge a little early. Just thinking about it made him start shaking again.

Mark and Steve wasted no time. Kevin had no sooner pulled out onto the highway than they were in their own pickup truck, following some distance behind. Steve checked his watch.

"It won't be long now," he said.

"So where do we dump him?" asked Mark.

"What's wrong with the river? He's heading there anyway."

It must have been that last beer, Kevin was thinking to himself. He must have chugged it down too fast or something; his stomach was letting him know about it. On top of that, he had to go to the bathroom. On top of that, he was really getting sleepy. He spent a few miles debating what to do, but finally he figured he had better pull over before he just plain keeled over.

A garishly painted, sagging, low-overhead hamburger joint was just ahead. He pulled off the highway and managed to bring the truck to a safe stop beside the building.

He didn't notice the pickup truck that pulled off the highway and then waited some hundred yards behind him.

"Terrific!" said Mark angrily. "So what's he going to do, keel over right in front of that hamburger place? I thought that stuff was supposed to hit hard and fast!"

Steve only shook his head. "Maybe he just has to go to the bathroom. We'll have to wait and see."

It looked like Steve was right. Kevin stumbled and staggered his way into the men's restroom behind the building. For a minute or so they stared at the restroom door. Steve looked at his watch again. Time was getting short.

"If he comes out and gets back on the road, the stuff should hit him before he reaches the bridge."

"If he even comes out!" Mark muttered. "What if we have to drag him out of there?"

No. Here he came, out the restroom door, looking a little better. As the two men watched, Kevin climbed back into his truck and pulled back out onto the highway. They followed him, waiting for something to happen.

It did. The truck began to swerve, first to the left, then back to the right.

"There he goes!" said Steve.

Up ahead was the Judd River Bridge, a steel span over a very deep chasm carved out by the Judd River. The little truck kept speeding along crazily, veering clear over into the left lane, then back again into the right lane, and then over onto the shoulder.

"He's fighting it, trying to stay awake," Steve observed.

"It's probably watered down with too much beer."

The truck went over onto the shoulder, and the tires began to wobble and dig into the soft gravel. The rear wheels spun and threw rocks, and the truck fishtailed along for several feet, heading for the bridge, but by now the driver had no control and seemed to have slipped into sleep with his foot on the gas pedal. The truck roared and accelerated, then shot across the road, roared across the wide turn-off just before the bridge, leaped upon a clump of alder saplings, and finally soared off the rocky precipice and into the river canyon below.

Mark and Steve pulled to a stop on the bridge just in time to look over the side and see the truck sinking wheels-up into the river.

"Score one more for Kaseph," said Steve.

Another driver in an oncoming car screeched to a halt and jumped out of his auto. Soon another vehicle pulled up. The bridge was starting to get clogged with excited people. Mark and Steve eased away, making their way off the bridge.

"We'll call the fire department!" Mark shouted out his window.

And away they went, never to be seen or heard from again.

30

Kate. Sandy. The Network. Bernice. Langstrat. The Network. Omni. Kaseph. Kate. Sandy. Bernice.

Marshall's thoughts went around and around as he stood at the sliding glass door just off the kitchen and watched daylight ebb slowly away from the backyard, from the delicate orange wash of sunset to the sad, ever deepening gray of nightfall.

Maybe it was the longest time he had ever spent in just one spot in his whole life, but maybe this right here and now was the end of the life he had always known. Sure, he had gone through several little attempts at denial, at trying to prove to himself that these cosmic characters, these far-out conspirators, were nothing but wind, but he kept coming back to the cold, hard facts. Harmel was right. Marshall was now out on his ear, like everybody else. Believe it, Hogan. Hey, it's happened whether you believe it or not!

He was out, just like Harmel, just like Strachan, just like Edie, just like Jefferson, Gregory, the Carluccis, Waller, James, Jacobson . . .

Marshall rubbed his hand over his head and stopped the train of names and facts coursing through his brain. Such thoughts were beginning to hurt; each one of them seemed to punch him in the stomach as it passed through his brain.

But how did they do it? How could they be so powerful that they actually destroyed lives on a personal level? Was it only coincidence? Marshall couldn't settle that question. He was too close to it, having lost his own family and having the Network to blame, but also himself. It would be so easy to blame the conspiracy for tampering with his family and turning his wife and daughter against him, and undoubtedly they had tried it. But where could he draw the line between their responsibility and his?

All he knew was that his family had fallen apart and now he was out, just like all the others.

Wait! There was a noise at the front door. Could it be Kate? He stepped to the kitchen door and looked toward the front room.

Whoever it was ducked around a corner very hurriedly as soon as he showed his face.

"Sandy?" he called.

For a moment there was no answer, but then he heard Sandy reply in a very strange, cold tone of voice, "Yes, Daddy, it's me."

He almost broke into a run, but he forced himself to take it easy and walk lightly to her bedroom. He looked in and saw her going through her closet, moving rather hurriedly and nervously, and she showed a definite discomfort at his watching her.

"Where's Mom?" she asked.

"Well . . ." he said, trying to come up with an answer. "She's gone to her mother's for a while."

"She's left you, in other words," she replied quite directly.

Marshall was direct too. "Yeah, yeah, that's right." He watched her for a while; she was grabbing clothing and belongings and throwing them into a suitcase and some shopping bags. "Looks like you're leaving too."

"That's right," she said, without slowing down or even looking up. "I felt it coming. I knew what Mom was thinking, and I think she was right. You get along so well all by yourself, we may as well let you have it that way for keeps."

"Where will you go?"

Sandy looked up at him for the first time, and Marshall was chilled and even sickened by the look in her eyes, a strange, glassy, maniacal expression he had never seen before.

"I'll never tell you!" she said, and Marshall couldn't believe the way she said it. It was not Sandy at all.

"Sandy," he said gently, pleadingly, "can we talk? I won't put any pressure or demands on you. Could we just talk?"

Those very strange eyes glared at him again and this person who used to be his loving daughter responded with, "I'll see you in hell!"

Marshall immediately sensed those all too familiar sensations of fear and doom. Some *thing* had come into his house.

Hank answered the door and immediately felt a certain check in his spirit. Carmen stood there. She was dressed neatly and conservatively this time, and her demeanor was much more down to earth; yet Hank had his qualms.

"Well, hi," he said.

She smiled disarmingly and said, "Hello, Pastor Busche."

He stepped aside and motioned for her to come in. She stepped inside the door in time to see Mary coming from the kitchen.

"Hello, Mary," she said.

"Hello," said Mary. She took an extra step and gave Carmen a loving embrace. "Are you all right?"

"Much better, thank you." She looked at Hank, and her eyes were full of repentance. "Pastor, I really owe you an apology for the way I acted before. It must have been very alarming for you both."

Hank hemmed and hawed a little and finally said, "Well, we certainly were concerned for your welfare."

Mary moved toward the living room and said, "Won't you have a seat? Can I bring you anything?"

"Thank you, no," said Carmen, sitting down on the sofa. "I won't be staying long."

Hank sat in a chair opposite the sofa and looked at Carmen, praying a mile a minute. Yes, she looked different, like she'd gotten a lot of loose ends finally tied together in her life, and yet . . . Hank had seen a lot in the last few days, and he had the distinct impression that he was seeing more of the same thing this very moment. There was something about her eyes . . .

Sandy backed up a little and narrowed her eyes at Marshall like a wild bull about to charge. "You get out of my way!"

Marshall remained in the bedroom door, blocking it with his body. "I don't want a big fight, Sandy. I won't stand in your way forever. I just want you to think for a moment, okay? Can you just calm down and give me an audience just one last time? Huh?"

She stood there rigidly, breathing heavily through her nose, her lips shut tightly, her body crouched a little. It was simply unreal!

Marshall tried to calm her down with his voice as if approaching a wild horse. "I'll let you go anywhere you want. It's your life. But we don't dare part without saying what needs to be said. I love you, you know." She didn't respond to that. "I really do love you. Do you—do you believe that at all?"

"You—you don't know the meaning of the word."

"Yeah . . . yeah, I can understand that. I haven't done very well these past years. But listen, we can put it back together. Why let this thing go in the shape it's in when we could heal it?"

She looked him over again, observed how he was still standing in the doorway, and said, "Daddy, all I want right now is to get out of here."

"In a minute, in a minute." Marshall tried to speak slowly, carefully, gently. "Sandy . . . I don't know if I can explain it to you very clearly, but remember what you said yourself about the town that one Saturday, how you thought—what was it? Aliens were taking over the town? Do you remember that?"

She didn't answer, but she seemed to be listening.

"You don't know how right you were, how true that theory really was. There are people in this town, Sandy, right now, that want to take the whole town over, and they also want to destroy anyone who gets in their way. Sandy, I'm someone who got in their way."

Sandy began to shake her head incredulously. She wasn't buying it.

"Listen to me, Sandy, just listen! Now . . . I run the paper, see, and I know what they're up to, and they know that I know, so they're just doing what they can to destroy me, take away my house, the newspaper, undermine my family!" He looked at her in earnest, but had no idea if any of this was getting through. "All that's happening to us . . . it's what they want! They want this family to fall apart!"

"You're crazy!" she finally said. "You're a maniac! Get out of the way!"

"Sandy, listen to me. They've even been using you against me. Did you know those cops in town are trying to find anything they can to put me away? They're trying to pin a murder rap on me, and it even sounds like they're accusing me of abusing you! That's how terrible this whole thing is. You have to understand—"

"But you did it!" Sandy cried. "You know you did it."

Marshall was stunned. All he could do was stare at her. She *had* to be crazy. "Did *what*, Sandy?"

She actually broke down and tears came to her eyes as she said, "You raped me. You *raped* me!"

Carmen seemed to be having a very difficult time getting around to whatever she had come to tell them. "I—I just don't know how to begin . . . it's just so difficult."

Hank reassured her, "Oh, you're among friends."

Carmen looked at Mary sitting at the other end of the sofa, and then at Hank, still sitting opposite her. "Hank, I just can't live with it anymore."

Hank said, "Then why don't you just give it over to Jesus? He's the Healer, you know. He can take away your regrets and your sorrows, believe me."

She looked at him and only shook her head incredulously. "Hank, I am not here to play games. It's time we were truthful and cleared the air once and for all. We're just not being fair to Mary."

Hank didn't know what she was talking about, so he just leaned forward and nodded, his way of telling her he was listening.

She continued, "Well, I guess I'll just have to say it and get it out. I'm sorry, Hank." She turned to Mary, her eyes filling with tears, and said, "Mary, for the last several months . . . ever since our first counseling appointment . . . Hank and I have been seeing each other on a regular basis."

Mary asked, "What do you mean by that?"

Carmen turned to Hank and implored him, "Hank, don't you think you should be the one to tell her?"

"Tell her what?" Hank asked.

Carmen looked at Mary, took her hand, and said, "Mary, Hank and I have been having an affair."

Mary looked startled, but not very stunned. She did pull her hand away from Carmen's. Then she looked at Hank.

"What do you think?" she asked him.

Hank took another good look at Carmen and then nodded to Mary. Mary turned directly toward Carmen, and Hank got up out of his chair. They both looked intently at Carmen, and she began to look away from their eyes.

"It's true!" she insisted. "Tell her, Hank. Please tell her."

"Spirit," said Hank firmly, "I command you in the name of Jesus to be silent and come out of her!"

There were fifteen of them, packed into Carmen's body like crawling, superimposed maggots, boiling, writhing, a tangle of hideous arms, legs, talons, and heads. They began to squirm. Carmen began to squirm. They moaned and cried out, and so did Carmen, her eyes turning glassy and staring blankly.

Outside the room, Krioni and Triskal watched from a distance.

Triskal fumed, "Orders, orders, orders!"

Krioni reminded him, "Tal knows what he's doing."

Triskal pointed toward the living room and cried, "Hank's playing with a bomb in there. You see those demons? They'll tear him apart!"

"We have to stay out of it," Krioni said. "We can protect Hank's and Mary's lives, but we cannot keep the demons from doing whatever they might do . . ." Krioni was having trouble with it himself.

Sandy got louder and louder. Marshall felt that any moment he would lose control of her altogether.

"You . . . you let me out of here or you're going to be in big trouble!" she nearly screamed.

Marshall could only stand there in total dismay and horror. "Sandy, it's me, Marshall Hogan, your father. *Think*, Sandy! You know I never touched you, I never molested you. I only loved you and cared for you. You're my daughter, my only daughter."

"You did it to me!" she cried hysterically.

"When, Sandy?" he demanded. "When did I ever touch you wrongly?"

"It was something my mind had blocked out for years, but Professor Langstrat brought it out!"

"Langstrat!"

"She put me under hypnosis, and I saw it like it was yesterday. You did it, and I hate you!"

"You never remembered it because it never happened. *Think,* Sandy!"

"I hate you! You did it to me!"

Nathan and Armoth, from outside the house, could see the hideous deceiving spirit clinging to Sandy's back, its talons deep in her skull.

Alongside them was Tal. He had just given them their special orders.

"Captain," said Armoth, "we don't know what that thing might do."

"Preserve their lives," said Tal, "but Hogan must fall. As for Sandy, see to it that a special detachment follows her at a distance. They'll be able to move when the time is right."

Just then, with a very low, stealthy trajectory, Signa floated in for a landing.

"Captain," he reported, "Kevin Weed is dead. It worked."

Tal gave Signa a strange, knowing look and smile. "Excellent," he said.

The fifteen spirits in Carmen were foaming and frothing, wailing and hissing. Hank held Carmen down gently, one hand on her right hand, one hand on her left shoulder. Mary stood beside him, clinging to him a little out of her own timidity. Carmen moaned and twisted, her eyes glaring at Hank.

"Let us go, praying man!" Carmen's voice warned, and the sulfurous odor coming from deep inside her was strong and nauseating.

"Carmen, do you want to be delivered?" Hank asked.

"She can't hear you," said the spirits. "Let us alone! She belongs to us!"

"Be silent and come out of her!"

"No!" Carmen screamed, and Mary was almost sure she saw a puff of yellow vapor from Carmen's throat.

"Come out in the name of Jesus!" said Hank.

The bomb exploded. Hank was thrown backward. Mary leaped aside. Carmen was on top of Hank, clawing, biting, mauling. Her teeth clamped onto his right arm. He pushed and pounded with his left.

"Demon, let go!" he ordered.

The jaws opened. Hank gave all the shove he had and Carmen's body staggered backward, twitching and shrieking. Her hands found a chair. Instantly it shot upward and came down with a crash, but Hank scurried out of the way. He dove for Carmen and tackled her as she was grabbing another chair. Her leg came up like a catapult and flung him across the room where he thudded into the wall. Her fist was right behind him. He dodged it. It rammed a hole in the plaster. He was looking into the eyes of a beast; he smelled the sulfurous breath hissing through the bared teeth. He jerked himself away. Sharp fingernails snagged and tore at his shirt. Some dug into his flesh. He could hear Mary screaming, "Stop it, spirit! In Jesus' name, stop it!"

Carmen doubled over and clapped her hands over her ears. She staggered and screamed.

"Be silent, demon, and come out of her!" Hank ordered, trying to keep his distance.

"I won't! I won't!" Carmen screamed, and her body careened toward the front door. She hit it full force. The center of the door caved in with a loud crack. Hank ran to the door and pulled it open, and Carmen flew out the door and down the street. As Hank and Mary watched her go, all they could do was hope the neighbors wouldn't see.

"Sandy," said Marshall, "this isn't you. I know it isn't you."

She said nothing, but like the strike of a rattlesnake she pounced at him, trying to get through the door. He held his hands up to protect his face from her flying fists.

"Okay, okay!" he told her, stepping aside. "You can go. Just remember, I love you."

She grabbed her suitcase and a shopping bag and bolted for the front door. He followed her down the hall toward the living room.

He came around the corner. He looked to see her, but all he saw was the lamp that smacked into his skull. He heard and felt the blow in every part of his body. The lamp fell to the floor with a crash. Now he was on one knee, slumped against the couch. His hand went to his head. He looked up and saw the front door still standing open. He was bleeding.

His head was so light he was afraid to try to stand up. His strength was gone anyway. Nuts, now there's blood on the rug. What will Kate say?

"Marshall!" came a voice above him. A hand rested on his shoulder. It was a woman. Kate? Sandy? No, Bernice, squinting at him through blackened eyes. "Marshall, what happened? Are you—are you still there?"

"Help me clean up this mess," was all he could say.

She scurried into the kitchen and found some paper towels. She brought them back and pressed a wad of them against his head. He winced at the pain.

She asked him, "Can you get up?"

"I don't want to get up!" he answered crossly.

"Okay, okay. I just saw Sandy drive off. Was this her doing?"

"Yeah, she pitched that lamp at me . . ."

"It must have been something you said. Here, hold still."

"She's not herself at all, she's gone crazy."

"Where's Kate?"

"She's left me."

Bernice settled to the floor, her bruised face the picture of shock, dismay, and exhaustion. Neither of them said anything for a few moments. They just stared at each other like two shot-up soldiers in a foxhole.

"Man, you're a mess!" Marshall finally observed.

"At least the swelling's gone down. Don't I look foxy?"

"More like a raccoon. I thought you were supposed to be resting at home. What are you doing here, anyway?"

"I just got back from Baker. And I have nothing but bad news from there too."

He anticipated it. "Weed?"

"He's dead. The truck he was driving went off the Judd River Bridge and into that big canyon. We were supposed to have met each other. He'd just gotten a call from Susan Jacobson, and it sounded pretty important."

Marshall's head fell back against the couch, and he closed his eyes. "Aw, great . . . just great!" He wanted to die.

"He called me this afternoon, and we set up the appointment. I imagine either my phone or his was bugged. That accident was set up, I'm sure of it. I got out of there fast!"

Marshall took the wad from his head and looked at the blood on it. He placed it back over the gash.

"We're going down, Bernie," he said, and went on to tell her about his whole afternoon, his meeting with Brummel and Brummel's buddies, his loss of the house, his loss of the paper, his loss of Kate, of Sandy, of everything. "And did you know that I've made it a habit to molest my daughter besides having an affair with my reporter?"

"They're cutting you up into little pieces, aren't they?" she said very quietly, her throat constricted with fear. "What can we do?"

"We can get the heck out of here, that's what we can do!"

"You're going to give up?"

Marshall only let his head sink downward. He was tired. "Let somebody else fight this war. We were warned, Bernie, and we didn't listen. They got me. They got all our records, any proof we ever had. Harmel blew his brains out. Strachan's getting as far away from it as he can. They took out Weed. Right now I think I'm just barely alive and that's all I have left."

"What about Susan Jacobson?"

It took some extra effort and willpower to make himself think about it. "I wonder if she even exists, and, if so, if she's alive."

"Kevin said she had the goods and she was getting ready to get out of wherever she was. That sounds to me like a defection, and if she has the evidence we need to seal this thing up—"

"They took care of that, Bernie. Remember? Weed was our last contact with her."

"Want to toy with a theory?"

"No."

"If Kevin's phone was bugged, they know what Weed and Susan talked about. They heard it all."

"Naturally, and Susan's as good as dead too."

"We don't know that. Maybe she managed to get away. Maybe she was going to meet Kevin someplace."

"Ehhh . . ." Marshall passively listened.

"What I'm toying with is that somewhere there must be a recording in somebody's hands of that phone call."

"Yeah, I suppose there is." Marshall felt half-dead, but the half of him that was still alive was thinking. "But where would it be? This is a big country, Bernie."

"Well . . . like I said, it's a theory to toy with. It's all we have left, really."

"Which sure isn't much."

"I'm dying to know what Susan had to say—"

"Please don't use that word 'dying.' "

"Well, think for a minute, Marshall. Think of all the people who seem to have responded to the alleged bug. There were the Windsor cops who knew they could find you at Strachan's after you told me you'd be there—"

"It's not likely they'd have the recording equipment. They're too far away."

"So somebody who did have the recording equipment must have tipped them off."

Marshall got an idea, and a little bit of color returned to his face. "I'm wondering about Brummel."

Bernice's eyes brightened. "Sure! Like I said, he and the cops in Windsor are in cahoots all the time."

"He fired Sara, you know. She wasn't there today. She'd been replaced." New ideas began to form in Marshall's mind. "Yeah . . . she talked to me on the phone and ratted on Brummel a little. She said she'd help me out if I could help her out . . . we agreed to deal . . . and Brummel fired her! He must have heard that conversation too." Then it hit him. "Yeah! Sara! Those filing cabinets! Brummel's filing cabinets!"

"Yeah, you're cooking, Marshall, just keep going!"

"He had his filing cabinets moved out into Sara's reception area to make room for some new office equipment. I saw it there, sitting right in his office, and there was a wire coming out of the wall . . . he said it was for the coffeemaker. But I didn't see any coffeemaker!"

"I think you might have it there!"

"It was telephone wire, not appliance cord." Excitement made his head hurt, but he said anyway, "Bernice, it was telephone wire."

"If we could find out for sure that the recording equipment is there in his office . . . if we could find any tapes of phone conversations . . . well, that might be enough to bring some kind of charges at least: illegal wiretapping—"

"Murder."

That was a chilling thought.

"We need Sara," Marshall added. "If she's on our side, now's when she can prove it."

"Whatever you do, don't call her. I know where she lives."

"Help me up."

"*You* help *me* up!"

31

Hank and Mary were still shaking as he took a careful look at the front door.

He shook his head and whistled his astonishment. "She cracked the doorjamb. Look at this! The stop is moved out about an inch."

"Well, how about changing your shirt?" Mary asked, and Hank remembered that half his shirt was gone.

"Here's another one for the rag box," he said, slipping the shirt off. Then he winced a little. "Oooo!"

"What's wrong?"

As the shirt came off Hank raised his arm to have a look, and Mary gasped. Carmen's teeth had made some very impressive welts. The skin was broken in some places.

"We'd better put some peroxide on those," said Mary, hurrying into the bathroom. "Come here!"

Hank went into the bathroom, still carrying the torn shirt. He held his arm out over the sink, and Mary started dabbing the wounds.

She was astonished. "Goodness! Hank, she bit you in four different places. Look at this!"

"Boy, I hope she's had all her shots."

"I knew that woman was up to no good the first time I saw her."

The doorbell rang. Hank and Mary looked at each other. What now?

"Better go answer it," said Hank.

She went out into the living room while Hank finished cleaning his arm.

"Hank!" Mary called. "I think you'd better come out here!"

Hank went out into the living room, still carrying the torn shirt in his hand and sporting the bite marks on his arm.

Two policemen stood at the door, an older, taller one and a younger, new-on-the-force type. Yeah, the neighbors must have thought something terrible was happening in here. Come to think of it, they were right.

"Hi there," said Hank.

"Hank Busche?" the older one asked.

"Yeah," he answered. "This is Mary, my wife. You must have received a call from the neighbors, right?"

The big officer was looking at Hank's arm. "What happened to your arm?"

"Well . . ." Hank wasn't sure how to answer. Even the truth would sound like a pretty tall tale.

No matter. He didn't have time. The younger officer grabbed Hank's shirt right out of his hand and unfolded it, holding it up in both hands. The older one happened to have the rest of Hank's shirt discreetly hidden behind his back. Now he produced the torn piece and made a quick comparison of the materials.

The older one nodded to the younger one, and the younger one got out a pair of handcuffs and rather forcefully twisted Hank around. Mary's mouth dropped open and she squealed, "What on earth are you doing?"

The older one started rattling off the prisoner's liturgy. "Mr. Busche, we are placing you under arrest. It's my duty to advise you of your rights. You have the right to remain silent, anything you say can and will be used against you . . ."

Hank had an idea, but he asked anyway, "Uh . . . mind telling me what the charges are?"

"You oughta know," snapped the older one.

"Suspected rape," said the younger.

"What?" Mary exclaimed.

The younger one held up his hand as a warning. "Just stay out of this, lady."

"You're making a mistake!" she pleaded.

The two officers led Hank down the front walk. It happened so fast that Mary hardly knew what to do. She ran after them, pleading, trying to reason with them.

"This is crazy! I don't believe this!" she said.

The younger one just told her, "You'll have to stay out of the way or face charges of obstructing justice."

"Justice!" she cried. "You call this justice? Hank, what should I do?"

"Make some calls," Hank answered.

"I'm going with you!"

"We can't allow you in the squad car, ma'am," said the older one.

"Make some calls, Mary," Hank repeated.

They strong-armed him into the car and closed the door. The two officers got in and away they went, down the street, around the corner and out of sight, and Mary remained there on the curb all by herself, without her husband, just like that.

Tal and his warriors and couriers knew where to look and they knew what to listen for; so they heard the telephones ringing all over town, they saw the many people roused from their televisions or from their sleep by the phone calls. The entire Remnant was buzzing with the news of Hank's arrest. The praying began.

"Busche has fallen," said Tal. "Only Hogan remains." He turned to Chimon and Mota. "Does Sara have the keys?"

Chimon answered, "She had several keys copied before she left her job at the police station."

Mota looked across the town as he said, "They should be meeting with her right about now."

Sara, Bernice, and Marshall conferred in a tight, hushed little huddle in the middle of Sara's small kitchen. Except for the light from one lamp out in the dining room, there were no other lights on in the house. Sara was still up, fully dressed. She was packing to move.

"I'll take whatever I can squeeze into my car, but I'm not staying around past tomorrow, especially after tonight," she said in a near whisper.

"How are you set for money?" Marshall asked.

"I've enough gas money to get out of the state, and after that I don't know. Brummel didn't give me any severance pay."

"Just booted you right out?"

"He didn't say so, but I've no doubt he overheard that conversation I had with you. I didn't survive very long after that."

Marshall handed her a hundred dollars. "I'd give you more if I had it."

"That's all right. I'd say we have a deal." Sara passed a set of keys to him. "Now listen carefully. This one here is for the main door, but first you have to deactivate the burglar alarm. That's this little key here. The box is around the back, just above the garbage cans. You just open the cover and flip the switch off. This key here, with the round head, is to Brummel's office. I don't know if that equipment is locked up or not, but I don't have any key for it. You'll just have to take the risk. The night dispatcher is still posted at the fire station, so there shouldn't be anyone else there."

"What do you think of our theory?" Bernice asked.

"I know Brummel's very protective of that new equipment in there. Ever since he had it installed, I've not been allowed in his office and he keeps the door closed. It's the first place *I'd* look."

"We'd better go," Marshall said to Bernice.

Bernice gave Sara a hug. "Good luck."

"Good luck yourselves," Sara replied. "Be very quiet going out."

They sneaked away in the darkness.

Later that night Marshall picked up Bernice at her apartment and they rode together downtown.

Marshall found a good spot to hide the Buick just a few blocks from Courthouse Square, a nice vacant lot with lots of overgrown shrubs and trees. His slipped the big car down into the jungle and turned off the engine. For a moment he and Bernice just sat there wondering what the next move should be. They thought they were ready. They had even changed into dark clothes, and they had brought flashlights and rubber gloves.

"Sheesh!" said Marshall. "The last time I did something like this was when we kids stole the neighbor's corn."

"How did that turn out!"

"We got caught, and boy, did we get it!"

"What time does your watch say?"

Marshall checked his watch with his flashlight. "1:25."

Bernice was clearly nervous. "I wonder if real burglars work this way. I feel like I'm in some kind of hokey movie."

"How about some charcoal for your face?"

"It's black enough now, thank you."

They both sat there for a few more moments, trying to build up the nerve to proceed.

Bernice finally said, "Well, are we going to do it or aren't we?"

"Die all, die merrily," Marshall replied, opening his door.

They tiptoed up an alley and through a few yards until they reached the back of the courthouse/police station. Fortunately, the town hadn't gotten the funds together yet for any floodlights over the parking lot, so the darkness was pretty concealing.

Bernice couldn't help feeling petrified; only sheer determination kept her carrying on. Marshall was nervous, but for some reason he felt an odd exhilaration in doing something so sneaky and dirty against these enemies. As soon as they had crossed the parking lot they ducked into a nearby shadow and stood tightly against the wall. It was so nice and dark there that Bernice didn't want to leave.

About twenty feet down the wall were the garbage cans, and above them a small gray panel. Marshall got there quickly, found the right key, opened the little door, and found the switch. He signaled to Bernice, and she followed him. They walked quickly around to the front of the building, and now they were in the open, facing the large parking area between the police station and the town hall. Marshall had the key ready, and they were able to get into the building without delay. Marshall quickly closed the door behind them.

They rested just a minute and listened. The place was deserted and dead quiet. They heard no sirens or alarms going off. Marshall found the next key and went to Brummel's office door. So far Sara had predicted right on the money. Brummel's door opened too. They both ducked inside.

And there sat the cabinetry housing the mysterious equipment—if it was truly there. Marshall clicked on his flashlight and kept the beam subdued under his hand so that it would not play on the walls or shine out the window. Then he swung open the lower left cabinet door. Inside he found some shelves on roller tracks. He pulled the upper one out . . .

And there sat a recording machine with a good supply of tape. "Eureka!" Bernice whispered.

"Must be signal activated . . . switches on automatically whenever an input comes in."

Bernice clicked on her flashlight and checked the other door on the lower right. Here she found some files and folders.

"It looks like a catalog!" she said. "Look—names, dates, conversations, and what tape they're on."

"That handwriting looks familiar."

They were both astounded at how many names were on the list, how many people were being listened in on.

"Even Network people," Marshall observed. Then he pointed to a listing near the bottom of one page. "There *we* are."

He was right. The *Clarion* phone was listed, the conversation noted as being between Marshall and Ted Harmel, recorded on tape 5-A.

"Who in the world has the time to list all this stuff?" Bernice wondered.

Marshall only shook his head. Then he asked, "When was that conversation between Susan and Weed?"

Bernice thought for a moment. "We'll just have to check all of today, yesterday . . . who knows? Weed didn't say exactly."

"Maybe that call came in today. There's no record of that here."

"It must be on the tape that's on the machine now. Those calls haven't been logged yet."

Marshall wound the tape back, put the machine into play, flipped on the speaker switch, and set the volume down low.

Conversations began to unfold from the recording, a lot of everyday, innocuous stuff. Brummel's voice was in a lot of them, talking business. Marshall ran the tape ahead on Fast Forward a few times, skipping over several conversations. Suddenly he recognized a voice. His own.

"You already ran once, remember?" came his recorded voice. "As long as you're alive, Eldon, you're going to be living with this and they're going to know it . . ."

"Eldon Strachan and I," he told Bernice.

It was scary hearing his very words coming out of the machine, words that could tell the Network anything and everything.

Marshall skipped forward some more.

"Man, this whole thing is crazy," came a voice.

Bernice brightened. "That's him! That's Weed!"

Marshall wound the tape back and flipped it to Play again. There was a gap, then the abrupt start of a conversation.

"Yeah, hello?" said Weed.

"Kevin, this is Susan."

Bernice and Marshall listened intently.

Weed replied, "Yeah, I'm listening, man. What can I do?"

Susan's voice was tense and her words hurried. "Kevin, I'm getting out, one way or another, and I'm doing it tonight. Can you meet me at The Evergreen tomorrow night?"

"Yeah . . . yeah."

"See if you can bring Bernice Krueger with you. I have materials to show her, everything she needs to know."

"Man, this whole thing is crazy. You ought to see my place. Somebody came in here and tore it all up. You be careful!"

"We're *all* in great danger, Kevin. Kaseph's moving to Ashton to take over everything. But I can't talk now. Meet me at The Evergreen at 8. I'll try to get there somehow. If not I'll call you."

"Okay, okay."

"I have to go. Good-bye, and thanks."

Click. The conversation was over.

"Yeah," said Bernice, "he called to tell me about this."

"It wasn't much," said Marshall, "but it was enough. Now the only question is, did she manage to get away?"

A key rattled in the front door. Bernice and Marshall never moved so fast. She replaced all the files, and Marshall slid the machine back inside the cabinet. They closed the cabinet doors.

The front door opened. The lobby lights came on.

They ducked behind Brummel's big desk. Bernice's eyes were full of one question: What do we do now? Marshall gestured to her to keep cool, then he made fists to show her they might have to fight their way out.

Another key worked at Brummel's office door, and then it opened. Suddenly the room was flooded with light. They heard someone going to the cabinets, opening the doors, sliding out the machine. Marshall figured the person's back had to be toward them. He raised his head to take a quick peek.

It was Carmen. She was winding the tape back to the beginning and preparing to make more entries in the record.

Bernice took a look also, and both of them felt the same rage and indignation.

"Don't you ever sleep?" Marshall asked Carmen right out loud. That startled Bernice and she jumped a little. It startled Carmen and she jumped a lot, dropped her papers, and gave a short little scream. She spun around.

"What!" she gasped. "What are you doing here?"

Marshall and Bernice both stood up. From their battered and dark-clothed appearance, this looked like anything but a nonchalant, cordial visit.

"I might ask you the same thing," Marshall said. "Do you have any idea what time it is?"

Carmen looked them both over, and she was speechless.

Marshall could certainly think of some things to say. "You're a spy, aren't you? You were a spy in our office, you wiretapped our phones, and now you've run off with all our investigation materials."

"I don't know—"

"—what I'm talking about. Right! So I suppose you do this every night too, go over all the recorded phone conversations and log them, listen for anything the big boys might want to know."

"I wasn't—"

"And what about all the *Clarion's* business records? Let's take care of that first."

She suddenly broke down crying, saying, "Ohhh . . . you don't understand . . ." She went out into the reception area.

Marshall was right on her heels, not about to let her out of his sight. He took her by the arm and spun her around.

"Easy, girl! We have some real business to take care of here."

"Ooohhh!" Carmen wailed, and then she threw her arms around Marshall as if she were a frightened child and sobbed into his chest. "I thought you were some burglar . . . I'm glad it was you. I need help, Marshall!"

"And we want answers," Marshall snapped back, unaffected by her tears. He sat her down in Sara's old chair. "Have a seat and save your tears for some soap opera."

She looked up at both of them, her mascara running down her cheeks. "Don't you understand? Don't you have any heart? I came here for help! I've just had a terrible experience!" She built up the strength to say it, and then burst out in a fit of tears, "I've been raped!"

She collapsed to the floor, sobbing uncontrollably.

Marshall looked at Bernice, and Bernice looked at Marshall.

"Yeah," said Marshall unsympathetically, "there seems to be a lot of that going around these days, especially among the people your bosses want out of the way. So who was it this time?"

All she did was lie there on the floor and cry.

Bernice had something boiling inside her. "How do you like my looks tonight, Carmen? I think it's interesting that you were the only one who knew I'd be going out to visit Kevin Weed. Did you tip off the thug who beat me up?"

She still lay there on the floor crying, not saying a word.

Marshall went into Brummel's office and returned with some of the files, including the notes Carmen had written that very night.

"It's all in your handwriting, Carmen, my dear. You've been nothing but a spy from the very beginning. Am I right or am I right?"

She kept crying. Marshall took hold of her, lifting her from the floor. "C'mon, get up!"

It was just as he saw her hand come off the silent alarm button in the floor that the front door burst open and he heard a voice holler, "Freeze! Police!"

Carmen was no longer crying. As a matter of fact, she was smirking. Marshall put his hands up, and so did Bernice. Carmen ran behind the two uniformed police who had just come in. Their guns were trained right on the two burglars.

"Friends of yours?" Marshall asked Carmen.

She only smiled an evil smile.

Just then Alf Brummel himself came into the building, fresh out of bed and in his bathrobe.

"What's going on here?" he asked, and then he saw Marshall. "What . . . ? Well, well, who do we have here?" Then he actually chuckled a bit. He walked up to Marshall, shaking his head and showing those big teeth. "I don't believe this! I just can't believe it!" He looked at Bernice. "Bernice Krueger! Is that you?"

Bernice had nothing to say, and Brummel was too far away to spit on.

Oh no. Now they had a full house. Juleen Langstrat, also in a bathrobe, walked in the door! She sidled up to Brummel, and the two of them stood there looking proudly at Marshall and Bernice, as if they were trophies.

"Sorry for disturbing all of you like this," said Marshall.

Langstrat smiled lusciously and said, "I wouldn't have missed this for the world."

Brummel kept on grinning with those big teeth and told the policemen, "Read them their rights and take them into custody."

The opportunity was too good to pass up. There stood the two cops trying to do their job, and there were Brummel and Langstrat, standing just a little in front of them. The situation was perfect, and it had been building up inside Marshall for a long time. Instantly, with all his weight, he dove into Brummel's stomach and toppled Brummel and Langstrat backward into the two cops.

"Run, Bernie, run!" he shouted.

She ran. She didn't stop to consider if she had the courage or the will or even the speed. She just ran for all she was worth, down the long hallway, past all the office doors, straight for the exit at the end. The door had a crash bar. She crashed into it, it opened, and she stumbled out into the cool night air.

Marshall was in the middle of a tangle of arms, hands, bodies, and shouts, hanging on to as many of them as he could. He was almost enjoying it, and he didn't try that hard to get away. He wanted to keep them all busy.

One cop recovered and ran after Bernice, bursting out through that back door. He was close enough on her trail to pick up the sound of footsteps heading up the back alley, and away he went in hot pursuit.

Here was Bernice's chance to find out what kind of shape she was in, cracked rib and all. She chugged down the alley, taking long strides, making her way through the blurry dark; she longed for her glasses, or at least a little more light. She heard the cop hollering at her to stop. Any moment he would fire that warning shot. She made a sharp left through a yard and a dog started barking. There was a space of light between two low-hanging fruit trees. She headed for that and encountered a fence. Two garbage cans helped her over with a clatter that told the cop where she was.

Bernice stomped through a freshly tilled garden, flattening several unseen bean poles. She ran onto a lawn, turned back toward the alley, knocked over some more cans, clambered over a fence, and kept running. The cop seemed to be fading back a little.

She was getting desperately tired and could only hope that he was, too. She couldn't keep this up much longer. Every panting breath brought a sharp pain from that cracked rib. She couldn't breathe.

She whipped around one house and doubled back through a few more yards, raising a tumult of barking from tattletale dogs, then crossed a street, and dove into some woods. The branches lashed at her and entangled her, but she plowed through them until she reached another fence bordering a service station. She ran along the fence, found an old dumpster just on the other side, went just a little further—and then her eyes were attracted by a fragment of street light filtering through the leaves and illuminating a pile of rubbish some litterbug had dumped. She grabbed the first thing her hand found, an old bottle, then dropped to the ground, trying not to breathe too loudly, trying not to cry from the pain.

The cop was moving rather slowly through the woods, groping his way along in the dark, snapping twigs under his feet, huffing and puffing. She lay there silently, waiting for him to pause to listen. Finally he did stop and fall silent. He was listening. She pitched the bottle over the fence. It bounced off the top of the dumpster and shattered on the pavement behind the service station. The cop came crashing through the woods and up to the fence. He climbed over and stood still behind the station.

Bernice could not see him from where she was, but she listened very intently. So did he. Then she heard him walk slowly along the back of the station and stop. A moment passed, and then he walked away at a normal pace. He had lost her.

Bernice remained where she was, trying to calm the pounding of her heart and the rushing of blood in her ears, trying to calm her nerves and her panic, and wishing the pain would go away. All she wanted to do was gasp deep breaths of air; she couldn't seem to get enough.

Oh, Marshall, Marshall, what are they doing to you?

32

Marshall was facedown on the floor, his pockets emptied, his hands cuffed behind him. He was being very cooperative with the cop who stood over him with his gun drawn. Carmen, Brummel, and Langstrat were in Brummel's office going over the tape that Marshall and Bernice had listened to.

"Yes," said Carmen, "here's my notation of the tape counter. I thought the tape hadn't run very far for such a long period of surveillance. The recordings continue after this stopping point. They wound the tape back."

Brummel stepped out of his office and stood over Marshall. "So what did you and Bernice listen to?"

"Big band jazz, I think," Marshall answered. That response brought Brummel's heel down on Marshall's neck. "Aaauu!"

Brummel had another question. "So who gave you the keys to this place? Did Sara?"

"Ask me no questions, I'll tell you no lies."

Brummel muttered, "I'll have to put out an APB on her too!"

"Don't bother," Langstrat said from the office. "She's gone now and she's nothing. Don't bring trouble back once you're rid of it. Just concentrate on Krueger."

Brummel told the cop who was guarding Marshall, "Ed, go out and see if you can help John. Krueger's the one we really need to round up."

But just then John came back in through the door at the end of the hall, and he did not have Bernice in tow.

"Well?" Brummel demanded.

John only gave a timid shrug. "She ran like a scared rabbit, and it's dark out there!"

"Aw, terrific!" Brummel moaned.

Marshall thought it really was terrific.

Langstrat's voice came from the office. "Alf, come listen to this."

Brummel went into his office, and Marshall could hear the conversation between Weed and Susan being replayed.

Langstrat said, "So they've heard this conversation. We picked it up from Susan's end today." The dialogue between Susan and Weed came to an end. "Unless I miss my guess, Krueger could very well be headed for The Evergreen Tavern in Baker to meet Susan—" She broke into laughter.

"I'll have it staked out, then," said Brummel.

"Get a stakeout on her apartment also. She'll want to get to her car."

"Good idea."

Brummel and Langstrat came out of the office and stood over Marshall like vultures over a carcass.

"Marshall," Brummel gloated, "you're in for quite a downhill slide, I'm afraid. I've enough against you to put you away for good. You should have gotten out of this thing while you had the chance."

Marshall looked up at that silly grinning face and said, "To use a cliché, you'll never get away with this, Brummel. You don't own the whole court system. Sooner or later this thing's going to go beyond your reach; it's going to get bigger than you are."

Brummel only smiled a smile that Marshall longed to kick into oblivion and said, "Marshall, a lower court decision is all we need, and I'm sure we can manage that. Let's face it. You're nothing but a liar and a third-rate burglar, not to mention a child molester and a possible murderer. We have witnesses, Marshall: fine, upstanding citizens of this community. We'll see to it that you have the fairest of trials, so you would have no grounds for appeal. It could go very hard for you. The judge might give you a break, but . . . I don't know."

"You mean Baker, the wheeler-dealer?"

"I understand he can be a very compassionate person . . . under the right circumstances."

"So don't tell me. You're going to book Bernice on charges of prostitution? Maybe you can dig up those hookers again, that bogus cop again, set the whole thing up."

Brummel chuckled mockingly. "That all depends on the evidence at hand, I guess. We can book her for burglary, you know, and the two of you set that one up yourselves."

"So what about the laws against illegal wiretaps?"

Langstrat answered that one. "We know of no wiretaps. We don't do that sort of thing." She paused for effect, then added, "And they wouldn't find anything even if they did believe you." Then something occurred to her. "Oh, and I can sense what you're thinking. Don't put your hopes in Susan Jacobson. We've received the sad news today that she was killed in a terrible motor vehicle accident. The only people Ms. Krueger can expect to meet at The Evergreen Tavern will be the police."

Bernice felt faint. Her rib cage felt like it was shattered; her bruises throbbed without mercy. For the better part of an hour she didn't have the strength or the nerves to get up from where she lay in the brambles. She tried to think what to do next. Every wisp of wind through the trees was an approaching policeman to her; every sound brought new horror. She looked at her watch. It was going on 3 in the morning. Soon it would be day, and there would be no more sneaking around. She had to get moving, and she knew it.

She slowly struggled to her feet, then stood there, slightly crouched, under the low hanging branches of a vine-tangled madrona, waiting for enough blood to circulate through her brain for her to stay standing.

She took a step, then another. She gained confidence and started moving ahead, feeling her way through the trees and underbrush, trying to fend off the scratching branches.

Back out on the street, it was quiet and dark. The dogs were no longer barking. She began to plot her course for her apartment, about a mile across town, making the trip in quick dashes from tree to hedge to tree. Only once did a vehicle drive by, but it was not a squad car; Bernice hid behind a large maple tree until it had passed.

She could not distinguish her physical pain and sickness from her emotional exhaustion and despair. A few times she got confused and lost her bearings and couldn't make out any of the street signs, and it was then that she almost cried, slumping against a fence or a wall.

But she remembered Marshall throwing himself into the jaws of those lions for her sake, and she couldn't let him down. She had to make it. She had to get out of town, get free, meet Susan, get help, do *something*.

For nearly an hour, block by block, step by step, she worked her way along and finally approached her apartment building. She cautiously followed a circuitous route around it, wanting to check it from all sides. Finally, from behind a neighbor's station wagon, she thought she could make out the telltale rack of lights atop one car parked at the end of the block. From that position, the occupants of that car would have a perfect view of anyone trying to get into any apartment. So that was out.

The back of the building was much easier to sneak into; there were small parking stalls along a dark, narrow alley, the lighting was poor, the parking stalls could not be seen from ground level up above. It was a terrible place to park a car in terms of security, but perfect for Bernice tonight.

She darted across the street a block away and out of view of that squad car, then doubled back and slipped into the alley, staying close to the dank, concrete retaining wall as the alley dipped down below the grade. She reached her Toyota, removed the little magnetic key box from under the bumper, and used those emergency keys to open the door.

Oh, so near and yet so far! There was no way she could start her car and get away without being heard on this very still night. But there were some things she could make very good use of. She clambered in as quickly as she could and closed the door after her enough to extinguish the dome light. Then she opened the ashtray in the front console and emptied the quarters, dimes, and nickels into her pocket. Just a couple of bucks, but it would have to do. In the glovebox she found her prescription sunglasses; now she could see better and use them to conceal her black eyes.

There was nothing else to do but get out of town, maybe get some sleep somewhere, somehow, and then, one way or another, get out to Baker and The Evergreen Tavern by 8 that coming night. That was all, but it was enough. She strained to think of anyone she knew that *they* would not know, any friend who could still aid and abet a fugitive from the law, without questions.

Her mental list of names was too short and too doubtful. She started walking, making her way toward Highway 27 while searching her mind for any other ideas.

Down below the courthouse, alone in a cell at the end of the dismal cellblock, Hank lay on his cot, asleep at last.

It had not been the most enjoyable of evenings: they had stripped him, searched him, fingerprinted him, photographed him, and then stuck him in this cell with no blanket to keep warm. He had asked for a Bible, but they wouldn't allow him to have one. The drunk in the next cell had thrown up during the night, the writer of phony checks in the cell after that had a very dirty mouth, and the mugger in the next cell turned out to be a very vociferous, opinionated Marxist.

Oh well, he thought, Jesus died for them and they need His love. He tried to be kind and share some of God's love with them, but someone had told them that he was an accused rapist, which put somewhat of a damper on his testimony.

So he had lain down, identifying with Paul and Silas and Peter and James and every other Christian who had ever spent time in a forlorn prison even though innocent. He wondered how long his ministry would survive, now that his reputation had been so blasted. Would he still be able to hang on in his already shaky pastorate? Brummel and his buddies were sure going to make full use of this. For all he knew, they had been the ones who set it up. Ah well, it was in the Lord's hands; God knew what was best.

He prayed for Mary and for all his new, motley sheep, and mentally recited memorized Scripture to himself until he dropped off to sleep.

In the very early hours of the morning Hank was awakened by footsteps coming down the cellblock and the jingle of the guard's jail keys. Oh no. The guard was opening his cell door. Now Hank would have to share the cell with . . . a drunk, a mugger, a *real* rapist? He pretended he was still asleep, but he opened one eye just a little to have a look. Oh brother! This hoodlum was big and grim looking, and from the bandage and bruise on his head it looked like he had just been in a brawl. He was muttering something about having to be stuck in a cell with a rapist. Hank started praying for the Lord's protection. This big character had to weigh twice as much as he did, and he looked violent.

The new guy flopped down on the other cot and breathed that heavy kind of breath one associates with bears, dragons, and monsters. *Lord, please deliver me!*

Rafar strutted back and forth on his hilltop overlooking the town, allowing his wings to trail and wave like a regal cape behind him. Demon messengers had been bringing him regular reports of how his final preparations of the town were going. So far it had been nothing but good news.

"Lucius," Rafar called with the tone one would use in calling a child, "Lucius, come here, won't you?"

Lucius stepped forward with all the dignity he could muster, trying to get his wings to wave and undulate like Rafar's.

"Yes, Ba-al Rafar?"

Rafar looked down at him gloatingly, a wry smile on his face, and said, "I trust you have learned from this experience. As you have so clearly seen, what you could not do in years, I have accomplished in days."

"Perhaps." That was all Lucius would give him.

Rafar thought that was funny. "And you disagree?"

"One could think, Ba-al, that your work was merely the capstone on the years of my labor wrought before your coming."

"Years of labor nearly undone by your blundering, you mean!" Rafar retorted. "Which does give one pause. Having won the town for the Strongman, do I dare now leave it in the hands of one who nearly lost it before?"

Lucius did not like the sound of that at all. "Rafar, for years this town has been my principality. *I* am the rightful Prince of Ashton!"

"You *were*. But honors, Lucius, reward deeds, and in deeds I do find you lacking."

Lucius was indignant, but he controlled himself in the presence of this giant power. "You have not seen my deeds because you have not chosen to look. Your will was set against me from the beginning."

Lucius had said too much. Immediately he was snatched from the ground by Rafar's burly fist around his throat, and now Rafar held him up and looked him straight in the eye.

"I," said Rafar slowly and fiercely, "and only I, am the judge of that!"

"Let the Strongman judge!" Lucius responded very brazenly. "Where is this Tal, this adversary whom you were to vanquish, whose little pieces you were to hurl across the sky as your victory banner?"

Rafar allowed a slight smile to cross his face, even though his eyes kept their fire. "Busche, the praying man, is defeated and his name sullied. Hogan, the once tenacious hound, is now a worthless and defeated wretch. The traitorous Maidservant is destroyed, and her scum of a friend is also eliminated. All others have fled."

Rafar waved his hand over the town. "Look, Lucius! Do you see the fiery hosts of heaven descending over the town? Do you see their flashing and polished swords? Do you see their numberless guard posted around about?"

He sneered at Lucius and Tal at the same time. "This Tal, this Captain of the Host, now commands a stricken and debilitated army, and he is afraid to show his face. Again and again I have defied him to confront me, to stop me, and he has not appeared. But don't worry. As I have spoken, so shall I do. When these other pressing matters are settled, Tal and I *will* meet, and you will see it take place . . . just before I vanquish *you!*"

Rafar held Lucius high as he called to another demon, "Courier, take word to the Strongman that all is ready and that he may come at his will. The obstacles are removed, Rafar has completed his task, and the town of Ashton is ready to fall into his hands"—Rafar dropped Lucius as he said it—"like a ripe plum."

Lucius bolted up from the ground and flew away in a humiliated flurry while the demonic ranks laughed and laughed.

33

E dith Duster had felt a certain stirring in her spirit before she went to bed that night. So when she was awakened abruptly by two luminous beings in her bedroom she was not entirely surprised, even though awestruck.

"Glory to God!" she exclaimed, her eyes wide, her face enraptured.

The two tall men had very kind and compassionate faces, but their expressions were serious. One was tall and blond, the other dark-haired and youthful. Both towered as high as the ceiling, and the glow from their white tunics filled the room. Each had a magnificent golden scabbard and belt, and the handles of their swords were purest gold, with fiery jewels.

"Edith Duster," said the big blond one in a deep, resonant voice, "we are going into battle for the town of Ashton. The victory rests on the prayers of the saints of God. As you fear the Lord, pray, and call others to prayer. Pray that the enemy will be vanquished and the righteous delivered."

Then the dark-haired one spoke. "Your pastor, Henry Busche, has fallen prisoner. He will be delivered through your prayers. Call Mary, his wife. Be a comfort to her."

Suddenly they were gone, and the room was dark once again. Edith knew somehow that she had seen them before, perhaps in dreams, perhaps as unimpressive, normal people here and there. And she knew the importance of their request.

She rose and grabbed her pillow, placed it on the floor, and then knelt upon it there beside the bed. She wanted to laugh, she wanted to cry, she wanted to sing; there was a burden and a power deep within her, and she clasped her shaking hands together there upon the bed, bowed her head, and began to pray. The words flowed forth from her deepest soul, an outcry on behalf of God's people and God's righteousness, a plea for power and victory in the name of Jesus, a binding of the evil forces that were trying to take the very life, the very heart of that community. Names and faces cascaded before her mind's eye and she interceded for all of them, pleading before the throne of God for their safety and salvation. She prayed. She prayed. She prayed.

From high above, the town of Ashton was spread out like an innocent toy village on a patchwork quilt, a small and unpretentious community still sleeping, but now awash with the slowly rising flood of predawn gray and pink that grew over the mountains in the east. As yet, nothing stirred in the town. There were no lights being switched on; the milk truck was still parked.

From somewhere in the skies, beyond the pink-edged clouds, a solitary, rushing sound began. One angelic warrior, soaring like a gull, spiraled quickly and covertly downward, until his form was lost in the patterns and textures of the streets and buildings far below. Then another appeared and he too dropped quietly into the town, disappearing somewhere within it.

And Edith Duster kept praying.

Two appeared, their wings swept back, their heads sharply downward, diving like hawks into the town. Then came another, gliding along a more shallow path that would carry him to the far side of town. Then four, dropping in four different directions. Then two more, then seven . . .

Mary was awakened from fitful sleep on the couch by the telephone.

"Hello?" Her eyes brightened immediately. "Oh, Edith, I'm so glad you called! I've been trying to reach you, I haven't even gone to bed, I must have your number written down wrong, or the phones aren't working . . ." Then she started crying, and told Edith all about the events of the previous night.

"Well, you just rest and be quiet until I get there," said Edith. "I've been on my knees all night and God is moving, yes He is! We'll get Hank out of there and more besides!"

Edith grabbed her sweater and her sneakers and was off to Mary's house. She had never felt younger.

John Coleman awoke early that morning, so shaken by a dream he couldn't get back to sleep. Patricia knew the feeling—the same thing had happened to her.

"I saw angels!" John said.

"I did too," said Patricia.

"And . . . and I saw demons. Monsters, Patty! Hideous things! The angels and the demons were fighting it out. It was—"

"Terrible."

"Awesome. Really awesome."

They called Hank. Mary answered. They got the story of last night, and they went right over.

Andy and June Forsythe couldn't sleep all that night. This morning Andy was crabby, and June just tried to stay out of his way. Finally, as Andy tried to eat some breakfast, he was able to talk about it. "It must be the Lord. I don't know what else it could be."

"But why are you so crabby?" June asked as tenderly as she could.

"Because I've never felt this way before," Andy said, and then his voice started to quiver. "I . . . I just feel like I have to pray, like . . . like something's really got to be settled and I can't rest until it is."

"You know," said June, "I really know what you mean. I don't know if I can explain it, but I feel like we haven't been alone all night. Somebody's been here with us, filling us with these feelings."

Andy got wide-eyed. "Yeah! That's it! That's the feeling!" He grabbed her hand with great joy and relief. "June, honey, I thought I was going crazy!"

Just then the phone rang. It was Cecil Cooper. He had had a very disturbing dream that night, and so had many others. Something was up. They didn't wait to gather to pray. They started praying right then and there.

From north, from south, from east and west, from all directions, and so very silently, heavenly warriors continued to drop into the town like snowflakes, walk into the town like people, sneak into the town like guerrillas, glide through fields and orchards into the town like bush pilots. Then they hid themselves and waited.

Hank woke at about 7; the nightmare had not ended. He was still in the cell. His new cellmate continued snoring for another hour until the guard brought in breakfast. The big man said nothing, but took the little plate that was handed through the bars. He didn't look too excited about the burnt toast and cold eggs. Perhaps this would be the time to break the ice.

"Good morning," Hank said.

"Good morning," the big man replied very half-heartedly.

"My name is Hank Busche."

The big man slid his plate out under the door for the guard to pick up. He hadn't touched the food. He stood there, looking out through the bars like a caged animal. He did not respond to Hank's introduction, nor did he tell Hank his name. He was obviously hurting; his eyes seemed so longing, and so vacant.

All Hank could do was pray for him.

Step, step, stumble, then step again. All morning long, through fields of corn, pastures of cows, thick forests, Bernice trudged along, slowly making her way north on a meandering route that ran roughly parallel to Highway 27, somewhere off to her left. The sound of the vehicles roaring along the highway helped her get her bearings.

She was beginning to trip over her own feet, her thoughts getting sluggish. Row upon row of cornstalks marched past her, their big green leaves brushing against her with a steady, almost annoying rhythm. The dirt under her feet was softly tilled and dusty. It was working into her shoes. It absorbed the strength from her strides.

After crossing the sea of corn, she came to a very long and very narrow grove of trees, a windbreak planted between the fields. She went into the middle of it and immediately found a patch of soft, grassy ground. She checked her watch: 8:25 A.M. She had to rest. She would get to Baker somehow . . . it was the only hope . . . she hoped Marshall was okay . . . she hoped she wouldn't die . . . she was asleep.

By the time lunch was brought in, Hank and his cellmate were a little more ready to eat. The sandwiches weren't that bad and the beef vegetable soup was quite good.

Before the guard got away Hank asked him, "Say, are you sure I couldn't have a Bible somehow?"

"I told you," the guard said rudely, "I'm waiting on authorization, and until I get it, no dice!"

Suddenly the big silent cellmate burst out, "Jimmy, you've got a stack of Gideon Bibles in your desk drawer and you know it! Now give the man a Bible."

The guard only sneered at the man. "Hey, you're on that side of the bars now, Hogan. *I'll* run the show out here!"

The guard left, and the big man tried to shift his attention to his lunch. He looked up at Hank, though, and quipped, "Jimmy Dunlop. He thinks he's a real man."

"Thanks for trying, anyway."

The big man heaved a deep sigh and then said, "Sorry for being rude all morning. I needed time to heal up from yesterday, I needed time to check you out, and I guess I needed time to get used to the idea of being in jail."

"I can sure identify with that. I've never been in jail before," Hank tried again. He extended his hand and said, "Hank Busche."

This time the man took it and gave him a firm shake. "Marshall Hogan."

Then something clicked for both of them. Before they had even dropped their hands again, they looked at each other, pointed at each other, and both began to ask, "Say, aren't you . . . ?"

And then they stared for a moment and didn't say anything.

The angels were watching, of course, and brought Tal word.

"Good, good," said Tal. "Now we'll just let those two talk."

"You're the pastor of that little white church," Marshall said.

"And you're the editor of the paper, the *Clarion*," Hank exclaimed.

"So what in the wide world are you doing here?"

"I don't know if you'd be able to believe it."

"Kid, you'd be amazed—*I'm* amazed—at what I'd believe!" Marshall lowered his voice and leaned close as he said, "They told me you were in here for rape."

"That's right."

"That sounds just like you, doesn't it?"

Hank didn't quite know what to make of that statement. "Well, I didn't do it, you know."

"Doesn't Alf Brummel go to your church?"

"Yes."

"Ever cross him?"

"Uh . . . well, yes."

"So have I. And that's why I'm in here, and that's why you're in here! Tell me what happened."

"When?"

"I mean, what really happened? Do you even know this girl you supposedly raped?"

"Well . . ."

"Where'd you get those bite marks on your arm?"

Hank was getting some doubts. "Say, listen, I'd better not say anything."

"Was her name Carmen?"

Hank's face said a yes that was almost audible.

"Just thought I'd take a stab at it. She's really a treacherous gal. She used to work for me and last night she told me she'd been raped and I knew then that it was a lie."

Hank was completely flabbergasted. "This is too much! How do you know about all this?"

Marshall looked around the cell and shrugged. "Ah well, what else is there to do? Hank, have I got a story for you! It's going to take a few hours. You ready for that?"

"If you're ready to hear mine, I'm ready to hear yours."

"Hello? Ma'am?"

Bernice jolted awake. There was someone leaning over her. It was a young girl about high school age, maybe older, with big brown eyes and black, curly hair, dressed in bib overalls, a perfect farmer's daughter.

"Oh! Uh . . . hi." It was all Bernice could think of to say.

"Are you all right, ma'am?" the girl asked in a slow and easy drawl.

"Um, yes. I was just sleeping. I hope that's all right. I was out for a walk, you know, and . . ." She remembered her bruised face. Oh, great! Now this kid will think I've been mugged or something.

"You looking for your sunglasses?" the girl asked, reaching down and picking them up. She handed them to Bernice.

"I . . . uh . . . guess you're wondering what happened to my face."

The girl only smiled a disarming smile and said, "Aw, you ought to see how I look when I first wake up."

"I take it this is your property? I didn't mean to—"

"No, I'm just passing through, like you are. I saw you lying here and thought I'd check up on you. Can I give you a lift anywhere?"

Bernice was about to say an automatic no, but then she looked at her watch. Oh no! It was almost 4 o'clock in the afternoon. "Well, you wouldn't happen to be going north, would you?"

"I'm heading up toward Baker."

"Oh, that's perfect! I could catch a ride with you?"

"Right after lunch."

"What?"

The girl walked out of the trees to the next field of corn, and then Bernice noticed a shiny blue motorcycle parked in the sun. The girl reached into a side saddle and brought out a brown paper sack. She returned and set that sack in front of Bernice, along with a carton of cold milk.

"You eat lunch at 4 in the afternoon?" Bernice asked with a conversational chuckle.

"No," the young lady answered with a chuckle of her own, "but you've come a long way, and you have a long way to go, and you need something to eat."

Bernice looked into those clear and laughing brown eyes, and then at the simple little lunch bag in front of her, and she could feel her face turning red and her eyes filling up.

"Eat up, now," said the girl.

Bernice opened the paper bag and found a roast beef sandwich that was truly a work of art. The beef was still hot, the lettuce crisp and green. Below that was a carton of blueberry yogurt—her favorite flavor—still cold to the touch.

She tried to keep her emotions down, but she began to quake with weeping, and the tears ran down her cheeks. Oh, I'm making a fool of myself, she thought. But this was so altogether different.

"I'm so sorry," she said. "I'm just . . . very touched by your kindness."

The girl touched her hand. "Well, I'm glad I could be here."

"What is your name?"

"You can call me Betsy."

"I'm—well, you can call me Marie." It was Bernice's middle name.

"I'll just do that. Listen, I have some cold water too, if you want that."

There came another wave of emotion. "You're a wonderful person. What are you doing on this planet?"

"Helping you," Betsy answered, running to her motorcycle for the water.

Hank sat on the edge of his cot, enraptured by the story Marshall was relating.

"Are you serious?" he responded suddenly. "Alf Brummel is into witchcraft? A board member in my church?"

"Hey, call it what you want, bub, but I'm telling you, it is spacy! I don't know how long he and that Langstrat have been bosom buddies, but enough of her cosmic consciousness crud has rubbed off on him to make him dangerous, and I mean that!"

"So who's in this group again?"

"Who *isn't* in it? Oliver Young's in it, Judge Baker's in it, most of the cops on the local police force are in it . . ." Marshall went on to give Hank just a small segment of the list.

Hank was amazed. This had to be the Lord. So many of the questions he had had for so long were finally finding their answers.

Marshall kept going for another half an hour or so, and then he started losing momentum. He had come to the part about Kate and Sandy.

"That's the part that hurts the most," he said, and then started looking out through the bars instead of into Hank's eyes. "It's a whole other story in itself, and you don't need to hear it. But I sure went over and over it this morning. It's my fault, Hank. I let it happen."

He heaved a deep breath and wiped wetness from his eyes. "I could have lost everything; the paper, the house, the—the battle. I could have taken it if I only had them. But I lost them too . . ." Then he said the words, "And that's how I ended up here," and he stopped. Abruptly.

Hank was weeping. He was weeping and smiling, raising his hands up to God, shaking his head in wonderment. To Marshall, it looked like he was having some kind of religious experience.

"Marshall," Hank said excitedly, unable to sit still, "this is of God! Our being here is no accident. Our enemies meant it for evil, but God meant it for good. He's brought the two of us together just so we could meet, just so we could put the whole thing together. You haven't heard my story yet, but guess what? It's the same! We've both been coming up against the exact same problem from two different sides."

"Tell me, tell me, I want to cry too!"

So Hank began telling how he suddenly found himself the pastor of a church that didn't seem to want him . . .

Betsy's motorcycle flew like the wind up Highway 27, and Bernice held on tight, sitting behind her on the soft leather seat, watching all the scenery go by. The whole trip was exhilarating; it made her feel like a kid again, and the fact that both of them wore helmets with dark face shields made Bernice feel all the more safe from discovery.

But Baker was coming up rapidly, and with it the risks and dangers and the big question of whether Susan Jacobson would even be there or not. Part of Bernice wanted to stay on the motorcycle with this sweet, likable kid and just keep right on going to . . . wherever. Any life had to be better than this one.

The landmarks became familiar: the Coca-Cola sign, and that big lot full of firewood for sale. They were coming into Baker. Betsy let off the throttle and started whining down through the gears. Finally she pulled off the highway and bumped along to a stop in a gravel parking lot just in front of the aged Sunset Motel.

"Will this do for you?" Betsy shouted through her face shield.

Bernice could just make out The Evergreen up the highway. "Oh, yeah, this will do just fine."

She climbed off the motorcycle and struggled with the chin strap of her helmet.

"Leave it on a while," said Betsy.

"What for?"

Bernice's eyes immediately gave her a good reason that *she* would know of: a squad car from the Ashton precinct just happened to drive by, slowing down as it entered Baker. Bernice watched as it then signaled left and pulled into the parking area in front of The Evergreen Tavern. Two officers got out and went inside. She looked down at Betsy. Did she know?

She didn't act like it. She pointed to a little diner attached to the motel. "That's Rose Allen's little cafe. It looks like a terrible place, but she makes the best homemade soup in the world and she sells it cheap. It'd be a great place to kill some time."

Bernice removed her helmet and set it on the bike.

"Betsy," she said, "I owe you a very great debt. Thank you so very much."

"You're welcome." Even through the face shield that smile shone brightly.

Bernice looked at the little cafe. No, it didn't look very nice. "The best soup in the world, eh?"

She turned back to Betsy and stiffened. For a moment she felt she would stumble forward as if a wall had suddenly disappeared in front of her.

Besty was gone. The motorcycle was gone.

It was like awaking from a dream and needing time to adjust one's mind to what was real and what was not. But Bernice knew it had not been a dream. The tracks of the motorcycle were still plainly visible in the gravel, leading from where it had left the highway to the spot directly in front of Bernice. There they ended.

Bernice backed away, stunned and shaken. She looked up and down the highway, but knew even as she did that she would not see that girl on her motorcycle. As a matter of fact, as a few more seconds went by Bernice knew she would have been disappointed if she had. It would have been the end of a very beautiful *something* she had never felt before.

But she had to get off the highway, she kept telling herself. She was sticking out like a sore thumb. She tore herself away from that spot and hurried into Rose Allen's little cafe.

Dinner came through the bars at 6. Marshall was ready to eat the fried chicken and cooked carrots, but Hank was so much into his story that Marshall had to prompt him to eat.

"I'm really getting to the good part!" Hank protested, and then he asked, "How are you keeping up with this?"

"A lot of it is new," Marshall admitted.

"What were you again? Presbyterian?"

"Hey, don't blame them. I'm just me, that's all, and I always thought that spooks only come out on Halloween."

"Well, you always wanted an explanation for Langstrat's strange pull, and how the Network could have all that powerful influence on people, and what may have really been tormenting Ted Harmel, and especially who these spirit guides might be."

"You're—you're asking me to believe in evil spirits."

"Do you believe in God?"

"Yes, I believe there's a God."

"Do you believe in a devil?"

Marshall had to think for a moment. He noticed that he'd gone through a change of opinion somewhere along the line. "I . . . well, yeah, I guess I do."

"Believing in angels and demons is simply the next step after that. It's only logical."

Marshall shrugged and picked up a drumstick. "Just keep going. Let me hear the whole thing."

34

Bernice killed another hour and a half in Rose Allen's cafe, buying a bowl of Rose's soup—Betsy was right, it was good—and eating it very slowly. She kept her eye on Rose the whole time. Boy, if that woman made one move toward that telephone, Bernice was going to be *out* of there! But Rose didn't appear to think a beat-up woman in her cafe was all that unusual, and nothing happened.

When 7:30 rolled around, Bernice knew she would have to try for that meeting one way or another. She paid Rose for the soup out of the change in her pocket and stepped outside.

It looked like that police car that had stopped at The Evergreen was gone now, but the light was getting poor and it was too far away for Bernice to tell for sure. She would just have to take it one step at a time.

She walked along carefully, her eyes looking in all directions for police, stakeouts, suspicious vehicles, anything. The parking lot of The Evergreen was overflowing, and that was probably typical for a Saturday night. She kept her sunglasses on, but apart from that she looked every bit like the Bernice Krueger the police were searching for. What else could she do?

As she approached the tavern, she looked here and there for any escape routes. She did notice a trail going back into the woods, but had no idea how far it went or where it eventually led. All in all, there didn't seem to be too many places to run or hide.

The back of The Evergreen Tavern was the one part of the building nobody seemed to care about at all; the three old cars, the forgotten refrigerators, the dented beer kegs, and the piles of delaminating tables and rusting, broken-through chairs were parted just enough to allow a narrow pathway to the back door.

This door also scraped an arc in the linoleum. The music from the jukebox hit Bernice like a wave, as did the smoke from cigarettes and the sickeningly sweet smell of beer. She closed the door after her, and found herself in a dark cavern full of silhouettes. She cautiously looked over, under, and around her sunglasses, trying to see where she was and where everyone else was without taking the sunglasses off.

There had to be someplace to sit in here. Most of the booths were full of loggers and their girlfriends. There was one chair in the corner. She took it and settled in to survey the room.

From this spot she could make out the front door and could see people coming in, but she could not distinguish their faces. She did recognize Dan behind the bar; he was pouring beers while trying to keep a bridle on things. Her ears verified that the shuffleboard game was in full swing, and two video games against a far wall were bleeping and burpling through the quarters.

It was 7:50. Well, just sitting here wasn't going to work; she felt too obvious, and she simply couldn't see. She got up from her chair and tried to mingle with the crowd, staying close to the walls.

She looked at Dan again. He was a little closer and he could have been looking back at her, but she didn't know. He didn't act like he recognized her, or cared if he did. Bernice tried to find an unobtrusive spot from which to look at the people at the front tables. She joined a small group around one of the video games. These people in the front were still silhouettes, but none of them could have been Susan.

There was Dan again, leaning over one table and pulling the front windowshade half down. Some of the people nearby didn't like it, but he gave them some explanation, and left it that way.

She decided to go back to her chair and wait. She worked her way back to the shuffleboard game, then went slowly behind the crowd toward the back of the room.

Then a thought hit her. She had seen that pulling-down-the-windowshade trick in some movie. A signal? She turned her head toward the front, and at that exact moment the front door opened. Two men in uniforms came in. Police! One pointed right at her. She moved as quickly as she could for the back door. It was nothing but dark in front of her. How in the world was she even going to *find* that door?

She could hear a shout over the noise of the crowd. "Hey! Stop that woman! Police! You! Hold it!"

The people around her began muttering, "Who? What woman? *That* woman?" One other voice out of the blackness said, "Hey, lady, I think he's talking to you!"

She didn't look back, but she could hear the shuffling of chairs and feet. They were coming after her.

Then she saw the green exit sign over the back door. Forget about keeping cool! She broke into a run toward that light.

People were hollering everywhere, coming to help her, wanting to see what was going on. They got in the policemen's way, and the police started hollering, "One side, please! Get out of the way! Stop her!"

She couldn't see the latch or knob or whatever that door had. Hoping it had a crash bar, she slammed her body against it. It didn't have a crash bar, but she could hear something break and the door opened anyway.

It was lighter out here than inside. She could make out the path through all the junk and raced through it, running for all she was worth just as she heard the backdoor crash open again. Then came the sound of their footsteps. Could she get out of sight before they got clear of all that junk?

She tore off her sunglasses just in time to spot the trail through the woods, on the other side of the fence.

It was amazing what a person could do when scared enough. Planting her hands on the top of the fence, she swung her body up and vaulted over it, tumbling down into the brush on the other side. Without stopping to congratulate herself, she scrambled up that trail into the woods like a scared rabbit, ducking to avoid the low-hanging branches she could see and being whipped in the face by the ones she couldn't.

The trail was soft and clear, and kept her footsteps quiet and muffled. It was darker in the woods, and at times she had to stop abruptly just to see where the trail led next. During those times she would also listen for her pursuers; she could hear some kind of yelling going on far behind her, but it seemed no one had thought of this trail.

There was light up ahead. She came to a gravel back road, but hesitated in the trees long enough to look up and down that road for cars, cops, anyone. The road was quiet and deserted. She stepped out quickly, trying to decide which way to go.

Suddenly, at an intersection a little way down the road, a car appeared, pulling onto this road and heading her way. They had to have seen her! There was nothing to do but keep running!

Her lungs were laboring, her heart was aching and felt like it would pound itself apart, her legs felt like lead. She couldn't help crying out in anguish and fear with each exhalation as she ran across a field toward a cluster of buildings in the distance. She looked back. A figure was after her, running swiftly in hot pursuit. No! No! Please don't chase me, just let me go! I can't go on like this!

The buildings were getting closer. It looked like an old farm. She was no longer thinking, only running. She couldn't see; her eyes were doubly blurred now with tears. She was gasping for breath, her mouth was dry, the pain from her rib cage shot up and down her whole side. The grass whipped against her legs, almost tripping her with every step. She could hear the footsteps of her pursuer swishing through the grass not far behind her. Oh, God, help me!

Ahead was a large, dark building, a barn. She would go for it and try to hide. If they found her, they found her. She could run no further.

She stumbled, trudged, dragged one foot after the other around one end, and found the big sliding door half open. She practically fell through it.

Inside, she found herself in inky blackness. Now her eyes were useless to her. She stumbled ahead, her arms out in front of her. Her feet were shuffling through straw. Her arms bumped into boards. A stall. She went further. Another stall. She could hear the footsteps coming around the corner and through the door. She ducked into one of the stalls and tried to quell her gasping. She was on the verge of fainting.

The steps slowed. The pursuer was encountering the same darkness and trying to feel his way along. But he was coming closer.

Bernice backed further into the stall, wondering if there might be some way to hide herself. Her hand encountered some kind of handle. She felt downward. A pitchfork. She took it in her hands. Could she really use this thing in cold blood?

The footsteps moved ahead methodically; the pursuer was checking each stall, working his way through the barn. Now Bernice could see a small beam of light sweeping here and there.

She held the pitchfork high as her cracked rib punished her in protest. You're going to be very sorry you ever chased me, she thought. She was playing by jungle rules now.

The footsteps were very close now. The little beam of light was just outside the opening. She was ready. The light shined in her eyes. There was a slight gasp. Come on, Bernice! Throw the pitchfork! Her arms would not move.

"Bernice Krueger?" asked a muffled, female voice.

Bernice still didn't move. She held the pitchfork high, still panting for air, the little shaft of light illuminating her crazed, blackened eyes and her terrified face.

Whoever it was stepped back abruptly at the sight of her and whispered, "Bernice, no! Don't throw it!"

That made Bernice want all the more to throw that thing. She was whimpering and gasping, trying to get her arms to move. They would not.

"Bernice," came the voice, "it's Susan Jacobson! I'm alone!"

Bernice still did not put down the pitchfork. For the moment she was beyond rationality, and words meant nothing.

"Do you hear me?" came the voice. "Please, put the fork down. I won't hurt you. I'm not the police, I promise you."

"Who are you?" Bernice asked finally, her voice gasping and quivering.

"Susan Jacobson, Bernice." She said it again slowly. "Susan Jacobson, your sister Pat's old roommate. We had an appointment."

It was as if Bernice suddenly recovered from a hallucination or a sleepwalking nightmare. The name sank into her mind at last and awoke her.

"You . . ." she panted. "You gotta be kidding!"

"I'm not. It's me."

Susan shone her little penlight on her own face. The black hair and pale complexion were unmistakable, even though the black clothes were replaced now with jeans and a blue jacket.

Bernice lowered the pitchfork. Then she dropped it and let out a muffled wail, putting her hand over her mouth. She suddenly realized she was in terrible pain. She sank to her knees in the straw, her arms around her rib cage.

"Are you all right?" Susan asked.

"Turn out that light before they see you," was all Bernice would say.

The light clicked off. Bernice could feel Susan's hand touching her.

"You're hurt!" Susan said.

"I . . . I try to keep everything in perspective," Bernice gasped. "I'm still alive, I've found the real live Susan Jacobson, I haven't had to kill anybody, the police haven't found me . . . and I have a cracked rib! Oooooohhh . . ."

Susan put her arms around Bernice to comfort her.

"Gently, gently!" Bernice cautioned. "Where in the world did you come from? How did you find me?"

"I was watching the tavern from across the street, waiting to see if you or Kevin would show up. I saw the police go in, and you running out the back, and I knew it was you right away. We college kids used to hang around here a lot, so I knew about that trail you took, and I knew how it emptied out onto that road out there. I drove around, thinking I could head you off and let you jump into my car, but you were too far ahead of me and you took off running."

Bernice let her head drop a bit. She could feel herself getting emotional again. "I used to think I'd never seen a miracle, but now I don't know."

Hank finished his whole story and, with Marshall's prodding, had also put away most of his dinner. Marshall began to ask questions, which Hank answered from his knowledge of the Scriptures.

"So," Marshall asked and mused at the same time, "when the Gospels talk about Jesus and His disciples casting out unclean spirits, that's what they were really doing?"

"That's what they were doing," Hank answered.

Marshall leaned back against the bars and kept right on thinking. "That would sure explain a lot of things. But what about Sandy? Do you suppose that she—she's . . . ?"

"I don't know for sure, but it could be."

"What I talked to yesterday. . . that wasn't her. She was just crazy; you wouldn't have believed it." He caught himself. "Aw, then again, you probably would."

Hank was excited. "But don't you see what's happened? It's a miracle of God, Marshall. All along, you were looking into all this racketeering and intrigue, and wondering how these things could be happening so smoothly and so forcefully, especially in the individual lives of so many people. Well, now you have your 'how.' And now that you've told me what you've found out and all that you've been through, I have my 'why.' All this time I've been encountering demonic powers in this town, but I never really knew just what they were up to. Now I know. It has to be the Lord who brought us together."

Marshall gave Hank a wry smile. "So where do we go from here, Preacher? They've locked us in, they haven't allowed us any communication with our families, friends, lawyers, or anyone. I have a feeling that our constitutional rights aren't going to have much to do with it at this juncture."

Now Hank leaned back against the cold concrete wall and thought about it. "That part only God knows. But I have a very strong feeling that He got us into this, and that He also has a plan for getting us out."

"If we must talk about strong feelings," Marshall countered, "I have some pretty strong feelings that they just want us out of the way while they finish once and for all what they've started. It's going to be interesting to see what's left of the town, our jobs, our homes, our families, and everything else we treasured once we get out of here. *If* we get out of here."

"Well, have faith. God's in control here."

"Yehhh, I just hope He hasn't dropped the ball."

As the two women sat there in the straw, in the dark, Bernice tried to explain everything to Susan: her battered face, her cracked rib, what she and Marshall had been through, and the death of Kevin Weed.

Susan digested it all for a moment, and then said, "It's Kaseph's way. It's the Society's way. I should have known better than to have brought Kevin into it."

"Don't—don't blame yourself. All of us are in this thing whether we really want to be or not."

Susan forced herself to be unemotional and calculating. "You're right . . . at least for now. Someday soon I'll sit down and really think about it, and I'll weep over that man." She stood up. "But right now there's too much to do and too little time. Do you think you can walk?"

"No, but that hasn't stopped me so far."

"My car is rented, and I have too many important materials in it to leave it sitting out there. Come on."

With careful and very quiet, well-picked steps, Susan and Bernice made their way to the big barn door. It was very quiet out there.

"Want to go for it?" Susan asked.

"Sure," said Bernice, "let's do it."

They started back across the expansive field toward the road where Susan had left her car, using one tree that jutted up against the starry sky as their heading. As they crossed the field again, Bernice noted how much shorter the trip seemed now that she was not fleeing for her life.

Susan led the way to where her car was parked. She had pulled it off the road a little way and nestled it in among some trees. She began fumbling in her pocket for the keys.

"Susan!" said a voice from the woods.

The two of them froze.

"Susan Jacobson?" came the voice again.

Susan whispered excitedly. "I don't believe it!"

Bernice answered, "I don't believe it either!"

"Kevin?"

Some bushes began to move and swish, and then a man stepped out of the woods. There was no mistaking that lanky frame and that lazy walk.

"Kevin Weed?" Bernice had to ask again.

"Bernice Krueger!" said Kevin. "You made it. Aw, that's great!"

After a short moment of speechless amazement and surprise, the embraces came automatically.

"Let's get out of here," said Susan.

They piled into her car and put some miles between themselves and Baker.

"I got a motel room in Orting, up north of Windsor," said Susan. "We can go there."

It was okay with Bernice and Kevin.

Bernice said very happily, "Kevin, you've just made a liar out of me! I thought for sure you were dead."

"I'm alive for now," Kevin said, not sounding too sure about anything.

"But your truck went into the river!"

"Yeah, I know. Some jerk stole it and crashed it. Somebody was trying to kill me."

He realized he didn't make much sense, so he started over. "Hey, I was on my way to meet you at the bridge like you said. I stopped at The Evergreen to have a few, and I bet some guy slipped me a mickey—you know, put something in my beer. I mean, I got *stoned*.

"I was driving down the road to meet up with you, and I was really spacing out, so I pulled over at Tucker's Burgers to throw up or get a drink of water or go to the bathroom or something. I fell asleep in the men's room, man, and I must have slept there all night. I woke up this morning and went outside and my truck was gone. I didn't know what happened to it until I read about it in the paper. They must still be searching the river for my body."

"It's obvious Kaseph and his Network have us all marked," said Susan, "but . . . I think somebody's looking out for us. Kevin, something very similar happened to me: I ran away from Kaseph's ranch on foot, and the only reason I got away was because all the security personnel went chasing somebody else who was trying to get away in one of the big moving vans. Now who in their right mind would try that, and at just that precise moment?"

Bernice added, "And I still haven't figured out who in the world that Betsy was."

Susan had been formulating her theory for days. "I think we'd better start thinking about God."

"*God?*"

"And angels," Susan added. She quickly recounted the details of her escape, and concluded, "Listen, somebody came into that room. I know it."

Kevin piped up, "Hey, like maybe it was an angel that stole my truck."

And then Bernice recalled, "You know, there was something about Betsy. It made me just cry. I've never run into anything like that before."

Susan touched her hand. "Well, it looks like we're all running into *something*, so whatever we do we'd better pay attention."

The car continued to speed along back roads, taking a slightly roundabout route toward the little resort town of Orting.

Like two comrades-in-arms, Marshall and Hank were beginning to feel they had known each other all their lives.

"I like your kind of faith," Marshall said. "It's no wonder they've tried so hard to get you out of that church." He chuckled a little. "Boy, you must feel like the Alamo! You're the only thing standing between the Devil and the rest of the town."

Hank smiled weakly. "I'm not much, believe me. But I'm not the only one. There are saints out there, Marshall, people praying for us. Sooner or later something's going to break. God won't let Satan have this town that easy!"

Marshall pointed his finger at Hank, even shook it a little. "See there? I like that kind of faith. Good and straight, laid right on the line." He shook his head. "Sheesh! How long has it been since I've heard it come across like that?"

Hank seasoned his words with salt, but he knew the time had come to say it. "Well, Marshall, since we're talking so straight here, right on the line, what do you say we talk about you? You know, there could be some more reasons God put us in this cell together."

Marshall was not defensive at all, but smiling and ready to listen.

"What are we going to do, talk about the fate of my eternal soul?"

Hank smiled back. "That's exactly what we're going to talk about."

They talked about sin, that aggravating and destructive tendency of man to stray from God and choose his own way, always to his own hurt. That brought them around to Marshall's family again, and how so many attitudes and actions were the direct result of that basic, human self-will and rebellion against God.

Marshall shook his head as he saw things in this light. "Hey, our family never did know God. We only went through the motions. No wonder Sandy wouldn't buy it!"

Then Hank talked about Jesus, and showed Marshall that this Man whose name was so casually thrown around and even trampled upon in the world was far more than just a religious symbol, a lofty untouchable personality in a stained-glass window. He was the very real, very alive, very personal Son of God, and He could be the personal Lord and Savior of anyone who asked Him to be.

"I never thought I'd be lying here listening to this," Marshall said suddenly. "You're really hitting me where it hurts, you know that?"

"Well," said Hank, "why do you suppose that is? Where's the pain coming from?"

Marshall took a deep breath as he took the time to think. "I guess from knowing that you're right, which means I've been wrong a long, long time."

"Jesus loves you anyway. He knows that's your problem, and that's what He died for."

"Yeah . . . right!"

35

The motel in Orting was nice, quaint, homey, just like the rest of this town situated along the Judd River on the border of the national forest. It was a stopping place for sportsmen, built and decorated in a pleasing hunt-and-fish, hike-in-the-woods motif.

Susan wanted no trouble or attention, so she paid for two more occupants for the room that night. They went into the room and pulled the shades.

They all made a stop in the bathroom, but Bernice remained just a little longer, carefully rewrapping her ribs and then washing her face. She looked herself over in the mirror and touched her bruises very gingerly, whistling at the sight. It could only get better from here.

In the meantime, Susan had flopped her big suitcase on the bed and opened it up. When Bernice finally came out, Susan took a small book from the suitcase and handed it to her.

"This is where it started," she said. "It's your sister's diary."

Bernice didn't know what to say. A diamond would not have been a greater treasure. She could only look down at the little blue diary in her hands, a last surviving link with her dead sister, and struggle to believe it was really there. "Where . . . how did you get this?"

"Juleen Langstrat made sure no one ever saw it. She had it stolen from Pat's room and she gave it to Kaseph, from whom I stole it. I became Kaseph's girl, you know; his Maidservant, he called it. I had regular access to him all the time, and he trusted me. I came across the diary one day while I was straightening up his office, and I recognized it right away because I used to watch Pat write in it almost every night in our dorm room. I sneaked it out, read it, and it woke me up. I used to think Alexander Kaseph was . . . well, the Messiah, the answer for all mankind, a true prophet of peace and universal brotherhood . . ."

Susan made a face like she was getting sick. "Oh, he filled my mind with all that kind of talk, but somewhere deep inside I always had my doubts. That little book right there told me to listen to the doubts and not to him."

Bernice thumbed through the pages of the diary. It went back a few years, and seemed very detailed.

Susan continued, "You may not want to read it just now. When I read that diary . . . well, it made me sick for days."

Bernice wanted the end of the story. "Susan, do you know how my sister really died?"

Susan said angrily, "Your sister Pat was methodically and viciously done away with by the Universal Consciousness Society, or I should say, the forces behind it. She made the same fatal mistake I've seen so many others make: she found out too much about the Society, she showed herself to be an enemy of Alexander Kaseph. Listen, what Kaseph wants, he gets, and he doesn't care who has to be destroyed, murdered, or mutilated to make sure of it." She shook her head. "I had to be blind not to have seen it happening to Pat. It was right out of the textbook!"

"So what about some man named Thomas?"

Susan answered directly, "Yes, it was Thomas. He was responsible for her death." Then she added rather cryptically, "But he wasn't a man."

Bernice was slowly catching on to this new game with its very weird rules. "And now you're going to tell me it wasn't a woman either."

"Pat was taking a psychology class, and one of her requirements was that she be in a subject pool for psychology experiments—it's in the diary, you'll read it all. A friend persuaded her to volunteer for an experiment involving relaxation techniques, and it was during that experiment that she had what she called a psychic experience, some kind of insight into a higher world, she called it.

"I'll make it short; you can read it for yourself later. She became extremely enamored by the experience and saw no connection between this 'scientific' exploration and the 'mystical' practices I was into. She kept going back, kept taking part in the experiments, and finally contacted what she called a 'highly evolved, disembodied human' from another dimension, a very wise and intelligent being named Thomas."

Bernice struggled with what she was hearing, but knew she held the documentation for Susan's account, her sister's diary. "So who was this Thomas really? Just a figment of her imagination?"

"Some things you're just going to have to accept for now," Susan replied with a sigh. "We've talked about God, we've toyed with the idea of angels; now let's try evil angels, evil spirit entities. To the atheistic scientists, they might appear as extraterrestrials, often with their own spaceships; to evolutionists they might claim to be highly evolved beings; to the lonely, they might appear as long-lost relatives speaking from the other side of the grave; Jungian psychologists consider them 'archetypal images' dredged from the collective consciousness of the human race."

"What?"

"Hey, listen, whatever description or definition fits, whatever shape, whatever form it takes to win a person's confidence and appeal to his vanity, that's the form they take. And they tell the deluded seeker of truth whatever he or she wants to hear until they finally have that person in their complete control."

"Like a con game, in other words."

"It's all a con game: Eastern meditation, witchcraft, divination, Science of Mind, psychic healing, holistic education—oh, the list goes on and on—it's all the same thing, nothing but a ruse to take over people's minds and spirits, even their bodies."

Bernice reviewed memory after memory of their investigation, and Susan's claims fell right into place.

Susan continued, "Bernice, we are dealing with a conspiracy of spirit entities. I know. Kaseph is crawling with them and takes his orders from them. They do his dirty work. If anyone gets in his way, he has numberless resources in the spiritual realm to clear away the problem in whatever manner is most convenient."

Ted Harmel, Bernice thought. The Carluccis. How many others? "You're not the first person to try to tell me all this."

"I hope I'm the last person who will have to."

Kevin piped in. "Yeah, I remember how Pat talked about Thomas. He never sounded like he was human. She acted like he was more of a god. She had to ask him before she'd even decide what to eat for breakfast. I—I thought she'd found some guy, you know, some male chauvinist type."

Susan eased into the bottom line of the story. "Pat had given her will over to Thomas. It didn't take long; it usually doesn't once a person really submits to a spirit's influence. No doubt he took control of her, then terrified her, then convinced her that—well, the Hindus call it karma; it's the delusion that your next life will be better than this one because you've earned enough brownie points. In Pat's case, a self-inflicted death would be nothing more than a way to escape the evil of this lower world and join Thomas in a higher state of existence."

Susan gently flipped the pages of the diary still in Bernice's hands, and found the last entry. "There. The last thing in Pat's diary is a love letter to Thomas. She planned to join him soon, and she even mentions how she'll do it."

Bernice could feel revulsion at the thought of reading such a letter, but she began to work her way through the last few pages of her sister's diary. Pat wrote in a style of someone under a very strange, lofty-sounding delusion, but it was clear she was also disoriented by an irrational fear of life itself. Terrible pain and spiritual anguish had taken over her soul, changing her from the happy-go-lucky Patricia Krueger that Bernice had grown up with to a terrified, aimless psychotic completely out of touch with reality.

Bernice tried to read on, but she began to feel old wounds reopening; emotions that had waited for this very moment of final revelation burst from their hiding places like a river through an opened floodgate. The scrawled and ambling words on the pages blurred behind a sudden cascade of tears, and her whole body began to quake with sobs. All she wanted to do was shut out the world, disregard this gallant woman and this poor, disheveled logger, lie down on the bed, and cry. And she did.

Hank slept peacefully on his cot in the cell. Marshall was not sleeping at all. He sat up in the dark, his back against the cold, hard bars of the cell, his head drooping, his hand making nervous little trips around his face.

He had been shot through the guts. That's what it felt like. Somewhere he had lost his armor plating, his strength, his strong and tough facade. He had always been Marshall Hogan, the hunter, the hound, the stay-out-my-way getter of whatever he wanted, a foe to be reckoned with, a guy who could take care of himself.

A lump, that's what he was, and nothing but a fool. This Hank Busche was right. Just look at yourself, Hogan. Don't worry about

God dropping the ball; you dropped it a long time ago. You blew it, man. You thought you had everything under control, and now where's your family and where are you?

Maybe you've been tricked by these demons Hank's been talking about, and then maybe you've even fooled yourself. Come on, Marshall, you know why you shortchanged your family. You were copping out, singing the same old tune again. And you enjoyed working with that good-looking reporter, didn't you? Teasing her, tossing paper wads at her, for crying out loud! How old are you, sixteen?

Marshall let his own mind and heart tell him the truth, and much of it felt as if he had known it somewhere but had never listened. How long, he began to wonder, had he been lying to himself?

"Kate," he whispered there in the dark, his eyes glistening with tears. "Kate, what have I done?"

A big hand reached across the cell and nudged Hank's shoulder.

Hank stirred, opened his eyes, and said quietly, "Yeah, what's up?"

Marshall was weeping and he said very quietly, "Hank, I'm just no good. I need God. I need Jesus."

How many times in his life had Hank said the words? "Let's pray."

After several minutes had passed, Bernice began to feel the flood subsiding. She sat up, still sniffling, but trying to get back to the business at hand.

"That's what woke me up," Susan reiterated. "I thought these beings were benevolent; I thought Kaseph had all the answers. But I saw them all in their true form when I read what they did to my best friend, your sister."

Kevin asked, "So is that why you came up to me at the carnival and got my number?"

"Kaseph had a special meeting in town with Langstrat and some other vital conspirators, Oliver Young and Alf Brummel. I came to Ashton with Kaseph, tagging right along as I always did, but when I got the opportunity I sneaked away. I had to take the chance that maybe I'd see you somewhere. Maybe it was God again; it was nothing short of a miracle that I spotted you at the carnival. I needed a friend on the outside I could confide in, someone obscure."

Kevin smiled. "Yeah, that describes me pretty well."

Susan continued, "Kaseph never liked to feel that he didn't have complete control of me. When I slipped away to the carnival, he probably told the others that he'd already sent me there and that they would meet me. When he found me and dragged me behind that silly booth, he talked to them like I had gone ahead and picked out that spot."

Bernice said, "And that's when I came across you and snapped your picture!"

"And then Brummel slipped some bills to those two hookers and some instructions to a few of his Windsor friends, and you know the rest."

Susan went to her suitcase. "But now for the really big news. Kaseph is making his move tomorrow. There's a special meeting scheduled with the Whitmore College regents at 2 in the afternoon. Omni Corporation—as a front for the Universal Consciousness Society—plans to buy Whitmore College, and Kaseph is closing the deal."

Bernice's eyes widened with horror. "Then we were right! He *is* going for the college!"

"It's good strategy. The whole town of Ashton is practically built around that college. Once the Society and Kaseph get established there at Whitmore, they'll have overwhelming influence over the rest of the town. Society people will come in like a swarm and Ashton will become another 'Sacred City of the Universal Mind.' It's happened enough before, in other towns, in other countries."

Bernice pounded the bed in frustration. "Susan, we have records of Eugene Baylor's financial transactions, evidence that might show how the college was undermined. But we haven't been able to make any sense of it all!"

Susan pulled a little canister out of her suitcase. "Actually, you only have half the picture. Baylor's no fool; he knew how to cover his tracks so his embezzlements on behalf of Omni wouldn't be noticed. What you need is the other side of those transactions: Kaseph's own records." She held the canister out for them to see. "I didn't have room for all that material. I did photograph it, though, and if we could get this film developed—"

"We have a darkroom at the *Clarion*. We could print that film right away."

"Let's check out of here."

They scrambled.

The Remnant continued to pray. None had been able to see or even hear from Hank since his arrest. The police station was manned at all times by strange police no one had ever seen in Ashton before, and none of these officers knew anything about how to visit anyone in jail, or how to bail them out, nor would they let anyone in to find out. It seemed Ashton had become a police state.

Fear, anger, and prayer increased. Something terrible was happening to the town, and they all knew it vividly, but what could be done in a town with deaf authorities, in a county whose offices were closed for the weekend?

The phone lines continued to hum, both in the town and going out across the country to relatives and friends, all of whom dropped to their knees to intercede and called their own authorities and legislators.

Alf Brummel stayed away from his office, avoiding any distraught Christians with sermons to deliver about their pastor's constitutional rights, or an official's duty to the will of the people, or anything else. He remained in Langstrat's apartment, pacing the floor, worrying, sweating, waiting for 2 o'clock on Sunday afternoon.

Grandma Duster kept praying and reassuring everyone that God had everything under control. She reminded them of what the angels had told her, and then many recalled what they had dreamed, or heard in their mind while praying, or seen in a vision, or felt in their spirits. And they continued to pray for the town.

And everywhere, from every direction, new visitors continued to arrive in the town of Ashton, riding in on passing hay trucks, hitchhiking in like summer backpackers, gliding in through the cornfields and then through the back streets, roaring in like wild bikers, bussing in like high schoolers, hiding in the trunks and under the bellies of every vehicle that traveled through on Highway 27.

And steadily the nooks, crannies, unused rooms, and countless other hiding places all over the town became alive with still, silent figures, their burly hands upon their swords, their golden eyes piercing and alert, their ears tuned to one particular sound from one particular trumpet.

Above the town, concealed in the trees, Tal could still look out across the wide valley and see Rafar in the big dead tree, overseeing the activities of his demons.

Captain Tal continued to watch and wait.

In the remote valley, a rapidly growing cloud of demon spirits churned for a radius of two miles all around the ranch, towering as high as the mountaintops. Their numbers were beyond counting, their density such that the cloud totally obscured anything within it. The spirits danced and wailed like drunken brawlers, waving their swords, raving and drooling, their eyes wild with madness. Myriads of them paired off, jousting, sparring, testing one another's skills.

In the darkened center of the cloud, in the big stone house, the Strongman sat with narrowed eyes and a crooked smirk that deepened the folds of his sagging face. In the company of his generals, he took time to gloat over the news he had just received from Ashton.

"Prince Rafar has satisfied my wishes, he has fulfilled his mission," the Strongman said, and then bared his ivory fangs with a drooling smile. "I will like that little town. In my hands, it will grow like a tree and fill the countryside."

He savored the next thought: "I may never have to stir myself from that place. What do you think? Shall we have our home at last?"

The tall and loathsome generals all muttered affirmatively. The Strongman rose from his seat, and the others snapped to a stiff and upright stance of attention.

"Our Mr. Kaseph has been calling me for some time now. Prepare the ranks. We will leave immediately."

The generals shot out through the roof of the house into the cloud, shrieking their orders, assembling their troops.

The Strongman unfolded his wings in a regal manner, then floated like a monstrous, overweight vulture into the basement room where Alexander Kaseph, sitting cross-legged on a large cushion, chanted the Strongman's name again and again. The Strongman alighted right in front of Kaseph and observed him for a moment, drinking in Kaseph's worship and spiritual groveling. Then, with a swift movement, the Strongman stepped forward and let his huge frame dissolve into Kaseph's body as Kaseph twitched and writhed grotesquely. In a moment the possession was complete, and Alexander Kaseph awakened from his meditation.

"The time has come!" he said, with the Strongman's look in his eyes.

36

Susan turned the rented car into the little gravel parking area behind the *Ashton Clarion*. It was 5 in the morning, and just beginning to get light outside. Somehow, as far as they knew, they had not been seen by any of the police. The town seemed quiet, and the day promised to be pleasant and sunny.

Bernice went to a special hiding place behind a pair of dented garbage cans and found the key to the back door. In a quick and silent moment, all three were inside.

"Don't turn any lights on, make any noise, or go near any windows," Bernice cautioned them. "The darkroom's in here. Everybody come in before I turn on the light."

All three squeezed into the little darkroom. Bernice closed the door and then found the light switch.

She prepared her chemicals, double-checked the film, then got the little developing tank ready. She switched off the light, and they stood in total blackness.

"Freaky," Kevin said.

"This will only take a few minutes. Boy, I haven't the slightest idea of what's happening to Marshall, but I don't dare try to find out."

"What about your answering machine? There might be some messages on it."

"That's a thought. I can check that as soon as I get this film all loaded in here. I'm almost finished." Then Bernice had another thought. "I wonder about Sandy Hogan, too. She pitched a lamp at her father and ran out of the house."

"Yes, you were telling me about that."

"I don't know where she'd go, unless she's decided to run off with that Shawn character."

"With who?" Susan asked abruptly. "Who did you say?"

"Some guy named Shawn."

"Shawn Ormsby?" Susan asked.

"Oh-oh, it sounds like you know him."

"I'm afraid Sandy Hogan could be in real trouble! Shawn Ormsby appears quite a few times in your sister's diary. He's the one who got Pat involved in those parapsychology experiments. He encouraged her to continue them, and he's the one who eventually introduced her to Thomas!"

The darkroom light clicked on. The developing tank was loaded and ready, but all Bernice could do was stare white-faced at Susan.

Madeline was not a beautiful, golden-haired, highly evolved, superhuman from a higher dimension. Madeline was a demon, a hideous, leather-skinned monster with sharp talons and a subtle, deceiving nature. For Madeline, Sandy Hogan had been a very easy and vulnerable prey. Sandy's deep wounds concerning her father made her an ideal subject for the candy of illusionary love Madeline was able to dangle before her, and now it seemed that Sandy would follow whatever course Madeline said was right for her life, believing whatever Madeline said. Madeline loved it when she got people to that point.

Patricia Krueger, though, had been a challenge. Then, disguised as handsome, benevolent Thomas, this demon had quite a struggle getting Patricia to believe he was really there; it had taken some very heavy-handed hallucinations and well-timed coincidences, not to mention the very best of his psychic signs and wonders. It wasn't enough to just bend keys and spoons; he had to carry out some very impressive materializations as well. Finally he had succeeded, though, and fulfilled Ba-al Lucius's bidding. Pat had ceremonially done away with herself, and she would never know the love of God again.

But what of Sandy Hogan? What would the new Ba-al, Rafar, want done with her? The demon, now calling himself—or herself—Madeline, approached the great prince on his big dead tree.

"My lord," said Madeline, bowing low with respect, "do I understand that Marshall Hogan is defeated and powerless?"

"He is," said Rafar.

"And what would you wish for Sandy Hogan, his daughter?"

Rafar was about to answer, but then hesitated, giving the matter a little more thought. At length he said, "Do not destroy her, not yet. Our foe is as subtle as I, and I would like one more assurance against any success of this Marshall Hogan. The Strongman comes today. Hold her against that time."

Rafar dispatched a messenger along with Madeline to visit Professor Langstrat.

Shawn was awakened by an early morning phone call from the professor.

"Shawn," said Langstrat, "I've heard from the masters. They want some extra assurances that Hogan will not be an obstacle to today's business. Is Sandy still there with you?"

Shawn could look out from his bedroom into the living room of his small apartment. Sandy was still on the couch, still asleep.

"I still have her."

"The meeting with the regents will take place in the Administration Building, the third-floor conference room. A room across the hall, 326, has been reserved for us and the other psychics. Bring Sandy with you. The masters want her there."

"We'll be there."

As Langstrat hung up the phone, she could hear Alf Brummel clattering about in the kitchen.

"Juleen," he called, "where's the coffee?"

"Don't you think you're nervous enough?" she asked him, leaving her bedroom and going into the kitchen.

"I'm just trying to wake up," he muttered, shakily putting a pot of water on the stove.

"Wake up! You haven't even slept, Alf!"

"Have you?" he retorted.

"Quite well," she said very mildly.

Langstrat, primly dressed, looked ready to leave for the college. Brummel was a wreck, his eyes sunken, his hair disheveled, still in a bathrobe.

He said, "I'll just be glad when this day is over and everything quiets down. As chief of police, I think I've broken about every law in the books."

She put her hand on his shoulder and said reassuringly, "All this new world growing around you will be your friend, Alf. *We* are the law now. You've helped to bring in the New Order, an ultimately good deed that deserves reward."

"Well . . . we'd better make good and sure of that, that's all I have to say."

"You can help, Alf. Several of the prime leaders will be meeting just across the hall the same time as the closure meeting this afternoon. With our combined psychic energies, we can assure that nothing will stand in the way of complete success."

"I don't know if I even dare go out in public. I guess the arrests of Busche and Hogan have a lot of people riled—*church* people, I might add! This rape charge hasn't hurt Busche nearly as much as it was supposed to. Most of the people in the church are coming at *me*, wondering what *I'm* trying to pull!"

"You will be there," she said plainly. "Oliver will be there, as will the others. And Sandy Hogan will be there."

He spun and looked at her in horror. "What? Why is Sandy Hogan going to be there?"

"Insurance."

Brummel's eyes widened, and his voice trembled. "Another one? You're going to kill another one?"

Her eyes grew very cold. "I do not kill anyone! I only let the masters decide!"

"So what have they decided?"

"You are to let Hogan know that his daughter is in our hands and that he would be very wise not to interfere with anything that happens from this day forward."

"You want *me* to tell him?"

"Mr. Brummel!" Her voice was chilling. She stepped toward him intimidatingly, and he backed up a few steps. "Marshall Hogan happens to be in your jail. You are in charge of him. You will tell him."

With that, she stepped out the front door and went off to the college.

Brummel stood there for a moment, nonplussed, frustrated, afraid. His thoughts swam about like a school of frightened fish. He forgot why he was even in the kitchen.

Brummel, you've had it. What makes you think you're not just as dispensable as anyone else the Society considers a commodity, a tool, a pawn? And, let's face it, Brummel. You are a pawn! Juleen's using you to do her dirty work, and now she's setting you up as nothing less than an accessory to murder. If I were you, I'd start looking out for Number One. This whole plan will be found out sooner or later, and guess who'll be caught holding the bag?

Brummel kept thinking about it, and his thoughts ceased to swim about. They all began to run the same direction. This was madness, utter madness. The masters say this and the masters say that, but what's it to them? They don't have wrists that can be handcuffed, they don't have jobs to lose, they don't have faces they could be afraid to show around town someday.

Brummel, why don't you stop Juleen before she totally ruins your life? Why don't you stop all this madness and be a real, genuine lawman for once?

Yeah, thought Brummel. Why don't I? If I don't, we're all going to sink on this crazy ship.

Lucius, the deposed Prince of Ashton, stood in the kitchen with Alf Brummel, the chief of police, having a little discussion with him. This Alf Brummel always was rather flimsy; perhaps Lucius could make use of this commodity.

Jimmy Dunlop arrived at the courthouse at 7:30 Sunday morning, ready to begin his shift. To his surprise the parking lot was full of people: young couples, old couples, little old ladies; it looked like a misplaced church picnic. Even as he pulled in, he could see every eye focusing on his policeman's uniform. Oh, no! Now they were coming his way!

Mary Busche and Edith Duster recognized Jimmy right away; he was the young and very rude officer who turned them away from visiting Hank last night. Now they were right up at the head of this crowd, and although none of these people had any intention of doing anything rash or improper, they were not about to be trodden on.

Jimmy had to get out of his car whether he wanted to or not. He did have to report to work today.

"Officer Dunlop," said Mary, quite brazenly, "I believe you told me last night that you would arrange for me to visit my husband today."

"If you'll excuse me," he said, trying to push his way past.

"Officer," said John Coleman respectfully, "we're here to ask that you honor her request to see her husband."

Jimmy was a police officer. He did represent the law. He had a lot of authority. The only problem was, he didn't have any guts.

"Uh . . ." he said. "Listen, you'll have to break up this gathering or face possible arrest!"

Abe Sterling stepped forward. He was an attorney who was a friend of a friend of an uncle of Andy Forsythe and he had been gotten out of bed last night and invited for just this occasion.

"This is a legal, peaceful gathering," he reminded Jimmy, "according to the definition of RCS 14.021.217 and the decision rendered in Stratford County Superior Court in *Ames versus the County of Stratford.*"

"Yeah," said several, "that's right. Listen to the man."

Jimmy was flustered. He looked toward the front door of the courthouse. Two officers from the Windsor precinct were guarding the fort. Jimmy walked toward them, wondering why they were letting this continue.

"Hey," he asked them with a subdued voice, "what's all this about? Why didn't you get rid of these people?"

"Hey, Jimmy," said one, "this is your town and your ball game. We figured you had the answers, so we told them to wait until you got here."

Jimmy looked at all the faces looking back at him. No, ignoring this problem would not make it go away. He asked the officer, "How long have all these people been here?"

"Since about 6. You should have been here then. They were having a regular church service."

"And they can *do* that?"

"Talk to that lawyer of theirs. They have the right to peaceful demonstration as long as they don't impede the regular conduct of business. They've been behaving themselves."

"So what do I do now?"

The two officers only looked at each other somewhat blankly.

Abe Sterling was right behind Jimmy. "Officer Dunlop, you are within the law to hold a suspect for up to seventy-two hours without charges, but seeing as the suspect's wife does have the right to contact her husband, we are ready to file suit in Stratford County Superior Court requiring you to appear and show just cause why she has been denied that right."

"You hear that?" someone piped up.

"I'll . . . uh . . . I'll have to talk to the police chief . . ." Under his breath he was cursing Alf Brummel for getting him into this mess.

"Where is Alf Brummel, anyway? This is his *pastor* he's thrown in jail," Edith Duster declared.

"I—I don't know anything about it."

John Coleman said, "Then we as citizens are asking you to find out. And we would like to talk to Chief Brummel. Can you please arrange that?"

"I'll—I'll see what I can do," Jimmy said, turning for the door.

"I wish to see my husband!" Mary said quite loudly, stepping forward with her jaw set firmly.

"I'll see what I can do," Jimmy said again, and ducked inside.

Edith Duster turned to the others and said, "Just remember, brothers and sisters, we are not contending against flesh and blood, but against the principalities, against the powers, against the world rulers of this present darkness, against the spiritual hosts of wickedness in the heavenly places." She got several Amens to that, followed by someone starting a worship song. Immediately the whole Remnant took up the song and sang it loudly, worshiping God and making His praise heard in that parking lot.

Rafar could hear the praise from where he stood on the hill above the town, and he glowered at these saints of God. Let them whine over their fallen pastor. Their singing would be curtailed soon enough when the Strongman and his hordes arrived.

Countless spirits were arriving in the town of Ashton—but they were not the kind Rafar desired. They rushed in under the ground, they filtered in under the cover of occasional clouds, they sneaked in by riding invisibly in cars, trucks, vans, buses. In hiding places all over the town one warrior would be joined by another, those two would be joined by two more, those four would be joined by four. They too could hear the singing. They could feel the strength coursing through them with every note. Their swords droned with the resonance of the worship. It was the worship and the prayers of these saints that had called them here in the first place.

The remote valley was now a huge bowl of boiling, swirling ink accented by myriads of glowing, yellow eyes. The cloud of demons had multiplied so that it filled the valley like a boiling sea.

Alexander Kaseph, possessed by the Strongman, stepped out of his big stone house and got into his waiting limousine. All the papers were ready for signing; his attorneys would meet him at the Administration Building on the Whitmore College campus. This was the day he had waited and prepared for.

As the limousine carrying Kaseph—and the Strongman—made its way up the winding road, the sea of demons began to shift in that direction like the turn of the tide. The drone of countless billions of wings rose in pitch and intensity. Streams of demons began to trickle over the sides of the big bowl, flowing out between the mountain peaks like hot, sulfurous tar.

In the darkroom at the *Ashton Clarion,* Bernice and Susan stood at the enlarger, looking down at the projected image of the negatives Bernice had just developed.

"Yes!" said Susan. "This is the first page of the college embezzlement records. You'll notice the name of the college doesn't appear anywhere. However, the amounts received should match exactly the amounts dispersed from the college records."

"Yes, the records we have, or our accountant has."

"See here? It's been a pretty steady flow of funds. Eugene Baylor has been skimming and channeling college investments just a little at a time into various accounts elsewhere, every one of which is actually a front organization for Omni and the Society."

"So the so-called investments have all been going into Kaseph's pocket!"

"And I am sure they will comprise a substantial part of the monies Kaseph will use to buy the college out."

Bernice moved the film forward again. Several frames of financial records rolled by in a blur.

"Wait!" said Susan. "There! Go back a few frames." Bernice rolled the film back. "Yes! There! I got this from some of Kaseph's personal notes. It's hard to make out the handwriting, but look at this list of names."

Bernice did have trouble making out the handwriting, but she had written those names herself quite a few times.

"Harmel . . . Jefferson . . ." she read.

"You haven't seen these yet," Susan said, pointing to the bottom of a very lengthy list.

There, in Kaseph's own writing, were the names Hogan, Krueger, and Strachan.

"I take it this is some kind of hit list?" Bernice asked.

"Exactly. It goes on for hundreds of names. Notice the red Xs after many of them."

"They were disposed of?"

"Bought out, driven out, maybe murdered, maybe ruined reputations or finances or both."

"And I thought *our* list was long!"

"This is the tip of the iceberg. I have other documents that we need to get photocopied and stored somewhere safe. It could all work into a very good case against not only Kaseph but the Omni Corporation—evidence that could prove a long history of wiretapping, extortion, racketeering, terrorism, murder. Kaseph's creativity in these areas knows no bounds."

"The ultimate gangster."

"With an international mob, don't forget, unnaturally unified by their common allegiance to the Universal Consciousness Society."

Just then Kevin, who had been running off photocopies of Susan's stolen documents, hissed at them, "Hey, there's a cop out there!"

Susan and Bernice froze.

"Where?" asked Bernice. "What's he doing?"

"He's across the street. It's a stakeout, I'll bet!"

Susan and Bernice went carefully toward the front to look. They found Kevin crouched in the doorway of the copier room. It was broad daylight now, and light was streaming in the front office windows.

Kevin pointed to a plain old Ford parked across the street, just visible through the front windows. A plainly dressed man sat behind the wheel, doing nothing in particular.

"Kelsey," said Weed. "I've had some run-ins with him. Dressed in his civies and driving an old Ford, but I'd know that face a mile away."

"More of Brummel's doing, no doubt," said Bernice.

"So what do we do now?" Susan asked.

"Get down!" Kevin hissed.

They ducked into doorways just as another man came up to the front window and looked inside.

"Michaelson," said Kevin. "Kelsey's partner."

Michaelson tried the door. It was locked. He looked through the other front window, and then he walked out of sight.

"Time for another miracle, huh?" Bernice said, a little sarcastically.

Hank awoke early that morning and thought for sure that some great miraculous intervention of God had occurred, or that he was about to ascend into heaven, or that the angels had come to rescue him, or . . . or . . . or he just didn't know what. But as he lay there on his cot, half asleep, still in that semiconscious state where you're not too sure of what is real and what isn't, he heard worship songs and hymns floating around his head. He even thought he could hear Mary's voice singing among all those other voices. For a long time he just lay there enjoying it, not wanting to wake up for fear that it might go away.

But Marshall exclaimed, "What the heck is that?"

He heard it too? Hank woke up at last. He jolted up from his cot and went to the bars. The sound was coming in through the window at the end of the cellblock. Marshall joined him and they listened together. They could hear the name "Jesus" being sung and praised.

"We've made it, Hank," said Marshall. "We're in heaven!"

Hank was crying. If those people out there only knew what a blessing this was! Suddenly he knew he was not in prison any longer, not really. The gospel of Jesus Christ was not imprisoned, and he and Marshall were now two of the freest men in the world.

The two of them listened for a while, and then, startling Marshall a little, Hank started singing too. It was a song painting Jesus Christ as a victorious warrior and the church as His army. Hank knew all the words, of course, and belted them right out.

A little embarrassed, Marshall looked around. The two car thieves in the next cell were still too dumbfounded to complain yet. The phony check writer only shook his head and went back to his paperback novel. Some other guy in the last cell, offense unknown, cursed a little, but not too loudly.

"C'mon, Marshall," prodded Hank. "Jump in! We just might sing ourselves out of this place."

Marshall only smiled and shook his head.

Just then the big door at the end of the cellblock burst open and in strode Jimmy Dunlop, his face red and his hands shaking.

"What's going on in here?" he demanded. "Do you know you're causing a disturbance?"

"Oh, we're just enjoying the music," Hank said, all smiles.

Jimmy shook his finger at Hank and said, "Well, you cut that religious stuff out right now! It has no place in a public jail. If you want to sing, you do it in church somewhere, not here."

Yeah, thought Marshall, I think I know the words well enough by now. He started singing as loudly as he could, singing right at Jimmy Dunlop.

It brought a very satisfying response from Jimmy. He turned on his heels and got out of there, slamming the door after him.

Another song began, and Marshall thought that maybe he'd heard this one somewhere before, maybe at Sunday school. "Thank you, Lord, for saving my soul." He sang it loudly, standing next to that young man of God, the two of them holding on to those cell bars.

"Paul and Silas!" Marshall suddenly exclaimed. "Yeah, now I remember!"

From that point, Marshall wasn't singing for Jimmy Dunlop's sake.

Tal could hear the music from where he stood in hiding. His face was still a little grim, but he nodded his head with satisfaction.

A messenger arrived with the news. "The Strongman is on his way."

Another messenger informed him, "We have prayer cover now from thirty-two cities. There are fourteen more being raised up."

Tal brought out his sword. He could feel the blade resonating with the worship of the saints, and he could sense the power of God's presence. He smiled a slight smile and put the sword back. "Gather in the sources: Lemley, Strachan, Mattily, Cole, and Parker. Do it abruptly. The timing will be important."

Several warriors disappeared to their missions.

37

Sandy Hogan continued to primp in front of the mirror in Shawn's bathroom, nervously brushing her hair, checking her makeup. Oh, I hope I look okay. . . . whatever will I say, what will I do? I've never been to a meeting like this before.

Shawn had given her some explosively good news: Professor Langstrat had decided that Sandy was an excellent subject with exceptional psychic abilities, so much so that Sandy was now being considered as a prime candidate for a special initiation into some kind of exclusive fellowship of psychics, an *international* fellowship! Sandy now recalled hearing just a fleeting mention here and there of some kind of Universal Consciousness group, and it had always sounded like something very lofty, very secret, even sacred. She had never dreamed that she would be granted such an extraordinary opportunity, to actually meet other psychics and become a part of their circle of confidence! She could imagine the new experiences and the higher insights that could be achieved in the company of so many gifted people, all combining their psychic skills and energies in the continuing search for enlightenment!

Madeline, did you have something to do with this? Just wait until we meet again! I have a hug and a load of thanks to give you!

Bernice, Susan, and Kevin could do nothing but try to preserve the evidence Susan had gathered at so great a risk. Bernice made prints of all the pictures Susan had taken, then Kevin ran photocopies of the prints, along with copies of all the other material. Bernice looked about the building for a good hiding place to stash all the material. Susan looked over a map and pondered different escape routes out of town, different means of getting out, different people they could call once they did get out.

Then the telepone rang. They had ignored it before and let the answering machine squawk out its usual message. But this time, after the little beep tone, a voice said, "Hello, this is Harvey Cole, and I've completed working on those accounts you gave me . . ."

"Wait!" said Bernice. "Turn it up!"

Susan crawled over to the desk in the front office where the answering machine was sitting and turned up the volume.

Harvey Cole's voice continued, "I really need to get in touch with you as soon as possible."

Bernice snatched up the telephone in Marshall's office. "Hello? Harvey? This is Bernice!"

Susan and Kevin were horrified.

"What are you doing?"

"The cops are going to hear this, man!"

Harvey said through the telephone and also through the turned-up answering machine, "Oh, you're *there!* I heard you were arrested last night. The police won't tell me anything. I didn't know where to call . . ."

"Harvey, just listen. Got a pen or a pencil?"

"Yeah, now I do."

"Call my uncle. His name is Jerry Dallas; his number is 240-9946. Tell him you know me, tell him it's an emergency, and tell him you have materials to show Justin Parker, the county prosecutor."

"What? Not so fast."

Bernice labored through the information again, more slowly. "Now, this conversation is probably being listened to by Alf Brummel or one of his lackeys on the Ashton Police Force, so I want you to make sure that if anything happens to me that information will still go to the prosecutor so he'll wonder what's going on in this town."

"Am I supposed to write that down too?"

"No. Just make sure you get in touch with Justin Parker. If you possibly can, get him to call us here."

"But, Bernice, I was going to say, it's pretty clear that the funds have been going out, but the records don't show where—"

"We have the records that show where. We have everything. Tell my uncle that."

"Okay, Bernice. You really are in trouble, then?"

"The police are after me. They'll probably find out I'm here because I'm talking to you and our phone has been bugged. You'd better hurry!"

"Yeah, yeah, okay!"

Harvey hung up quickly.

Susan and Kevin looked at each other and then at Bernice.

She looked back at them and could only say, "Call it a gamble."

Susan shrugged. "Well, we didn't have any better ideas."

The phone rang again. Bernice hesitated, waiting for the answering machine to go through its little recitation.

Then came the voice. "Marshall, this is Al Lemley. Listen, I've got some pretty stirred-up feds here in New York that want to talk to you about your man Kaseph. They've been tracking him for quite some time, and if you can supply them with any good evidence, they'd be interested . . ."

Bernice picked up the phone again. "Al Lemley? This is Bernice Krueger. I work for Marshall. Can you bring those men to Ashton today?"

"What? Hello?" Lemley was taken aback. "Are you real or a recording?"

"Very real, and very much in need of your help. Marshall's in jail and—"

"In jail?"

"A bum rap. It's Kaseph's doing. He's taking over the Whitmore College today at 2, he has Marshall in the slammer to keep him out of the way, and I'm a fugitive at large. It's a long story, but your friends will love it and we've secured the documents to prove every word of it."

"What was the name again?"

Bernice labored through her name again and had to spell it twice. "Listen, they've bugged this phone, so they probably know where I am now, so would you please hurry up and get here and bring all the good guys you can find? There are none left in this town."

Al Lemley knew enough. "Okay, Bernice, I'll do anything and everything I can. And those eight-balls who've bugged your phone had better be warned that if things aren't downright peachy by the time we get there, there will most certainly be trouble!"

"Make it the Administration Building on the Whitmore College campus at or before 2."

"See you then."

Now Kevin and Susan were beginning to lighten up a bit.

"What was that you wanted?" asked Susan. "Another miracle?"

The phone rang again. Bernice didn't wait this time, but snatched it right up.

A voice said, "Hello, this is State Attorney General Norm Mattily, calling for Marshall Hogan."

Susan couldn't hold down a little squeal. Kevin said, "All right, all right!"

Bernice spoke to Mattily. "Mr. Mattily, this is Bernice Krueger, a reporter for the *Clarion*. I work for Mr. Hogan."

"Oh . . . uh, yes . . ." Mattily seemed to be conferring with someone else. "Yes, uh, Eldon Strachan is standing right here with me, and he tells me there's some kind of trouble there in Ashton—"

"The worst kind. It's all coming together today. We've gained some substantial evidence to show you. How soon can you get here?"

"Well, I wasn't planning on doing *that* . . ."

"The town of Ashton is going to be taken over by an international terrorist organization at 2 o'clock today."

"What?"

Bernice could hear the muffled voice of Eldon Strachan, probably pounding away at Mattily's other ear. "Uh . . . well, where is Mr. Hogan? Eldon is concerned for his safety."

"I am sure that Mr. Hogan is not at all safe. He and I were ambushed by the local mobsters last night during a routine investigation. Marshall fought them off while I fled. I've been in hiding ever since and I have no idea what's happened to Mr. Hogan."

"What on earth! Are you . . ." Eldon kept on talking in Mattily's other ear. "Well, I'm going to need some kind of concrete evidence, something that will wash legally . . ."

"We have it, but we'll need your direct and immediate intervention. Can you come, and bring some *real* police with you? It's a matter of life and death."

"This had better be on the up and up!"

"Get here, please, before 2. I would advise meeting us at the Administration Building on the Whitmore College campus."

"All right," said Mattily, his voice still sounding a bit hesitant, "I'll get down there and see whatever it is you have to show me."

Bernice hung up and the phone immediately rang again.

"*Clarion*."

"Hello, this is County Prosecutor Justin Parker. With whom am I speaking?"

Bernice clapped her hand over the receiver and whispered to Susan, "There *is* a God!"

Alf Brummel could not stand it anymore. Things were getting out of his control, things that had a lot to do with his own future and security. He could not stay away from the police station any longer. He had to be there to be sure of what was going on, to keep things from becoming irreversibly messed up, to . . . oh, where were those car keys?

He got into his car and raced through town to the station.

The Remnant was still singing in the parking lot when he arrived, and by the time he knew who they were and why they were there, it was too late to sneak away. He had to pull in and park.

They converged on his car like a voracious swarm of mosquitoes.

"Where have you been, chief?"

"When's Hank going to get out?"

"Mary would like to see him."

"What in blazes do you think you're doing to that man? He hasn't raped anyone!"

"You'd better be ready to kiss your job good-bye!"

Best foot forward, Alf, if you intend to save the rest of you. "Uh, where is Mary?"

Mary waved to him from the front steps of the courthouse. He tried to make a beeline for her, and once the people saw the direction he was heading, they were more willing to make way for him.

Mary started asking him questions as soon as he was within earshot of her shouts. "Mr. Brummel, I would like to see my husband, and how dare you allow this travesty!"

Brummel had never in his life seen sweet, seemingly vulnerable Mary Busche so feisty.

He tried to think of what to say. "It's been a real madhouse around here. I'm sorry I've been away . . ."

"My husband is innocent and you know it!" she said quite firmly. "We don't know how you intend to get away with this, but we are here to see that you don't."

With that comment, a flurry of shouts in agreement thundered up from the crowd.

Brummel tried the intimidation approach. "Now listen to me, all of you! No one is above the law, regardless of who they are. Pastor Busche has been accused as a sexual offender, and I have no choice but to carry out my duties as an officer of the law. I can't help it if we are friends or fellow church members, this is a matter of law—"

"Bunk!" came a deep-throated shout near Brummel.

Brummel turned toward the voice to correct it, but then turned pale as he saw the face of Lou Stanley, his old comrade-in-arms.

Lou stood his ground firmly, one hand on his belt, the other pointing right into Brummel's face as he said, "You've talked about pulling a stunt like this many times, Alf! I've heard you say that all you needed was the right opportunity. Well, now I'm saying that you've done it. I'm accusing you, Alf! If anybody wants my testimony in any court of law against you, they've got it!"

A cheer and some jeers went up.

Then Brummel got another shock. Gordon Mayer, the church treasurer, stepped to the front of the crowd, and he too pointed his finger right in Brummel's face.

"Alf, simple dissent is one thing, but flat-out conspiracy is quite another. You'd better be really sure of what you're doing."

Brummel was backed against the wall. "Gordon . . . Gordon, we have to do what's best . . . we . . ."

"Well, count me out!" Mayer said. "I've done enough for you!"

Brummel turned away from his two former comrades, only to come face to face with the suddenly cleaned-up Bobby Corsi!

"Hey, Chief Brummel," said Bobby. "Remember me? Guess who I'm working for *now.*"

Brummel was speechless. He began to walk toward the police department door, as if there would be some shelter in there from all this disaster.

Andy Forsythe did not block his way, but walked close enough to him to cause him to stop.

"Mr. Brummel," said Andy, "there's a young wife back there who would still like her requests considered."

Brummel walked more briskly. "I'll see what I can do, all right? Let me check the status of things. Just wait. I'll be with you in a moment."

As quickly as he could, he ducked through the door and locked it behind him just in time. The crowd followed him like a wave and pressed up against the door, blockading him inside.

His new receptionist sat wide-eyed at the reception desk, looking out the window at all the angry faces.

"Should . . . should I call the police?" she asked.

"No," said Brummel. "They're just some friends here to see me."

With that, he disappeared into his office and closed the door.

Juleen, Juleen! This was her fault! He was sick of her, sick of this whole thing!

He saw a note on his desk. Sam Turner had left a message to call. He rang the number, and Sam answered.

"How's it looking, Sam?" Brummel asked.

"No good, Alf. Listen, I've been on the phone all morning, and no one wants to call any emergency congregational meeting. They have no intentions of voting Hank out, and few of them buy this rape business. Let's face it, Alf, you blew it."

"*I* blew it?" Brummel exploded. "*I* blew it? Wasn't this your idea too?"

"Don't you say that!" came Turner's reply very threateningly, "Don't you ever say that!"

"So now you're not going to stand by me either."

"There's nothing to stand by, Alf. The plan just didn't fly. Busche is a boy scout and everybody knows it, and you just won't get this rape charge to stick."

"Sam, we were in this together! It was going to work!"

"It didn't, buddy. Hank's in to stay, that's the way I see it, and I'm withdrawing from this whole thing. You do what you have to, but you'd better do something, or your name won't be worth a dung heap by the time this is over."

"Well thanks a lot, *buddy!*" Brummel angrily hung up.

He looked at the clock. It was just about noon. The meeting would take place in two hours.

Hogan. He still had to get a message to Hogan about Sandy. Oh brother, here was another of Juleen's fine messes. Sure, Juleen, you bet! I'm already pegged with this bum rap against Busche, and now you want me to go on record as an accessory to whatever you have planned for Sandy Hogan.

And what about Krueger? Who had she been able to snitch to about this whole thing? He bolted from his office and went down the hall to the dispatch room.

"Anything yet on that fugitive?" he asked the lone dispatcher.

The dispatcher stuffed a bite of peanut butter sandwich into his cheek and said, "No, it's been pretty quiet."

"Nothing even at the *Clarion?*"

"There's a strange car parked out back, but it's out of state and they haven't traced the plates yet."

"They haven't . . . ! Get those plates traced! Check that building! Somebody could be in there!"

"They haven't seen anybody—"

"Check the building!" Brummel exploded.

The receptionist called from up the hall, "Captain Brummel, Bernice Krueger is on the telephone. Should I take a message?"

"Nooo!" he screamed, running up the hall to his office. "I'll take it in here!"

He slammed his office door behind him and grabbed his telephone. "Hello?" He hit the second button on his phone. "Hello?"

"Mr. Alfred Brummel!" came a very condescending voice.

"Bernice!"

"It's time we had a talk."

"All right. Where are you?"

"Don't be an absolute idiot. Listen, I'm calling to give you an ultimatum. I've been talking to the state attorney general, the county prosecutor, and the feds. I have evidence—and I mean some really hard stuff—that will blow your little plot wide open, and they're all on their way here to see it."

"You're bluffing!"

"You have the conversations on tape, no doubt. Just play them back."

Brummel smiled a bit. She had given away where she was. "And just what is your ultimatum?"

"Spring Hogan. Now. And call off your manhunt for me. In two hours I intend to show my face in this town, and I want no harassment, especially since I'll be accompanied by many very special guests!"

"You're at the *Clarion* right now, aren't you?"

"Yes, of course I am. And I can see . . . what's his name? Kelsey, sitting out there in that old heap, he and his partner Michaelson. I want you to call those guys off. If you don't, all the big boys in the world will know what happened to me. If you do, it can only help you."

"You're . . . I still say you're bluffing!"

"Play your little bugging machine, Alf. See if I'm telling you the truth. I'll wait to see that car pull away."

Click. She hung up.

Brummel dashed to the cabinet and opened the doors. He pulled out the recorder. He hesitated, thought furiously, froze for a moment. He shoved the recorder back into the cabinet, slammed the doors shut, and dashed down the hall to the dispatch room.

The dispatcher was still munching on his sandwich. Brummel reached right across his lap and grabbed the microphone, throwing the talk switch.

"Units two and three, Kelsey, Michaelson, 10-19. Repeat: 10-19 immediately."

The dispatcher looked up with delight. "Hey! What happened? Did Krueger turn herself in?"

Alf Brummel never was good at comebacks for stupid or ill-timed questions. He dashed up the hall to the front desk and dialed the courthouse.

"Get me Dunlop."

Dunlop picked up the other end.

"Jimmy, Hogan and Busche are being released on personal recognizance. Turn them loose."

Jimmy gave him some more dumb questions.

"Just do what you're told and leave the paperwork to me! Now go!"

He slammed down the phone and disappeared into his office. The receptionist continued looking out the window at all those people. They were starting to sing again. It sounded kind of nice.

Bernice, Susan, and Kevin waited nervously for either a very good or a very bad thing to happen. Either Brummel would play ball, or they would be getting high on tear gas within minutes. But then they heard an engine starting up across the street.

"Hey!" said Kevin.

Susan still wrung her hands a little. Bernice just watched, unwilling to believe anything good too quickly.

The old Ford pulled away, with both Kelsey and Michaelson in it.

Bernice didn't want to wait around. "Let's pack all this stuff in that suitcase again and get over to the courthouse. Marshall's going to need a catching up."

"You don't have to tell me twice!" said Kevin.

All Susan could say was, "Thank you, God. Thank you, God!"

Alf Brummel heard only one short segment of one telephone conversation, the one between Bernice and State Attorney General Norm Mattily. He knew Mattily's voice, and, yes, it made perfectly good sense that Eldon Strachan would go to Mattily, *if* Strachan had some genuinely reliable information.

Brummel cursed aloud. Reliable information! All Mattily had to do was find this blankety-blank recorder sitting here, tapped illegally into all those phones!

The receptionist buzzed him. He reached over to his desk and hit the intercom switch.

"Yeah?" he said very crossly.

"Juleen Langstrat on line two," she said.

"Take a message!" he said, and flipped off his switch.

He knew why she was calling. She was going to nag him, remind him to be there at the afternoon meeting involving Sandy Hogan.

He opened the other cabinet door and pulled out the records and stored tape recordings. Where in the world could he stash all this stuff? How could he destroy it?

The receptionist buzzed him again.

"What?"

"She insists that you talk to her."

He picked up the telephone, and Langstrat's oily voice came over the line.

"Alf, are you ready for today?"

"Yes," he answered impatiently.

"Then please come as soon as you can. We must prepare the energies of the rooms before the meeting begins, and I want to have all things in unison before Shawn arrives with Sandy."

"So you're really going to bring her into this?"

"Only as a safeguard, naturally. Marshall Hogan is out of the way, but we must be sure we keep him there, at least until all our efforts and visions have been fulfilled and the town of Ashton has been afforded its victorious leap into Universal Consciousness." She paused to relish the thought for a moment, and then asked rather nonchalantly, "And have you heard any news of our runaway burglar?"

Before he even knew why he was doing it, he lied. "No, nothing yet. She's out of the way."

"Certainly. I'm sure she'll be found soon enough, and after today she will have no hope at all."

He said nothing to that. He was suddenly distracted by a thought that poured over him like a ten-foot wave: *Alf, she believed you. She really doesn't know!*

"You will be here immediately, Alf?" she asked and ordered at the same time.

She doesn't know what's been happening, was all Brummel could think. She's vulnerable! *I* know something *she* doesn't!

"I'll be right over," he said mechanically.

"See you soon," she said with an authoritarian finality, and hung up.

She doesn't know! She thinks everything is going fine and there will be no trouble! She thinks she'll get away with it all!

Brummel let his thoughts race as he considered his options, his newly acquired exclusive knowledge, and the strange sense of power it gave him. Yes, it was all as good as over, and he was probably going to go down . . . but he had the power to bring that woman, that spider, that witch, down with him!

Suddenly he had no desire to destroy the tapes and the records. Let the authorities find them. Let them find everything! Maybe he'd even show them.

As for the Plan, if Kaseph and his Society are so all-knowing and so invincible, why should you tell them anything? Let them find out for themselves!

"Wouldn't it be nice to see your dear Juleen sweating for once?" asked Lucius.

"It would be nice to see Juleen sweating for once," Brummel muttered.

38

Hank and Marshall stepped out the basement door of the courthouse and found themselves all alone. Their friends were still congregated at the police department door, singing, talking, praying, demonstrating.

"Praise the Lord," was all Hank could say.

"Oh, I believe it, I believe it," Marshall answered.

It was John Coleman who first spotted them and let out a whoop. The others all turned their heads and were shocked and ecstatic. They came running up to Hank and Marshall like chickens to feed.

But they all made room for Mary, even gave her loving pushes forward as she ran by. The Lord was so good! Here was Hank's dear Mary, weeping and hugging and kissing and whispering her love to him, and he could hardly believe it was really happening. He had never felt so separated from her before.

"Are you all right?" she kept asking him, and he kept telling her, "I'm just fine, just fine."

"It's a miracle," said the others. "The Lord has answered our prayers. He got you out of prison just like Peter."

Marshall understood when they virtually ignored him. This was Hank's moment.

But what was going on over there? Through the heads, shoulders, and bodies Marshall noted Alf Brummel ducking quickly out the front door and into his car. He sped away. The creep. If I were him, I'd duck out too.

And here came . . . No! No, it couldn't be! Marshall started easing his way through the crowd, craning his neck to see for sure if the passengers in this just arriving car were who they seemed to be. Yes! Bernice was even waving to him! And there was Weed, alive! That other gal, the one driving . . . she couldn't be! But she had to be! Susan Jacobson, back from the dead, no less!

Marshall made his way through Hank's admirers and broke into a very brisk, wide-grinned walk to where Susan was just parking the car. Wow! When these people pray, God listens!

Bernice burst from the car and threw her arms around him.

"Marshall, are you all right?" she said, almost crying.

"Are you all right?" he asked her back.

A voice behind them said, "Oh, Mrs. Hogan, I've really wanted to meet you."

It was Hank. Marshall looked at the man of God, standing there all smiles, with his little wife by his side and God's people all behind him, and he felt the hug go out of his arms.

Bernice slipped limply out of the embrace.

"Hank," said Marshall with a broken kind of tone Bernice had never heard from him before, "this is not my wife. This is Bernice Krueger, my reporter." Then Marshall looked at Bernice and said with great love and respect, "And a good one, too!"

Bernice knew immediately that something had happened to Marshall. It didn't surprise her; something had been happening to her too, and she could see in Marshall's face and detect in his voice that same inner brokenness she had been feeling in herself. Somehow she knew that this young man standing next to Marshall had something to do with it all.

"And who is your fellow jailbird here?" she asked.

"Bernice Krueger, meet Hank Busche, pastor of Ashton Community Church and a very recent, very good friend of mine."

She shook his hand, shoving all her thoughts and emotions aside. Time was running out.

"Marshall, listen carefully. We have a sixty-second crash course to give you!"

Hank excused himself and returned to his excited flock.

When Bernice introduced Susan to Marshall, he thought he was extending his hand to nothing less than a miracle.

"I'd heard that you'd been killed, and Kevin too."

"I'm looking forward to sharing the whole story with you," Susan replied pleasantly, "but right now our time is very short and there's a lot you need to know."

Susan opened the trunk of her car and showed Marshall the contents of her battle-weary suitcase. Marshall loved every minute of it. It was all there, everything he thought he'd lost to sticky-fingered Carmen and these creeps, this "Society."

"Kaseph is coming to Ashton today to close the deal with the college board of regents. At 2 o'clock, the papers will be signed and the Whitmore College campus will be quietly sold to Omni Corporation."

"The Society, you mean," said Marshall.

"Of course. It's a key move. When the college goes, the town will ultimately go with it."

Bernice burst in with her news about Mattily, Parker, and Lemley, not to mention Harvey Cole's untangling of Baylor's records.

"So when do they get here?" Marshall asked.

"Hopefully in time for that board meeting. I told them to meet us there."

"I just might invite myself to the meeting. I know they'll all be very happy to see me."

Susan touched Marshall's arm and said, "But you need to be warned that they've been working on your daughter Sandy."

"Don't I know that!"

"They might have her under their influence right now; it's Kaseph's style, believe me. If you try to make a move against him, it could endanger her."

Bernice told Marshall about Pat, about the diary, about the mysterious friend named Thomas, and about that deceiving devil's advocate, Shawn Ormsby.

Marshall looked at them for a moment, then called, "Hank, this is where you and your people come in!"

A summer Sunday in Ashton is usually one of the happiest, carefree days of the week. The farmers jaw with each other; the storeclerks enjoy a leisurely pace; other business owners close up shop; moms, dads, and kids think of fun things to do and neat places to go. Many lawnchairs are occupied, the streets are a lot quieter, and families are usually together.

But this sunny, summer Sunday did not feel right to anyone: one farmer had a cow bloating on him while another had a tractor with a burned out magneto that no one seemed to have in stock; and though neither farmer was in any way responsible for the other's problems, they still got into a fight about it. The storeclerks working today were having trouble counting change, and were getting into very uncomfortable discussions with the customers whose change they were trying to count. Every business owner had no desire but to get out of his or her business, because no matter what it was, it was doomed to fail sooner or later. Many wives were nervous and wanted to go somewhere, anywhere, they didn't know where; their husbands would load the kids into all the station wagons, then the wives wouldn't want to go anymore, then the kids would get into fights in the cars, then their parents would get into fights, and then the families would go nowhere while the station wagons remained parked in all those driveways with screams coming through their windows and their horns honking. The lawnchairs either ripped through under their owners' bottoms or just plain couldn't be found; the streets were hectic with frantic drivers driving with no destination in mind; the dogs, those ever vigilant dogs of Ashton, were barking and howling and whining again, this time with their fur bristling, their tails up and their faces toward the east.

Faces toward the east? There were many. Here a college adminstrator, there a Post Office employee, over here a family of potters and weavers, over there an insurance salesman. All over the town, certain people who knew a certain destiny and a certain sympathetic spiritual vibration stood silently, as if worshiping, their faces toward the east.

And there was no small stir around the big dead tree. Rafar rose from his big branch, his gamemaster's seat of power, and stood on the hill, looking out over the little town of Ashton with his leering yellow eyes as his hordes of attending spirits gathered around him. His muscular arms rippled, his expansive black wings rising behind him like a royal train, his jewels gleaming and glittering in the sun.

He too looked toward the east.

He waited until he saw it. Then his breath sucked in through his fangs like a gasp of surprise, but this was no surprise. It was the highest kind of thrill, a demonic exhilaration such as he felt only rarely, a precious and very ripe fruit to be enjoyed only after much labor and preparation.

His black-haired hand grabbed the golden handle of his sword and he pulled the blade from its sheath, making it sing and drone and shimmer with blood-red light. The attending demons all gasped and cheered as Rafar held the sword high, bathing the whole gathering in its sinister red light. The huge wings suddenly disappeared into a blur and with a rush of wind and a blast of power they carried him into the air, out over the wide valley, out over the little town, out into the open where he could be seen from any part of the town or any hiding place near it.

He climbed to a lofty height, then hovered, his sword still in his hand. His head turned this way and that, his body slowly rotating, his eyes shifting about.

"Captain of the Hosts of Heaven!" he bellowed, and the echoes of his booming voice traveled back and forth across the valley like thunder. "Captain Tal, hear me!"

Tal could hear Rafar perfectly. He knew Rafar was about to make a speech, and he knew what the demon warlord was about to say. He too was watching the eastern horizon as he stood hidden in the forest, his chief warriors beside him.

Rafar continued to look everywhere for any sign of his adversary. "I who have never yet seen your face in this, our adventure, now show you mine! Behold it, you and your warriors! For today I place this face forever in your memory as the face of him who vanquished you!"

Tal, Guilo, Triskal, Krioni, Mota, Chimon, Nathan, Armoth, Signa—all were there together, gathered for this moment, gathered to listen to this long-awaited oration.

Rafar continued, "Today I place the name of Rafar, Prince of Babylon, forever in your memory as the name of him who remains bold and stands undefeated!" Rafar took a few more quick turns, looking all around him for any sign of his archenemy. "Tal, Captain of the Hosts of Heaven, will you dare to show your face to me? I think not! Will you even dare to assail me! I think not! Will you and your motley little band of highwaymen dare to stand in the path of the powers of the air?" Rafar threw in a derisive chuckle. "I think not!"

He paused for effect, and allowed himself a mocking grin. "I give you leave, dear Captain Tal, to withdraw yourself, to spare yourself the anguish awaiting you at my hand! I grant to you and to your warriors now the occasion to turn away, for I do pronounce that the battle's decision is made already!" Rafar then pointed his sword toward the eastern horizon and said, "Look to the east, captain! There is the outcome clearly written!"

Tal and his chiefs were already looking toward the eastern horizon, their attention rapt and unswerving, even when a young messenger came soaring in with the news—"Hogan and Busche are free! They've—" He stopped in midsentence. His eyes followed every other gaze to the east, and he saw what so held their interest.

"Oh, no!" he said in a whisper. "No, no!"

At first the cloud had been only a distant fingertip of blackness poking up over the horizon; it could have been a raincloud, or factory smoke, or a distant, haze-darkened mountain appearing suddenly. But then, as it drew nearer, its borders expanded outward like the slowly emerging edge of a blunt arrowhead stretching slowly and surely across the horizon like a dark shroud, like a steadily rising tide of blackness blocking out the sky. At first, one direct glance could contain it all; in just a few minutes, the eyes had to sweep back and forth, from one end of the horizon to the other.

"Not since Babylon," Guilo said quietly to Tal.

"They were there," said Tal, "every one of them, and now they're back. Look at the front ranks, flying multiple layers over, under, and within."

"Yes," said Guilo, observing. "Still the same style of assault."

A new voice said, "Well, so far, Tal, your plan is working very well. They've all come out of hiding, and in countless numbers."

It was the General. He was expected.

Tal answered, "And hopefully they are planning on a rout."

"At least your old rival is, to hear him boast."

Tal only smiled and said, "My General, Rafar boasts with or without reason."

"What of the Strongman?"

"By the shape of the cloud, I would say he precedes it by just a few miles."

"Having possessed Kaseph?"

"That would be my guess, sir."

The General looked carefully at the approaching cloud, now a deep, inky black and spread like a canopy across the sky. The deep, rumbling drone of the wings was just becoming audible.

"How do we stand?" the General asked.

Tal answered, "Prepared."

Then, as the sound of the wings grew louder and the shadow of the cloud began to fall across the fields and farmlands beyond Ashton, a reddish tint began to spread through the cloud as if it were burning from within.

"They've drawn their swords," said Guilo.

Why am I so afraid? Sandy wondered.

Here she was, holding Shawn's hand, going up the front steps of the Administration Building on campus, about to meet some people who had to be the real keys to her destiny, her stepping-stone to real spiritual fulfillment, to higher consciousness, maybe even to self-realization, and yet . . . all the talk could not remove a nagging fear she felt deep within her. Something just wasn't right. Maybe it was just a normal nervousness such as one would feel before a wedding or any other very significant event, or maybe it was that last remaining shred of her old, discarded Christian heritage still holding her, pulling her back as if with a leash. Whatever it was, she tried to ignore it, overcome it with reason, even use relaxation techniques she had learned in her college yoga class.

Come on, Sandy . . . steady breaths now . . . focus, focus . . . realign your energies.

There, that's better. I don't want Shawn or Professor Langstrat or anyone to think I'm not ready to be initiated.

All the way up the elevator she talked and prattled and tried to laugh, and Shawn laughed along, and by the time they reached the third floor and the door numbered 326, she thought she was ready.

Shawn opened the door, saying, "You'll love this," and they went in.

She didn't see them. To Sandy, this was only the staff lounge, a very pleasant room with soft carpet, leather-upholstered couches, and massive burl coffee tables.

But the room was occupied, very densely and hideously, and the yellow eyes glared and stared at her from all around, from every corner and chair and wall. They were waiting for her.

One hissed out asthmatically, "Hello there, child."

Sandy extended her hand to Oliver Young. "Pastor Young, what a pleasant surprise," she said.

Another let out a long, drooling snicker and said, "I'm very glad you could make it."

Sandy gave Professor Juleen Langstrat an embrace.

She looked around the room and recognized many of the college faculty, some of her own professors, even some business people and blue-collar workers from around town. There, in the corner, stood the new owner of what used to be Joe's Market. These thirty people looked like a cross section of Ashton's best.

The spirits were all ready and waiting. Deception showed her off like a trophy. Madeline was there, smiling wickedly, and beside her, or it, was another demon accomplice, with loop after loop of heavy glistening chains draped over his bony hands.

In the cloud, the myriads of demons were haughty, wild, drunk with the anticipation of victory, of slaughter, of unprecedented power and glory. Below them, the town of Ashton was a mere toy, such a very small little hamlet in such a vast countryside. Layer upon layer of spirits droned steadily forward, and myriads of yellow eyes peered down at the prize. The town was quiet and unguarded. Ba-al Rafar had done his work well.

A series of harsh screeches came from the front ranks of the cloud—the generals were calling out orders. Immediately the demon commanders on the fringes of the cloud relayed the orders to the swarms behind each of them, and as the commanders flew out from the cloud and began to drop downward, followed by their countless squadrons, the edges of the cloud began to wilt and stretch toward the ground.

In the large, formally furnished third-floor conference room, the regents began to gather. Eugene Baylor was there with a pile of financial records and reports, smoking a cigar and feeling chipper. Dwight Brandon looked just a little somber, but he was conversational enough. Delores Pinckston was not feeling well at all, and only wanted to get the whole thing over with. Kaseph's four lawyers, very professional, sharp-as-a-whip types, came in smirking. Adam Jarred strolled in and seemed more concerned with going fishing afterward than with the business they would be conducting. Every once in a while, someone would look at his watch or at the fancy clock on the wall. It would soon be 2 o'clock. Some were feeling just a little nervous.

The evil spirits that had come into the room with them were feeling nervous also—they realized they would soon be in the presence of the Strongman. This would be their very first time.

Alexander M. Kaseph's long, black, chauffeur-driven limousine entered the city limits and turned onto College Way. Kaseph sat in regal splendor in the back, cradling his briefcase in his lap and taking a lustful look out the tinted windows at the beautiful town passing by. He was making plans, envisioning changes, deciding what he would keep and what he would remove.

So was the Strongman, sitting inside him. The Strongman laughed his deep, gargling laugh, and Kaseph laughed the same way. The Strongman couldn't remember when he had been so pleased and so proud.

The cloud was drooping down at the edges as it continued to move forward, and Tal and his company kept watching from their hiding place.

"They're lowering their perimeter," said Guilo.

"Yes," said Tal with fascination. "As usual, they intend to contain the town on all sides before actually descending into it."

As they watched, the edges of the cloud dropped like black curtains that gradually wrapped around the town; demons were slipping into place like bricks in a wall. Every sword was drawn, every eye was wary.

"Hogan and Busche?" Tal asked a messenger.

"They are moving into place, along with the Remnant," the messenger answered.

Kaseph's limousine cruised toward the college, and Kaseph could see the stately, red brick buildings reaching up through the maples and oaks all around the campus. He looked at his watch. He would be right on time.

As the limousine passed through an intersection, a green, unmarked squad car pulled out onto College Way and began to follow. Its driver was Chief of Police Alf Brummel. He looked grim and very nervous. He knew whom he was following.

As the limousine and then the squad car passed through another intersection, the light changed and a stream of cars all turned right onto College Way and followed behind. The first car making the turn was the big brown Buick.

"Well, well!" said Marshall as he, Hank, Bernice, Susan, and Kevin all noticed the two cars they were following.

"Did you recognize Kaseph?" Susan asked Bernice.

"Yes, good old Pudgy himself."

Marshall had to wonder, "So what's up here? It looks like the meeting is still on, regardless."

Bernice said, "Maybe Brummel didn't believe me after all."

"Oh, he believed you, all right. He did everything you told him to do."

"So why hasn't Kaseph called this whole thing off? He's walking right into it."

"Either Kaseph thinks he's untouchable, or Brummel hasn't told him anything."

Hank looked behind them. "Looks like they all made it through the light."

The others looked back. Yes, there was Andy, driving his Volkswagen bus crammed with praying believers, and there came Cecil Cooper's pickup with the cab and the bed full. The ranch wagon of John and Patty Coleman followed behind that, and somewhere back there was the former pastor, James Farrel, driving a good-sized van carrying Mary and Grandma Duster and several others.

Marshall looked ahead, and then behind, and then concluded, "This is going to be one heck of a meeting."

39

At Juleen Langstrat's direction, all the smiling psychics, along with Sandy and Shawn, made themselves comfortable in the plush chairs and couches, arranged in a rough circle around the room.

"This is a significant day," said Langstrat warmly.

"Yes, indeed!" said Young.

The others also agreed. Sandy smiled back at them all. She was very impressed with the reverence they all seemed to have for this great woman, this great pioneer.

Langstrat assumed a lotus position in her big chair at the head of the group. Several others who had the desire and the flexibility did likewise. Sandy just relaxed where she was, settling into the couch and resting her head back.

"Our purpose here is to combine our psychic energies to assure the success of today's venture. Our long awaited goal will soon be realized: the Whitmore College campus, and afterward the whole town of Ashton, are going to become a part of the New World Order."

Everyone in the room started applauding. Sandy applauded as well, even though she didn't really know what Langstrat was talking about. It did sound vaguely familiar, though. Was it her own father who had said something about people wanting to take over the town? Oh, but he couldn't have been talking about the same thing!

"I have a wonderful new Ascended Master to introduce to you," said Langstrat, and faces all around the room immediately lit up with excitement and expectation. "He has lived long and traveled far, and has learned the wisdom of countless ages. He has come to Ashton to oversee this project."

"We welcome him," said Young. "What is his name?"

"His name is Rafar. He is a prince from long ago, and once ruled in ancient Babylon. He has lived many lives, and now returns to let us benefit from his wisdom." Langstrat closed her eyes and breathed deeply. "Let us call him, and he will speak to us."

Sandy could feel a queasiness in the pit of her stomach. She thought she felt chilled. The gooseflesh on her arms was real enough. But she brought these feelings under discipline, closed her eyes, and began her own relaxation, listening intently for the sound of Langstrat's voice.

The others also relaxed and went into a trance. For a moment the room was silent except for the deep breaths being drawn and expelled by everyone present.

Then the name formed on Langstrat's lips. "Rafar . . ."

They all echoed, "Rafar . . ."

Langstrat called the name again, and continued to call, and the others let all their thoughts narrow down to that one name as they spoke it softly.

Rafar was standing by the big dead tree, gleefully watching as the cloud spread over the town. At the sound of the call, his eyes narrowed with a very crafty expression and his mouth stretched slowly into a fang-baring grin.

"The pieces now fall into place," he said. He turned to an aide. "Any word from Prince Lucius?"

The aide was happy to report, "Prince Lucius says he has surveyed all fronts and finds no trouble or resistance."

Rafar roused ten demon monsters with a sweep of his wing, and they gathered at his side in an instant.

"Come," he said, "let us finish this business."

Rafar's wings clapped downward, and he shot into the air, his ten rogues following him like a regal honor guard. High above, the cloud stretched across the sky like an oppressive, light-blocking shroud, its shadow of evil and spiritual darkness falling over the town. As Rafar sailed over Ashton in a high arc, he could look up and see the myriads of yellow eyes and the red swords waving in salute. He waved his own sword back, and they cried out jubilantly, their numberless swords bristling downward like a wind-stirred, inverted field of crimson wheat. They filled the air with sulfur.

Ahead and far below was the Whitmore campus, the ripest of

ready plums. Rafar eased the whirring of his wings and began to drop toward the Administration Building.

As he descended, he saw the big limousine carrying the Strongman come up the circular drive and stop right at the building's front door. The sight filled him with exhilaration. This was it: *the* moment! He and his demon escorts disappeared through the roof of the building just as the Strongman and his human host emerged from the car . . . and just a little too soon to see a stream of cars not far behind that limousine, now finding parking spots here, there, and everywhere.

Alf Brummel got out of his car in one hurried jolt. He stood there for just a moment, building up courage, and then started for the main door of the building with stiff, jittery strides.

Marshall parked the Buick, and the five of them got out. All around, they could hear car doors slamming as the Remnant found parking spaces and then each other.

"Brummel doesn't look too happy," Marshall observed.

The other four looked just in time to see Brummel go through the front door.

"Maybe he's going to warn Kaseph," said Bernice.

"So where are all our powerful friends?" Marshall asked.

"Don't worry. . . at least not too much. They said they'd be here."

Susan said, "I'm quite sure the meeting is to take place in the third-floor conference room. It's where the board of regents usually meets."

"So where do I find Sandy?" Marshall asked.

Susan could only shake her head. "That I don't know."

They hurried toward the building, and from every direction the Remnant converged on the front steps.

Lucius could sense the tension in the air, like one huge rubber band pulled to its limit and about to snap. As he dropped quietly out of the sky and alighted on the roof of Ames Hall, right across the commons from the Administration Building, he could see the cloud still lowering its perimeter, spreading a thick drapery all around the town. The atmosphere became thick and choking with the presence of so many foul spirits.

Suddenly he heard a frantic flapping behind him and turned to see a little sentry demon, a petty creature, a busybody, flitting up to speak to him.

"Prince Lucius, people are gathering below! They are not *ours!* They are saints of God!" the little thing gasped.

Lucius was irritated. "I have eyes, little insect!" he hissed. "Pay them no mind."

"But what if they start praying?"

Lucius grabbed the little demon by one wing, and it fluttered about in pitiful little circles at the end of his arm. "Silence, you!"

"Rafar must know!"

"Silence!"

The little creature settled down, and Lucius brought him to the edge of the roof for a brief lesson.

"So what if they do pray?" Lucius said with a fatherly tone. "Has it helped them to this point? Has it slowed our progress one iota? And you have seen the power and might of Ba-al Rafar, have you not?" Lucius couldn't help the sarcastic tone with which he added, "You know that Rafar is all-powerful, and undefeatable, and does not need our help!" The little demon listened with wide eyes. "Let us not bother the great Ba-al Rafar with our petty worries! He can handle this endeavor . . . all by himself!"

Tal remained steady and kept watching. Guilo grew more and more restless, pacing about, looking from one end of the town to the other.

"Soon the perimeter will be entirely enclosed," he said. "They will have enveloped the entire town, and there will be no escape."

"Escape?" said Tal, his eyebrows raised.

"Purely a tactical consideration," Guilo replied with a shrug.

"The moment is approaching very quickly now," said Tal, looking toward the college. "In just a few minutes, all the players will be in their places."

The demons in the conference room could feel *him* coming, and they braced themselves. The hair bristled on their arms, necks, and backs. A darkness, a crawling cloud of evil was coming down the hall. Quickly each one looked himself over to make sure nothing was out of place, that his appearance was impeccable.

The door opened. They froze in respect and homage.

And there he stood, the Strongman, nothing less than the most horrible nightmare.

"Good day to you," he said.

"Good day to you, sir," the regents and lawyers answered Alexander Kaseph as he entered the room and started shaking their hands.

Alf Brummel had no desire to meet up with Alexander Kaseph. He even waited to take a different elevator. When the elevator opened on the third floor, he peeked to see if the coast was clear before he stepped out. Only after he heard the big door to the conference room down the hall click shut did he make his way down the hall himself, going very quietly to Room 326.

He stood for a moment outside the door, listening intently. It was pretty quiet in there. The session must be underway. He turned the knob very slowly and cracked the door just enough to see in. Yes, there was Langstrat in meditation, her eyes closed. She was the only one Brummel was worried about, and for now she wasn't looking.

He stepped into the room quietly and found a chair halfway around the circle from Langstrat. He looked around, sizing up the situation. Yes, they were calling for a certain spirit guide. He had never heard this particular name before. This entity must be some new personage brought in for the project today.

Oh no. There was Sandy Hogan, also meditating. She was calling the name as well. Well, Brummel, what do you do now?

Outside, the Remnant was ready for orders. Hank and Marshall gave them a very brief rundown on the present situation, and then Hank concluded, "We really don't know what we're going to encounter in there, but we know we have to go in, at least to see if we can locate Sandy. There's no question that this is a spiritual battle, so you know what you all have to do."

They all knew, and they were ready.

Hank continued, "Andy, I'd like you and Edith and Mary to take charge out here and lead in the prayer and worship. I'll be going inside with Marshall and the others."

Marshall conferred with Bernice. "Stay here and keep an eye out for our visitors. The rest of us will go in and see if we can find where this meeting is taking place."

Marshall, Hank, Kevin, and Susan went into the building. Bernice went to a vacant spot on the steps and sat down there to watch and wait. She could not help but observe the Remnant. There was something about them that felt all too familiar, and very . . . well, very wonderful.

Rafar and his ten escorts had been in the lounge for quite some time now, just listening and watching. Finally Rafar stepped up behind Langstrat and sank his talons deep into her skull. She twitched and gagged for a moment and then slowly, hideously, her countenance took on the unmistakable expressions of the Prince of Babylon himself.

"Indeeeeeeeeed!" said Rafar's deep, guttural voice from Langstrat's throat.

Everyone in the room shuddered. Several eyes popped open with a start, and then widened at the sight of Langstrat, her eyes bulging, her teeth bared, her back arched like a crouching lion. Brummel could only cringe and wish he could disappear into his chair before that thing spotted him. But it was looking at Sandy, drooling.

"Indeeeed!" the voice said again. "Have you come together to see your vision truly fulfilled? So it shall be!" The creature sitting in the chair pointed a crooked finger at Sandy. "And who is this newcomer, this searcher for the hidden wisdom?"

"S—Sandy Hogan," she answered, her eyes still closed. She was afraid to open them.

"I understand that you have walked many pathways with your instructor, Madeline."

"Yes, Rafar, I have."

"Descend within yourself again, Sandy Hogan, and Madeline will meet you there. We will wait."

Sandy had only a fraction of a second to wonder how she would ever be able to relax herself into an altered state. Then a slimy, death-like spirit behind her clapped his bony hand down on her head, and she went under immediately. Her eyes rolled upward, she wilted in her chair, and she felt her body dissolving away, along with her rational thoughts and nagging fears. All outside sensations began to vanish, and she was floating in pure, ecstatic nothingness. She heard a voice, a very familiar voice.

"Sandy," the voice called.

"Madeline," she answered. "I'm coming!"

Madeline appeared deep within some endless tunnel, floating forward, her arms outstretched. Sandy moved toward the tunnel to meet her. Madeline came into sharp focus, her eyes sparkling, her smile like warming sunshine. Their hands met and grasped each other tightly.

"Welcome!" said Madeline.

Alf Brummel watched it all happen. He could see the dopey, ecstatic look on Sandy's face. They were going to take her! All he could do was sit there and fidget and shake and sweat.

Lucius floated silently down through the roof of the Administration Building and landed on the third floor, folding his wings behind him. He could hear Rafar bellowing and boasting in the lounge; he could hear the Strongman going through his preliminaries in the conference room. So far they had no fears or suspicions.

He heard the elevator opening down the hall and then the footsteps of several people. Yes, this would be Hogan the hound and the praying man, Busche, and the one person the Strongman would be the most loath to see alive: the Maidservant.

Suddenly there was a flutter of wings and a frantic gasping. A demon shot down the hall toward him, wings rushing, his face filled with terror.

"Prince Lucius!" it cried. "Treachery! We've been tricked! Hogan and Busche are free! The Maidservant is alive! Weed is alive!"

"Silence!" Lucius cautioned.

But the demon just kept spouting. "The saints are gathered and are praying! You must warn the Ba-al—"

The demon's ranting ended abruptly in a choked gargle, and he looked at Lucius with his eyes full of horror and questions. He began to shrivel. He clawed at Lucius in an effort to remain upright. Lucius pulled his sword out of the demon's belly and swung it in a fiery arc through the ebbing body. The demon disintegrated, dissolved in a puff of red smoke.

Outside on the front steps, even as passersby stared and gawked, the Remnant was in prayer.

Sandy could see other beautiful beings emerging from the tunnel behind Madeline.

"Oh . . ." she asked, "who are these?"

"New friends," said Madeline. "New spirit guides to take you higher and higher."

Alexander Kaseph began to exchange important documents and contracts with the regents and the attorneys. They were discussing all the little loose ends that needed sewing up. Most of it was minor. It would not take long.

The cloud finally formed a complete enclosure around the town of Ashton. Tal and his company found themselves trapped under a thick, impenetrable tent of demons. The spiritual darkness became deep and oppressive. It was difficult to breathe. The steady drone of the wings seemed to permeate everything.

Suddenly Guilo whispered, "They're descending!"

They all looked up and could see the ceiling of demons, that boiling red and yellow tinted blanket of black, starting to settle downward, coming closer and closer to the town. Soon Ashton would be buried.

Several cars were just turning onto College Way. The first carried County Prosecutor Justin Parker, the second Eldon Strachan and State Attorney General Norm Mattily, the third Al Lemley and three federal agents. As they passed through an intersection, a fourth car turned right and joined the procession. This car just happened to carry that true-blue accountant Harvey Cole, with a sizable stack of papers beside him on the seat.

Tal now held a golden trumpet in his hand, gripping it very tightly, every muscle and every tendon tensed.

"Get ready!" he ordered.

40

Marshall, Hank, Susan, and Kevin walked quietly down the hall, listening for any sounds and checking the numbers on all the doors. Susan gestured toward the conference room, and they paused just outside. Susan recognized Kaseph's voice. She nodded to the others.

Marshall put his hand on the doorknob. He gestured to the others to wait. Then he opened the door and stepped inside. Kaseph sat at the head of the big conference table, and the regents and the four attorneys were seated around it. The demons in the room immediately drew their swords and backed up against the walls. Not only was this the very unexpected newspaperman, but he was accompanied by two very mean-looking heavenly warriors, a huge Arabian and a fierce African who looked more than ready for a fight!

The Strongman knew this meant trouble, but . . . not that much trouble. He looked at the intruders defiantly, even grinning just a little, and said, "And just who are you?"

"The name is Marshall Hogan," Marshall told Kaseph. "I'm the editor of the *Ashton Clarion*—that is, as soon as I prove to the right people that I still rightfully own it. But I understand you and I have had a lot to do with each other, and I think it's time we met."

Eugene Baylor did not like the looks of this at all, and neither did any of the others. They were speechless, and some looked like frightened mice with nowhere to run. They all knew where Hogan was supposed to be, but now, suddenly, shockingly, he was in the worst possible place: Here!

The Strongman's eyes took on an icy stare, and the demons attending him drew strength from the thought that the Strongman was invincible and diabolically clever. He would know what to do!

"How did you get *here*?" Kaseph asked for them all.

"I took the elevator!" Marshall snapped. "But now I have a question for you. I want my daughter, and I want her unharmed. Let's deal, Kaseph. Where is she?"

Kaseph and the Strongman only laughed derisively. "Deal, you say? You, a mere man, wish to deal with me?" Kaseph took a few side glances at his team of lawyers and added, "Hogan, you have no idea what kind of power you're dealing with."

The demons snickered along. Yes, Hogan, the Strongman cannot be tampered with!

Nathan and Armoth were not laughing.

"Oh, no," said Marshall. "That's where you're wrong. I do know what kind of power I'm dealing with. I've had some really good lessons all through this thing, and some good lectures from my friend here."

Marshall opened the door and in came Hank—and Krioni, and Triskal, this time under no orders of peace.

The Strongman jumped up, his jagged jaws gaping. The demons in the room started trembling and tried to hide behind their swords.

"Relax, relax!" said a lawyer. "They're nothing!"

But the Strongman could feel the presence of the Lord God enter the room with this man. The demon monarch knew who this was. "Busche! The praying man!"

And Hank knew whom he faced. The Spirit was crying it out very loudly within Hank's heart, and that face . . .

"The Strongman, I presume!" said Hank.

Sandy asked Madeline again, "Madeline, where are we going? Why are you hanging on to me so?"

Madeline would not answer but kept pulling Sandy deeper and deeper into the tunnel. Madeline's friends were all around Sandy, and they did not seem kind or gentle at all. They kept pushing her, grabbing her, forcing her along. Their fingernails were sharp.

The people around the conference table were shocked and nonplussed, suddenly finding themselves in the presence of a hideous creature; they had never seen such an expression on Kaseph's face before, and they had never heard such a vicious voice. Kaseph rose from his chair, his breath hissing through his teeth, his eyes bulging, his back arched, his fists clenched.

"You cannot defeat me, praying man!" the Strongman bellowed, and the demons around him clung with desperate hope to those words. "You have no power! *I* have defeated *you!*"

Marshall and Hank stood their ground unflinchingly. They had tackled demons before. This was nothing new or surprising.

Kaseph's attorneys could not think of anything to say.

Marshall reached over and opened the door. With her head held high and her face full of determination, Susan Jacobson, the Maidservant, stepped into the room, followed by the very angry Kevin Weed, and four more towering guards with them. The room was getting crowded, and tense.

"Hello, Alex," said Susan.

Kaseph's eyes were full of shock and fear, but still he gasped and sputtered, "Who are you? I don't know you. I've never seen you before."

"Don't say anything, Alex," an attorney advised him.

Hank stepped forward. It was time for battle.

"Strongman," Hank said in a firm and steady voice, "in the name of Jesus, I rebuke you! I rebuke you and I bind you!"

Madeline would not let go! Her hands felt like icy steel as she pulled Sandy along. The tunnel was getting dark and cold.

"Madeline!" Sandy cried. "Madeline, what are you doing? Please let go of me!"

Madeline kept her face forward and would not look back at Sandy. All Sandy could see was that long, flowing, blonde hair. Madeline's hands were hard and cold. They were hurting Sandy's wrists, cutting into them.

Sandy cried in desperation, "Madeline! Madeline, please stop!" Suddenly the other spirit guides pressed in all around her. They were clamping onto her, and their steely hands hurt. "Please, don't you hear me? Make them stop!"

Madeline turned her head at last. Her hide was soot-black and leathery. Her eyes were huge yellow orbs. Her jaws were the jaws of a lion, and saliva dribbled off her fangs. A low guttural growl rumbled out of her throat.

Sandy screamed. From somewhere in this blackness, this tunnel, this nothingness, this altered state, this pit of death and deception, she screamed from the depths of her tortured and dying soul.

Tal leaped from the earth. He exploded in a burst of wings and light. The ground dropped away and the town became a map below him as he shot over Ashton like a comet, piercing the spiritual darkness

like a fiery arrow, illuminating the whole valley like a prolonged lightning bolt. He climbed, he circled; his wings were a blurred flurry of
jewels.

The trumpet went to his lips, and the call went forth like a shock
wave to shake the heavens. It echoed across the valley and back again,
and back again, and back again. With wave after wave it washed over
the ground, it deafened the demons it soared down the streets and
rumbled through the alleys, it rang in every ear with volley after volley
of notes, building higher and sounding longer, and the still, thick air
was shattered with the sound. Tal blew and blew as he soared over the
town, his wings flashing, his garments glowing.

The moment had come.

The Strongman was suddenly silent. His big eyes rolled back and
forth.

"What was that?" he hissed.

The demons all around him were shaken and looking at him for
answers, but he had none.

The eight heavenly warriors drew their swords. That was answer
enough.

Rafar screamed through Langstrat, "*I* am speaking here! Let nothing else draw your attention!"

The demons in the room tried to pay attention again, as did the
psychics they controlled.

For a fraction of a moment, Madeline's grip weakened. But only
for a moment.

But they all knew they had heard something.

The evil warriors in the cloud steadily settled downward upon the
town; but now their eyes were dazzled by the sudden appearance of
one lone angel tracing brilliant streaks of light across the sky below
them. And what was this horribly loud trumpet all about? Were not the
heavenly forces already defeated? Did they dare to think they could
possibly defend this town?

Suddenly tiny bursts of light appeared all over the town far below,
flashes that did not dissipate but remained and grew brighter. They
thickened and grew in numbers and density. The town was on fire; it
was disappearing under myriads of tiny lights, as numerous as grains of
sand. It was blinding!

The eerie screams began at the center of the cloud and rippled outward across the layers upon layers of demons: "The Host of Heaven!"

Thunderous shouts began the moment Tal touched down on his hill and raised his blazing sword high above his head.

"For the saints of God and for the Lamb!"

Tal shouted it, Guilo shouted it, myriads of heavenly warriors shouted it, and the entire landscape from one end of the valley to the other, the entire town, and even the forested hills surrounding Ashton erupted in brilliant stars.

From the buildings, streets, alleys, sewers, lakes, ponds, vehicles, rooms, closets, nooks, crannies, trees, thickets, and every other imaginable hiding place, flaming stars shot into the air.

The Host of Heaven!

Sandy was tumbling, struggling. The thing called Madeline had both her arms; the other spirits held her legs, her neck, her torso. They were biting her. From somewhere the mocking voice of the Ascended Master, Rafar, said, "Take her, Madeline! We have her! We cannot fail now."

Sandy tried to get out of the trance, out of the altered state, out of the nightmare, but she couldn't remember how. She heard the metallic clinking of chains. No! NOOOOO. . . .

"You cannot defeat me!" the Strongman screamed, and his demons hoped, or rather wished it were true.

"Be quiet and come out of him!" Hank ordered.

His words threw the demons against the walls and hit the Strongman like a left hook.

Kaseph hissed and spat curses and obscenities at the young minister. The regents around the table were all speechless; some ducked under the table. The lawyers were trying to calm Kaseph down.

"I want my daughter!" Marshall said. "Where is she?"

"It's all over," said Susan. "I've given them all the right documents! The feds are coming to hang you, and I'm going to tell them everything!"

From behind the other three Kevin shouted, "Kaseph, you think you're so tough, let's step outside and settle this man to man!"

The descending cloud of demons and the rising fireball of angels began to collide in the skies over Ashton. Thunder began to rip the sky in response to the terrific clash of the spiritual forces. Swords flashed, and a hail of screams and shouts echoed across the sky. The heavenly warriors mowed through the ranks of demons like blurring scythes. Demons began to fall out of the sky like meteors, spinning, smoking, dissolving.

Tal, Guilo and the General streaked toward the college, swords ready, the town a blur beneath them. A very strong regiment of angelic hosts had pushed its way through the demonic offensive and began cordoning off the college campus. Soon there would be an angelic canopy over the college within the demonic canopy over the town. The breaking of the enemy's strength would begin there.

"They have nearly contained the Strongman!" Guilo shouted over the roar of the wind and their wings.

"Find Sandy!" Tal ordered. "There is no time to spare!"

"I'll take the Strongman," said the General.

"And Rafar will soon get his wish," Tal said.

They fanned out, shot forward with a new burst of speed, and began cutting their way through the demons who were still trying to blockade the college. The demon warriors fell upon them like an avalanche, but for Guilo this was good sport. Tal and the General could hear his uproarious laughter through the thudding sounds of his blade going through demon after demon.

Tal was busy himself, being such a valuable prize for the demon lucky enough to vanquish him. The most horrible warriors were singling him out, and they didn't fall easily. He skidded through the air sideways, slammed one spirit with his sword, went into a blurred spin and split the next warrior with the force of a saw-blade. Two more dove down at him; he shot toward them, impaled the first as he passed it, grabbed its wingtip and whipped around in a tight circle, coming up behind the other, his blade like a bullet. They vanished in a cloud of red smoke. He slipped through the clutches of several more, then dove and zigzagged toward the college, cutting demons down as he went. He could hear Guilo still roaring and laughing somewhere over his left shoulder.

The conference room was quickly losing its calm atmosphere.

Delores Pinckston was distraught. "I knew it! I knew it! I knew we were all getting in too deep!"

"Hogan," fumed Eugene Baylor, "you're only bluffing. You have nothing."

"I have *everything*, and you know it."

Kaseph was beginning to look very ill. "Get out! Get out of here! I'll kill you if you don't leave!"

Was this the real Kaseph that Marshall had been tracking down all this time? Was this the ruthless occult mobster who controlled such a vast international empire? Was he actually *afraid?*

"You're sunk, Kaseph!" said Marshall.

"You're defeated, Strongman!" said Hank.

The Strongman began to shake. The demons in the room could only cower.

"So let's deal," Marshall offered again. "Where's my daughter?"

Brummel was about to have a heart attack, and he wished he really could. It was horrible! The others were sitting around the room listening raptly to this beast speaking through Langstrat, and actually relishing what was happening to Sandy. She trembled and shook in her chair, moaning, screaming, struggling against some unseen assailant.

"Let me go!" she screamed. "Let me go!"

Her eyes were wide open, but she was seeing unspeakable horrors from another world. She gasped for air, pale with terror.

She's going to die, Brummel! They are going to kill her!

The hulking, bug-eyed creature sitting in Langstrat's chair was bellowing in a voice that made Brummel's insides quiver. "You are lost, Sandy Hogan! We have you now! You belong to us, and we are the only reality you know!"

"Please, God," she screamed. "Get me out of here, please!"

"Join us! Your mother has fled, your father is dead! He is gone! Think of him no longer! You belong to us!"

Sandy went limp in her chair as if she had been shot. Her face suddenly numbed with despair.

Brummel could take no more. Before he had time to realize what he was doing, he jumped out of his chair and ran to her. He shook her gently and tried to speak to her.

"Sandy!" he pleaded. "Sandy, don't listen to them! It's all a lie! Do you hear me?"

Sandy could not hear him.

But Rafar could. Langstrat jumped up from her chair and screamed at Brummel in that same, deep, devilish voice, "Be silent, you little imp, and step aside! She belongs to *me!*"

Brummel ignored her. "Sandy, don't listen to this lying monster. This is Alf Brummel talking to you. Your father is all right."

Rafar's rage grew so that Langstrat's body nearly burst from the intensity of it. "Hogan is defeated! He is imprisoned!"

Brummel looked right into Langstrat's—and Rafar's—crazed eyes and shouted, "Marshall Hogan is free! Hank Busche is free! I released them myself! They are free, and they are coming to destroy you!"

Rafar was stymied for a moment. He simply could not believe the ravings of this weak little man, this insignificant little puppet who had never before acted in this brazen fashion. But then Rafar heard a very inappropriate snicker coming from behind Brummel, and he saw a familiar face laughing him to scorn.

Lucius!

Tal and Guilo swooped down into the Administration Building, but Tal suddenly stopped short.

"Wait now! What is this?"

Lucius drew his sword and said, "You are not so mighty, Rafar! Your plan has failed, and I am the only true Prince of Ashton!"

Rafar's sword rang from its sheath. "Do you dare to oppose *me?*"

Rafar's sword cut through the air with a rush of wind, but Lucius stopped the big blade with his own; the force of the blow almost knocked him over.

The many demons in the room were startled and confused. They let go of their hosts. What was *this?*

Kaseph was indignant with his lawyers and even threw some punches at them. "Stop it! You will not tell me what to do! This is *my* world! *I* am in charge here! *I* say what is and what is not! These people are fools and liars, every one of them!"

Susan spoke directly to Kaseph. "You, Alexander Kaseph, are responsible for the murder of Patricia Krueger *and* the attempted murder of myself and Mr. Weed here. I have the many lists I helped you write up, lists of people who ended up dead by your order."

"Murder!" exclaimed one regent. "Mr. Kaseph, is this true?"

"Don't answer that," said a lawyer.

"No!" Kaseph screamed.

Several other regents looked at each other. They knew Kaseph pretty well by now. They didn't believe him.

"How about it, Kaseph?" Marshall said grimly.

The Strongman wanted with all his evil heart to lunge at this brazen hound and maul him, and he would have, guards or no guards—if not for that horrible praying man who stood in the way.

Langstrat stalked like a lion toward Brummel, as many of the psychics, having lost their spirit guides, came out of their trances to see what in the world had happened.

"I will vanquish you for this treachery!" she hissed at him.

"What is this?" Oliver Young demanded. "Have you both gone mad?"

Brummel stood his ground and pointed a shaking finger at Langstrat. "You will no longer rule over me. This plan will not succeed for your glory. I will not let it!"

"Be quiet, you little fool!" Langstrat ordered.

"No!" Brummel shouted, driven on by the crazed and brazen Lucius. "The Plan is doomed. It has failed, just as I knew it would."

"And *you* are doomed, Rafar!" Lucius screamed, dodging the lethal thrusts of Rafar's sword. "Do you hear the battle outside? The Hosts of Heaven are everywhere!"

"Treachery!" Rafar hissed. "You will pay for your treachery!"

"Treachery!" some of the demons cried.

"No, Lucius speaks the truth!" others shouted back.

Sandy forced herself to look into those evil yellow eyes and plead, "What's—what's happened to you, Madeline? Why have you changed?"

Madeline only cackled and answered, "Do not believe what you see. What is evil? It is but an illusion. What is pain? It is but an illusion. What is fear? It is but an illusion."

"But you lied to me! You deceived me!"

"I have never been other than I am. It is you who have deceived yourself."

"What are you going to do?"

"I am going to set you free."

Just as Madeline spoke those words, Sandy's arms suddenly dropped with such a ponderous weight that she almost fell to the ground.

Chains! Links upon links of glistening, heavy chains hung around her wrists and her arms. Crooked hands were whipping them around her. The cold and bruising links slapped against her legs, her body, her neck. She could no longer struggle against them. She tried to scream, but her breath was gone.

"Now you are free!" Madeline said gleefully.

Brummel started speaking for himself. "The authorities . . . the state attorney general . . . Justin Parker . . . the feds! They know everything!"

"What?" some of the psychics cried, jumping out of their seats. They started to ask questions, to panic.

Young tried to keep order, but he was failing.

Rafar dropped his hold on Langstrat so he could better handle this traitorous upstart.

Langstrat snapped out of her trance and could feel the psychic energy in the room collapsing.

"Get back in your seats, everyone!" she shouted. "We have not accomplished our purpose here!" She closed her eyes and called out, "Rafar, please return! Bring order!"

But Rafar was busy. Lucius was smaller, but he was very quick and very determined. The two swords flashed about the room like fireworks, burning and clanging. Lucius flitted about Rafar's head like a pesky hornet, jabbing, swinging, and slashing. The whole room was filled with Rafar's swirling wings and his chugging breath, and his big sword traced fiery red sheets through the air.

"Traitor!" Rafar screamed. "I'll cut you to pieces!"

Langstrat moved toward Brummel with wild eyes. "Traitor! I'll tear you apart!"

"No," Brummel muttered with widened eyes, his hand going to his side. "Not this time . . . no more!"

Young shouted at them both, "Stop it! You don't know what you're doing!"

The demons in the room were dividing into camps.

"Prince Lucius speaks the truth!" said some. "Rafar has led us to our doom!"

"No, it is *Lucius* who is the enemy's fool!"

"You are the fools, but we will save ourselves!"

More swords flashed into view.

Rafar knew he was losing control.

"Fools!" he roared. "This is a trick of the Enemy! He is trying to divide us!"

It only took that one brief moment when Rafar's eyes were on his quarreling demons and not on Lucius's sword.

It only took that one moment of terror to push Brummel over the edge. He pointed his police revolver at the wild-eyed Langstrat.

Lucius's blade sang through the air and slipped just under Rafar's parrying sword. The tip ripped deeply through Rafar's hide and opened his flank with a deep, gushing wound.

Langstrat made just one wrong move and the bullet thudded into her chest.

In the conference room they all heard the shot. Marshall was out in the hall in an instant.

41

Bernice leaped from her spot on the front steps. It was Eldon Strachan with Norm Mattily himself, and Justin Parker, and that had to be Al Lemley—and those three guys in their nice three-piece suits had to be FBI! Oh, and there was Harvey Cole with a stack of papers under his arm.

She ran up to them, her black eyes wild with excitement. "Hello! You made it!"

Norm Mattily's eyes got big. "What's happened? Are you all right?"

Bernice had paid a lot for these bruises; she was going to use them. "No, no, I've been attacked! Please hurry inside! Something terrible is happening!"

The VIPs ran into the building with serious business in their eyes and guns in their hands.

Tal had seen enough. He shouted the order to Guilo, "Go in!" and then soared out of the building to signal for more troops.

Smoke and red tar were pouring from Rafar's side, but his rage spelled certain doom for the rebellious Lucius. The light of a thousand angels beamed in through the windows. They would be in the room in an instant, but that was all the time Rafar needed. He whipped his plank-sized sword in vicious circles over his head. He brought it down in blow after blow upon Lucius as the defiant demon's little sword parried every blow with a loud clang and a shower of sparks.

The roar of angels' wings outside grew louder, louder. The floors and walls rumbled with the sound.

Rafar let out a roar and brought the blade straight down. Lucius blocked the blow, but collapsed under the power of it. The blade ripped through the air in a flat circle and caught Lucius under the arm. The arm went spinning into space, and Lucius cried out. The blade came down again, passed straight through Lucius's head, shoulders, torso. The air filled with boiling red smoke.

Lucius was gone.

"Kill the girl!" Rafar shouted to Madeline.

Madeline drew out a horrible, crooked knife. She placed it gently in Sandy's hand. "These chains are the chains of life; they are a prison of evil, of the lying mind, of illusion! Free your true self! Join me!"

Shawn had a knife ready. He placed it in the entranced Sandy's hand.

Rafar staggered through a wall just as the light of a million suns exploded into the room with a deafening thunder of wings and the warcries of the Heavenly Host.

Many demons tried to flee, but were instantly disintegrated by slashing swords. The whole room was one huge, bombastic, brilliant blur. The roar of the wings drowned out every sound except the screams of falling spirits.

Kaseph leaped from his chair and fell across the table. The regents and lawyers shied away and pressed against the wall. Some headed for the room's other door.

Hank, Susan, and Kevin watched from a safe distance. They knew what was happening.

Kaseph's face seemed numb with death and his mouth hung open as the most hideous scream came out of him.

The Strongman was face to face with the General. His demons

were gone, washed away by an overwhelming tide of angels that were still roaring through the room like an avalanche. The General's sword moved faster than the ponderous Strongman could even anticipate. The Strongman fought back, screaming, slashing, swinging. The General just kept coming at him.

Marshall was out in the hall, listening for any disturbance. He thought he heard a commotion from down the hall.

Sandy still held that knife, but now Madeline was hesitating and looking around frantically. The chains still held Sandy tightly, an iron cocoon.

Guilo could see the chains wrapped tightly around her, the horrible demonic bondage they had used to enslave her.

"No more!" he shouted.

He raised his sword high above his head and brought it down, trailing a wide ribbon of light. The tip passed through the many windings of those chains like a series of small explosions. The chains burst outward and away from her, writhing like severed snakes.

Guilo's big fist clamped onto the fleeing Madeline's grisly neck. He jerked her backward, spun her around, and hacked her into vanishing particles.

Sandy felt herself spinning, then rushing upward as if she were a rocket in an elevator shaft. Sounds began to register on her ears. She could feel her physical body again. Light registered on her retinas. She opened her eyes. A knife fell from her hands.

The room was in chaos. People were screaming, running back and forth, trying to calm each other down, fighting, arguing, trying to escape from the room; several men were wrestling Alf Brummel to the floor. There was a haze of blue smoke and a strong smell like fireworks.

Professor Langstrat was lying on the floor, with several people huddled over her. There was blood!

Someone grabbed her. Not again! She looked to see Shawn holding her arm. He was trying to comfort her, trying to keep her in her chair.

The monster! The deceiver! The liar!

"Let me go!" she screamed at him, but he wouldn't let go.

She hit him in the face, then pulled away from him; she leaped to her feet and ran for the door, bumping into several people and stepping on some others. He went after her, calling her name.

She burst through the door and stumbled out into the hall. From somewhere down the hall she heard a familiar voice shouting her name. She screamed and ran for that voice.

Shawn went after Sandy. He had to contain this woman before all control was lost.

What! Before him, filling the entire hallway with fiery wings, stood the most frightening being he had ever seen, holding a terrible flaming sword right at his heart. Shawn braked to a stop, his shoes skidding on the floor.

Marshall Hogan appeared suddenly, running right through that being. A huge fist slammed into Shawn's jaw, and the whole matter was settled.

"C'mon, Sandy," Marshall said, "we'll take the stairs!"

Rafar, somewhere inside that shaking, besieged building, knew he had to get out. He tried to get his wings to stir. They only quivered. He had to build up the strength. He could not be defeated in the presence of these petty warriors; he would not go to the abyss!

He sank to one knee, his hand holding his oozing side, and let his rage grow inside him. Tal! This was all Tal's doing! No, clever captain, you'll not gain your victory this way!

The yellow eyes burned with new fire. He tried again. This time his wings roused themselves and went into a blurred rushing. Rafar gripped his sword tightly and turned his eyes skyward. The wings surged with power and began to lift him up through the building, faster and faster, until he soared up through the roof and into the open air . . . and found himself face to face with the very captain he had taunted and challenged time and again.

All around them the battle raged; demons—and Rafar's great victory—fell like smoking, burning rain from the sky. But for one very short moment of awe and mutual horror, Tal and Rafar remained frozen.

They had met at last! And each could not help but be numbed by the memories he had of the other. Neither remembered the other looking so fierce.

And neither could be entirely sure of winning this contest.

Rafar shot sideways, and Tal braced himself for a blow, but—Rafar was fleeing! He dashed away across the sky like a bleeding bird, trailing a stream of ooze and vapor.

Tal went after him, wings rushing, dashing this way and that through falling demons and charging angels, looking far ahead through the wild flurry of the battle clashing and thundering all around. There! He spotted the demon warlord dipping down toward the town. He would be hard to find in that maze of buildings, streets, and alleys. Tal quickened his speed and closed the distance. Rafar must have seen him coming up from behind; the evil prince shot ahead with a surprising burst of speed and then dropped suddenly and sharply toward an office building.

Tal saw him disappear through the roof of that building and dove after him. The black tar roof came at him, growing in an instant from the size of a postage stamp to more than the eye could see. Tal plunged through it.

Roof, room, floor, room, then pull up, then down a hall, through a wall, up again, turn back, follow that smoke, through an office, follow up a wall, dip through a floor, rush along, the passing walls slap, slap, slapping the eyes and rushing past like speeding freight cars.

A smoking black missile followed by a flaming comet roared down the hall, down through several floors, back up again, right through the office and over all the desks, up through the ceiling panels, up through the roof and out into the open sky again.

Rafar was soaring, dashing, looping, zigzagging through falling demons, doubling back, ducking down side streets, but Tal stayed right on his tail and retraced his every turn perfectly.

How much longer could that bleeding demon keep this up?

The other door of the conference room burst open, and the body of Alexander Kaseph rolled across the hallway floor. He was retching and screaming.

The General swung his sword at the Strongman again and again, weakening him, cutting him more and more frequently as the Strongman continued to lose his power.

"You will not defeat me!" the Strongman still boasted, as did Kaseph, but the boast was empty and futile. The Strongman was gushing red vapor and tar like a wretched and broken sieve. His eyes were full of evil and hate and he slashed with his big sword, but the prayers . . . ! The prayers could be felt everywhere, and the General could not be defeated.

Bernice had her group of vindicators gathered in the lobby downstairs, and she was trying to figure out where to start explaining everything when Marshall and Sandy burst out of the stairway door.

"Get yourselves upstairs!" Marshall hollered, holding his weeping daughter. "Someone's been shot!"

Lemley's feds went right into action. "Call the police! We'll cordon off the building!"

Bernice remarked, "I see some cops outside there . . ."

The police had come purely in response to a call about all these religious fanatics assembled on the campus. They were trying to break up the gathering when Norm Mattily and one federal agent ran out to them, identified themselves, and ordered them to close off the building.

Brummel's men were no fools. They obeyed.

Rafar darted and weaved all over the sky, still trailing a stream of red smoke from his wound. With that telltale marker it was easy to follow him, and Tal kept up the chase unrelentingly. Rafar sped toward a very large warehouse several blocks away.

He shot through the outside wall at about the third floor, and Tal dove into the building after him. This floor was open, with no places to hide; Rafar dove immediately to a lower floor, and Tal followed that trail of smoke. The gray, concrete floors came up at them.

Tal came out on the first floor and could see the smoke trail veering off sideways and corkscrewing through the distant wall. He shot after it. The wall slapped around him as he passed through.

Impaled!

A burning edge cut through his side! He spun and spun from the impact and the sword went flying from his hand. He tumbled to the floor, doubled up with pain.

There stood Rafar, bent and wounded, his back against the wall Tal had just come through. He had been waiting in ambush. The tip of his ugly sword was still draped with part of Tal's tunic.

No time to think! No time to feel pain! Tal dove for his fallen sword.

Crash! Rafar's sword came down with a shower of sparks. Tal rolled and fluttered out of the way. The big red sword ripped through the air again, and the keen edge whistled just over Tal's head. Tal clapped his wings and jerked sideways several feet.

Whoosh! That horrible sword sliced the air with brilliant red streaks. Rafar's eyes turned from yellow to red, his mouth frothed with putrid foam.

The huge wings roared, and Rafar came at Tal like a pouncing cat. His powerful arm raised that blade to strike again.

Tal lurched forward and ducked under Rafar's raised arm, his head butting into Rafar's chest. The sulfur exploded from those huge lungs as Tal spun around Rafar's body and beyond the tip of that red blade as it slashed through the air.

This was what Tal needed: he was now between Rafar and his fallen sword. He dove at it, grabbed it, and turned.

Clang! The blade of hell came down upon Tal's sword with a flash of fire. They faced each other, swords held ready. Rafar was grinning.

"So now, Captain of the Host, we are alone together, and evenly matched. I am opened, and you are opened. Shall we assail each other for *another* twenty-three days? We will be finished long before that, eh?"

Tal said nothing. This was Rafar's way; cutting words were part of his strategy.

The swords met again, and again. An envelope of darkness began to fill the room: Rafar's creeping, growing evil.

"Is the light fading?" Rafar sneered. "Perhaps it is your *strength* we now see ebbing away!"

Saints of God, where are your prayers?

Another blow! Tal's shoulder. He returned with a swipe that caught Rafar under the ribs. The air was filling with darkness, with red vapor and smoke.

Several more clashes of the fiery blades . . . ripping hides, tearing garments, more darkness.

Saints! Pray! PRAY!

When the police reached the third floor, they thought at first that Kaseph was the gunshot victim. They found out differently when this wild animal threw them off as if they weighed nothing.

"You cannot defeat me!" he screamed.

The General slashed at the Strongman again, and the Strongman screamed again. The swords clashed and sang and flashed with fire.

"You cannot defeat me!"

The police aimed their guns. What was this nut going to do next?

Hank shouted, "No, take it easy! It's not him!"

They did not understand that statement at all.

Hank stepped forward and gave it one more try: "Strongman, I know you can hear me. You *are* defeated. The shed blood of Jesus has defeated you. Be silent and come out of him and depart from this region!"

Now the police were aiming at *Hank!*

But the Strongman could take no more of this praying man's rebukes. He wilted. His sword dropped. The General took one swipe with his flashing blade, and the Strongman was gone.

Kaseph collapsed to the floor and lay there as if dead. The lawyers and regents shouted from the conference room, "Don't shoot!" and came out with their hands raised whether ordered to or not. The police still did not know who to arrest.

"In here!" someone shouted from the lounge. The police ran in and found the pitiful wreck that Alf Brummel had become, and the very deceased Juleen Langstrat.

42

Rip! Rafar's sword took off a corner of Tal's wing. Tal kept darting and flitting, dodging and swinging, and he clipped Rafar's shoulder and thigh. The air was filled with the stench of sulfur; the evil darkness was thick like smoke.

"The Lord rebuke you!" Tal shouted.

Clang! Rip!

"Where is the Lord?" Rafar mocked. "I see Him not!"

Whoosh!

Tal screamed in pain. His left hand hung useless.

"Lord God," Tal cried, "His name is Rafar! Tell them!"

The Remnant were not praying so much now; instead they watched all the excitement and the police dashing in and out of the Administration Building.

"Wow!" said John Coleman. "The Lord's really answering our prayers!"

"Praise the Lord!" Andy replied. "That just goes to show . . . Edith! Edith, what's wrong?"

Edith Duster had sunk to her knees. She was pale. The saints gathered around.

"Should we call an aid car?" someone asked.

"No! No!" Edith cried. "I know this feeling. I've felt it before. The Lord is trying to speak to me!"

"What?" asked Andy. "What is it?"

"Well, quit your gabbing and let me pray and I'll tell you!"

Edith started to weep. "There's still an evil spirit out there," she cried. "He's doing great mischief. His name is . . . Raphael . . . Raving . . ."

Bobby Corsi spoke up. "Rafar!"

Edith looked up at him with wide eyes. "Yes! Yes! That's the name the Lord's impressing upon me!"

"Rafar!" Bobby said again. "He's the big wheel!"

Tal could only back away from the fearsome onslaught of the demon prince, his one good hand still holding his sword up for defense. Rafar kept swinging and slashing, the sparks flying from the blades as they met. Tal's arm sank lower with each blow.

"The Lord . . . rebuke you!" Tal found the breath to say again.

Edith Duster was on her feet and ready to shout it to the heavens. "Rafar, you wicked prince of evil, in the name of Jesus we rebuke you!"

Rafar's blade zinged over Tal's head. It missed.

"We bind you!" shouted the Remnant.

The big yellow eyes winced.

"We cast you out!" Andy said.

There was a puff of sulfur, and Rafar bent over. Tal leaped to his feet.

"We rebuke you, Rafar!" Edith shouted again.

Rafar screamed. Tal's blade had torn him open.

The big red blade came down with a clang against Tal's, but that angelic sword was singing with a new resonance. It cut through the air in fiery arcs. With his one good hand, Tal kept swinging, slashing, cutting, pushing Rafar back. The fiery eyes were oozing, the foam was bubbling out the mouth and fizzing down the chest, the yellow breath had turned deep crimson.

Then in one horrible, rage-empowered swipe, the huge red sword came sizzling through the air. Tal went tumbling backward like a tossed rag toy. He fell to the floor stunned, his head spinning, his body drenched in fiery pain. He could not move. His strength was gone.

Where was Rafar? Where was that blade? Tal tried to turn his head. He strained to see. Was that his enemy? Was that Rafar?

Through the vapor and darkness he could see Rafar's battered frame swaying like a big tree in the wind. The demon did not move, he did not charge. As for the sword, the huge hand still held it, but the blade now hung limply, the tip resting on the floor. The breaths were coming in long, slow wheezes. The nostrils spewed deep red clouds. Those eyes—those hate-filled eyes—were like huge, glowing rubies.

The dripping, foaming jaws trembled open, and the words gargled through the tar and the froth. "But . . . for . . . your . . . praying saints! But for your saints . . . !"

The big beast swayed forward. He let out one last hissing sigh, and rumbled to the floor in a cloud of red.

And it was quiet.

Tal could not breathe. He could not move. All he could see was red vapor spreading along the floor like thin fog and darkness all around that huge body.

But . . . yes. Somewhere the saints were praying. He could feel it. He was healing.

What was that? From somewhere the sweet music found its way to him. It soothed him. Worship. The name of Jesus.

He lifted his head up from the floor and let his eyes explore the cold, concrete room. Rafar, the mighty, loathsome Prince of Babylon, was gone. Nothing remained but a shrinking cloud of darkness. Above the cloud of darkness light was coming through, almost like a sunrise.

He could still hear the music. It echoed throughout the heavenlies, washing them clean, clearing away the darkness with God's holy light.

And his heart was the first to tell him: You've won . . . for the saints of God and for the Lamb.

You've won!

The light grew and grew, blossoming, filling the room, and the darkness continued to shrink and ebb and fade away. Now Tal could see light coming in through the windows. Sunlight? Yes.

The Heavenly Host? Yes!

Tal struggled to his feet and waited for more strength. It came. He stepped forward. His gait became firm and steady. Then, like unfurling silk spun from sparkling diamonds, he spread his wings, fold by fold, inch by inch. They blossomed outward from his shoulders and back, and he let them grow strong.

He drew a deep breath, took the handle of his sword in both hands, held it out in front of him, and the wings took over. He was into the air, climbing into the fresh, light-washed sky, looking straight up and seeing no darkness, no oppression, no clouds.

What he did see was light: light from the Heavenly Host as they swept the sky clean from one end to the other. The air was so fresh, the smells were so clean.

He sailed over the little town and back to the college just in time to see the many flashing lights of squad cars and aid cars and official cars parked everywhere.

Where was Guilo? Oh, where was that blustery Guilo?

"Captain Tal!" came the shout, and Tal dropped toward Ames Hall where his burly friend awaited him with an almost crushing bear hug.

"Surely the battle is over?" Guilo roared happily.

"*Is* it?" Tal wanted to know.

He looked all around to make sure. Yes, in the very great distance he could see the last fleeing fragments of the cloud scattering in all directions, swept away by the heavenly forces. The sky was a very lovely blue. Below them he could see the faithful Remnant still singing and cheering. It looked like the police were going through some kind of final clean-up.

Norm Mattily, Justin Parker, and Al Lemley huddled around Bernice and her new friend.

"Well, everybody," said Bernice, "I'd like you to meet Susan Jacobson. She has a lot to show you!"

Norm Mattily took Susan's hand and said, "You are a very brave woman."

Susan could only point at Bernice through tears of relief and say, "Mr. Mattily, look right there. You're looking at bravery personified."

Bernice looked at the stretcher being carried out of the building by two medics. Juleen Langstrat was completely covered with a white sheet. Behind the stretcher came Alf Brummel, handcuffed and escorted by two of his own officers.

Behind Brummel came the number-one man himself, Alexander M. Kaseph. Susan stared at him long and hard, but he never raised his eyes. He got into the squad car with a federal agent without saying a word.

Hank and Mary were embracing and crying because it was over . . . and yet it was just beginning. Look at all these fired-up saints! Hallelujah—what God could do with a bunch like them!

Marshall held Sandy as if he had never held her before. Both of them had lost count of how many times they had each said they were sorry. All they wanted to do now was get caught up on some badly missed love.

And then . . . what was this, some kind of fairy tale? Forget the doubts and the questions, Hogan, that's *Kate* coming your way! Her face was shining, and boy, did she look good!

All three of them held on to each other, and the tears dripped all over everybody.

"Marshall," Kate said with tearful giddiness, "I couldn't possibly stay away. I heard you were *arrested!*"

"Aw," Marshall said, giving her a loving squeeze, "how else was God ever going to get my attention!"

Kate cuddled close to him and said, "Wow, this does sound promising!"

"Just wait'll I tell you about it."

Kate looked around at all the people and the activity. "Is this the end of your . . . big project?"

He smiled, held his two favorite girls, and said, "Yeah, it is. You *bet* it is!"

The General touched Tal on the shoulder. Tal looked and saw that big, golden trumpet in the General's hand.

"Well, captain," said the silver-haired angel, "how about doing the honors? Sound the victory!"

Tal took the trumpet in his hand and found he could not see through a sudden flow of tears. He looked down at all those praying saints and that little praying pastor.

"They . . . they will never know what they have done," he said. Then he took a breath to sober up and turned to his old buddy-in-arms. "Guilo, how about you?" He pushed the trumpet toward the big angel.

Guilo was reluctant. "Captain Tal, you are always the one who sounds the victory."

Tal smiled, gave Guilo the trumpet, and sat down right there on the roof. "Dear friend . . . I am just too tired."

Guilo thought about that for one short moment, then started guffawing, then slapped Tal on the back and sailed into the air.

The victory signal went forth loud and clear, and Guilo even did a tight corkscrew climb for effect.

"He loves to do that!" said Tal.

The General laughed.

So Hank had Mary and his little newborn church; Marshall had his family back together again, ready to patch things up; Susan and Kevin would be busy for a while as state witnesses; Bernice figured Marshall would let her cover the story to its final end.

But as Bernice stood there, bruised and exhausted, she felt very separate, far away from this happy crowd. She was glad for them, and her professional, public-minded side acted the part very well. But the rest of her, the real Bernice, couldn't smile away that same old burden of deep sorrow that had been her closest companion for so long.

And now she missed Pat. Perhaps it was the mystery of her death and the obsession with finding the answers that kept Pat alive in her heart for so long. Now there was nothing left to delay the final step Bernice had never been able to take: saying good-bye.

And there was that strange yearning deep in her heart, something she had never felt before she met that strange girl, Betsy; had she really been touched by God somehow? If she had been, what was she to do about it?

She started walking. The skies were bright again, the air was warm, the campus was quiet. Maybe a walk along the red brick pathways would calm her and help her to think, help her to make sense of all that was happening around her and inside her.

She paused under a big oak tree, thought of Pat, thought of her own life and what she would ever do with it, and then let herself cry. She thought maybe she should pray. "Dear God," she whispered, but then she couldn't think of what to say.

Tal and the General were assessing the situation below them.

"I would say this whole thing has left the town in quite a mess," said the General.

Tal nodded. "The college won't be the same for a long time, what with the investigation by the state and federal authorities, not to mention all that money to be tracked down."

"So do we have a good contingent to set the town back in order?"

"They're assembling for that now. In the meantime Krioni and Triskal will remain with Busche; Nathan and Armoth will remain with Hogan. Hogan's family will have a good church where they can heal, and—" Tal suddenly noticed one downcast figure standing alone across the campus. "Hold on." He got the attention of one particular angel. "There she is. Let's not let her get away."

Bernice finally thought of one little sentence to pray. "Dear God, I don't know what to do."

Hank Busche. The name just came to her. She looked back toward the Administration Building. That pastor and his people were still there.

You know, said a voice inside her, *it wouldn't hurt to talk to that man.*

She looked at Hank Busche, and then at all those people who seemed so happy, so at peace.

You've been calling out to God. Well, maybe that preacher can introduce the two of you once and for all.

He sure did something for Marshall, Bernice thought.

There's something back there that you need, girl, and if I were you I'd find out about it.

The General was eager to be gone. "We're needed in Brazil. The revival is going well, but the enemy is concocting some plan against it. You should like that kind of a challenge."

Tal rose to his feet again and drew his sword. Just then, Guilo returned with the trumpet. Tal told him, "Brazil."

Guilo laughed excitedly and drew his sword also.

"Wait," said Tal, looking below.

It was Bernice, timidly making her way toward the young pastor and his new flock. By the quiet surrender in her eyes, Tal could see she was ready. Soon the angels would be rejoicing.

He waved his approval to the little curly-haired angel sitting in the crook of the big oak, and she smiled and waved back, her big brown eyes sparkling. Her glowing white gown and golden slippers suited her much better than bib overalls and a motorcycle.

The General asked with pleasure in his voice, "Shall we be going?"

Tal was looking at Hank when he said, "Just a moment. I want to hear it one more time."

As they watched, Bernice found her way to Hank and Mary. She began to weep openly, and spoke some quiet but impassioned words to them. Hank and Mary listened, as did the others nearby, and as they listened, they began to smile. They put their arms around her, they told her about Jesus, and then they began to weep as well. Finally, as the saints were gathered and Bernice was surrounded with loving arms, Hank said the words, "Let's pray . . ."

And Tal smiled a long smile.

"Let's be off," he said.

With a burst of brilliant wings and three trails of sparkling fire, the warriors shot into the sky, heading southward, becoming smaller and smaller until finally they were gone, leaving the now peaceful town of Ashton in very capable hands.

**If you enjoyed reading *This Present Darkness*
you'll want to get these other Frank Peretti
titles, available at your local Christian
bookstore from Crossway Books:**

PIERCING THE DARKNESS

*The light shines in the darkness,
and the darkness has not overcome it.*

John 1:5, RSV

The veil between the natural and supernatural is opened again with *Piercing the Darkness,* sequel to Frank Peretti's thriller, *This Present Darkness.* In the tiny farming community of Bacon's Corner, the hosts of heaven and Satan's hordes come face-to-face in a titanic spiritual struggle centering around Sally Beth Roe, a young drifter with a dark past. Fast-paced action propels this story, which begins when someones tries to kill Sally. Was it a case of mistaken identity, or is someone trying to mastermind a cover-up? The suspense intensifies when a high-powered anti-Christian group files a child abuse lawsuit against the superintendent of the local Christian school. Before it's all over the media, the police and a humanistic think tank get involved. And Marshall Hogan's investigation uncovers secret occult societies and murder.

Across a vast panorama of heart-stopping action—including Sally's attempts to escape the relentless pursuit of a mysterious group called Broken Birch—*Piercing the Darkness* compellingly illustrates the reality of spiritual warfare, and the ability of God's truth to burst through the darkness of humanism and New Age beliefs. But it is also a personal story about how the fervent prayers of devoted Christians help a young woman find refuge from the darkness that had claimed her soul, and real forgiveness from her tragically sinful past.

Sally's journey is a penetrating portrayal of our times, a reflection of our wanderings, and a vivid reminder that while the powers of evil are great, the redemptive power of the Cross is even greater. A soul stained by the darkness of sin can still be turned toward the light of God's love and forgiveness.

THIS PRESENT DARKNESS
AUDIO CASSETTE and CD

You've never experienced this riveting best-seller in such a powerful way! The book that changed the way Christians view spiritual warfare and set a new standard for fiction in Christian publishing is available on audio cassette—and read by author Frank Peretti, who, besides his phenomenal success as a writer, is also a master storyteller. These two 90-minute tapes are packed with special music, stirring effects, and all the drama and excitement of the full-length novel.

PIERCING THE DARKNESS
AUDIO CASSETTE and CD

Peretti reads Peretti . . . again. This time it's the audio version of his second #1 seller, *Piercing the Darkness*. Read by the author himself, this audio abridgment is fortified with dramatic sound effects and music that bring to life all the intrigue and spiritual impact of the beloved novel on two 90-minute cassettes. Great for listening to in the car, while working around the house, or to enjoy as a family.

PROPHET

John Barrett, anchorman for the city's most-watched evening newcast, knows something is wrong. The facts don't add up. So he determines to find the real news—the truth. It won't be easy, though. He's caught his producer reworking a story to fit her own prejudices, then lying to cover her tracks. And she appears to be hiding something much bigger.

Prompted by extraordinary spiritual experiences, Barrett begins to uncover the story that no one wants to hear—of ruthless power, blind ambition and political intrigue. As he confronts the politically correct attitudes of the news team, Barrett finds that they are in league with desperate forces that will stop at nothing to keep the lid on the story, even if it means his job . . . or his life.

Once again, Frank Peretti has woven a prophetic tale for our times. Winner of numerous book awards and with more than 800,000 copies sold, *Prophet* carries all the hallmarks of Frank's blockbusting fiction—plenty of edge-of-the-seat action, nail-biting suspense, breakneck pacing, and blow-you-out-of-the-water spiritual impact. But more than this, it penetrates to the very heart of a struggle that threatens to tear our society to pieces—the struggle over which vision of moral authority will define our nation. And it provides a grippingly courageous witness that the Truth alone can set us free.

TILLY
AUDIO CASSETTE, VHS and DVD

Kathy looked at the little gravestone again. Now she could see it clearly. It bore just that one name: Tilly.

Tilly. She couldn't take her eyes away. She didn't want to. She stooped down to look. Only one date. Only one. Nine years ago.

Kathy and Dan Ross are just like any other young couple . . . except for the secrets that lie buried in their souls. When Kathy is captivated by that simple name "Tilly" on a small grave marker, both her life and Dan's are changed forever.

Originally presented as a radio drama on "Focus on the Family," *Tilly* is the deeply moving story of a woman's struggle to reconcile herself with a long-ago abortion, and a couple's efforts to ultimately move forward with their lives. This powerful tale of forgiveness will shake the most stoic soul.

THE COOPER KIDS
ADVENTURE SERIES

Brilliant cover art enhances the exciting four-volume set of Frank E. Peretti's "Indiana Jones-style" adventure stories. They're books that will build sound values in kids ages 9-14 while keeping them glued to their seats. More than 500,000 copies sold!

BOOK 1:
THE DOOR IN THE DRAGON'S THROAT

Jay and Lila Cooper have been on adventures with their archaeologist father before, but nothing like this! As they make their way through the dark and mysterious cavern called The Dragon's Throat, they can't help thinking about the other exploration parties that tried to open the Door leading into it. All fled in panic or died terrible deaths!

What really lies behind the Door? Incredible riches from a lost kingdom? Some ancient evil? They must find the key and discover for themselves the truth about the Nepurian legends. One thing is for certain: Jay and Lila have been protected in many dangerous circumstances before. But will they be able to overcome whatever force lurks behind the Door in the Dragon's Throat? Join them as they solve this dreaded desert mystery, which ends with a gigantic clash between the forces of good and evil.

BOOK 2:
ESCAPE FROM THE ISLAND OF AQUARIUS

When Jay and Lila travel with their adventurous father to an exotic South Sea island to find a missionary who has vanished, they discover some very strange things going on. It appears that the arrogant, tyrannical leader of the island colony is the man they've been sent to find. But if that's true, then why is he acting so strange? As the Coopers attempt to solve the mystery, they encounter several deadly perils—poisonous snakes, fierce biting insects, bone-crunching earthquakes. In fact, the very foundations of the island seem to be jarring loose. Jay, Lila and their dad must find a way to overcome the evil that holds the colonists in a death grip—before the entire island breaks apart.

A thrilling tale filled with heart-stopping danger that will captivate readers to the last page.

BOOK 3:
THE TOMBS OF ANAK

When Jay and Lila Cooper enter the cave-tombs of Anak with their father, they hope to find a co-worker who has unaccountably disappeared. Instead, they stumble onto a frightening religion and new mysteries that soon put them all in incredible danger.

Who or what is Ha-Raphah? How does he hold the local villagers in such overwhelming fear? Knowing they can't avoid confronting this villian—whatever he is—the Coopers desperately search for answers. As they begin to unravel the mystery, Jay, Lila and their dad face even more perilous adventures. Will they understand the truth in time to avoid disaster, or will they be swept away in a last desperate attempt by Ha-Raphah to preserve his evil powers?

The Tombs of Anak is a spine-tingling thriller as current as today's newscasts, yet as timeless as the age-old struggle between good and evil.

BOOK 4:
TRAPPED AT THE BOTTOM OF THE SEA

When Lila insisted on leaving her father's teaching expedition to go back to the States, she never suspected that her flight would be hijacked! Now she is a prisoner, trapped at the bottom of the sea in a locked, top-secret weapons pod with no way of escape. Meanwhile, her dad, Dr. Jake Cooper, her brother Jay, and daring adventurer-journalist Meaghan Flaherty are trying to pick up Lila's trail.

Pursued by angry terrorists, and with a cannibal tribe ahead of them, they island-hop in a remote corner of the Pacific, hoping against hope to find the plane. But will they reach Lila before her air runs out and before the pod is found by another hostile group searching for it?

This breathtaking adventure is complete with exciting sea chases, daring deeds and narrow escapes.